To

The Dark Reflection

I wrote this!

M A CLARKE

Other novels by the author:

Lunaria

The Horizon Conspiracy

The Dark Reflection First Edition

www.tekamuttmedia.com

ISBN: 978-0-9929585-7-2

CONTENTS

DEDICATION

For my mates back home.

CHAPTER ONE

*woosh!*

"Whoa!" Ellie and Johanna both cried as the exploding fireball singed their eyebrows. Then they fell about in hushed fits of giggles.

"That was awesome! Do it again!" Ellie urged her sister in a loud whisper.

"Alright," Johanna replied, grinning.

They were sitting on the roof of their parents' cottage under a canopy of stars. Both had rabbit skin patchwork cloaks draped over their shoulders to ward off the chilly midnight air. A small leather-bound book lay on the thatch between their crossed legs, open on a page titled *Pyromancy - The Basics.*

Johanna glanced at the page, reminding herself of the words, then sat up straight. She cupped her hands together, closing a ball of air between her palms, and muttered the spellphrase. "*Ignus spareet.*" Light spilled out between the cracks of her fingers, and her skin glowed as a flame appeared within. She slowly lifted one hand away, revealing a gently swirling ball of flame nestled within her upraised palm.

Ellie's round, blue eyes shimmered in the firelight as she

gaped in awe at her big sister. "It's so pretty," she murmured, entranced by the flickering flames.

Johanna raised the fireball at arm's length above her head and whispered a second phrase. "*Ignus projeet!*" The fireball shot from her hand and leapt into the sky. It popped above the treetops, illuminating the surrounding woods in a soft glow. The light fizzled out, returning the woods to a peaceful moonlit twilight.

Ellie grinned as fiery sprinkles fluttered down around them like confetti, blinking out of existence. She beamed at her big sister, and demanded in an excited whisper, "Again!"

"Hold on a minute," Johanna said, wheezing. "That one took it out of me. I need to recharge." She picked up a banana from a bowl of fruit wedged into the thatch beside the open book, and began to peel it.

Ellie gave a wistful sigh, and laid back on the thatch, crossing her arms behind her head so she could look up at the stars. "So you're gonna be a wizard, eh, Hanna?"

Johanna had the banana half way to her mouth, but paused at this. "No, I'm going to be a *mage*."

Ellie continued the conversation whilst lying on her back. "Don't you want to be a wizard?"

"Girls can't become wizards."

"Why not?" said Ellie.

"*Boys* become wizards, girls become *mages*. Its tradition," Johanna explained patiently, taking a bite of her banana. A moment of satisfying silence suggested the issue was settled.

"What's the difference?" said Ellie.

"Nuff-ing," Johanna said through a mouthful of mush, feeling very uncouth, but her sister's ignorance needed to be addressed. She swallowed, and added, "Mage is just the female equivalent of wizard. It's very simple Eleanor."

Ellie sat up, scrunching her nose in disgust. "Hate when you call me that."

"And I'll hate it if you start calling me a *wizard*," Johanna said.

"Fine," Ellie submitted, shrugging her shoulders. "Just

seems a bit unnecessary, using different words for the same thing."

"That's just the way it is."

"It's dumb. What if I was able to do magic, and I wanted to be called a wizard. Who could stop me?"

"Let's just be thankful you can't—" Johanna hesitated, trying to think of a better phrase than her sister's plebeian use of *do magic*. She finished with, "—that you're not attuned."

"*Wizard* still sounds cooler than *mage*," Ellie said.

"I don't mind it," Johanna said fondly. "Sai Mage rolls off the tongue much better than Sai Wizard. Sai Mage is elegant."

"What does Sai mean?"

"It's the proper prefix. Like *ser* for knights and soldiers. *Sai* for wizards and mages. You'd know all of this if you read a book once in your life."

"Books are a mystery to me," Ellie said whimsically with a yawn and a stretch, poking her slender arms sideways out of the cloak. She flopped back on the thatch again just in time to see a shooting star. "Ooh, that was a big'un."

Johanna glanced up at the sky, but by then the star had burnt out and disappeared. She always seemed to look too late. The girls sat in peaceful silence, staring up at the sky together. The only sounds were the gentle rustle of the woodland leaves swaying in the breeze, and Johanna's soft chewing as she finished her banana.

Ellie piped up in another loud whisper, "You ready yet?"

"Almost," Johanna said, feeling a little re-energised. "You have the patience of a nibbet, you know that?"

"And proud of it." Ellie sat up and eagerly leaned forward. "Do it, sis!"

"All right, all right," Johanna said, smiling. She couldn't even pretend to be agitated. Practicing her pyromancy was always fun, with or without an audience. But it was nice to be appreciated, especially by her little sister.

Johanna whispered into her cupped hands, "*ignus*

spareet," and summoned another cute little fireball. She could feel the nutrition of the banana being sucked out of her body already, fuelling the flames, and making her stomach grumble unhappily. It didn't matter, she had Mother's entire fruit bowl up there.

Johanna pulled her hands apart and the swirling spherical flame licked the air, lapping up oxygen. Now she leaned in close, the fire setting her pale cheeks aglow and transforming her hazel eyes into pools of shimmering gold. "*Ignee dividay,*" she whispered.

The fireball separated into two smaller balls, one in each palm.

"Hoo!" Ellie squealed with delight, eyes darting between the two fireballs.

With a flick of her wrist, Johanna gently tossed one into the air. It arced upwards and over before coming back down to land in her other hand. She had smoothly flipped the second fireball into her right hand and tossed that one as well. "*Ignee dividay,*" she repeated and the first ball became two even smaller fireballs. She tossed them again and again, splitting each one every time they looped around. Soon enough, she was juggling a dozen tiny glowing balls so close together that they made a swirling ring of fire.

Ellie stared in mesmerised fascination. Her eyes and slackened jaw both expanded into incrementally wider O's each time the fireballs split. "How come it doesn't burn you?" she asked after a while, eyes fixed on the dancing orbs.

"Because they're mine," Johanna replied distractedly. She had a look of deep concentration on her face.

"So, you can never hurt yourself with your own fire?"

"Hmm..." Johanna's eyes didn't leave the fireballs, but she frowned. "No, it's possible. Because what if—?"

She fumbled.

A fireball dropped from her hand and fell into the dry thatched roof beside Ellie's knee. A sharp twang of hot smoke stung Johanna's nostrils.

Ellie gave a loud yelp and flinched away.

Johanna, with her concentration shattered, fumbled two more before blurting in panic, "*Ignus projeet!*" The remaining fireballs shot into the sky and fizzled out.

"Here!" Ellie cried, diving forwards to smother the burning thatch with her cloak. Both sister's drummed the cloak with their hands, patting out the flames.

Footsteps sounded from inside the house. Rapid and with purpose. A moment later, Julia McKree appeared in the garden, illuminated by the oil lantern in her outstretched arm. She wore a cotton night gown and her hair was a tangled bird's nest of brown curls. She swung the lantern around, and squinted towards the girls on the roof. "What on Kellamon…?" Then her eyes went wide. "Girls! What are you doing up there?"

Ellie had always been the faster thinker when it came to lying. "Midnight snack! See!" She tipped the fruit bowl towards their mother. An apple rolled out and tumbled down the roof to splat on a paving stone.

Julia planted her free hand on a hip. "*Eleanor McKree…*" She spoke in that specific tone that only a mother can achieve when they know their children are telling porkies.

Ellie cringed. "I'm not lying, mum!"

"Did I accuse you of lying?" Julia said. "Which of you screamed a moment ago?"

"Oh. You heard that?"

"I imagine you woke the whole village! Johanna, has your tongue lost its wiggle? Tell me why you're on the roof."

Johanna lifted her hands away from the cloak and sat up straight, scratching the back of her neck. "We were, um. Just… stargazing!" That was believable. And it wasn't even a lie. Johanna felt a moment of pride, surprised by her own ability to come up with a feasible explanation that might get them both out of trouble.

A small wheezing figure burst out of the hedge behind Julia at that moment, giving the two girls and their mother such a fright that, this time, they all yelped.

"Sorry!" the figure panted. He hunched over, clutching his knees. "Are you all right, Mrs McKree?"

"Markus!" Julia sighed, clutching her chest. "We are fine, thank you."

Markus, a boy the same age as Johanna, lived in the neighbouring cottage down the lane. He looked up at the sisters with flushed red cheeks. "I ran here when I heard the scream. I was watching you juggle from my bedroom window. Then when I saw you drop one, I—"

As soon as Markus said the word *juggle,* Ellie and Johanna both closed their eyes in a wince.

"You were watching them *what?*" Julia cut in. "Good grief Johanna, tell me you were not juggling fireballs on the thatched roof of our home?"

Johanna's mind drew a panicky blank. She looked desperately at Ellie, as if she could somehow pluck a good excuse out of her sister's mind that would keep her from being grounded. But of course that didn't work. Johanna couldn't read minds any more than Ellie could read beyond the opening page of a novel.

"Oh my word that explains the fruit. And I'm not blind, I can see the spellbook Miss Henlowe lent you!" Julia shrilled. "Both of you, *get down this instant!*"

"Yes, mother," Johanna muttered in defeat. She closed her book and began to crawl down the sloping thatch.

Ellie tentatively lifted her cloak off the singed patch of roof and checked it for damage. It didn't seem so bad, although being the middle of the night made it rather difficult to see properly. She slipped the cloak back over her shoulders and shimmied down. She felt a bit guilty. It had been her idea to go up there in the first place, but that didn't stop her from hoping to slink away while Johanna received an onslaught of telling-off. By the time they had both climbed down, using the big water barrel as a stepping stone, Markus had already done just that. He was nowhere to be seen.

Wait until I see him again, Johanna fumed. *He's such a dope!*

"Our whole house could've burned to the ground!" Julia said. "I'm of a mind to ground you into next month for this. *Both* of you." She wagged a finger at Ellie as she dropped down beside her sister.

"What did I do? I'm not the family wizard," Ellie pointed out.

Johanna shot her a sideways glare.

"You encouraged her, I have no doubt, missy," Julia said. "One who condones the crime deserves a share of the punishment."

Johanna looked up to meet her mother's eyes, feeling truly ashamed. "Mother... I'm sorry."

"Me too," Ellie said, staring at the grass. Then the implications of being locked indoors tomorrow made her jerk her head up to plead forgiveness. "Please don't ground us. Dad promised to take me on his next hunt!"

"You should've thought of that before you stole my basket of fruit and started messing about on the roof. But what good will it do?" Julia's tone softened. Her voice lowered to barely above a whisper, all anger drained out of it. "You're going to be gone next week. Come here."

Julia put down the lantern and swept her daughters into a tight hug. "Why can't you just use your senses for once?" She kissed them one after the other on the top of the head. When she released them, Johanna saw tears in her eyes, and she was forcing a sad smile.

"I'll still be here, mum," Ellie reminded her. "It's only Hanna going to the city."

Julia chuckled, squeezing Ellie's arm. "I know, honey. But how long will you stick around? You spend more time in the woods than at home! You take after your father, always out exploring."

"And I'll be home for winter," Johanna added. "Miss Henlowe doesn't tutor once the snow comes. I'll be back before you know it."

"I know, I'm just feeling emotional," Julia said. "My two girls, growing up so fast. It's frightening!"

They all giggled.

Ellie pointed up at the sky suddenly. "There's another one!" A bright glare streaked across the sky, the longest shooting star Ellie had ever seen.

This time, even Johanna caught the tail end of it.

"Wow," their mother cooed. "What a beautiful clear night. I can see why you girls wanted to be out here."

The soft *clip-clop* of horse hoofs echoed towards them, and they all turned to look down the garden path.

"Dad!" Ellie cried, unwinding herself from her mother and taking off towards the lane. She disappeared into the shadows and out of sight. Johanna and Julia ambled after her, walking side by side.

Frank McKree rode out of the gloom into view. His face and torso were hidden beneath his hooded green cloak, and a few feathered arrow shafts poked out of the quiver above the back of his head. Slung over Gilbert's ample rump was a small doe carcass. Squeezed in between that and Frank's back, Ellie had found a spot to sit, her legs dangling over Gilbert's side barely past the midpoint of his ribs, and sat with her arms wrapped tightly around her father's chest.

"Good evenin', mi'ladies," Frank greeted them, pulling his hood back and shooting them a wide, puzzled smile. "Didn't expect a welcoming party at this hour." He reined Gilbert up. The giant lumbering horse exhaled a snort as Ellie and Frank dismounted. "Look what I caught for Sunday's supper."

"Mmm, venison," Johanna said, licking her lips.

"Nope," said Frank. He scooped Ellie up by the waist and slung her over his shoulder like a sack of potatoes. "A fresh, wild Eleanor!"

Ellie shrieked with delight, kicking her feet in the air.

"Be *quiet*!" Julia said, chuckling. "We'll wake the neighbours."

"Takes an earthquake to wake those two codgers," Frank said, referring in good humour to his own parents, who lived in the cottage directly beside their own. Grandpa and Grandma McKree would be snoring peacefully in their beds, despite all the commotion outside. "What are you lot doing out here in the middle of the night, anyway?" Frank asked when the girls had stopped giggling. He put Ellie back on her feet and hoisted the deer carcass off of Gilbert. "I had planned to surprise you all in the morning with this."

"Well, you won't *believe* what I caught the girls doing just now," Julia started.

Johanna felt her cheeks warming up.

"I'll take Gilbert back to his stable," Ellie said and slipped away, tugging on the reins causing the horse to amble after her.

Frank cocked an eyebrow. "Do I want to know?"

"Let's talk about it tomorrow." Julia stepped forward to receive a scratchy kiss from her stubble-chinned husband. "You smell terrible, honey."

"And your hair looks like a woodpecker's been at it," Frank retorted, swinging the deer onto his shoulder and carrying it towards the house.

Johanna smiled to herself, knowing that everything would be okay. It was a close call, but her parents were not the sort to punish for *almost* burning the house to cinders.

CHAPTER TWO

Ellie McKree found Harbrook a marvellous place to grow up, and at fourteen years of age, was finally allowed to start discovering what lay beyond the borders. She already knew the village back to front, having spent her childhood wandering around and exploring every nook and cranny. She could tell you where the fishes' favourite eddies were in the Mana River. She knew about the secret blackberry bush farmer Cribs had in the back corner of his field. And she knew the quickest route from one house to any other, and all the shortcuts in between. Admittedly, this wasn't too difficult, seeing as Harbrook was made up of only two dozen buildings, but even as a child Ellie had impressed her father with how quick she could get from one side of the village to the other without using the main road.

Johanna and Ellie used to explore together when they were younger, but to Ellie's immense sadness, her big sister was growing distant ever since she discovered her *attunement*, whatever that really meant. Now, Johanna preferred to read a book indoors than to catch moths around the cottage. It had taken her a lot of convincing to clamber up onto the roof to show Ellie what she had been learning, but after nearly setting fire to the house, Ellie knew it would be a long time before she could convince her sister to do anything as fun as that again.

And she would be leaving soon… Moving to the big city.

"How can she abandon us like that, Dad?" Ellie asked her father as they walked down the lane, heading for the western woods.

"She's not *abandoning* us, Ells," Frank assured her. "She's just following her dream. We have to understand that."

"I don't understand it *at all*," Ellie said in a tone of bewilderment. "How many people live in the city, again?"

"Well, I don't know exactly, but it's at least five thousand."

"Five *thousand*!" Ellie said. "That's like… it's at least… what, ten Harbrook's?"

Frank laughed. "More like a hundred. Darune is huge and bustling, their market alone is about the size of our little village. Johanna will make lots of friends."

"It sounds awful," Ellie said. "And it smells, doesn't it? Markus said that when he visited with his parents, he saw a stream of poo running down the side of the road. *Human* poo!"

"Haha, it's true. Though I wish that lad would keep his trapper shut. Don't want him putting the lass off now, do we?"

"He was trying to put her off. Everyone knows he fancies Hanna," Ellie explained.

"Is that so?" Frank said, cocking a brow.

"He told her about the noise and the smell, and finally the poo, but she still wants to go." Ellie kicked a clod of dirt into the hedgerow.

"You can have her room when she goes."

That lit Ellie's face up, her blue eyes gaped at Frank. "Seriously?"

"Yeah. But don't tell her," Frank winked.

Ellie gasped for joy. Now she walked with a bounce in her step, already making plans for where to put her collection of dried insects in Johanna's room. Her brown ponytail bobbed up and down, brushing against her bow, which was slung around one shoulder, the same way Frank carried his. They strolled under the morning sun, chatting and joking and enjoying each other's company.

They entered the shadowy cool woodland, sticking to the rutted lane that wound its way through the trees. After a short while, Frank steered them off the track and they wandered into the woods proper, heading north, which would take them into the boar's territory.

"Keep an eye out for tracks, eh?" Frank said, holding aside an elasticated branch for Ellie to slip past.

"Will do," she said, keenly eyeing the ground. A carpet of brown cedar leaves covered the whole area, making it difficult to pick up a trail, but Ellie relished the challenge. She was so excited to finally be on a real hunt with her father, and eager to impress him.

Well, *real hunt* was an exaggeration. Ellie knew it wasn't really that important. Not like one of his bounties. The boar they were trying to hunt was nothing but a pest, so there'd be no reward other than the satisfaction of bringing the local cucumber thief to justice.

"There's a waterhole not far from here," Frank said. "Pig's gotta drink, so I say we check there and see if we can find a print or two."

"Okay," Ellie said, grinning.

She followed him to the waterhole, and noticed the ground becoming squishier the closer they got. Mud oozed around the edges of her hide boots, which were worn and moulded to her feet like slippers. Ellie had made all of her own clothing from the skins that Frank brought home, including the two rabbit skin cloaks she and her sister liked to wear. Ellie didn't need the cloak today, so had donned her lighter goat fleece vest, a reed skirt and a leather utility belt, which held her two knives, one for piercing and one for skinning. A quiver of arrows and her old crooked ash bow finished the apprentice huntress look.

Frank meanwhile had opted for his green cloak, which

hung down his back as far as his knees, and his soft doe skin trousers which were light enough to run in, should the need arise. He left deep boot prints in the soft mud which Ellie amused herself by trying to walk in herself. Her own feet were swallowed by his bear-like prints, and she had to stretch to mimic his long strides.

Frank stopped suddenly and hunkered down and Ellie almost tripped over him.

"Here we go," he said, pointing at the ground. "Ells, look here. Tell me what you see."

She hunkered beside him and studied the area. The waterhole was just a big puddle, fed by a small ditch that meandered up the gentle slope to their left. Ellie spied a whole bunch of footprints scattered in the mud, all varying shapes and sizes. Frank could probably recount the entire story of who'd been here and which way they'd gone, but Ellie was still trying to grasp the basics and it boggled her mind as she looked at the mishmash of indents.

"Is that a badger?" She pointed to a clean footprint that had four easily identifiable toes and a set of pads, similar to a dog's paw.

"Very good," Frank said. "What else?"

"And that," she gestured to a pair of long footprints parallel to one another, which were smudged by a half dozen other prints, but still easily identifiable due to being twice the size of everything else. "Is that a honeyroo?"

"Easy one," Frank said with a nod.

"I haven't seen a roo lately," Ellie said.

"There's a few still about," Frank said. "Most live near the hives out east. Come now, I'm waiting for you to hit the jackpot."

Ellie chewed her lip, surveying the prints the way an artist might examine her subject. She couldn't see any obvious signs of a boar. There were a few bird prints, but those were just about the easiest things to recognise, and she knew her dad wouldn't be impressed if she identified those now. *I just don't see anything!*

"Not seeing it?" Frank said, as if reading her mind. He slowly raised his hand and extended a finger towards a patch of mud a few feet to their right.

Ellie followed his finger but still couldn't pick anything out of the hodgepodge of animal tracks. "Aargh, where, Dad?" she groaned in frustration.

"Right there. A boar. Heading that way." He pointed to a busy section of mud that looked as though it had been trampled by a group of foxes having a party, and flicked his finger upwards, gesturing past the puddle, deeper into the woods.

"How can you see that?" Ellie frowned, annoyed at herself.

"See the way the mud sinks lower at these two points. A boar is heavy, their trotters sink lower than a deer's hoof, say."

"I thought you said boars have two toes. That looked like a 3-talon bird print to me."

"Some fat bird!" Frank laughed.

Ellie exhaled a disgruntled sigh.

"Chin up, lil' missy. You'll get there. Hunting's a patient game."

Ellie never did have much patience. But she was determined to get this.

"Come on," Frank said, rising to his feet and adjusting the strap of his shoulder pack, which contained their lunch. "Let's follow him, shall we?"

They hiked a little further, and Frank showed Ellie how to maintain a pursuit without veering off course. You had to read the forest from the eyes of the animal you were tracking. A boar was quite low to the ground, so it would have no trouble squeezing under low branches and such. But it was also heavy, so would avoid softer areas like bogs, opting to walk around them instead.

When they reached a grove of cedar trees, Frank hunkered to study the prints again. Here, they seemed to double back on themselves, as if the boar had walked in both directions at different times.

"It's a cross-point," he declared.

"What does that mean?" said Ellie.

"It means that our boar friend probably has a den somewhere over there." He pointed in the direction they had been travelling, which Ellie guessed as due east. "He comes this way for water, then does a little loop that we were just following, and returns through here to get back home. I'd say we found a perfect spot for an ambush."

Ellie felt a tingle of excitement. "Oooh, yes."

"Pick a tree," Frank grinned.

The cedar trees had very convenient horizontal branches running around their trunks, which made for a perfect set of ladder footholds. They each climbed into a tree above the cross-point of tracks, and settled themselves on thick branches about fifteen feet above the ground.

"Keep an eye out, eh, Ells?"

"I will," she replied, her blue eyes shining and alert.

"Gonna have to be silent now," Frank whispered, pressing his index finger to his mouth.

Ellie nodded, and looked back at the ground.

They waited for two minutes. Ellie's stomach grumbled noisily. She couldn't help but laugh.

"Here," Frank said, trying to hide a smirk as he tossed her a couple of chunky oat cookies that Julia had baked for them. "Eat 'um quietly."

She bit into a cookie and a cluster of crumbs tumbled to the ground. As she munched, she listened to the birds tweeting and the leaves blowing in the wind. With every passing minute, Ellie found herself growing tense, like a slingshot being drawn, ready to fire. *Come on, piggy! Where are you?*

A rustle of leaves grabbed her attention. A startled squirrel froze dead in its tracks on a branch a couple of trees over, staring at her with big round eyes.

Ellie heard a tiny voice inside her head squeak, *wassat?*

When Ellie smiled at the squirrel, it bolted, scurrying

away in the opposite direction, leaping from branch to branch until it was out of sight.

What followed was an agonisingly long period of waiting. Sitting still for more than five minutes was a remarkable achievement for Ellie. After twenty-five minutes, she was finally rewarded.

The boar came sniffing and snorting down the track from their right, exactly as Frank said it would. Ellie's arm muscles went rigid, and her neck turned to stone. She exchanged a glance with Frank, who mouthed *shhh* silently. She nodded.

The boar was pretty small, she thought. Probably a sow, and not too old. Her tusks were a smooth, clean white, pointing skyward through her slobbering lips. Her head was bent to the ground as she sniffed and searched for food. To Ellie's absolute glee, the boar came right up to her tree and there she stopped. Ellie could hear her snuffling the ground, then she started to chew on something.

My cookies! She's eating the crumbs!

Frank had silently slipped his bow around and was knocking an arrow. He drew back, but grimaced by turning his nose up. Ellie mouthed *what?* He gestured back with thumb and forefinger forming an O. He split the O by jerking his finger and thumb apart – a signal that meant *no clear shot.* Now, he pointed to his knife which hung at his belt, then jabbed the finger at Ellie's own waist.

He wants me to use my knife? Ellie's eyes went wide. She drew her hunting knife from its holster and gripped it in white knuckles. Frank mimed a slashing motion with his hand.

Ellie felt blood rushing to her arms, as adrenaline kicked in. *Okay, here goes.*

She shimmied forwards as quietly as she could, until she was practically hanging over the boar. The boar froze, as if hearing something, and looked ready to bolt.

Ellie leaped from the tree.

She landed with her feet on either side of the boar's flank

and her crotch slammed against its back. The impact jolted her knife from her hand, and it fell into the mud. The pig screeched and took off. Ellie leaned forward and it carried her with it. She was riding the panicking boar into the woods. This had not been her intention at all.

Come to think of it, what *was* her plan? Her brain ricocheted around inside her skull as the squealing boar bounded away in a crazed panic, trying to shake her off. Without her knife, she had no way of killing the poor creature regardless. All she'd done was frighten and piss it off.

A low branch flew at her face cancelling any further thought on the matter. She saw stars and white pain flared through her head, and then she was rolling in sticky cedar leaves, tumbling over and over before finally coming to a stop. Lying face down in a clump of muddy leaves, she blinked and tried to roll over, but everything hurt, her head swam and she felt that the best thing to do would be to sleep. Yes, a little nap should make everything feel better.

"Ells? Ellie?" Someone was rocking her rudely. Sharp jolts of pain shot through her temples with every shake.

"Ow." She winced, lifting a hand to her face.

"You okay, Ellie?" Frank looked into her eyes, upside-down. She realised she was lying in his lap. He was sitting on the ground cross legged, a look of fatherly concern creasing his face.

"Hey, Dad." She flushed red with embarrassment. "I uhh… I think I need more practice."

"You lunatic," he said in a scolding tone. "What were you thinking, jumping out of the tree like that?"

"I thought you wanted me to." She groaned.

"What on Kellamon gave you that idea?"

"My knife. You said to use my knife."

"To cut the leaves that were blocking my shot!" he said.

"What?"

"You silly girl. Cripes, did you really think you had to jump onto the poor creature's *back*?" A hint of his sarcasm was returning now, so she knew her injuries couldn't be as bad as they felt.

"I uhh, yeah," was all she could manage. Ellie felt bitterly disappointed in herself. What a foolish mistake. Of course father wouldn't teach her such a ridiculous method of hunting, but she'd gotten so caught up in the moment and just wanted to nab her first kill.

Frank dabbed her forehead with a gentle pad of something soft. It felt like leaves.

Ellie winced, but the pain didn't last long. "That feels good," she muttered.

"We need to wrap your arms. You have a few scrapes, not to mention those splinters."

She slowly sat upright and looked at her bare arms. They were indeed scratched up, one particularly nasty graze throbbed on the flat part of her forearm near the elbow. And at several points along the same arm, tiny wooden needles had jabbed themselves under the skin. "Ouch," she said, feeling very glum.

"Least you landed in the right place to deal with those," Frank said. "Here, wrap these around your arm." He gave her a handful of cedar leaves, which were sticky to the touch. "The sap will stick to your arm, and we'll be able to pull the splinters out later. Come on, let's get you home."

CHAPTER THREE

In the abandoned ghost city of Archdale, the Prime Wizard Jason Brockhurst finished preparing his experiment to prove once and for all that dragons really existed.

Jason and his son Garrod stood next to the dried-up well in the middle of the old town square. Jason wore the long maroon coloured Prime robes, while Garrod displayed the navy cloak of an acolyte. Together, father and son waited at the centre of the experiment.

Surrounding the two Brockhursts were one hundred prisoners, standing in a wide circle. Each captive was chained and manacled at the ankles, their hands bound with coarse rope behind their backs, and gagged with a piece of cloth between their teeth. Paired with each prisoner waited a guard, another one hundred men armed with spears, swords and shields.

Jason adopted his trademark pose of observation – thumb and forefinger pinching his chin, the free hand cradling the elbow. He turned on his heel to survey the men, nodding with approval. This moment was thirty years in the making. At sixty-two, he would not get another chance to prepare such an event in his lifetime. The thought tugged his lips into a nervous, excited smile.

He cleared his throat to hide it.

"Heed today, Garrod," he spoke softly to his son. "When a Brockhurst dreams…"

"Nothing stands in his way," Garrod finished the family motto, placing a hand on his father's shoulder and giving it a proud squeeze.

A long, drawn out cough of thunder rumbled in the distance. The overcast sky bulged overhead, ready to rain, but biding its time for the moment. The weather made no difference to Jason. He was finally ready. The time had come to see where his research and long laid plans would lead him.

It had to be in this city. Once the pinnacle of attunement in the Darune Province, Archdale had rotted into a crumbling ruin of derelict castles, weed-infested cobblestone streets and a population of zero. Archdale, a dead city. Hard to believe the Brockhurst family used to call it their home.

"Make way!" a bellowing voice called from outside the ring of prisoners. "Step aside, make way for the Prince!"

A gap parted in the ring, and Prince Leo stepped into the circle, followed closely by his hulking personal guardsman. To Garrod's bemusement, Leo was dressed in leather armour, and a sword hung in a sheath from his belt. He carried a silver knight's helmet in his hand and strode into the middle to join Jason and Garrod by the crumbling well. A conniving grin played on the lips of the prince's juvenile face. He was only a few years younger than Garrod, but a life of privilege in the capital separated their maturity by a gulf of years. Leo was the delinquent son of the king, and Jason owed him a debt too great to count.

"I see you have my riff-raff in order," Leo said, referring to the prisoners. "Didn't give you any trouble on the road, I hope?"

"No, Highness," Jason said. "A few tried to escape in the Everdusk, but were quickly tracked down." He pointed to a batch of prisoners standing next to each other in the ring. Their once-white rags were stained a deep brownish red along the front of their bellies, and their bare feet were heavily pockmarked with sores. "They were suitably punished."

"Nothing too *painful*, I hope. Need something left for today, right?" Leo cocked an eyebrow at both of the wizards, an unsubtle conspiring glint in his eye.

"Quite," Jason said, bowing his head a fraction.

Garrod cleared his throat. "We are ready to begin, sire. You may wish to remain outside of the circle." He spoke with a strained effort, uncomfortable about using courtesy to an unattuned man that had no obvious value at a wizard's ritual.

Leo didn't seem to hear him. He was eyeing the circle ponderously, stroking his fluffy goatee beard with thumb and forefinger. Garrod was about to say something more curt, when Leo turned sharply to Jason, and this time the boyish excitement was replaced with a hard, stony expression. "I'm going through first."

"Excuse me, Highness?" Jason said, flabbergasted.

Leo straightened his back and lifted his chin in defiance. "If the rift – no, *when* the rift opens, I want to be first through the breach."

"I'm not sure that's wise," Jason interjected. "The soldiers here, their role—"

"I care not," Leo said, shaking his head. "I have dreamed of slaying a dragon ever since I was a boy. What we do here may be remembered in history for centuries. I pulled many strings to aid you, providing you with scoundrels and soldiers for this fanciful endeavour. Now I come to claim my reward. I have risked too much to walk away empty handed, ser wizard."

His ignorant use of the title *ser* when addressing his father caused a ripple of embarrassment to crawl up Garrod's spine. *Oh, yes, such risk,* he thought. Pilfering dungeon inmates that were scheduled to hang, just so he could watch them die up close. Was there even a law against that? And the king would never punish his dearest son, regardless. *You have a warped idea of risk, my witless friend.*

"So be it," Jason said to Leo.

Garrod's jaw dropped open, but he closed it quickly. He knew better than to argue with his father today. It took a monumental effort, but he held his tongue.

"Will your guardsman be accompanying you?" Jason said, glancing to the prince's bodyguard.

"No," Leo said brightly. "Wait outside the ring, Rodrik. I will not have you steal my glory." He said it in cocky jest, but clearly meant it. Rodrik, a hulking mass of muscle, bowed his head to the prince and retreated a step, exchanging a disbelieving shrug with the wizards when Leo turned his back on him. He pushed his way through the ring of prisoners and stepped out.

Jason inhaled a deep breath. "Let's begin."

He instructed Garrod and Leo to form a triangle of points with himself around the inner edge of the circle, standing a couple of feet away from the prisoners, facing the crumbling well in the centre.

Garrod's confidence in his father's abilities kept him mostly level headed about what was about to happen, but as he took up his position, he gulped and the drumbeat of his steady heart quickened a tad.

Jason lifted a hand to the brooding grey sky, signalling the guards for silence. He bellowed at the top of his lungs, "Commence!"

He said nothing else. There were no other words necessary. Garrod understood that since fleeing Archdale from the calamitous dragon thirty years ago, his father had spent every spare waking moment conducting research, all in preparation for this day. He understood that the rift is closer than most people could comprehend, and it did not require potions or spells or mystical ancient chants to gain access to it.

The simple key to the rift was pain. Intense, concentrated *pain.*

At Jason's command, one hundred armed guards drove one hundred spears through the back of one hundred prisoners' kneecaps.

Despite the gags in their mouths, an orchestra of screams erupted into the still air, piercing the quiet of the abandoned city with deafening clarity. Garrod almost covered his ears to block out the cacophony, but he resisted. He stared across the circle at the wailing prisoners opposite him, blood spraying out of their exposed knee joints, dripping from the ends of the metal spikes that protruded through the cartilage and bone. Some of the victims toppled forwards, collapsing on the cobblestones, others threw back their heads, trying to howl at the sky but choking on the gags.

The soldiers pulled their weapons back out in unison. The prisoners wailed.

Garrod could smell iron now. Steaming blood trickled past his feet in thin rivulets between the cobblestone cracks, drowning the small weeds that grew there. He looked across to his father, who was now frowning intently as he studied the faces of the prisoners. Garrod turned around to look into the eyes of the men directly behind him just a few paces away.

He passed his gaze over them, and stopped on one particular man with blue eyes and a shock of greasy red hair. The man had tears streaming down his face and looked at Garrod in a way that defined regret and self-pity. Garrod did not feel sorry for him. He couldn't allow himself to. The redhead was a criminal, guilty of murder, or treason, or some other heinous act that was only redeemable through death. At least here today, he would be part of something important, something much bigger than himself. To die with purpose was more than the likes of he deserved.

The soldier behind him rammed his spear through the red haired man's other knee, in perfect synchronicity with the other ninety-nine soldiers.

More screams. Garrod noted a change in the tone, a

higher pitch.

The prisoners had reached the required levels of pain calculated to trigger whatever phenomenon caused the rift to open. Garrod looked into the red haired man's eyes again as he lay choking and gasping on the ground. He was staring straight ahead towards the well. His eyes glazed over. The prisoner's jaw went slack, his pupils dilated as his eyes stretched wider than seemed natural. He was staring not at Garrod, but *through* him, gaping at something behind him. Something that his mind was struggling to comprehend.

"It's open!" Leo cried in awestruck jubilance from the other side of the circle.

Garrod swivelled and saw the prince holding onto the shoulder of his nearest prisoner, tilting his head slowly up, admiring something unseen above the well between himself and Garrod. To his right, Jason Brockhurst was doing the same thing, holding a prisoner and staring in awe towards the centre point of the circle. They'd created a physical connection with their prisoners, which allowed them to see what they were seeing.

Garrod put his back to the well and stepped in front of his red haired prisoner. He took a deep breath, hunkered down and reached out to grip the man's shoulder.

A shadow enveloped Garrod. The sky, which had been dim before, now turned darker than dusk. Garrod sensed a heavy gravitational force tugging at his back, looming over him.

At length, he spun to face whatever they had unleashed. It took a moment for his eyes to focus, and his vision swam.

Garrod looked at the spot where the well had been a moment ago, but found it gone. In its place, rising up from the cobblestones and filling the majority of the space within the circle of prisoners, was a dome-shaped black void, almost as tall as the derelict buildings that enclosed the town square.

Garrod felt a sting of anxiety flood over him as he stared into that empty abyss. As his eyes adjusted, he saw a shimmering purple light form deep inside the pitch black. The light expanded, inheriting the dome shape of its container, seeming to either grow in size or race towards him, he couldn't tell which. The light flickered and danced like the flames of a violet bonfire. It expanded to fill the arch of darkness before him, but a thick border of black nothingness separated the purple fire from the outside air.

That is the rift.

The flickering arch of purple light settled, becoming easier to look at. It reminded Garrod of a church window, and then he realised it *was* a window, but rather than looking out on a pleasant courtyard, this window led to another world… maybe even another *universe.*

On the other side, Garrod could see eggs in a giant nest. A clutch of them sitting in exactly the spot where the well should be. The view wavered in the hazy purple light, as if he was looking at the nest through a wall of rippling water. The eggs were scaly and speckled with rounded lumps, lying in a bed of prickly twigs.

My Kella. Father was right. Dragon's eggs!

An astonished smile broke across Garrod's face. He could no longer see his father, the rift blocked him from view, but he knew he must be able to see the eggs as well. As could Leo.

As if summoned by that very thought, the prince of Darune appeared inside the window on the other side of the nest. He materialised in thin air, shimmering into existence and fading from a transparent shadow into a solid form. He had donned his silver helmet and lofted his sword above his head, holding it in a ready-stance as he approached the nest.

Through the haze, Garrod saw the young prince's eyes light up beyond the slit of his helmet, as he gaped at the eggs.

"Soldiers, proceed!" Jason Brockhurst's voice cried out, muffled somehow by the rift's presence. The soldiers now touched the shoulders of their assigned prisoner and a wave of gasps spun around the circle as they suddenly saw it too.

Fifty of the armed men stepped forward into the circle. The ones near Garrod brushed past him, raising their shields in a defensive position as they marched into the rift. Garrod watched in fascination as they faded out of existence, before reappearing in the purple glow of whatever world was on the other side.

He was overcome with awe and amazement, but had the wit to remember the plan. Half of the soldiers would go in first, and assuming they made it through unscathed, Jason and Garrod would follow with the second half of soldiers.

The first group surrounded the dragon's nest, most looking around at whatever lay beyond the rift's border that Garrod could see. All seemed well enough.

Garrod called out to Jason. "You were right, father! Do you see the eggs?"

"I do," Jason replied, having to shout to be heard over the wailing prisoners and distortion caused by the rift. "I'm going to…" He stopped short. There was a commotion stirring among the soldiers near the nest. Garrod heard faintly, like an echo over a wide valley, a harsh guttural shriek.

Something moved across Garrod's view, just inside the portal. Something big, hairy, and inhuman. The soldiers on the left raised their swords and sprang backwards, flinching away from something. A head loomed into view, the head of an enormous weasel-like creature. Only it couldn't possibly be a weasel, because weasels didn't have fangs on the outside of their mouths, or forked tongues. This one had both. And it was the size of a bull. It appeared to be infected with some kind of disease, because the skin hung off the side of its face in scabby flaps, exposed raw flesh swarmed with clusters of blood-sucking nibbets.

The weasel creature lunged into the group of soldiers and chaos erupted. It pounced on one soldier and tore his head clean off with a ferocious bite. Before the others could react, the weasel's tail whipped around with rib cracking force and swiped five men away out of sight.

A soldier behind Garrod cried out. "What's happening in there?"

They're being killed, Garrod thought grimly. *Was this a terrible mistake?*

The soldiers in the rift were slashing at the monster now, stabbing and hacking chunks of meat off, and Prince Leo threw himself into the fray.

A second weasel appeared from the right, head-charging through the pack of men and tossing them into the air. Two soldiers were hewn in half by its terrible jaws and a third swung his sword arm straight into the thing's mouth as it clamped its fangs shut. The man stumbled backwards, the stump of his arm spewing blood and he collapsed on the ground.

Leo charged the second weasel with his sword aimed down, seemingly with the intent to stab it in the eye. The weasel snarled and darted away, and Leo's sword bit the ground.

Another beast appeared.

It came from the sky. A hideous, monstrous black condor, with talons as big as a horse and a wingspan that completely blotted out the sky. It landed on the nest. Garrod had never seen such ferocity in any animal before, and he recognised its crazed aggression for what it was: a mother defending its children.

"Not a dragon nest," he muttered almost incoherently. His heart rate went up another notch, now beating against his ribs in what one might call mild panic.

"Garrod!" his father called. "I have to help them! I'm going through!"

Garrod tore his eyes away from the hypnotic rift. "What?" he cried. "It's a slaughterhouse in there!" Garrod let go of his prisoner, half expecting the rift to disappear as he severed his connection with one of its creators, but it remained. It seemed that now he could see the rift, he was powerless to unsee it. He ran around the circle, skirting the edge of the bulging darkness that was the border between his world and that of the hazy purple other-world.

He reached his father just as Jason was shouting his final command. "Onwards! Save the prince!" The remaining fifty soldiers stepped forwards now and marched bravely into the rift. If they were scared, they didn't show it.

Garrod grabbed his father's arm, intending to stop him from following. But in a fit of mad bravery, Garrod heard himself say, "I'm with you, father."

Jason patted his son's hand, and gave him a proud smile. His eyes gleamed with anticipation. Despite the carnage that was happening in there, there was nothing Garrod could do or say that would prevent him from entering the rift. No man alive could stop a Brockhurst from following his dream.

Father and son turned to face the darkness, and stepped over the threshold between the two worlds.

Garrod's ears popped as the town square retreated at his back, and the darkness engulfed him. All concept of presence completely disappeared and he found himself floating in a tunnel of emptiness between two gateways of light. Ahead was the purplish portal to whatever world those monsters lived in. And behind, he saw his own world through another gateway. This portal also flickered and danced like a flame in the wind, but it glowed a soft inviting orange hue, the polar opposite of the repulsive sickly purple that tinted the other.

Garrod's resolve wavered. Whatever insanity had lured him this far disappeared in a wave of fear. He paused in the void, while his father walked on. He watched as though in a dream, his father stepped through the boundary of the other world and joined the fray.

Jason summoned a fireball in his palm and cast it at one of the weasels, disintegrating its whiskers and scorching its fangs a charred black. The weasel yelped and fled away from the new combatant.

The giant vulture was defending its eggs by pecking any soldier within range of its bloody, jagged beak. Grisly flesh dangled from its tip, it jerked its head this way and that, impaling soldiers through the back or stabbing them right through the neck.

One of the eggs hatched.

A micro version of the condor exploded out of a scaly green eggshell and its yellow eyes glared at the intruders like a cat that has been rudely interrupted during a nap. It stumbled out of the nest and flopped onto the ground. A soldier accidentally stepped backwards and tripped over its long neck. The hatchling, which was about half the size of the men, squawked and jabbed its beak at the man's face, instinctively going for his eyes, and plucked one out. The soldier screamed, lifting a hand to his oozing eye socket and swinging a fist at the bird with the other. The hatchling's beak clamped around the man's exposed neck and sliced him open in four deep strips. Blood sprayed, and the man went limp.

A second egg burst open amid the carnage and then a third and fourth. Leo cut off the head of one bird as soon as it lunged out of its egg. The mother lashed its heavy tail fan and caught him in the side of the head as she spun to fend off more attacks on the opposite side of the nest. Leo took the blow and fell to the ground. One of the hatchlings leapt onto his back and started pecking at his leather armour with the force of a blacksmith's hammer on an anvil. Leo screamed as his spine shattered. He awkwardly tried to swing his sword at the hatchling on his back but he couldn't roll the feathery monstrosity off. The bird caught a glimpse of his face and tried forcing its beak between the eyehole of his silver helmet.

Garrod stared in grim fascination as the hatchling jabbed at Leo's face again and again, shifting and turning to follow his desperate attempts to turn away from the onslaught. Eventually, the bird broke through, and the beak plunged into the helmet. A small piece of dripping gore was attached to the tip of its beak when it raised its head. The bird jerked open its beak, swallowing Leo's eyeball and a slice of his brain. The prince convulsed on the ground for a moment, then lay still.

Garrod was frozen in a mortified trance, hardy believing the horror he was witnessing. He was apparently safe between the worlds inside the rift. The monsters couldn't see him. He lingered, hesitating about whether to move forward or turn back. He didn't know if it would be a one-way trip or not.

The sight of Jason being heaved aside by a retreating soldier spurred Garrod into action. He couldn't let his father die in there. Gulping once more, his heart thundering in his chest now like a woodpecker, he strode forwards through the gateway.

An intense flood of power radiated through him as he emerged in the other world and into the heart of the chaos. It felt like coming up for air after nearly drowning in a river.

Garrod aimed one palm towards the giant condor and instantly launched a fireball at the underside of the mother's wings. It screeched a terrible cry as feathers burned away, tearing a hole in the wing that would prevent it from ever flying again. Jason joined his son and together, they hurled a volley of flames at the monster until it toppled over sideways, crushing a group of soldiers and a weasel creature that had been engaged in battle on the other side of the nest.

Garrod noticed how easy it was to summon fireballs here, but did not have time to process how that could be. And though he didn't notice at the time, he later reflected on the location of the vulture's nest. He recalled the crumbling ruin of the cobblestones. The similarities to Archdale's town square were obvious. He wondered whether he would have found the remains of the well hidden beneath that cluster of twigs and branches that formed the bird's nest, but he didn't have the chance to find out.

There might have been thirty men left alive by the time the enraged mother was taken down in a smoking ruin of burnt feathers and charred skin. The remaining weasel creature had chased a group of soldiers into a corner of the ruinous buildings, cutting them off from retreat.

Is retreat even an option?

Garrod looked around at the rift, a dome of wavering orange light all around them. It was fading, losing its vibrancy. Garrod could see the prisoners lying on the cobblestones on the other side, but now and then they faded and he caught glimpses of ruinous buildings through the diminishing haze. Garrod took his father's arm and said, "We must go, or else we'll be stranded here."

Jason gave the rift a disdainful glance, then turned to look up at the sky. On this side, there were no clouds, but the sun seemed pale and weak, struggling to penetrate the strangely thick, acrid air. "No, son. I have to stay. You go."

"What?" Garrod couldn't believe what he was hearing. "You can't stay here, father. Look at this place! It's full of monsters and decay. There is something very wrong with this world."

Jason smiled at his son. "Precisely. Only a dragon could live in such a place. That's why I have to stay."

"*Why?*" Garrod demanded. "What's so important about finding a dragon?"

"Don't you remember?" Jason looked a mixture of puzzlement and shame. "How could you, I suppose? You were just a boy when it came."

Garrod glanced nervously at the rift again. The shimmering orange portal that marked the way home to his world beckoned, growing fainter and fainter. Now he could see the ruinous buildings beyond the dome's borders, even more decrepit than the ones in Archdale.

"There's no time," Jason said, tears forming in his eyes. "Farewell, my son."

And with that, he turned and ran past the nest, heading for the group of men that had been cornered by the giant weasel. Garrod watched him go, lost for words and torn between going after him and retreating through the rift.

"Squark!"

He turned sharply to face the nest. The last egg had hatched. Out of it shambled a horribly deformed baby condor, the size of a dog. It had black stubby wings and one yellow eye bulged bigger than the other, with a crooked beak that bent downwards at its tip.

The hatchling lunged at Garrod, stretching its neck towards him, trying to bite off his nose.

Garrod caught it with outstretched arms and stumbled backwards. He fell on his back on the cobbles, the baby bird scrabbling on top of his chest, pecking downwards at the stones on either side of his head. The black void that marked the boundary of the rift pulsed and thrummed in Garrod's mind, inches away. He sensed that it would collapse soon and he feared being stuck on this side forever, if he couldn't get the squawking, hideous beast off him in time.

He shoved the bird away, but it scrambled back, giving him no time to stand up. Craning his neck, he saw the gateway to his own world rippling like a flag caught in a strong breeze, flickering with that inviting orange fire glow. He longed to reach it and stretched his hand out across the threshold.

As if answering his will, the portal pulled him and the hatchling in. He passed through the rift and was spat violently out the other side.

It could only have taken a second to pass through the rift back into his world, but in that moment, time seemed to slow to a crawl. Garrod experienced the extremely unpleasant sensation of his mind being torn in two and put back together again. Only there were new parts being added, an alien conscience that had no place in his mind, but was somehow forced in anyway.

He heard a hissing, scratching sound inside his head. He sensed confusion and fear, that of an adolescent. He shook his head, trying to reject the invasive thoughts; he was a thirty six year old man with a mind full of memories and experience, he had no room for an outsider's fears.

He didn't know what was happening and that triggered a brutal resistance to flare up inside his will. Garrod fought for dominance over the other's presence in an effort to keep control of his mind.

The next thing he saw was a great fork of lightning streak across the sky in front of his nose. He was lying on his back, a rude cobblestone jabbing him in the ribs, rain pelting him in the cheeks and forehead.

He blinked and sat up, just as the thunder boomed. Another jolt of fear coursed through him, but it was alien, not his fear. He knew that because he had always *loved* storms. He had nothing to fear from them, so why was it scaring him now?

He rubbed his eyes and staggered to his feet. The rift was gone. A circle of dead prisoners lay strewn around the old well in the Archdale town square. The rain was washing away the blood.

Coork-ussss! A voice hissed in his mind. He clutched his forehead, grimacing with discomfort.

What happened to the bird creature that had attacked him? Did it come through with him?

Qaarrrrk-bussss!

That voice again.

No. Not a voice.

A squawk.

Is that your name? Garrod thought.

Crrrk-abusss.

"Corcubus?" Garrod muttered to himself. "You're inside my head, aren't you?"

Crrk-abusss!

The creature seemed incapable of saying anything else. And yes. The voice was coming from inside his own mind. Somehow, as Garrod and the hatchling had crossed the threshold between worlds, their spirits had been merged. He didn't know how it had happened, and he had no idea what he could do about it now.

A lesser man would panic. But Garrod swallowed the

fear and numbed it into submission. If he panicked, he'd be lost.

CHAPTER FOUR

Ellie climbed out of her bedroom window, silent as a shadowcat and shimmied along the upper frame of the kitchen window below. She could hear the muffled voices of Johanna and Grandma chatting about something or other downstairs, and the thunderous snoring of Grandpa in the living room. Their grandparents were housesitting while Julia and Frank were out visiting friends in Honeyville, the next village up the road. Clinging to a wooden support beam on the underside of the roof, Ellie leaned out until she could peek inside the window below her feet.

Sure enough, Johanna and Grandma were in there, an open book spread out between them on the kitchen table, the pair engaged in animated conversation, probably discussing characters from an old story. They would be there for hours. Plenty of time for Ellie to go and come back without them even noticing.

She crept a little further, until there was no chance of being spotted, and dropped onto the grass, bending her knees to soften the fall. A quick glance around the empty garden and… *Crap! Who's that?*

It was Markus. Walking along the lane, coming towards the McKree's cottage. She saw him intermittently as he passed behind the row of trees that separated their boundary from the lane. Ellie waited for him to go behind the next tree, then made a run for it, slipping into the woodland behind the house.

As far as Ellie knew, she had timed her getaway with perfection. But as she crossed the grass, a shaft of sunlight had glinted off the knife in her belt, catching Markus' eye. He saw her disappearing into the trees, thinking what a fortunate stroke of luck it was that Ellie was out of the house. Now, he would be free to talk to Johanna alone, which seemed a most exciting prospect. He pushed back his hair, which he'd just spent twenty minutes pruning, and strode up to the front door, knocking three times with a flourish.

Meanwhile, Ellie took off into the woods. She weaved between the trees, creeping through the thick layer of underbrush. Her bow was tucked over one shoulder and her two knives hung on either hip, tucked into her leather belt. With a quiver and ten arrows, she was armed and ready for battle. That hog didn't stand a chance this time.

As she made her way through the woodland towards the watering hole, she grinned to herself. Each step brought her further away from the house and closer to danger, but she reveled in the thrill of it. A small voice inside her head was whispering something about being patient, but she found it easy to ignore because there were so many other voices to listen to in the woods.

She heard them all in her head as she walked. Not human voices, they sounded strange and vague, often unintelligible. But not unwelcome. Ellie liked these voices, because they allowed her a special insight into the minds of animals. It was what made people say things like, "She has such a way with them, doesn't she?"

Without even thinking about it, she could open her senses and allow the snapshot thoughts of the many creatures seen and unseen in the woods to flow through her mind.

A sparrow in a tree glanced down, noting Ellie's presence, its tiny heart skipping a beat in a moment of fear as the human crunched through the fallen leaves. In Ellie's head, the sparrow spoke with a wiry, thin voice. Like all the animals, its thoughts bore closer resemblance to *feelings* than words, but her brain worked its mysterious magic to translate them into simple phrases: *Beware! Hunter below. Keep watch,* said the sparrow to itself. Ellie smiled, smug that even her petite frame could instil fear.

A squirrel perched on a tree branch watched her approach with similar thoughts: *Wassat? Danger! Climb!* It scurried up the trunk and out of sight just as Ellie walked past. She wasn't interested in squirrels or sparrows, though. This was, after all, a boar hunt.

At the watering hole, Ellie hunkered down to check for tracks. This time, she recognised the boar's footprints straight away. Two pointed prongs and a third pad at the back, leading away north, just like before. She stood and retraced her father's footsteps along the boar's track. When she came to the cedar trees that they had used as an ambush point the last time, she considered her options: *I could climb up there and wait for it to come back again, or I could keep following these tracks and see where they lead…*

Hardly a real choice at all. On she went, with the reckless confidence of youth and determination.

The tracks were easy to follow. The boar had pounded the underbrush from repeated journeys to and from the waterhole to wherever its hideaway was. Even when Ellie couldn't see individual footprints, she could just follow the trampled leaves.

After a while, she spied a fiery glow ahead, light from the setting sun. It teased her between the trees, which were thinning out as she reached the outer edge of the woods. The beaten track led all the way to where the woodland came to an abrupt end. The track continued out into the rocky, rolling hills beyond.

Ellie stopped when she reached the threshold, hunkering

next to the outermost tree. The blindingly bright sun shone directly in her face, making it difficult to scan the horizon, but she saw the boar tracks making a beeline for a lonely chestnut tree silhouette, out on the plains. A mound of grassy earth jutted up next to the tree, looking suspiciously like a den.

Found you!

Ellie licked her lips. She craned her neck to look up at the tree's branches. A gentle breeze came from her right, blowing south. All the leaves were leaning in that direction. *Father always says to keep downwind whenever possible.* That meant she would have to skirt the edge of the forest and creep out into the field to approach the den from behind, to ensure her scent didn't spook the boar into fleeing.

So that's what she did. Crouch-walking as stealthily as possible, she made her way behind the den in a wide circle, and when her leg muscles burned, she dropped onto her belly and crawled. In a rare moment that might have made her father proud, Ellie took her time on the approach. Once she was within range of her bow, the sun had begun its descent behind the horizon. The sky dimmed as the sun disappeared, signalling the onset of dusk.

The wind remained steady. Ellie thanked it for not giving away her position. The chestnut tree swayed to and fro against the breeze, its leaves rustling a sweet song.

Something snorted.

Ellie froze. The sound came from the den, now only a few dozen paces ahead of her.

Mrs Hog is home…

Her heartbeat quickened. She realised at this point that she had no plan to lure her out of the den. The mound's opening must have been on the opposite side, because all she could see from here was a slope of earth, little more than a grassy hump. The brief possibility of crawling up there and jumping down into the opening crossed her mind – element of surprise and all that – but she quickly dismissed the idea as ludicrous. The little scar on her forehead was a reminder not to try jumping on a wild boar ever again.

So, what could she do?

The chestnut tree swayed again, almost waving at her in greeting.

That wasn't a bad idea – a distraction. A lure. Ellie, still lying on her belly, unhooked her bow from around her shoulder and laid it on the stony ground. She pulled out three arrows and placed her quiver beside the bow.

She brushed her hand around in the thin grass and picked up a small but weighty pebble which fit snugly in her hand, then hunkered to one knee, keeping her head low.

Pulling her arm back, she took aim at the chestnut tree, and threw the pebble at it.

Her aim was true. It struck the tree trunk about six feet off the ground with a wooden *clunk*.

A voice, faint but wild, fuzzed out of the air and into Ellie's mind. She picked up two words:

Noise! Prey?

Ellie gulped. Somehow, that didn't seem like the voice of a boar. An icy shiver crawled through her bones, and for the first time since leaving the house, she had a moment of regret.

She forced it aside. *Just get ready to shoot it!*

Ellie grabbed her bow, nocked an arrow and drew, taking aim at the spot between the mound and the tree.

She held her breath.

Movement over the brow of the den. An animal, cautious, alert. It was covered in fur. And its ears were up, two triangular shapes. A bushy tail protrude from its rear.

Boar tails are short and stubby.

That's no boar. It's a fookin' wolf.

Ellie's arms tensed, almost releasing the arrow by mistake.

The wolf crept over to the tree, its nose low to the ground. It reached the area where the pebble must have landed and sniffed. Ellie had a clear shot, but she was too tense. *What if I miss? It'll see me, and then what?* She had no idea how fast wolves could run, but she estimated that if she was lucky, she *might* have enough time to knock a second arrow, if the first one didn't find its mark. But… even so. *It's a fookin' wolf!*

Nothing, the wolf thought. It dismissed the pebble and spun to go back to its den. As it turned, it spotted Ellie. She was completely exposed, kneeling in the open field, aiming an arrow at it. The wolf's ears pricked up and it lifted its head, staring right at her.

Prey!

Ellie's throat constricted violently, cutting off her air. *It's going to eat me.* A paralysing fear swept over her so suddenly, that every muscle in her limbs clenched, turning her arms and legs to stone. Her vision swam, the wolf began to shimmer in waves, as if she was seeing it through tears.

That wasn't right. She wasn't crying, and her eyes were fine. There really *was* a shimmer appearing in front of her. It seemed as if the air itself was breaking apart, splitting open from some tremendous pressure. The wolf cocked its head at her, its body wavering through the strange anomaly.

Ellie's clenched fingers jerked and she fumbled her bowstring. The nocked arrow flew. It shot through the weird hazy air bubble and sailed past the chestnut tree.

A total miss.

The wolf bounded forwards. Its ears drew back, its lips peeled upwards in a terrible snarl and it charged at her.

"*Ignus PROJEET*!"

The wolf's eyes suddenly glowed a bright orange, reflecting an enormous ball of fire. Ellie felt heat singing the hairs on the back of her neck, and a ferocious roar enveloped her from behind.

The wolf skidded to a halt in its tracks, its head bent in fear, as a giant fireball soared over Ellie's head and crashed into the chestnut tree. A mighty explosion of crackling leaves erupted from the branches, as the whole tree went up in flames.

The wolf turned and fled. It bolted to Ellie's right, away

from the burning tree and across the field, tail tucked firmly between its scampering legs, paws flicking up mites of soil. It bolted into the shadowy woods and disappeared out of sight.

Ellie found her breath, and let out a shuddering cry. She turned to see Johanna and Markus standing on the edge of the forest, looking her way. Johanna was leaning forwards, both palms outstretched towards Ellie, where she had cast the fireball. Johanna's knees buckled and she keeled over. Markus tried to catch her as she fell, but she slumped to the ground in a heap.

"Hanna!" Ellie cried, scrambling to her feet and breaking into a run.

Markus was saying something in a tone of distress, crouching beside Johanna on one knee and leaning over to peer into her pale face.

Ellie reached them, panting and gasping for breath. "*Hanna!*"

"Hey sis," Johanna croaked, looking up from the grass. "You okay?"

"That w-w-wolf!" Ellie stammered. She could still hear its awful voice inside her head and the terrible way it had looked at her as though she was nothing but an easy meal. "You saved me…" Now she was crying. Tears of sorrow, guilt, regret, relief.

"That fireball. I've never seen anything like it. That was the biggest fireball I've ever seen!"

"I don't feel so great," Johanna wheezed. Ellie had no idea the amount of energy it must have cost her sister to cast such an incredible blaze, and she did it to save her life.

"Thank you, Hanna!" she cried, falling to her knees and wrapping both arms around Johanna's neck. "How did you know I was here?"

"You didn't come down for supper." Johanna gasped for breath.

Markus squeezed her hand. "Don't talk. You need to rest." He looked to Ellie. "I saw you going into the woods.

I should have said something straight away, but I didn't… Your grandparents invited me to stay for tea, so I did. Then when it came time to eat, I remembered you were out here. I told Johanna I had seen you, and so we came looking for you. We found fresh footprints and followed them here."

"Patience of a nibbet," Johanna said softly, smiling up at Ellie. The words seemed to take a tremendous effort, and she lolled her head back to the ground and passed out.

"We have to get her home," Markus said. "She needs food and water, that fireball must have cost her a whole day's worth of energy, maybe more!"

"How do you know so much about it?" Ellie said raising an eyebrow.

"I, uhh, you know. Been reading about attunement."

"Uh huh," Ellie said. "Help me carry her." Ellie stood, wiping her eyes and nose on her sleeve.

They hoisted Johanna up, looping her arms over each of their shoulders. She was taller than Ellie, but shared her slender frame. Even so, Ellie never realised how awkward and cumbersome an unconscious person could be. *Huntresses have to deal with this all the time whenever they bring home a fresh kill. I need to get used to it!*

"Are you a good tracker or something?" she said, straining a bit.

"Not really," Markus said, pointing to the ground with his chin. "You left a nice easy trail of prints."

Ellie realised in a sudden rush that she was not as skilled as she thought she was. Not only had Markus seen her sneaking away, but she'd left such a clear set of tracks that anyone with eyes could have followed her. This bitter realisation fed her determination to improve herself.

That wolf encounter had scared her deeply, though. It wasn't the first time an animal had meant to harm her, but she had always had quick fight-or-flight instincts before. Usually flight, she was particularly good at running away from Farmer Cribs' overweight guard dog.

But the wolf had triggered a whole new response that

filled her with dismay: she had frozen in fear. What good was that to a huntress? Staring at the wolf as it prowled towards her was like staring death directly in the face, and now she knew how a rabbit felt when it spotted a hawk dive bombing it from above. Utterly helpless.

How could she ever become a master huntress if she couldn't master her own fear? Freezing couldn't be an option next time. Freezing meant death. Next time, she would fight or flee. But *not* freeze.

CHAPTER FIVE

"My son is *dead*?" King Victus howled, spittle flying from his cracked lips. His voice echoed around the grand chamber, fading out somewhere in the rafters high above.

"My sincerest condolences, Highness," Garrod said, kneeling before the king, his head bowed low. "I can only offer my deepest sympathies for your loss, on behalf of my father, whom I have also lost. Though his fate is not yet confirmed." He rose to his feet and looked the king straight in the eye. "It is for that reason I come to you now, humbly seeking aid in my time of need."

The king, sitting hunched in his throne, looked the definition of flabbergasted. "You ask my aid, mere moments after informing me of my son's death?"

Rodrik, Prince Leo's hulking bodyguard, shifted on his feet beside Garrod. The guard had escorted Garrod into the castle from outside, and now kept within striking distance, no doubt protocol for any visitors attending the king.

"I know the timing is ill," Garrod admitted. "But time is something I do not have the luxury of. I must act quickly if I am to have a chance of rescuing my father. If you can spare me some more prisoners, I know I can reopen the rift and—"

"How did he die?" King Victus croaked.

Garrod paused to consider, swallowing his frustration and trying to summon some genuine empathy. The man had lost his son. Garrod had no idea what that must be like, but he knew that without the king's assistance he would have no chance of rescuing his father. So, he had to appease him.

"Prince Leo died bravely," Garrod said. "Fighting monsters."

"Monsters?" King Victus said, cocking his head.

"Yes. I don't know how much Leo informed you of my father's plans, but we were searching for a dragon."

"Poppycock," Victus hissed. "I know Leo believed in such nonsense, but do not mock me in my own halls, Sai."

"I would never, Highness. It's the truth."

The king studied him warily. "Are you telling me my son met his end at the talons of a dragon?"

"No, sire. We didn't come across any dra—"

"Then how did he die?" Victus demanded in a shrill cry.

Garrod had to inhale a breath to steady his patience. He glanced over the other king's guards that stood to attention in a neat line along the dais, either side of the throne. *What a dull life, standing there all day to protect this royal dimwit.* An idea struck him. "Sire, if I may share with you a memory?"

"What do you mean?"

"I can show you what happened." Without waiting for an answer, Garrod opened the door to the king's mind, which was easy. King Victus had not a single attuned cell in his body. Garrod recalled the disastrous events of the rift experiment in Archdale. He pictured Leo dressed in his knightly finery, storming through the rift to assault what he thought was a dragon's nest, and projected the memory at the king.

"Ohh," the king groaned. "Leo…"

He was seeing the memory in his own mind, through the filter of Garrod's perception. The unfortunate side effect of that allowed the king to feel Garrod's embarrassment, the sneering way he perceived the foolish prince, and that hurt the king more than Garrod had anticipated.

"You despised him?" Victus sounded surprised. "After all he did to assist you?"

"I showed the prince respect and courtesy whenever he was present, sire."

"You let him enter that foul place by himself!"

"He would have it no other way," Garrod insisted. "Your son chose his role in the experiment. Who were we to deny him? Look, we sent soldiers in immediately after. And my father, he tried to save—"

"*Monsters!*" the king bellowed in fright. Garrod thought he meant himself and Jason, but Victus was referring to the literal monsters of the other world. He gaped in horror as the prince fought off the giant weasel creatures, and the hideous rotting condor and its screeching babies. When Leo fell, pinned by the weight of the hatchling hammering its beak into his spine, the king cried out in anguish.

"Stop!" Victus wailed, flapping his hands around in front of his face. "For the love of mercy, *stop it!*"

Garrod closed his mind. The memory receded into his subconscious, he stuffed it down next to the sleeping vulture, Corcubus. Garrod was grateful for the creature's unconsciousness. If it were awake, the king might have sensed it while he was experiencing Garrod's memory. And how exactly would Garrod be able to explain that he was now harbouring one of the same creatures that had murdered the prince inside his mind? Garrod couldn't even explain it to himself yet, nevermind the grieving king.

"My poor boy." The king slumped back in his throne, clutching his forehead and uttering a long, despairing moan. "To die in such a cruel way, in some unknown hell realm."

"I am glad you saw that."

"*Glad?*" Victus shrilled.

"Beg pardon, sire." *Fool! Speak wiser, or he'll never help you.* "I meant only that you now understand the peril in which my father now resides. That place is evil, like a dark reflection of our world. My father, he…" He *chose* to stay behind, Garrod knew, but he couldn't tell the king that. "He was still inside when the rift closed. Please, sire, do not make me beg for your assistance. Would you not do anything you could to bring your son back, if you had the choice?"

"Master Brockhurst, your father got what he deserved," the king said coldly. "To mess with such foul sorcery invites nothing but madness and death. I see now that is all you sinister conjurers are good for."

"Conjurers?" Garrod was almost lost for words. Whatever patience he had for the king drained away in an instant. He had never particularly liked King Victus, but now he pondered whether he had ever loathed anyone as much as he did in that moment. How dare he call his father's work *madness?* Garrod folded his arms and said, "Sai Jason Brockhurst is the Prime Wizard of Darune, the most respected man in the province."

"Since when is a *Sai* more respected than a *King*?" Victus sneered.

Garrod opened his mouth to retort, but managed to restrain himself. *I've lost him now.*

"I think I have unearthed the root of this land's problem," Victus went on. "There's been a thorn in my side ever since I shouldered the mantle of responsibility over this province. It has taken the loss of my own flesh and blood to see it, but I thank you Master Brockhurst for bringing it to my attention. The problem is *you*."

"What do you mean?" Garrod frowned.

"My son humoured your father's preposterous notions of rifts and dragons, and now they both lay dead, rotting in a hellplane. If that isn't the work of evil, then I'm a common peasant."

"Please, Highness. My father might still be alive, you must help me—"

"Do not presume to tell me what I must do in my own castle, wizard!" King Victus stood up violently from his throne, looking down at Garrod from the dais. "These dark practices should be cast aside for they are too dangerous for the likes of us to trifle with. Your father paid the price with my son's life, and I will not be so foolish as to help you continue his delusional work now. For the sake of our province, I command you to cease. The practices of wizards and mages will no longer be tolerated in Darune. I hereby ban all study of attunement within our borders."

Garrod churned with anger at being treated with such disrespect. He may be the king, but who was Victus to speak so derogatively of the attuned community? A third of the population of Darune was at least partially attuned. What did he hope to achieve by forbidding their practices? Did he intend to imprison half the city? *That* sounded like madness.

Crrrkabusss, the vulture within him stirred.

Garrod clenched his fists, which trembled with rage. He shot the king a glare and reopened Victus' mind, shoving the memory of Leo's death through the door. He forced the king to see the moment his son died. The flapping monstrosity hammered its beak against Leo's back, crushing his spine, and Garrod felt a smile curling his lips when the king wailed in grief.

"No, stop!" Victus cried, collapsing back in his throne.

But Garrod didn't stop. He let the memory continue, showing the king every gory detail of his son's demise. The bird pecking furiously at his son's helmet, again and again, finally breaking through and impaling his eye socket with its long razor beak.

"*No!*" King Victus covered a shaky hand over his mouth. Shaking as much as Leo's twitching corpse.

Garrod didn't close his mind voluntarily. Rather, Rodrik, the prince's meathead bodyguard, gave him a sharp whack on the skull with the butt of his spear. Garrod was brought to his knees in a searing flash of pain, and the memory vanished once again.

The king thrashed in his throne, shaking his head between his fists, as if trying to excavate the vision of what he'd just seen. "Curse you, wizard! Curse you to ashes in the wind! Be gone from my city by sundown, Sai. Return to your wretched tower in your wretched forest, and stay there. I banish you from Darune, under penalty of death. *Get out of my sight!*"

Garrod turned on his heel and strode away down the middle of the king's audience chamber. Corcubus was awake now, squawking and demanding food. It siphoned Garrod's energy, like a lamb slurping milk from a teat, and there was nothing Garrod could do to stop it.

The king hollered maniacally behind him. "Archdale was a lesson in calamity! I will never allow such to be repeated under my rule. Darune will never again suffer the folly of wizards!"

Garrod barely heard him. Corcubus' wailing had escalated to a high-pitched screech, threatening to scratch its way out of Garrod's throbbing skull. He clutched at his head and marched from the king's chamber shrouded in rage.

***

By the time Garrod reached the gates of the city, he had a pounding headache, but Corcubus had partially settled and was no longer screeching at least. Garrod could feel his energy being passively drained, nourishing the bird. His stomach growled, despite the fact that he ate during the journey here, and he'd been careful about using a minimal amount of power on the king. There could only be one explanation – his body had to share its resources with Corcubus. *I have to eat for two now, like some pregnant wench.* What an absurd notion.

The Brockhurst's family servant and advisor, Robert Anders waited with the horses at the city gates. He must have seen the haggard look on Garrod's face, because he quickly opened the leather satchel hanging on his horse and pulled out a skin of water. "Here, Sai. You look pale."

Garrod took the skin, uncorked it and drank deep. "Thank you, Robert. Do we have any food?"

"Plenty, I visited the market and gathered supplies for our return journey." The old man took the water skin back and began rummaging around in the satchel. "What would you like?"

"Anything."

"I assume the king didn't take the news of his son well?" Robert handed him a brown paper bag with something firm wrapped within.

"You could say that," Garrod said, taking out an apple and biting off a chunk. He ate quickly, taking several ravenous bites while Robert waited patiently for him to elaborate. "King Victus has abandoned my father to his fate. He has declared a province-wide ban on attunement study and barred me from the city."

"Good grief," Robert said with a wince. "What on Kellamon did you say to him?"

"Nothing but the naked truth. He responded like a spoilt child."

Robert shook his head in disappointment. "That sounds like Victus. But to forbid attunement entirely? Even for him, that's a drastic move. Are you sure you didn't provoke him, Garrod? I'm not blind, I see how drained you are. And you're devouring that apple. What did you do to him?"

He hadn't told Robert about Corcubus yet. In time, Garrod supposed he would have to, but for now, he wanted to see if he could keep the creature under control by himself. "I forced a memory on him. I showed him his son's death."

"Oh, Garrod," Robert said in an accusatory tone. "Well, that explains his overreaction. Why would you inflict that on him? That was petty."

"I only meant to show my father's bravery in trying to save that delinquent. Do you really think I would take pleasure in tormenting someone just because I can?"

"You always had a dark streak, Garrod," Robert said. "I helped raise you, a man in my position sees much."

Garrod harrumphed. He couldn't argue with Robert. The man was pushing seventy, and had more wisdom than every member of the king's government combined. Despite his uncanny knack for uncovering secrets, Garrod was glad to have him by his side.

Garrod tossed the apple core away, took out a strip of jerky, and meticulously chewed it. He could feel his strength returning with every bite. The pair watched a few peasants coming and going through the city gates. Once Garrod left the city, he wouldn't be able to return. Not that he cared. He belonged in the Everdusk to the north. His body felt the pull of home, tugging at him like gravity.

"I'm sorry about your father," Robert said, breaking the silence. "But without the king's aid, we have no way of acquiring the prisoners needed to perform another experiment. As much as it pains me to admit, your father is lost to us."

"Perhaps. But if we could just—"

"Garrod…" Robert's voice was kind now, trying to offer comfort. "It took your father almost thirty years, most of your life, to develop his research."

"I know," Garrod said, resigned. He took a long breath, the anger finally dulling. Now that he could think a little clearer, he knew what he needed to do. "I will continue his legacy."

"A noble proposition. What, specifically, do you have in mind?"

"I will return to the Towers alone," Garrod said. "I need you to remain here for a few more days, Robert."

"To what end?"

"The king only banished me. You should be free to come and go as you please. But try to be discreet. I want you to gather as many high-ranking wizards and mages that you can find. Over the coming days, I suspect most will be given a choice: surrender their skills, or be forced out of their homes. Find the ones that choose to leave, and invite them to Trinity Towers."

Understanding dawned on Robert's face. "You mean to take over as Prime, in your father's absence?"

"Yes." He found a sudden urge to have Robert's approval. "Do you think I am ready for such responsibility?"

Robert smiled, and placed a leathery hand on Garrod's shoulder, giving it a surprisingly firm squeeze. "I do."

"Thank you. It means a lot to hear that. I'll begin preparations at the Towers, first by organising a ceremony in honour of my father. I think the tutors will need closure before they accept me as the new Prime."

"I fear some will not accept it regardless, Garrod. Your father was the glue that held the college together for many years. I'll do my best to help you through the transitional period, so that the Towers can stand for another century. But this attunement ban is dire news for us. Anyone who agrees to remain at the college now will have to do so under full disclosure that they are renegades. The same goes for any future students. Many will not want to take such a risk."

Garrod smiled. "That is why I need you to convince them. You can pick out a vagabond better than anyone."

Robert grinned. "My roguish days are long behind me. But a scoundrel never forgets his roots. I'll see who I can find. Is there anything else I can do for you, Sai?"

"Bring more of this jerky with you when you return." *I can feel Corcubus absorbing it.* "See you in a few days."

"Swift and pleasant travels, Sai."

***

Three days later, Garrod arrived back at Trinity Towers, his ancestral home in the Everdusk Forest. He climbed the tallest tower to his father's chamber and locked himself inside. Corcubus harassed his dreams each night as he made his way back from Darune City. The hatchling was growing stronger, Garrod could feel it pushing and bulging against the confines of his mind, down in the depths of Garrod's subconscious. If he didn't find a way to control it or, better yet, exorcise it entirely, he feared it would break out and try to take over his body.

Corcubus was not of his world. The beast had come from the other place, and the only way to figure this madness out would be to understand what that place truly was. His father had kept journals for years, noting down all of his significant findings. They had to be stored somewhere up there in his father's chambers at the top of the Sun Tower.

There were three separate rooms at the top of the tower. The largest was the Prime Wizard's chamber, a wide open study featuring a hefty superoaken desk and Jason's plush leather reclining chair. Bookshelves lined the curved walls, and a panoramic glass window overlooked the back of the Towers' grounds, pointing north east, to a view of the magnificent superoak trees.

Adjacent to this was the wizard's bedroom. A simple affair, just big enough for the four-post bed and sturdy wardrobe. A rounded window looked south with a clear view of the other two towers that made up the Trinity, and the grounds' main entrance gate. The third room was a cosy privy, accessed via a door from the bedroom.

Garrod wandered around the chambers feeling like a prying thief. He had been up here before, but never by himself. This was where he had learned all he knew about attunement, taught by his father. It was the closest they ever came to a father-son relationship. At the very least, this was where they almost bonded.

The truth was, Jason and Garrod were not close in the way many fathers and sons can be. Garrod was not raised by Jason so much as simply co-existed in the same household. The role of raising him fell to servants like Robert Anders who had tutored him in math, language, spiritual guidance and laws of nature. The only time he spent with his father was during attunement studies. Jason taught Garrod everything he knew, which was a considerable amount. He had grown into a powerful wizard in his own right.

But when it came to the rifts, that other realm, and now Corcubus, he had entered uncharted territory. His father had never mentioned the idea of assimilating another creature in one's own mind. As far as Garrod knew, no such thing had ever occurred to another wizard or mage. If his father had known about it, he never relayed such information to Garrod. So, that was why, on a stifling mid-spring day, he locked himself in the Sun Tower and pored over his father's journals. He scoured them page by page, searching for a way to open another rift, and any clues as to how on Kellamon he'd ended up with the soul of a diseased baby fucking vulture living inside his head.

Flipping through the books, Garrod discovered his father had a flair for dramatisation, as if he hoped that someone might find his journals one day and read them. Under any other circumstances, Garrod would have felt guilty reading such personal accounts, but his father was gone now and it didn't matter.

He flipped through the pages until he found an entry dated twenty-seven years ago, the fateful day when Archdale was destroyed. It wasn't relevant to rifts, but Garrod's eye caught on the first sentence, and he decided to read the rest.

293rd Day, 10th Moon, 3047 KD

I saw a glimpse of oblivion today. It was only a glimpse, but it was enough to scar my mind for the rest of my days. My hand is trembling, making it difficult to hold the quill, but if I don't record this now, I fear my mind will wipe it from memory.

In short, my home is destroyed, and a dragon of death is responsible.

It happened in the dead of night. As per my usual habit, I wanted to sneak away to Trinity Towers while the city slept. Ever since my beloved Maria passed, I've lost my patience with the hustle and bustle of life in the city. She was always so good at dealing with the masses, but I have no time for them. I know it's selfish, but I wanted to leave before the morning rush of apprentices and patrons came knocking. Had I not been a stickleback for getting underway when the city was at its quietest, I would be dead along with everyone else. Such as it is, Garrod, Robert and I survived the calamity that I am about to describe, if I can summon the words.

It was at least three after midnight, because I remember the clock tower chime while Robert saddled the horses and I loaded the wagon. I returned to the house to double check my inventory, passing Robert on the way out, who cradled Garrod asleep in his arms. I made my final rounds of the house, locking the doors and setting the intruder traps. When I stepped outside again, that's when calamity struck.

Robert was fussing with Garrod's blanket in the back of the wagon, with his back to the city. So he didn't see the hazy shimmer appear in the sky just above the clock tower. I remember the way the stars shifted around it, one moment they were in their rightful place, the next they had jerked askew, but only in a small area above the clock. The stars faded out, replaced by an oval shaped hole of blackness, strikingly void of colour. Inside the void, a sickly bruise-coloured light shimmered. A rank odour wafted across the city, the stench of rotting vegetables that have been left to decay in a damp cellar. Then the light wavered, like a canvas fluttering in the wind, but I could see a shadow approaching from the other side of the portal. Yes! A portal! The hole in the sky above the clock tower was a portal to... somewhere rotten.

A dragon burst out of the sky portal. A nightmarishly huge creature, with a pale, bulbous body and black sails for wings, it swooped towards me before it banked to my right, soaring over the town square with an eerily silent flap of its gargantuan wings.

I stared in dumbstruck bewilderment, pointing up at the monster. Robert stepped down from the wagon, then he saw it too. I wasn't imagining it, nor was it some waking dream or shroom vision. The dragon made a full circle of the city, cocking its head as it surveyed the ground. I thought it was looking for a place to land, and half hoped it would do so near me, so that I could get a closer look at it.

It didn't land.

Instead, it opened its long snout and exhaled. Legends speak of fire-breathing dragons, or ice dragons, but this creature breathed insects. It rained down a plague of pestilence upon my city. A black cloud of blood-sucking nibbets erupted from its jaws, flooding down into the trader's district, and with it arose an almighty buzzing cacophony. There must have been a billion nibbets living inside that creature's belly, and it was spilling them into the streets like a deadly flood.

The screaming started then. The sleeping city was waking up to a nightmare.

Robert came out of nowhere, suddenly he filled my vision, a look of panic in his eyes.

"We have to go!" he cried, grabbing my hand. He pulled me to the wagon and bundled me under the canopy with Garrod. Had he not, I may have stood there until the plague spilled over the walls and devoured me, like the rest of the city. The dragon swooped around, blowing its filthy breath across everything, and I couldn't help picturing the blood-seekers slipping in through open windows, under doors and swarming throughout family homes, enveloping any living thing they could find and stripping the flesh from the bones. Children would be waking up screaming as the nibbets sucked the fluid from their eyes, while others would simply never wake up.

Robert had taken up the driver's position and whipped the horses into a frenzied canter, then a full gallop. We fled the city amid a clowder of stray cats down the main road.

Gaping out the back of the wagon, I watched the dragon make a final pass over the castle, before turning back towards the clock tower and the portal it had come from. It flew straight inside and disappeared. The portal vanished with it. After that, the stars returned to their rightful position and any trace of the anomaly in the sky had gone.

My son stirred, groaning as the wagon bumped across the drawbridge and sped out of the city gates onto the dirt road beyond. Even over the galloping hooves and rushing wind, the terrible buzzing was overwhelming. The cloud of nibbets had spread across the road in our wake, I could see a billowing black haze tumbling towards us, and when it reached the gates, the cloud exploded outwards and up, blocking my view of the city entirely. Archdale was gone, replaced by a writhing black mass of the swarm.

"Father, what's happening?"

I had no voice to even begin explaining the horrific situation to Garrod.

An arm of the swarm detached from the main bulk, probably sensing our movement. A million insects pursued us across the plains as we raced towards the safety of the Everdusk. The swarm moved with a speed unlike anything natural that I've ever seen. No nibbet should be able to outrun a pair of galloping horses. But they caught us up.

I let forth a fireball at the swarm's head, and sizzled a temporary hole in the cloud. But the bulk of the swarm darted sideways to dodge before reforming and continuing the pursuit. They smelled blood.

Garrod shrieked as nibbets crawled inside his blanket.

"Argh!" Robert cried from the driver's seat. I caught a glimpse of him swatting nibbets off the back of his neck, leaving deep red whelps on his skin, dripping blood.

"Put your hood up!" I ordered him.

I couldn't hold off the bugs with just my fireballs. I'd expel all of my energy within minutes, and we had many wheels to go before we'd reach the Everdusk. I saw no other option, but to ignite the wagon's canopy above our heads.

It went up like kindling, billowing out a

choking black smog, which kept the nibbets at bay for a while. Garrod and I took shelter under his blankets as the wagon's roof burned above us. The heat was unbearable. I shielded him from the flames with my own body, pressing ourselves flat against the floor.

The swarm didn't let up, though. Despite the countless nibbets that I incinerated, thousands continued the pursuit, occasionally breaking through the smoke and biting our flesh. My arms were covered in whelps by the time Robert gave a shout.

"The horses can't keep up this pace! We must ditch the wagon!"

As crestfallen as I was to abandon my precious belongings, what choice did I have?

"Go, Garrod, make your way forward."

"I'm scared, father!"

"I know."

I ushered him through to the driver's platform, and Robert, skilfully steering the horses with one hand, aided my son to climb atop the gelding on the left. I know not how he didn't fall. I summoned another fireball and hurled it skyward, exploding it just above our heads so that it would disintegrate more of the swarm. Then I climbed out and joined my son.

Robert took the second horse, and when we were all riding bareback, I smote the halters with another fiery explosion. The ropes connecting the horses to the wagon snapped and we broke free, tearing ahead of the dwindling wagon. Some of the swarm seemed to slow and investigate it as it rolled to a stop, perhaps smelling the blood we had all dripped over it. But the majority of the swarm kept chasing us.

Now, with no more shelter and nothing left to burn, I was forced into expunging more of my energy on casting fireballs to keep the nibbets at bay. I do not know how I managed to stay upright on the horse and cast so much fire. It was as if something within me had awoken, and somehow I knew it had to do with the dragon I had seen. Close proximity to the portal had bestowed on me a newfound level of energy, previously untapped by my body. I have no way of proving this, but somehow in my gut I know it's the truth.

We finally made it to the edge of the Everdusk. The horses, frothing at the mouth, had slowed to an exhausted canter, foaming and slathered with sweat, I could feel it seeping through my trousers as we bounced up and down. The soft glowing spores beckoned us on the horizon like a haven of safety. If we could make it to the trees, the nibbets should be forced to abandon their plight. No nibbet could survive in the Everdusk. At least, not the ones from our world.

Somehow, we made it. The horses carried us under the shelter of the trees, and the glow of the dusk spores embraced us in their warmth. The swarm flew into the forest and were choked by the spores. A rain of nibbets fell to the ground like a black hailstorm. The incessant buzzing died in an instant. A shocking silence moved in to replace it.

I slowed my horse, bringing it to a gradual standstill. But it collapsed, throwing Garrod and myself to the dirt.

The horse wheezed and panted in agony, twitching and writhing on the ground, its hind awash with clotting blood and hideous oozing pimples. It kicked violently at thin air a few times before its head slapped down against the dirt and didn't rise again. Its tongue lolled out and after a few shuddering final breaths, the horse died.

We found Robert a little farther down the road. His horse was hardly better off. It had more of its skin left, at least. But it also succumbed.

After summoning so many fireballs, I was utterly drained. Unable to walk any further, I collapsed on the side of the road, passing out to the sound of my screaming son.

Robert picked some duskfruit which he brought to me, and I managed to regain enough strength to survive the night. We sheltered in a fallen tree hollow, and then hiked the following day back to Trinity Towers.

I cannot get the dragon out of my head. Where did it come from? And what sort of creature is it, to have a plague living within it? It radiated power like nothing I've ever seen before. It has to be attunement of the kind wizards have only dreamed of. I must learn more. Whatever power the dragon wields, it's enough to open a gate from its world to ours... A rift. Yes, that's what I will call the portal, it is a rift between worlds. I want to learn such power. I must figure this out... it is my new dream. And when a Brockhurst dreams, nothing will stand in his way.

CHAPTER SIX

Johanna spent the next three days and nights in bed, sipping on Grandma's soup and being waited on by her grounded sister. When their mother had learned about Ellie's escapades, she almost screamed the roof off.

"You could have died!" she shrilled. "You have got to learn that your actions have consequences! You'll not go off hunting by yourself ever again, the woodland is completely forbidden. And worst of all, you've made your sister so ill that she can barely walk! What if she *dies*?"

Both Ellie and her mother were bawling as the conversation went on, until Frank stepped in to calm them both down. "Now, now, what's done is done. We're all safe. Ellie, your mother's right. You're not ready to hunt alone."

"I know, Dad," she sobbed. "I'm sorry."

"It's not me you should apologise to." He led her upstairs to Johanna's room. She lay sound asleep in bed, her long brown hair draped across a white pillow in a flowing cascade. She looked beautiful in her fragility. But that scared the life out of Ellie.

"She's not going to die, is she?" she pleaded.

"I don't think so," Frank said, but something in his uneasy tone made Ellie feel even more scared. "I don't understand this attunement stuff, but yer gra'ma says that she just has to regain her energy. She used up a lot of it to save you." He added softly, "Just let this be a lesson, Ells. If you don't learn to master your patience, one day you might get seriously hurt, or worse, someone else."

A fresh well of tears formed in her eyes and her lips curled down at the corners, trembling. "I'll try, Dad. I'll try."

"I know you will. Come here." He embraced Ellie in a fierce hug.

***

Johanna didn't remember much of the events that occurred during her recovery. She drifted in and out of consciousness, catching glimpses of her sister dabbing her face with a warm towel, or to offer her a drink of water. On the third day, she awoke feeling human again. She sat up in bed, rubbing her eyes.

A light headache and a growling stomach was all that remained of her ordeal. She held up her hand and looked at her open palm. The skin was hard, as if her entire palm had tried turning into a callous. *Must have been from the heat.* That really was the biggest fireball she'd ever cast. When she saw the wolf approaching her sister, Johanna had summoned everything she had and put it into that ball.

A long, drawn out grunt, the sort of sound one might expect a heavily congested warthog with a throat infection to make, gargled to Johanna's left. It made her jump. The cause became quickly apparent, as she saw her sleeping grandpa, leaning back in the armchair with his hands clasped across his ample girth. She giggled at the sight. That must have been what woke her up.

"Hey, Grandpa," she said softly, not expecting a reply.

But he stirred. His eyes fluttered open and his tongue sucked back inside his mouth. He blinked a few times and looked at her, smacking his lips before offering her a warm, beaming smile. "Ahh, the princess has awoken. How are you feeling?"

"I'm okay, thank you." Her stomach gave another embarrassingly loud growl. "A bit peckish," she said, feeling blood rush to her face.

"Well, that has to be a good sign. As are those rosy cheeks." He hauled himself out of the chair. "Was beginning to think you'd turn into a sheep. Never seen a girl so ghostly white! I'll fetch the handmaiden for ya." He ambled out.

Handmaiden? What's he talking about? Johanna smiled to herself. Grandpa was nothing if not quirky.

A moment later, Ellie burst into the room. "Oh thank Kella you're awake, sis!" She dived onto the bed and threw her arms around Johanna's neck.

"Whoa, careful little sis," Johanna said, taken aback at her sister's overbearing concern. But it felt good at the same time. Ellie radiated warmth and affection, which was rare enough from her.

"I'm so glad you're okay." Ellie pulled back and Johanna saw the glint in her eyes, something that was totally her sister. "Now I can finally go outside again!" Ellie said.

"Oh, gee. Is *that* what you were worried about?"

"I've been grounded for three days, Hanna! I've barely left your room. How are you feeling, anyway? You look *sooo* much better."

"I think I'm okay. I need to eat something, though."

"Oh!" Ellie said, eyes widening. "Of course! Wait right there."

"I'm not going anywhere," Johanna started to say, but Ellie was out the door before she could even finish.

She came back carrying a tray of soup and a fresh chunk of bread. "Grandma made this for you. It's full of goodness, she says. You have to eat it all."

Johanna had no trouble obeying that order. Ellie had to bring her two more helpings before Johanna's stomach finally settled down. When she was finished, she felt like a new person.

***

Tabitha Henlowe had a huge wiry bush of black curly hair, held down by a big red bandana. She wore several chunky necklaces of multi-coloured beads, and her clothes were baggy, flowing robes. She was the only southern woman the McKree family had ever met, and made for an exotic guest, according to Grandma and Grandpa. She was supposed to have been Johanna's pyromancy tutor, but when she paid the cottage a surprise visit just two days after Johanna's recovery, she brought with her some troubling news.

"I can't be takin' you under my wing, young'un. I'm so sorry to have to tell you," Tabitha said across the kitchen table, as she drank a mug of hot tea with Johanna and her parents.

"Why not?" Johanna said, her heart sinking.

"The king has thrown a tantrum and forbidden the study of attunement across the province," Tabitha said, giving a resigned sigh.

"What?" Johanna gaped. "Why? He can't do that! Can he do that? *Why?*"

"Honey, let the lady speak," Julia said, patting her daughter's hand in sympathy.

"Well, I don't rightly know the details. I wish I did, young'un." Tabitha gave a slow, ponderous shrug. "It has to do with his son, most reckon. Did you hear about Prince Leo?"

"Pfft," Frank scoffed. "You know where you are, Miss Henlowe? Harbrook doesn't exactly keep up to date with the happenings of the royal nincompoops."

Julia gave him a scolding look.

"What?" Frank said, innocently.

"What my husband means is that city news doesn't reach us very quickly down here," Julia explained apologetically.

"What does the prince have to do with attunement?" Johanna asked.

"He had a keen interest in it," Tabitha said. "And, well,

I don't know the details, but Prince Leo died last week. Apparently, he was involved with the Brockhursts, helping them carry out some research."

"The Brockhursts?" Johanna said in awe.

"Who's that, sweetie?" Julia asked.

"The Brockhursts!" Johanna said again. "They are the most famous attuned family in the whole of Darune, Mother."

"Never heard of 'em," Frank said, taking a gulp of his tea. "And as for the prince, well, that's a tough one for ol' Victus, even I wouldn't wish that on him. But I don't think the little twerp will be missed much."

"Frank!" Julia scolded.

"So I won't be moving to the city…" Johanna said softly, eyes cast downwards at her tea.

"I wouldn't recommend it," Tabitha said. "All the wizards and mages are being run out. I was one of the first, I packed my bags as soon as I heard the law had changed."

Johanna wiped a tear from her eye and sniffed. She'd been looking forward to moving to the city ever since her parents had agreed to let her go and learn pyromancy.

"Tell you what, though," Tabitha said. "How about we do some private tutoring here?"

Johanna looked up sharply, hope flaring in her hazel eyes. "Really?"

"Yup."

Julia cleared her throat.

Johanna looked to her mother, who was scratching the back of her neck. "Miss Henlowe," Julia said slowly. "Harbrook's not really – how do you say, *interested* in magic. The reason we agreed for Johanna to go to the city was because we knew how much it meant to her. But the people who live here prefer the simple life, one without anything unusual or, you know, mysterious."

Tabitha nodded solemnly. "I think I understand. Were it to happen, I would insist on finding somewhere a little secluded, where we wouldn't bother any of the local residents." She took out a bulbous, curving pipe. "May I?"

Julia looked to Frank and an unspoken agreement passed between Johanna's parents. "Go ahead," Julia said.

"Thank you." Tabitha stuffed some green herbs down into the pipe's funnel, then lifted the mouthpiece to her lips. Johanna watched in curious fascination at this, but felt a wave of excitement over what Tabitha did next. With her free hand, she cocked her thumb towards the pipe and a tiny flame spurted out of the air around the tip. She lit the herbs, sucked on the pipe, and inhaled a good drag. Then the thumb-flame just vanished.

Johanna's jaw gaped wide. "How did you do that?"

Julia crossed her arms, sitting back in the chair, unsure whether to be amazed or scared. Either way, she was impressed.

"Is that what you're going to teach my daughter?" Frank said, leaning forward, and pointing in mild disgust at the pipe.

"This? No," Tabitha said, holding the pipe up. "This, perhaps." She gave them all a thumbs up and another little flame popped out, jumping a short way into the air before disappearing.

"You didn't even say anything!" Johanna said, overwhelmed with excitement. "Look, I can only do it using the focus words."

"Honey—" Julia started, but was cut off.

"*Ignus spareet,*" Johanna said, summoning a little fireball in her palm.

"Not indoors!" Frank cried.

"Sorry," Johanna dismissed the flame by closing her fist and it puffed out of existence. "But didn't you *see?* Miss Henlowe can do it without speaking!"

"You've been reading the book I gave you," Tabitha smiled. "And you've been practicing."

"Oh, that's *nothing,*" Ellie said, appearing out of nowhere and striding into the room. She had a grubby face and stank of rodent droppings. "Hanna could burn the whole village down if she wanted. I've seen her make a fireball *this* big." She stretched her arms as wide as they could go, dropping flakes of mud onto the kitchen floor.

"Eleanor, you're filthy!" Julia said, rising to her feet and shooing Ellie out of the room. "Get in the bathtub right now. Go!" They both left the room, leaving Johanna with Frank and Tabitha.

Frank looked slightly embarrassed, Johanna more so, but Tabitha was smiling and watching Johanna with a cocked eyebrow. "That true?"

"What?"

"You summoned a big'un?"

"Oh. Well, yes, actually," Johanna blushed even redder, this time from modesty.

"She's a do-er," Frank said, tipping his mug of tea. "When Johanna wants something, she knows how to figure it out. You serious about tutoring her here in the village, Miss? Don't you have a home to get back to?"

"Honestly, I haven't figured that out yet, Mr McKree." Tabitha took another drag of her pipe, and blew a puff of smoke up towards the ceiling. "I can't go back to the city, unless I wanna live in the dungeons. But I don't wanna give up my pyromancy, neither. I figure I can camp somewhere out here, get a taste of nature for a while. Teaching young'un here a few tricks might be a fun distraction while I work out where to move to next."

"Oh, thank you!" Johanna cried. "That sounds wonderful!"

"Sure does," Frank agreed. "We got nature coming outta our ears down this way. Only, you don't need to worry about camping outside. Spring nights can get chilly, and there's pesky nibbets always looking for a snack. I'll ask my folks if you can't use the spare room next door. I'm sure you'll be comfy in there."

***

And so pyromancy teacher Tabitha Henlowe moved in with Grandma and Grandpa McKree next door. It was a very short-lived affair, because three days later, Harbrook received another surprise visit from a wizard of a very different nature, and Johanna's plans changed all over again.

Ellie led Johanna and Tabitha to a clearing in the woods that she knew of, wide enough to give them room to summon small-to-medium sized fireballs without the risk of setting alight to the entire woods, and deep enough to not disturb, or be disturbed by anybody else.

On their third day of practicing simple techniques in the clearing, Johanna and Tabitha came home to find a stranger in a black robe sitting at the kitchen table drinking a mug of tea.

"Hello," Johanna said, looking to her mother who was chopping vegetables.

"Ah, you're back," Julia said, wiping her hands on a towel. "Miss Henlowe, this gentleman arrived this afternoon, looking for you."

"Greetings, Sai Henlowe," the robed man said, rising to his feet. He had short black hair and a sharp, pointed nose. He wasn't much younger than Johanna's parents, which would put him in his early thirties, Johanna guessed. He had a somber face, with deep set dark brown eyes that sunk into his somewhat hollow cheekbones.

"Sai Brockhurst?" Tabitha said with surprise, shaking the wizard's hand. "What an unexpected face to see in these quiet parts."

"Brockhurst?" Johanna said softly, suddenly having trouble remembering her manners and almost gaping at the wizard.

Tabitha said, "This is the Prime Wizard's son, Sai Garrod."

He cocked his head, noticing Johanna for the first time and offered her a thin smile. "Greetings, Miss." He held out a hand.

Johanna shook it. His skin was dry as paper, and he

gripped with a firm shake. She had a little tingle run down her spine. *I just shook hands with a* Brockhurst. *And it's the Prime Wizard's own son!*

"What brings you here, Sai?" Tabitha asked.

"I came in search of you," Garrod said, pulling out a chair for Tabitha to sit.

Feeling more than a little star struck, Johanna tottered over to the counter to pour herself a glass of water from a ceramic jug. She offered Sai Brockhurst one, but he refused with a curt shake of the head.

"I had my servant, Robert, seek you out in Darune," Garrod said to Tabitha. "And when he learned of your whereabouts down here, I decided to come find you myself. A mage of your talents is not easy to find, and Victus is a fool for driving the likes of you out."

"Why, thank you," Tabitha bowed her head a little. "The ban is why I came here. I'm tutoring this young'un in the art of pyromancy. She's a natural."

"That is promising," the wizard said, shooting Johanna a brief smile.

Johanna blushed heavily. *A Brockhurst just complimented me? In my own home? Am I dreaming?*

"Yes, she's going to be a fine little fire mage," Tabitha said.

"No, I was referring to your tutoring."

Johanna's flush drained away like water down a crack. As if he'd be impressed by her, what was she thinking?

"I have a proposition I'd like to share with you," Garrod went on.

"Oh," Tabitha said. She seemed uncomfortable and glanced at Julia as if to apologise for having such a conversation in their home. Sai Brockhurst seemed oblivious to the potential awkwardness, perfectly content to talk openly in front of Johanna and Julia, two complete strangers to him. "What kind of proposal?" Tabitha asked.

"I am taking over as Prime at Trinity Towers, and would like to hire you as the new Head Pyromancer."

Trinity Towers? What an opportunity! The excitement in Johanna's heart at hearing the name of such a prestigious place came before the abrupt fear that Tabitha Henlowe might actually accept the job, which would result in losing her private tutor, just three days after they had started.

"Wow," Tabitha said, clearly taken aback. "What a proposal. Begging your pardon Sai, but I thought your father was the Prime of Trinity Towers. Has he fallen ill?"

"Not ill…" Now Garrod *did* seem uncomfortable with the presence of Julia and Johanna, and he cast them a quick wary glance. He paused a moment to consider his next words, then looked Tabitha in the eye and said, "My father is dead."

"Oh my goodness," Johanna blurted, not realising she had spoken aloud until Garrod looked at her and gave her a solemn bow of the head.

"I'm very pained to hear that, Sai," Tabitha said. "I apologise for asking."

"It was a perfectly reasonable question," Garrod said, dismissing the issue.

How did he die? Johanna wanted to know, and hoped Tabitha would ask, but Garrod swiftly brought the subject back to his proposal.

"Now, I don't expect you to make an immediate decision," he said. "I intend to make my way back to the Towers over the coming fortnight, and you can send a messenger, or—"

"Actually, that won't be necessary," Tabitha interrupted. "I can give you an answer straight away, Sai."

Johanna inhaled a sharp breath. *I'm going to lose her!*

"Really?" Garrod said in surprise.

"I've already given a lot of thought about my path now that I'm forbidden from practicing in the city, and this is too good'n opportunity."

Johanna's shoulders slumped as a wave of bitter disappointment crashed over her. She was about to leave the room, when Tabitha added, "On one condition. I wish to bring this young'un with me."

Sai Brockhurst's eyes widened, and he gave Johanna a curious inspection. "I don't see why that would be a problem. I'm arranging some preliminaries to test a batch of potentials. I can add her to the list of candidates."

"Not as a candidate, Sai," Tabitha shook her head. "Sorry, but I must honour my arrangement to tutor this young mage. I won't abandon her so early in her training. If you're serious about making me your Head of Pyromancy, I trust you'll have enough confidence to believe me when I say she has potential."

Garrod glanced at Johanna with a hint of impatience. "Of course," he bowed his head towards Tabitha. "I trust your judgment. But I cannot allow a student to enter Trinity without at least seeing some example of what she's capable of." He cocked his head at Johanna again in scrutiny. "Perhaps a demonstration of your skills, if you please?"

"It would be respectful if we went somewhere more private, Sai," Tabitha said, smiling. "And we just happen to know a good spot."

Garrod agreed, and followed them into the woods behind the house. Johanna had a kaleidoscope of butterflies in her stomach by the time they reached the clearing. *If I can impress him, I will go to Trinity Towers. Trinity… Towers… ohmygoodness…*

Tabitha and Garrod watched Johanna from the edge of the clearing. Tabitha looked stumpy, wise and kindly, while Garrod loomed over her like a brooding vampire from some old horror story, his body hidden within the long, draping black robe.

"Okay Johanna, show us what you're made of," Tabitha said, smiling encouragingly.

Johanna nodded. She inhaled a few deep breaths in an attempt to calm her nerves. It didn't work. She cupped her palms together in front of her lips, and said, "*Ignus sprite!*" Her voice box croaked and she mispronounced the focus spell entirely, and they all knew it. "Sorry! Hold on." She cleared her throat.

"She's still using the words," Garrod muttered under his breath, but Johanna still heard. It filled her with dismay.

She tried again, and this time got the words right. "*Ignus spareet,*" she whispered, and opened her palm to reveal a neat, spherical ball of flame. She willed her energy into it, making it grow. The fireball pulsed and seemed to breathe, expanding in incremental beats until it was almost too big for one hand. Then she began to split it apart.

"*Ignee dividay!*"

She tugged the ball into two, and then three, and started to juggle. Just as before, when she practiced on the roof with Ellie, she kept splitting the balls until she had twelve spinning fiery spheres dancing in her palms.

But she didn't stop there.

She'd never gone beyond twelve, but felt an urge to do so in front of this man. She started to split the fireballs again, now each one was the size of her thumbnail. They spun faster and faster, and she kept splitting them until she had twenty four fireballs, double what she had ever juggled before! And now they were moving so fast that the ring of fire merged into a hoop. It was no longer a group of individual fireballs, but a single searing ring of fire, spinning in her hands. Johanna uttered a laugh. She stole a quick glance at her audience, Tabitha was nodding and smiling, but Sai Brockhurst was stony faced and indecipherable.

Johanna gritted her teeth. *Does nothing impress him?* Her nerves were gone, the butterflies all sizzled by her will. She had to end on a flourish. So with great concentration, she bent her knees and sprang up, tossing the flaming ring into the air. "*Ignus projeet!*" The ring exploded in a sparkling firework display, raining fiery petals down around the clearing.

"Woohoo! Yeah, sis!" Ellie cried.

Johanna looked around in horror, wondering where Ellie could be, and spotted her sitting on the branch of a tree overlooking the clearing. *Was she watching me this whole time!?*

Sai Brockhurst and Sai Henlowe glanced her way, Tabitha smiling, Garrod looking irritated. The wizard walked over to Johanna. He bent over, carefully inspecting her face. "How do you feel?"

Johanna's heart was racing, and she felt the unmistakable tickle of hunger in her belly. Those fireballs had used up a fair bit of energy, but she had held enough back in case he asked for an extra demonstration.

"I feel a little nervous, to tell you the truth." She straightened, lifting her chin in an effort to boost her confidence. Mother had taught her that little trick.

"Where did you learn to do that?" he asked.

"I am self-taught, mostly. Sai Henlowe lent me a wonderful book."

"You like to read?" He cocked his head.

"Oh, yes. I believe books are a source of great knowledge. Don't you, Sai?"

"I do." He almost smiled. But not quite. "However, you must know that using focus words to cast your spells is the sign of an amateur."

She flushed a little, but determined not to show her agitation, answered with as much vigour as she could muster. "Yes. I only started practicing the art at the beginning of the spring."

"No, you are practicing *pyromancy*. The art, that is another matter entirely. One which we specialise in teaching at Trinity Towers."

"Oh. Well, yes. I think I understand."

"Perhaps you do. But the power of attunement doesn't come from books. Do you know where it truly comes from?"

"I think so," Johanna frowned. *He's testing me.* "The words are a way to focus the mind. The power comes from our mind, and we use the spellphrases to teach our mind how to summon the essence of the spell we wish to cast." She couldn't see Tabitha's face, but she hoped she was smiling. Johanna's eyes never left Sai Brockhurst's.

"Not a bad effort," he said, in a tone that suggested she could have done better. "Our power is born out of time and memory. We can use our memories as energy sources, the same way you currently use the focus words. Once you learn to master this, you will be capable of producing more efficient spells. Perhaps then you'll be able to juggle a few little fireballs without the urge to eat a three course meal straight after."

This time she flushed with embarrassment. *Could he hear my stomach or something?*

"So, let's try something more practical again. I want you to use time and memory to summon another fireball."

"Um. I'm not sure how to do that..."

"It's simple. Think of a memory, one that means a lot to you. A troubling event from your past, for example."

Johanna felt a sting of panic rising. She couldn't think of any memories like that. Her childhood had been one of playful fun. She lived with her parents, grandparents and sister in peace. "If I may ask, Sai, could you give me an example?"

"You wish to know one of my memories?" He cocked an eyebrow. "That *is* bold."

She opened her mouth to apologise, but thought better of it. Perhaps he was trying to see if she could hold her nerve.

After a moment, he went on. "Okay. When I was five years old, my home was destroyed. Almost everyone I ever knew was killed. My father, the family aide and I were the sole survivors. I remember fleeing with my father in the back of a wagon, chased by a plague of devouring nibbets. I remember fire, blood and screaming. We escaped, and fortunately only our horses were killed. My father told me that I lost my voice for a week, because I had spent the entire chase wailing my lungs out."

Johanna listened to this in dumbstruck horror.

"That is a powerful memory for me," Garrod said.

"Whenever I think about it, I am invigorated with a strong sense of memory, which gives me energy to use as fuel for my spells."

Johanna found her voice. "I'm sorry, Sai. I don't think I have any memory even a tenth as powerful as that."

"No. I suppose you wouldn't, would you?" His tone became scathing and mean. "How could you? A pretty little thing, growing up in the arse end of the world, where the biggest threat to your existence is perhaps a rainy day, or a flock of wild geese. How can you know anything of pain and suffering when you live in such an insignificant place?"

Johanna had never felt so offended in her life. She was stricken by his disdain, his self-importance, and total disregard for her family's way of life. "My grandpa built the farm that gives the entire village food, my father is a skilled hunter, my grandma is renowned throughout the village as a wise woman and my mother taught me the value of hard work and determination. I can't believe you would mock us, Sai. You don't even *know* us!"

The anger seemed to flow through her, giving her a burst of chaotic energy that needed to be released. A fireball had appeared in her palm. It gave her a fright so bad that she yelped and shot it straight down at the ground where it charred the grass in a small circular spot next to her right foot.

A beat later, she realised she had summoned it without saying the focus words.

"Oh my." She blinked in shock.

"Very impressive," Garrod said, smiling and clapping three times. "You were right, Sai Henlowe. This one has great potential."

"H-how did you do that?" Johanna stammered.

"That was all you," Tabitha said, stepping forwards. "I have seen other tutors use such a dirty trick before. While I would never choose to use that technique myself, I can't argue with its effectiveness."

"Apologies, Miss McKree," Garrod said, giving her a

small bow. "The tale about my home was the truth. My comments regarding yours were not. I hold no ill will towards Harbrook, nor any other village in these parts. I merely wanted to antagonise you. You see, when memory fails us, emotions will suffice. Anger is one of the purest emotions, capable of creating a lot of energy. A useful fuel, if used sparingly."

"Wow. I think I see." Johanna was taken aback. In summoning her first fireball without the aid of focus words, she'd taken her first step towards mastering her skills as a mage. The aftertaste of Garrod's harsh words lingered unpleasantly in her mouth, though.

Garrod turned to Tabitha. "Johanna may join us, Sai Henlowe. Consider this your formal invitation to enroll at Trinity Towers, Miss McKree."

"Seriously?" Johanna broke into a wide, toothy smile of pure relief. "Thank you, Sai!"

She looked towards her sister, still sitting in the tree. She thought she saw a look of concern on Ellie's face, but it quickly turned into a happy grin, and she shot Johanna a double thumbs up.

"I'll definitely accept!" Johanna said to Garrod. "I'll have to ask my parents, first, though."

***

Of course, they accepted.

The issue of Johanna being a fugitive if she ever went to Darune City wasn't an obstacle to prevent her from going. The people of Harbrook weren't exactly fond of the government, and why should they be? No king had ever set foot in Harbrook, let alone understood who its people were or what their lives entailed. The village was perfectly happy to run its own affairs without the input of a man a thousand wheels away. And as Frank McKree eloquently put it, Johanna's enrolment at this wizard's fancy college was a fine way to give two fingers to the king and his cronies, so he was all for it.

Grandma and Grandpa McKree were both full of encouragement for Johanna. They caught Garrod on his way down the path and interrogated him about the city's new ban on magic, finding Garrod's reluctance to back down both amusing and a sign of honesty. "Stick to your pitchfork, I say, lad," Grandpa said, giving Garrod a firm slap on the shoulder. "You wanna be a wizard, don't let no-one stop you, least of all some pompous twit that calls himself king."

"Thank you, I think. It is good to have the blessing of an elder such as yourself," Garrod said, seeming to find the entire conversation terribly awkward.

Meanwhile, Johanna explained the situation to her parents inside the cottage. Trinity Towers would reopen at the beginning of summer, and she had been invited to attend as soon as it did. All she had to do was travel to Darune City, where a representative of the college would meet all the potential students, in secret of course. From there, they would depart under disguise and embark along the road to the Everdusk Forest, where the Towers awaited.

Frank grinned, beaming with pride. "You go, my lass! Follow that heart to the ends of the world, and just see where you end up."

Julia was the most reluctant to see her daughter go. "I was just getting used to the idea of having you around for the summer," she said, wiping away a tear. "But now it seems I'm losing you for an entire year. Just make sure you visit for Winter's Feast, you hear?" She hugged Johanna fiercely.

"There's still a couple of weeks left of spring, mum. Let's make the most of it before we have to say goodbye."

"Too right!" Julia said, pulling back and caressing Johanna's cheek with a delicate hand. "And we'll come to see you off at Darune. We'll make a family trip of it, stop at a few inns along the way and enjoy some quality family time together. Oh, come here!" She pulled Johanna in for another hug.

***

That night, Johanna and Ellie sat on the roof again, not juggling fireballs this time, but simply hanging out, like they used to do as kids. For once, however, they felt the need to have a conversation, instead of just skylarking.

"I'm happy for you, sis," Ellie said, sitting cross-legged and fiddling with a long piece of thatched straw. "You're gonna be a great wiz… I mean mage."

Johanna smiled. "I hope so. It feels like my calling, you know? Like you with your hunting."

Ellie gave a wan smile.

"Is something the matter?" Johanna asked.

"I dunno. It's just something about that guy."

"*That guy*? You mean Sai Brockhurst? He's arguably the greatest wizard in Darune. His father certainly is at any rate." Then she remembered. "Or *was*… he died apparently. How awful is that? And yet, Sai Garrod is continuing his father's work, taking over the college. What an admirable determination."

"He said some horrible things about us."

"He didn't mean it. He was just teaching me a lesson. And it worked! Did you see I cast a fireball without using the words?"

"I saw it," Ellie smiled again, but it didn't reach her eyes.

"What is it?" Johanna probed. "You know you can tell me anything, little sis."

"I just got a funny feeling with that guy. I was, um, foraging. And I heard voices, that's how I knew you were in the clearing. But, I heard an extra voice among you guys."

"What do you mean an extra voice?"

"Well, it's hard to explain. But there seemed to be another voice, and it was coming from that guy."

"*Sai Brockhurst*," Johanna corrected impatiently.

"Yeah. He seemed to have another voice inside him."

"Don't be ridiculous. That doesn't make any sense. And besides, how would *you* be able to sense something like that? You're not attuned, like me."

"I know." Ellie sighed.

CHAPTER SEVEN

It took Garrod a fortnight to return to Trinity Towers. A frustrating journey for two reasons: the first being that he had to cut across a vast area of rugged countryside in order to avoid going near Darune City, effectively doubling his journey time. And the second reason had to do with Corcubus, the increasingly bothersome vulture creature fighting for control within his mind.

Corcubus was quickly turning into a major concern. The vulture became most active when Garrod fell asleep. One night after leaving the road, he'd taken shelter in an old cowshed, fallen asleep in one stall and tied up his horse in the adjacent one. That's not where he woke up the following morning, though. At some point in the night, Garrod had apparently sleepwalked across the field and collapsed next to a tree. He woke with scratches all over his arms and hands, and his robe had a tear down one side, a strip of the fabric clung to a jagged piece of tree bark, as if he'd been scratching himself against the trunk. He'd never sleepwalked before, so Corcubus had to be responsible. It was the only rational explanation. Birds roosted in trees, after all, right? The wretched creature must have tried climbing it.

He couldn't allow that to happen again.

When he closed his eyes, he could see the bird floating in a black void within his thoughts. Garrod imagined an iron cage and it appeared. The metal bars closed around the bird and its gate slammed shut. Corcubus whined and pecked at the bars inquisitively. Garrod imagined a cane and beat the bird with it. "Hurt me, and I hurt you, beast. It's simple." He whacked the cane across the bird's neck.

Coooorrrrk! Corcubus screeched in fear and pain.

He struck Corcubus again and again until the creature fell down and sprawled on the floor of its new cage.

"Now stay there," Garrod said, reopening his eyes. He made his way back across the field, returning to the stable and mounted his horse.

When Garrod finally made it back to Trinity Towers, he found preparations for the new teaching season well under way. Robert had hired a small army of janitors, gardeners and builders to spruce up the grounds. Windows were being polished, the gutters scraped, weeds plucked, and roof tiles mended.

Garrod met a stable boy at the main gates, who helped him dismount.

"Welcome home, Sai. How was the journey?" the boy asked, taking the reins.

"Troublesome," Garrod said, rubbing his forehead. He had another Corcubus-shaped headache. "Is Mr Anders present?"

"No, Sai," the lad said. "He's out on an errand. Might be back sometime this evening."

"Okay. Send him up to my father's chambers as soon as he returns."

"Yes, Sai. Of course."

He left the stable boy with the horse and crossed the courtyard to the Sun Tower. He scaled the inner spiral staircase up to the Prime's quarters, slumping down in the chair behind Jason Brockhurst's mighty desk. Garrod poured himself a goblet of duskfruit juice and gulped it down.

Coooorkabussss!

"Shut up," Garrod muttered. He imagined his mind cane and Corcubus cowered and hushed when he sensed it coming for him. Garrod smiled grimly to himself. "You're learning, at least."

An almighty yawn came bursting out of his throat. He hadn't slept properly since leaving Harbrook, and those nights camping outside had overtaken him. A small nap was called for.

He shuffled into the bedchamber, and drew the heavy drapes across the windows to block out the afternoon sun, stripped off his robe and collapsed in the bed.

He was softly snoring within a minute.

Cooorkabus?

Corcubus stirred. The creature peered from its cage, with two beady yellow eyes, searching for a sign that its captor was awake.

Crrrrk! It cooed.

A small wave of excitement ruffled through its matted, bloody feathers. The man was sleeping.

At this realisation, the cage door clicked open. Corcubus didn't know why, but he understood what it meant: freedom.

He hopped out of the cage, and stalked into Garrod's subconscious.

Garrod's eyes opened. But he saw nothing. He remained fast asleep. His irises took on a yellowish tint, the only suggestion that he was not himself.

Corcubus, controlling Garrod's body like a puppet, sat up in the bed. He swivelled his heavy, human head this way and that, surveying the room. It was dim and claustrophobic, as if his captor had chosen to seal himself in his own cage, like the one he kept poor Corcubus in.

A thin strip of light spilled under the door, which caught Corcubus' attention. He reached for it with his beak, but realised that he had no beak, and looked curiously down at the blanket covering his legs and feet. This body felt extremely cumbersome to him, but he sensed the two legs, two wings, no, *arms*, which were roughly where they were supposed to be.

He swung his legs out of the bed and made to stand, but clumsily toppled over and landed on the floor. Garrod might have woken up at this, but Corcubus was so deep within his neural core, Garrod himself had no connection to his senses. Someone could have poured a bucket of cold water on his head and he wouldn't have woken up.

Corcubus scrambled across the floorboards, dragging himself towards the door, and that enticing light. Light meant sunlight, sunlight meant sky, and sky meant freedom.

He spent a few moments jabbing at the light with his beak, Garrod's nose, scratching his face against the floorboards in an effort to look under the door. How to reach the light?

"Crrrk!" Garrod's voice box croaked in frustration.

Corcubus clumsily stood up, scraping Garrod's head up the door as he went, planting a nasty splinter in his cheek. He looked around the room and stumbled aimlessly along the wall, leaning on it for balance as he manoeuvred his clumsy, meaty legs.

A light breeze fluttered the drapes, and as they billowed inwards, more light spilled onto the floor for a brief moment. Corcubus was drawn to it. He reached the drapes and pushed them aside with Garrod's head, ducking into the narrow space behind them.

He staggered towards the window, which was ajar, and pushed his head against it. The window swung open, revealing a magnificent view. *Trees! Sky!* Corcubus realised he was high up in a roost made of stone. A sudden rush of raw instinct crashed over him, strong as a gust of wind.

Fly.

He spread his wings – arms – and inhaled the fresh air, marveling at the way the cool breeze caressed his naked, featherless skin. A weird sensation, but very pleasant.

Corcubus stretched his neck out of the window, peering straight down at the eighty foot vertical plummet to the ground below. So high! A giddy flush of anticipation fluttered through him.

Corcubus leaned forwards, stretching his neck out further and further, tilting his head to peer at the trees straight ahead, beyond the outer wall of the Tower grounds. Garrod's knees clattered against the window sill as Corcubus attempted to push himself through the gap. His arms snagged on the frame and Corcubus hissed and grunted in frustration.

Finally, with a monumental shove, he threw himself forwards.

Out of the window.

He flapped his arms once, twice, and then—

Terrifying panic.

He realised this body couldn't fly. Instead of soaring forwards, he was tumbling straight down, utterly helpless and out of control.

It took three seconds for Garrod's body to slam into the ground.

In that time, Corcubus did the only thing he could: he retreated back through his captor's subconscious and into the safety of his cage. Garrod's spirit bounced back to its natural place at the helm of his body's central nervous system. The little bone in Garrod's inner ear communicated with his brain to tell him that he was tumbling head over heels. Garrod awoke in mid-air, and had only a split second to curl his neck in a flinch before he collided with the ground. That last second flinch saved his life. Instead of landing on the crown of his skull, his shoulder blades struck first and then his legs flipped violently over his head, slamming both heels into the dirt.

He lay there, splayed on his back, staring up at the tower and the sky.

What happened? How did I get here?

He tried to move his arms but couldn't. He tried to move

his legs but couldn't. He tried to sit up… but couldn't.

Oh no. No, no, no. A rising fear began in the pit of his stomach and flooded across his chest, flowing down the arms that wouldn't respond, down his legs that were dead and lifeless, the panic and terror overloading every other thought.

I'm paralysed.

He blinked. His facial muscles were apparently the only responsive part of his body. The tower disappeared from view momentarily. It was beginning to wave and shimmer. It became clearer the more he panicked, and when the sky turned purple, he gave in to it.

The rift tore open around him. The tower transformed into a slanting, crumbling version of itself, and the trees just beyond the wall by his feet lost all of their leaves, black disfigured skeletons of their former selves.

Corcubus cried inside his head, *Corrrrk!*

It felt happy. It wanted to move. It recognised the desolation, and knew it was home.

"No!" Garrod growled through gritted teeth, fighting the fear and trying to drag his conscious back to his own realm.

A human head appeared high above him, leaning out of the crumbling tower window.

Garrod froze, staring up at the familiar face that was looking down at him. "Father?" Garrod croaked.

Jason Brockhurst was alive, he had somehow travelled from this world's version of Archdale and made it to Trinity Towers.

"Garrod?" Jason frowned for a moment, then gaped in sheer surprise. "My son!"

Garrod tried to respond, but his voice cracked and he coughed up a large spout of blood. He wanted desperately to pull his father through the rift that he had somehow opened. But as he thought of it, the rift shrank and swallowed him, his spirit was pulled back through, responding to his will to return home. The air shimmered around him and faltered for a moment in a black void. Then he blinked again and when he reopened his eyes, the sky was blue once more. Jason was gone. The crumbling, ruinous tower had returned to its present glory. The trees were green and billowing in the breeze, soaking up the late afternoon sun.

"Father!" he croaked again, spitting up more blood.

What just happened? I saw him! He's alive! My father is alive!

Despite the overwhelming distress, Garrod smiled. Blood dripped down the sides of his cheeks and stained the dirt a muddy maroon. Then he coughed, unable to breathe as more blood gushed up from his insides and tried to choke him.

A gardener that had been working on the side of the tower heard the noise and came to investigate. He found Garrod lying there, and rushed to help, turning him onto his side.

Garrod spat the blood out and exhaled a deep, ragged gasp. His airway cleared and he slowly regained his breath.

He couldn't move. But he was *alive*. And now he knew his father was, too.

CHAPTER EIGHT

The McKree family set out together from Harbrook on a cloudy morning in Grandpa's old hay cart, which he'd converted into a rustic traveler's wain with two benches running down the length of each side. He dangled apples on sticks in front of the noses of Bob and Slob, a couple of stocky ponies that he had bought from Farmer Cribs years ago. Bob and Slob must have been pushing twenty, but they had as much vigour as Grandpa himself, and enthusiastically pulled the cart down the lane.

"Goodbye, home!" Johanna waved to their cottage, feeling giddy with excitement and a happy sort of sadness. She had to take it all in, imprint the village into her mind, because she wouldn't see it again for a long time. She was off to Trinity Towers College for Wizards and Mages.

"I'll look after your room, don't worry big sis," Ellie said nonchalantly.

"You had better..." Johanna trailed off. "Wait, *what?*"

"Yeah, I'm moving in as soon as we get back."

"Mother!" Johanna cried in protest. "You can't let *her* sleep in my bed. She'll get it covered in grass and mud and *poop!*"

"I'm sorry dear," Julia said with sympathy. "But you're

going to be gone for a while, and your room is bigger than hers."

"Dad!"

"We'll change the sheets before you get back," he said unhelpfully.

Johanna could only gape in horror. Ellie sat there in the back of the wagon next to her parents with a very obnoxious grin plastered across her stupid face.

"What's all the racket back there?" Grandpa called over his shoulder as he tugged on the reins, steering the ponies left out of the lane onto the main road.

"Just a sisterly dispute," Frank chuckled. "You comfortable up there, ma? Plenty of room back here if you want."

"I'm fine," Grandma said cheerfully from the passenger seat in the front. "I like the wind in my hair."

The cart was a decent size, large enough for Johanna, her sister, both parents, and her leather trunk which was full of Johanna's clothes, plus another smaller case which was filled to bursting point with books. Even so, she'd had to leave a lot behind, because there was just no way to fit an entire bookshelf into a suitcase. "Just promise me one thing, Ellie," she said. "Don't touch my books."

"Why would I?" Ellie said, as if the very idea might give her some sort of disease.

An overdose of intelligence, perhaps, Johanna thought, which made her smile. Why waste time being mopey about her room, when she would be two thousand wheels away.

The cart bumped along the rutted road, rolling down the gentle hill and over the old stone bridge. Johanna took a final glance at the Mana River as it bubbled beneath them, and a little spine-fish leapt out of the current as if giving her a farewell wave. They passed her old school, and the farm behind it, and soon Harbrook village was dwindling behind her as they entered the open country.

"H'yup!" Grandpa called to Bob and Slob, who quickened their amble to a meaningful walk. Johanna stared back towards her home, with the intention of watching until it was out of sight, but the pull of what lied ahead was too much, and she turned to face the front long before Harbrook village dipped below the horizon behind them.

***

The journey to Darune City took three days, which meant stopping overnight at a few of the villages along the way for rest. One such stop occurred in Honeyville, a village of similar size and population to Harbrook, which got its name from the collection of honeybee apiaries scattered around the lush shrub land that the village had sprung up within.

Frank McKree often passed through on his way to Bridgton, the next town along the road, where he did most of his bounty hunting. But Honeyville wasn't without its own quaint troubles, making it a good place for any bounty hunter to make some extra pocket money. While Grandpa parked up in the village square outside the inn, Ellie ran over to the noticeboard like an excited child waking up for Winter's Feast.

"Is this it, Dad?" she cried, pointing at the board, which had about half a dozen posters pinned to it.

"Yup yup, let's take a look and see what's going on, shall we?" He ambled over and stood with his hands on Ellie's shoulders, surveying the bounty board over her head.

Johanna joined them, mildly curious. She had little interest in her father's choice of occupation, but it put food on the table, so she had a healthy level of respect for it.

"Ooh, what about this one?" Ellie said, tapping her finger on a poster. Johanna read it, feeling more uncomfortable with every sentence. It read:

WANTED: Hunter required for rat infestation. Location: Kindermann Homestead. Comments: Must be at least a hundred critters living under my old barn. I've tried poison, I've tried flooding 'em out, but they just keep popping up. Lookin' for a man with a sharp eye to camp out there with his bow and send as many as he can to ol' Kella.

REWARD: 5 bob per rat. Payment upon delivery of corpses.

"Actually," Ellie said at length. "That sounds boring. You might fall asleep on the job, Dad."

Frank laughed. "Well, gee, thanks for the vote of confidence."

"Dad's a bit overqualified to be a ratter, anyway," Johanna said. She cast her eye over the board.

The other posters all looked the same, as if the town had a template that you just filled in. The words 'WANTED' and 'REWARD' were both printed in red ink at the top and bottom of the page, creating an eye-catching header and footer which actually appealed to Johanna's interest in book-cover design. Everything else was scrawled in a messy handwritten style by people who either had a serious injury in their fingers or had only learned how to write in the last month.

"Ooh, how about a wolf hunt?" Frank gave a short, impressed whistle. "200 bobs."

"A w-wolf?" Ellie stammered, visibly tensing.

Frank leaned closer to read the poster. "Over at the Greenwold Estate, a large black wolf has been seen prowling around the lamb paddocks. Recommends a pair of hunters, or one especially skilled loner. Think I could do that?" He cocked an eye at Johanna and Ellie, oozing confidence.

"I… I don't wanna do that one," Ellie said quickly.

Frank laughed, and Johanna scoffed. "*You* aren't a huntress yet," Johanna said. "Besides, you can't take on a bounty until you're eighteen."

Ellie spun around with wide, mischievous eyes. "Dad said he's gonna take me on his next hunt. I brought my bow and knives and I'm *ready*!" Her enthusiasm wavered, and she gave a nervous laugh. "Not for a wolf, though."

Johanna felt a pang of sympathy for her sister, remembering Ellie's encounter with the lone wolf.

"All right, lil' missy," Frank said, rubbing his chin as he searched for another potential. "Aha, this one sounds perfect. A honeyroo!"

Johanna frowned. "What's dangerous about a honeyroo?"

Ellie pulled her hands up to her chest and curled them into a stumpy pair of claws, pouted a big O with her lips and began bouncing around on both feet. "They turn feral and eat babies!"

Johanna gave her sister a withering look.

Frank smirked at Ellie, then explained to Johanna. "They're not dangerous, but they certainly are a pest. They can bounce right over most farm fences, and churn up the seedlings with their big feet. They sometimes eat grass and berries, but their favourite food is honey straight out of a beehive."

"Their nose is like a big straw," Ellie said, now planting her nose against her shoulder and swinging her floppy arm about in some childish imitation of a mammoth trunk. "They slurp up the honey, and they don't even get stung because their skin is all stony and stuff."

"Are they difficult to hunt?" Johanna asked.

"I've caught a few. Definitely easier with a partner, because they get spooked easily, and just bounce away," Frank explained. "But they would never attack a human. Might be the perfect test for Ells, if it's still available when we head back this way." They both watched Ellie bouncing around the village square making confused bleating noises.

Frank howled then like a ravenous wolf and cried, "Oh look, a tasty 'roo, just what I need for my supper," and ran after Ellie with his hands stretched out in front of him. Ellie shrieked, dropping the honeyroo impression and legged it away from him.

Some passers-by cast them bemused looks, which Johanna interpreted as, "*Oh, must be Harbrookers… those weirdo's from down the road.*"

No, she thought, grinning to herself. *It's just the McKree's, on a family road trip to the city*. Though Johanna often felt too shy to join in with her sister and father's public displays of nonsense, she wouldn't have them any other way and felt a strong sense of familial pride. She realised for the first time that she was really going to miss them.

"Get in here!" Julia cried, appearing in the doorway of the inn and shooting apologetic glances around the square in embarrassment. Johanna went over to her, and gave her a tight hug. "What's that for, honey?" she said mildly.

"Just felt like it, Mum. Do we have a room?"

"Yup, 'Pa and 'Ma are already inside. Go fetch your luggage."

"Okay," Johanna said, pulling out of the hug. She hurried to the cart, wiping a single tear from her cheek.

***

Two days later, they arrived at the province's capital, Darune City. It was late afternoon, and Johanna needed to meet the Trinity Towers representative the following morning near the main city gates. She'd know who it was because they would be wearing a long brown robe, and should be surrounded by at least a dozen other teenagers like her.

But that was tomorrow. First, she had to enjoy her last night with her family, and wanted to savour every moment.

"Whoa," Grandpa rumbled to his ponies, shifting the apple sticks so that Bob and Slob could reach them. The cart rolled to a stop outside the biggest stable Johanna had ever seen.

They were at the far end of a sprawling cobblestoned street, ten times wider than their little dirt lane in Harbrook. Running along both sides of the street were many stores, selling all manner of items – clothes, ornaments, tools, a bookstore! Johanna had to resist running over to see what they had in stock.

She'd been a toddler the last time she came to the city, and couldn't have appreciated its abundance back then. That was the word that stuck in her mind as she looked around: *abundance*. There was just so much *stuff* crammed inside Darune's walls. People bustled to and fro in every direction, and there was a constant drone of noise that seemed to hover in the air. At first, she wondered what on Kellamon that drone could be, but quickly realised that it was just people talking. So many people, all living their lives, doing whatever city folk did in the afternoon. Harbrook was quiet as a graveyard compared to this, and Johanna, in a strange mix of disappointment and relief, wasn't sure that she *liked* it.

Johanna was impressed, however, definitely impressed. Until Ellie pointed out the human waste floating down a stream in the street's gutter.

"See? You see! It's a river of poo! Markus was *right*. I can't believe you wanted to live here, Hanna." It was the first thing she had said since they arrived. Ellie apparently didn't feel very comfortable here. There weren't enough trees, no wild animals other than stray dogs and cats, and aside from the rivers of filth, no muck to frolic in, Johanna supposed.

Johanna had been so excited at the prospect of living here only a month ago, but now that future had been stuffed into a pot, shaken around and tipped back out. The core idea remained – she was still moving away from home to study pyromancy, but now she was going to spend her summer learning all kinds of other wondrous things at Trinity Towers, the most respected school for attunement studies in the entire province, maybe even the *world*.

Darune City could keep its turd rivers. Trinity Towers and the Everdusk would be much, much better for her.

A long gurgling sound drew Johanna's attention. She found Ellie standing behind her, looking mournfully at her belly.

"I'm starving," she groaned.

"I think it's time for some grub," Grandpa said, helping Grandma down from the wagon.

"What say we take them to see old Freddy?" Grandma said longingly. "I could just about eat a double portion of pentini."

"Yes!" Ellie said, brightening in an instant.

"Who's Freddy?" Julia inquired with a curious smile.

"Oh, he's been here for years," Grandpa said. "Why, 'Ma and I used to come here every moon! Didn't we, snook'ums?" The old couple shared a tender, slightly disgusting kiss, which Johanna couldn't help but stare at.

I'll be gone for two seasons. What if Grandpa or Grandma dies in that time? Oh, Kella! The thought came unbidden and hit Johanna with a terrible clarity. For the second time, she realised she was *really* going to miss her family. Was she actually ready to leave them?

***

Freddy's pentini turned out to be a delicious taste of Darune Province. Freddy himself was an ancient old geezer that had apparently spent most of his life baking himself in a steaming hot kitchen, because every visible part of his skin was wrinkled and lined like Johanna's fingertips after spending too long in the washtub. But he sure knew how to cook. The meat melted in the mouth and the potatoes were crispy on the outside but fluffy in the middle. And the gravy… Johanna could've died happy as she mopped up the last of the gravy with a hunk of fresh bread.

Pentini got its name from the five ingredients that went into it. Each one was produced in a different corner of the province – Potatoes from the north, cheese from the south, beef came from the farms near Harbrook in the west, and exotic vegetables and herbs which grew in the warmer regions south and east of the city. It came served in a bowl, with everything mixed in together, either dry, or as the

McKree's liked it, doused in thick gravy, a specialty of the westerners, but admirably reproduced here in the city by Freddy.

"Thish is jusht aweshome," Ellie said with a mouthful. She swallowed and added, "Didn't think the city would have food like this."

"It brings us back, don't it dear?" Grandpa said, winking at his wife across the table.

Grandma simply said, "Oh it do." She had a beaming smile as wide as her face which made her look a youthful sixty-two, rather than her actual eighty-five.

The McKree's were sitting at a round table in the corner of the lively pub, while a bard played catchy tunes on a fiddle and people clinked and clanked their glasses in merriment at the bar on the other side of the room. A real jolly atmosphere.

Frank gulped beer from a big wooden stein, sighing with pleasure after each sip. "City's all right for a night or two. I could never live here, but I always like to visit, knowing I can go back home afterwards."

"Well said, honey," Julia agreed, offering her mug to say cheers.

Johanna hardly said a word during the meal, content to just let the conversation flow around her and soak in the sight of her family sharing the last supper they would eat together for a long time. It was simply a wonderful evening, the perfect farewell. She even managed to feel better about that scary thought of Grandpa and Grandma dying before she came home, which was good, because the next time the McKree's sat down to enjoy a family meal, there would indeed be two empty chairs.

CHAPTER NINE

Ellie awoke at dawn, surprised to find herself feeling anxious about saying goodbye to her big sister. It suddenly sunk in that they were about to be separated for the first time, and it didn't fully hit her until they went to the city gates to wave Johanna off.

A small gathering of other students were already waiting with the college representative by the time they arrived. Ellie eyed them up and down, wondering where they might have come from and how good at magic they were. She doubted any of them could summon a fireball as big as the one Johanna had made when she saved her from the wolf.

Sticking out of the crowd like goats in a paddock full of sheep were two familiar faces. The first was Tabitha Henlowe, Hanna's pyromancy tutor, a flash of blindingly white teeth smiling out from under her curly black hair, which was tied down with her trademark red silk bandana. And standing next to her was—

"Markus?" Johanna said, striding forwards, breaking away from the McKree's. "What are *you* doing here?"

Markus gave her a sheepish grin, and they shared a rather awkward hug. He pulled out of it with blushing cheeks. "I, err, meant to tell you last week, but you know, didn't find the time before we left for the city."

"Are you attuned?" Johanna said with wide, surprised eyes.

"Yeah, a little bit." He trailed off, looking around nervously in case anyone was listening. His voice dropped almost to a whisper. "You know, we shouldn't really talk about it here, and don't say *attuned* in public!"

Hanna's lips curled downwards in an expression of *eeek*, and she apologised. "I forgot about the new law."

Ellie stepped up and gave Hanna a playful rib jab with her elbow. "How's it feel to be a filthy scoundrel, sis?"

"Shut up!" Hanna hissed. "I'm not, I mean, we're not… *criminals*." She looked to Markus for help.

"She's technically right." He shrugged.

"Bahaha," Ellie cackled. "I think it's awesome. About time you got your hands dirty!" She exhaled a long sigh of pleasure which tapered off into something rather subdued. "I guess this is goodbye?"

Johanna threw her arms around Ellie's neck before she had time to blink. "I know!" She squeezed hard enough to cut off Ellie's air supply for a second or two, but Ellie didn't care. She just squeezed back, tears forming in her eyes due to the lack of oxygen.

Ellie had time to calculate that this was the longest hug they had ever shared, and when they finally broke apart, both girls had wet cheeks and glistening eyes.

Johanna turned to the rest of the family now and everyone got a tight squeeze and offered their own little final words to her. Ellie stood by holding onto her elbows and watched.

"You take care of yourself out there," Grandpa said, kissing Hanna's forehead.

"I will, Grandpa," she said, moving onto Grandma.

"Just keep learning, kiddo," Grandma said, and then leaned up to whisper in Johanna's ear, loud enough for Ellie to hear. "And don't be afraid to show off a little. Confidence is attractive." She looked straight at Markus then, who quickly turned away, pretending to admire the architecture of the big city gates.

Johanna flushed bright red, and pushed a strand of hair behind an ear as she drew back from Grandma, stifling an embarrassed laugh. Grandma winked and let her go.

Julia and Frank stood together, Frank with his arm draped over her shoulders. Mum was crying and Dad looked like he was trying very hard not to. Ellie had never seen him cry before, but supposed that now was as good a time as any.

"Goodbye!" Johanna sobbed happily, falling into her parents arms in a triple embrace.

Frank rubbed her back vigourously. "You'll knock 'em flat, lil' missy, I know you will. Just try your best, keep practicing and come home next year with some stories to tell. I wanna hear all about it."

"You will!" she said.

"Ohh, honey," Julia said, planting kisses on Hanna's head and cheeks, clutching the back of her head in a loving squeeze. "Just enjoy yourself, okay? I'm so proud of you."

Ellie sniffed a big glob of snot and wiped her eyes. "Oh let's get rid of her before we all drown!" she said, and they all laughed.

Johanna finally pulled away from her parents and inhaled a deep, shuddering breath. Grandma gave her a fresh white handkerchief from her pocket. "I knew this'd come in handy. Keep it and think of me whenever you blow your nose, eh?"

"Thanks, Grandma," Hanna said with a giggle. She folded it neatly, before putting it into her pocket.

"Excuse me?" said a woman, approaching from the crowd of students. "Are you here for the Edgehurst expedition?"

"Yes, I sure am," Hanna said, composing herself and smiling at the Trinity Towers representative. As expected, she was wearing a baggy brown robe, which looked pretty impractical to Ellie. It's a wonder she wasn't tripping up every step.

"I thought so," the woman said, returning the smile. She lifted up a little notepad and asked, "Your name, please?"

"McKree. Johanna McKree, from Harbrook."

The woman looked down through her list, a little nub of charcoal in her finger. She frowned. "I'm sorry, I don't have anybody by that name."

Ellie could practically see her sister's heart skipping a beat, but before she had an outright panic attack, Tabitha Henlowe came over and sorted the misunderstanding out. "Sai Clements, it's okay. This one is with me. Didn't Sai Brockhurst tell you about Johanna?"

"No," the woman called Clements said. "But he has been rather distracted lately, what with the, well, you know."

Death of his dad? Ellie presumed. Yeah, that had to be pretty distracting to say the least.

"Of course," Tabitha said, dismissing it with a wave. "Here, Johanna, let me help you with your bags. They're loading the coach."

"Allow me!" Markus stepped up and took hold of Johanna's leather case of books. When he tried to lift it, he must not have expected it to weigh as much as a mammoth and his cheeks bulged as he hefted it off the ground, wheezing and carrying it towards the waiting wagon.

Johanna picked up her bulging suitcase and offered her family a huge, beautiful smile. "Farewell! I will write as soon as I can."

"Goodbye, honey!" Julia said, waving and blowing kisses.

Frank smiled and waved too, as did Grandpa and Grandma.

"Don't do anything I wouldn't do!" Ellie cried, then quickly added, "No, wait, *do* do anything I wouldn't do!"

Johanna laughed, waving and smiling, casting a final glance across each of her family's faces, before turning her back on them and joining the queue of students filing into the coach.

The McKree's lingered until the group were ready to set off, which didn't take too long. Johanna and Markus were sitting next to each other, chatting away, but as they pulled away, she turned and waved some more. Most of the other students were waving too, at the various parents and guardians gathered at the gates.

It occurred to Ellie that this charade was clearly no merchant's trip to Edgehurst, as the official story told. Surely the city guards watching over the gate knew that. Perhaps they weren't yet taking the new law seriously, or maybe they just didn't want to get involved. Either way, the horse-drawn coach full of attuned young wizards and mages set out through the gates and began its three-day journey along the road to the sprawling Everdusk Forest, where Trinity Towers, and Prime Wizard Sai Garrod Brockhurst awaited them.

***

Sccrrrp, scrrrp, scrrrrp, went Ellie's knife as she slid the blade along the whetstone. She blew away the dust and carefully tested the edge with the tip of her thumb.

"Feels good?" Frank asked, glancing over.

"Yup, I think it's ready. Here." She handed him back the stone and he slipped it into his hunter's pack.

They were sitting on a bench outside the bounty office at Honeyville, just down the road from the inn they had stayed at three days before on their way to Darune City. Frank had picked up the honeyroo bounty and, just as he had promised, invited Ellie along as his apprentice.

In order to accept a bounty, and to make sure multiple hunters didn't turn up at the same time to carry it out, each hunter had to take the poster from the noticeboard, and bring it to the bounty office to let them know they were going to fulfil it. Every village had a hunter's outpost like this one, which carried out various tasks to help keep the bounty system organised and running efficiently. Honeyville employed a single man to run its office because it was such a small, close-knit community, it didn't need any more than that. The man, who Frank introduced to Ellie as Mr Huggins, had a big bushy beard and thick arms like tree trunks. He had an imposing physique, but spoke with a warm and kindly voice, the sort that Ellie often associated with animal lovers.

"Howdy Miss," Huggins said, smiling at her. "Following in yer pa's footsteps, are we?"

"I hope so," Ellie said softly, feeling uncharacteristically shy. She was nervous that he wouldn't let her join Frank on the bounty on account of her age, but needn't have worried. Westerners really didn't need rules and regulations to tell them how to run their lives. If Frank wanted to take his daughter on a hunt, that was his bloody prerogative, and Mr Huggins knew as well as any other person in Honeyville, Harbrook or Woodhurst that he wouldn't do it unless he felt she was ready.

Ellie didn't exactly understand all of that grown up mentality, but she sure sensed her father's good intentions to teach her, and knew that he was taking a risk bringing her along, because if he failed the bounty, it would be recorded on his hunter's license and his reputation might be permanently scarred.

"You need a bee suit?" Huggins asked Frank.

"Nah, we'll keep a good distance from the hives. Shouldn't bother the bees."

Ellie gulped. She hoped he was right. The honeyroo she could deal with, but being chased by a swarm of angry bees didn't sound like her idea of a good time.

"Fine lookin' bow, you make that yerself?" Huggins asked Ellie.

She bit her lip and nodded eagerly.

"It's ash, we have a few of 'em down in the woodland," Frank said. "I chopped her off a fine piece and she spent a whole week carving it into shape. Shoots a bit to the left, but she's got the hang of it and can hit a scarecrow from over a hundred yards clean in the chest."

"Corr," Huggins said, impressed. "Sounds like a good partner to be taking on a pesky 'roo with. Happy huntin', lil' missy."

Hearing the stranger say her father's old expression brought a smile to Ellie's lips. It seemed to confirm her membership of the hunters, like a secret passphrase that only they knew. Something like that, anyway. It made her feel giddy with excitement.

"You ready to set out?" her father said, rising from the bench and slinging his pack over a shoulder.

"Yes sir," Ellie said, jumping up and sliding her knife into its sheath at her hip.

"All righty, let's go."

They hiked out of the village centre and headed into the small woodland that surrounded Honeyville. Their target had last been seen north of the village in the flowery clearings that were owned by one of the beekeepers in the area. Huggins told them to expect around a dozen apiaries, spread out down a long clearing. Each apiary would be a batch of about five or six hives.

Ellie saw her first glimpse of these man-made wooden structures when they came out on the other side of the woods and into the wide, colourful field. "Wow," she cooed, taken aback by the fragrance of a thousand different flowers.

"Pretty nice up here, ain't it?" Frank said. "I always enjoy hunting 'roos."

"Those are the hives, right Dad?" Ellie said, pointing to a cluster of five wooden box-shaped hutches with slanting roofs. They looked like tiny, miniature houses, with slatted paneled walls and a little round hole cut into the base. They were more than a stone's throw away, but Ellie could just make out the tiny specks of movement flying in and out of the holes, and the gentle *buzz* drifted in the air towards them.

"Yup, they're busy making all that sweet honey for us. I

reckon we should go that way." He pointed to their left.

"Why?"

"Hunter's instinct. What do you reckon?"

Ellie considered it. "Yeah, sure. Lead the way."

Frank smiled at her and started walking. Ellie followed in his footsteps, casting her eye across the far side of the field, searching for movement in the trees. She had seen honeyroos before, so knew what to expect, and she started seeing them *everywhere*. That log looked like a tail… a fallen branch might have been a head poking around a tree… a bush moved and she watched it, expecting a big bounding roo to leap out of it, but nothing did. It's funny, when you're hunting for a specific creature, everything begins to look suspicious.

They skirted the edge of the clearing until they were way down on the left hand side, having passed three more apiaries and were approaching a fourth. Before they reached it, Ellie noticed one individual hive had been damaged. Its roof was off, lying upside down in the grass next to it, and some of the side paneling had been pulled away, revealing a dried up honeycomb jutting into the air.

"Could a roo do that?" Ellie asked, pointing to the damage as they came nearer.

"Yup. Definitely," Frank said. "They stand up on their tails and grab the roof in their paws. I've seen it. They have the top off, and that long nose just dives right in. They slurp louder than Grandpa's snoring, and can suck a hive half dry within ten minutes. They're smart enough not to take it all, knowing that if they come back tomorrow, they'll have a second meal. Judging by how crusty that comb looks, I'd say the roo's finished with it and moved on further down the clearing. Then again, he may just come back and try his luck with one of the others here."

Frank eyed the area, slowly sweeping his gaze back the way they had come, and further ahead, gauging whether or not this would be a good spot to lie in wait.

Ellie looked too, trying to judge her area of effect – she

could shoot an arrow at the damaged hive with ease, it was only about thirty yards away. The next closest hives were at least eighty yards back the way they had walked, and the group ahead might have been a hundred and twenty. If the roo showed up there, she'd have to rely on Frank to shoot it, so she hoped with slightly morbid wishful thinking that the roo showed up within range of her so she could try and nab the kill.

"I like it," Frank nodded. "Let's fall back to the tree line and see if he shows up."

Frank's instincts proved correct. After hiding near the base of some birch trees for less than an hour, Ellie spied movement in the bushes across the clearing, directly opposite them. The honeyroo stood about five feet tall and poked its head around a tree, scanning the area cautiously before it took two bounces into the open.

"He's here," Ellie whispered, tensing up.

"I see 'im," Frank whispered back. His nocked bow lay on the ground in front of him, so he picked it up very slowly and held it, ready to draw.

The honeyroo looked around and Ellie unconsciously reached out her senses to it, picking up its jumbled thoughts.

All clear. Food. Go.

The roo bounced quickly now, leaping over to the beehives in three gigantic hops and sniffed the air. Its ears and skinny straw-snout flapped comically as bees buzzed around its head. It picked a hive in the middle, the next one over from the one with the damaged roof and stood up on its tail to get a good sniff.

Ellie heard it thinking. *Food. Sweet. Yesyesyes.*

It was excited. She grinned.

Then the roo hopped a little to its left, and suddenly they couldn't see it anymore, because it was hidden behind the hive itself.

"Dammit," Frank whispered, holding his bow steady.

The roof of the hive tipped upwards, as the roo pushed it from behind. It tilted over, then slipped off and clattered on to the grass. The roo's long, narrow snout rose into the air and plunged down into the hive. They could see nothing now but its ears poking up over the top of the beehive. Nothing they could aim at.

"We have to move," Frank said softly. "Let's pincer it. I'll go left, you move right. It *will* see one of us and bolt the other way, so whoever's on that side can take the shot. You understand?"

Ellie nodded. That sounded like a good plan.

"Stay as low as you can, and move very slowly. That way."

She picked up her bow as softly as a mouse's footstep, and the two of them split up.

Ellie crept from cover into the clearing. She held her bow out in front, one hand firmly squeezing the leather-bound grip, and the other pinching the feathery end of an arrow and the bowstring, ready to draw. Her eyes never left the roo's flappy ears.

Slurrrp, it went, the sound of a greedy animal binging on its favourite snack.

She could only see its ears poking up over the hive's open top, but as she moved, its ears disappeared out of sight behind the adjacent hive, and Ellie took this opportunity to glance across and check on her father's progress. To her dismay, he was at least four steps behind.

Dammit, he wants me *to spook it!*

Of course he does, a little voice inside her head explained rationally. *He's more experienced than you. He knows that, and his hunter's instincts tell him to use you as the spook to ensure he can get the kill. Wouldn't you do the same in his boots?*

Ellie knew in her heart that yes, she absolutely would. But she *really* wanted to get the kill for herself. It would be amazing to come away from her first hunt with *that.* She didn't even care about the thirty bobbins share that Frank said he would give her. More than anything, she just wanted to nab the kill.

So, she slowed down. Let him catch up with her. Let him

overtake her… She crept forwards at a glacial pace, showing the kind of restraint and patience that Frank had been trying to teach her for flippin' months, but all the while never taking her eyes off the roo, and always, always listening to its mind.

Yum. Honey. Yesyesyes. Honey. Food. Wassat?

The ears pricked now. The slurping came to an abrupt halt. Ellie saw the roo's head pop up, its nose dripping with golden, glistening honey. It was looking away from her, towards her father.

Ellie froze in mid stride. She aimed her bow, and slowly drew back the bowstring.

Get ready, he's gonna bolt.

The roo licked its lips, staring intently towards Frank. She could just make out Frank's body shape in the corner of her eye, frozen like a statue in the wild grass. The roo must have been looking right at him, deciding whether or not he was just a harmless shrub, or a predator.

Flee!

The honeyroo panicked. It leaped backwards and swivelled in mid-air, bouncing once, twice, straight into Ellie's line of fire.

Jeepers he's fast!

Ellie fired the arrow. She aimed slightly ahead of it, the way she had been taught to hit a moving target, and the roo bounced right over it. The arrow sailed harmlessly into the woods, disappearing from sight.

"Dammit!" she hissed, scrambling to her feet and giving chase.

"Cut him off!" Frank cried, popping up and running forwards.

Ellie's movement caused the roo to rethink his escape plan and he jerked to the left, heading for the trees. Ellie sprinted after it, running parallel to its route as the roo bounced over a shrub and into the shelter of the denser trees.

Hide. Danger. Honey. Hide!

Ellie reached the trees herself and jumped over a fallen log, skidding to a halt on the other side of it. She crouched in the shadows, trying to listen to the honeyroo's panicky thoughts. *It wants to hide?* That meant it was still close. It could be just inside the tree line, hoping for the hunters to forget about it, intending to come back to the beehive and finish its meal when they had gone away.

But we're not going anywhere, Mr Roo. Ellie cocked her head, sensing the roo's presence and felt its movement coming from somewhere ahead of her to the left. So, she moved right.

Frank was hopefully doing the same thing on the other side, creating another pincer, just like before. It would be far more difficult to carry out now that they were among the trees, but Ellie supposed the basic principle still worked. She crept along, staying as low as she could, pulling another arrow from her quiver and nocking it into the string.

Hidden. Safe. Wait.

The roo wasn't moving any more. He thought he was safe. But Ellie knew better. She could sense his presence, coming from a large bushy fern on her left. She weaved between the trees, skirting a wide circle around the plant, meaning to approach it from behind and shoot it. Around she went, creeping through the trees.

A furry paw. She spied the paw through a thin patch of leafy shoots at the bottom of the bush. Ellie grinned.

Gotcha!

She took a few more cautious steps closer, trying to get as clean a view as possible of the fern and the area just beyond, where it would most likely flee to if she alerted it.

Its head popped up. It stared straight at Ellie for a whole second. Its eyes bulged, and she heard its singular thought:

Flee!

Ellie drew her arrow as fast as she could, anticipating its direction of flight and aiming straight ahead of it. The honeyroo leapt forwards, springing out of the bush and landing on its feet. As it did, Ellie took a shot. The arrow flew straight towards the roo, which was bending its knees to spring again. Its muscles writhed beneath its skin, and it moved a fraction slower than she'd anticipated. The arrow flew under its chin, close enough to trim several hairs out of its neck but nothing more.

Ellie heard a meaty *thunk*.

The honeyroo completed its bounce and leapt away into the woods. As it moved to Ellie's right, Frank came into view. Facing Ellie. He dropped his bow. Glanced down at the arrow in his chest.

Ellie's arrow.

They looked straight at one another.

Ellie's hand flew to her mouth. A scream tried to force its way out, and it bulged in her cheeks.

Frank was smiling as he fell to his knees, still looking at Ellie. Then he rolled over onto his side.

Ellie jerked into motion. "*Dad!*" she screamed, abandoning her bow and running to him. "*Daaaaad!*"

She fell to the ground beside him, staring in terror at the circle of blood spreading out across his shirt from the base of the arrow, which had buried itself in the middle of his chest.

Somehow, for some unfathomable reason, he was still smiling at her. "Good shot, Ells," he croaked.

How? How could he joke at a time like this? "I s-sh-shot you!" she cried. "I-I- didn- Oh k-kell-…" The words choked in her throat.

"It's okay." His voice was terrifying in its softness. "I'm so proud of you."

"Why?" Ellie said in a thin, high pitched whine. The forest swam around her.

"Promise me," Frank wheezed. "That you'll keep on… trying."

Ellie clutched his hand, squeezing it vigourously. He squeezed back, so strong, so firm, her father's hand, the one that had always been there when she needed it. But as she squeezed, she felt his grip weakening. Felt his life slipping away.

"Become the huntress I know you can be, lil' missy."

"Dad, I—"

"Say it," he said, still smiling that warm, terrible, beautiful smile.

"I promise," Ellie whispered, blinking away tears.

He nodded his head a barely perceptible amount. His eyes glazed over. All the squeeze went out of his grip.

"No, Dad, no. Dad! Come back! Come back, come back, don't go, oh Dad…" Ellie broke into wracking, painful sobs, tears streaming down her face.

What followed were several seconds of grief so pure, that words utterly fail to describe it. It's a grief reserved only for those responsible for extinguishing another life. A swift darkness blanketed Ellie's mind as she came so unexpectedly face to face with death. But worse still, that death had come via her hand, to one she loved so deeply, it was almost impossible to comprehend.

Such grief and pain has a power that those who are attuned can use.

A rift swallowed Ellie on the spot.

She found herself floating in a black abyss, devoid of sight, sound or smell. Her vision was the first sense to return, as a shimmering purple pinprick of light opened up around her. Soon, she was engulfed by the light, staring through a gateway to another world. A bruise-coloured mirror of the forest materialised around her and she became overwhelmed by the scent of its rotting, decomposing leaves.

Trembling and crying, she stared in confusion, completely failing to make sense of it. Movement rushed by beyond the skeletal black husks of the trees. Black movement, rippling fur, legs hammering the ground. A group of animals. Hunters. A *pack*…

The black wolves ignored her, running past as if she were invisible. Perhaps she was.

But then one, the last wolf, smaller than the rest, stopped

and looked at her.

Ellie felt the fear rolling over her like a blanket, and she fought to shrug it off, but it only enveloped her tighter. The wolf pup cocked its head, curious. It looked at her with four curious eyes. Four eyes and two tails. It was like no wolf she'd ever seen or heard of. It stalked closer, both sets of eyes gazing right at Ellie. Closer and closer.

It stepped into the rift with her.

Stay away! She tried to scream but nothing came out of her parched throat. Instead, a croaking, scratchy sound escaped between her lips that was part shriek, part cough, and something gave in her voice box. She felt her speech muscles slip into place again and she screamed, "*Get back!*"

The desolate forest vanished in an instant. The black dome around her shrank, spiraling and all-encompassing. She caught a glimpse of the wolf as it pricked its ears and flew towards her.

She screamed again and tumbled backwards, stretching her hands out to ward off the beast, but nothing could stop it. The wolf seemed to become *transparent* and its head plunged into Ellie's chest, disappearing.

Ellie felt herself being pulled violently backwards and she fell onto her buttocks in a bush.

"Agh! Ah!" she cried, gulping deep breaths. She stumbled to her feet, slapping herself along her chest, feeling for the wolf. She spun around wildly, searching for it, but it was gone. She was back in the Honeywoods. Her father lay on the ground a few feet away, the bloodstain now soaked across his entire shirt.

Arrrk?

The scratchy, hissing voice, louder than anything she had ever heard before, tore through her mind like a rusty sword. It was a terrifying, invasive voice, and plucked down Ellie's nerves like fingers strumming a guitar of fear.

"Where are you?" she cried aloud, looking for the wolf.

Where? Arkrussss! Where pack? Arroooooo! Arrrkrusssssss! Arooooooo!

The wolf howled inside her mind. It howled and Ellie covered her ears with both hands, but it didn't help.

Arrrkrussss! Arrkrussss!

She sensed the wolf panicking, adding to her own rising fear as she struggled to catch her breath, hyperventilating and clutching her head, grabbing fistfuls of her long brown hair, on the brink of tearing great clumps of it out.

The wolf in her head howled and Ellie screamed.

CHAPTER TEN

The Trinity Towers students had three days to get to know each other as they journeyed up the north-western road. There were thirteen in total, all of similar age to Johanna, with seven girls and six boys. Tabitha Henlowe rode in the front seat next to Sai Clements, the college representative, and the driver sat outside in the front, driving the four burly horses.

The coach had two rows of front-facing seats with a narrow aisle running down the middle between them. Students sat in pairs, with their luggage on every other seat. With three different stops along the way, the tutor's made sure that the students rotated their seating partner, in an effort to make sure everyone got to know at least two other people. They would be spending the next year all living together at Trinity Towers, and it was imperative that they got along.

During the first leg of the journey, Markus and Johanna sat together, she on the outside and he next to the aisle.

"So, what score did you get, Jo?" he asked shortly after the wagon had left the outer limits of Darune City.

She had been staring out of the window, lost in thoughts of her family she was leaving behind. She turned to him with distracted surprise. "Hmm?"

"Your preliminaries, I mean," he said. "What was your score?"

"Oh, what? I didn't have a preliminary."

Some of the other students overheard this and several heads turned in their direction. "Did you say you *didn't* take a preliminary?" a girl sitting across the aisle from Markus said in a tone of mild shock.

"Um, no. Should I have?" She felt her cheeks reddening. There was something about the accusatory way the other students were looking at her that made Johanna feel naked.

"Trinity Towers is the most prestigious academy for attuned in the entire country," another girl said. "How did you get invited without taking the tests?"

"Maybe she's a prodigy," a young boy said, sitting two rows ahead of her and craning his neck around to join in the conversation.

"She doesn't *look* like a prodigy," another boy said. He had round glasses and freckles on his nose. Then he frowned, and added, "What do prodigies look like, anyway?"

"Where are you from?" the first girl asked.

Johanna felt dizzy from spinning her head to keep up with all the probing questions. "Harbrook," she said in a meek voice.

"We're both from Harbrook," Markus added. "How about you guys?"

"We're Darunian," two girls sitting together said, then giggled at each other.

"You're friends?" Markus asked.

"Actually, we only met this morning at the gathering." They curled their pinkies together in a rather childish, but inarguably cute gesture. "We just clicked!"

Markus didn't seem to know how to respond to that.

"What about you?" Johanna said, asking the boys in front.

"I'm from Krillbottom," the freckled boy said, tipping

his glasses up onto his nose.

"Where's that?" Johanna asked, having never heard of the place.

"It's to the right of Darune."

"You mean east," the boy next to him corrected.

"Oh. Yeah. That's the one that goes right, right?"

"Not if you're looking south," the other boy said. "Then it would be *left.*"

"What?" Freckles said, frowning in utter bewilderment.

Johanna and Markus laughed.

"What's your name?" someone asked the boy.

"Herbert," said Freckles.

This triggered a round of name exchanges, as each student broke off into separate discussions about where they were from, what their parents did and which attunement specialty they were hoping to study.

To Johanna's relief, pyromancy seemed to be a popular choice, which meant she would have something in common with them. That whole preliminary business seemed close to putting her under a nasty spotlight. The last thing she wanted was to be singled out for something she had no control over. Tabitha Henlowe had somehow gotten her into the college just by asking Sai Brockhurst for a favour. That meant she was *really* lucky to be there. What if she'd been forced to take the test, and failed? The implication there was that some other students must have gone through that exact experience, and she had taken their place without even being tested. A wave of guilt washed over her at this thought, and she hoped nobody would bring the subject up again.

"I've been practicing my electro bolt," one of the girls across from Markus said in a hushed voice. Her name was Mallory, and she had tawny hair, green eyes and a chubby round face. She laid the back of her hand on her thigh and whispered, "*Sparkay-illit.*"

A bright flash flickered in her upraised palm making Johanna blink back sudden tears. It was accompanied by a fizzy crackle, and then the smell of charring wood.

"Mallory!" her friend Bella said, gasping and covering her mouth with a hand. "Look what you did!" Bella pointed to the blackened scorch mark now scarred across the back of the seat in front.

"Oops," Mallory said, feebly brushing the mark with her hand, succeeding only in making her fingertips go black.

"*Gustus-hoo!*" said a boy somewhere behind them. Johanna's hair ruffled against a sudden blast of warm air, and she yelped, along with Mallory and Bella. Markus leaned forwards with wide eyes against the gust that dissipated as it flew down the length of the coach.

"Who summoned the wind?" cried Sai Clements, rising from her chair and storming down the aisle towards them. "For goodness sake, don't spellcast inside the coach! And definitely not while we're still within earshot of the city. Sai Brockhurst has given me permission to dole out detentions to any students that misbehave, even before we get to the Towers. You're among the brightest mages and wizard apprentices in the province. *Please* act like it." She gave them a withering look, before returning to her seat next to Sai Henlowe. Tabitha was sucking on her lower lip, possibly trying to hide a smirk, then she turned around and the two tutors continued whatever discussion they had been having before the interruption.

Mallory turned towards the back, searching for the culprit that had cast the wind spell. "Was that you?" she said, directing it at a somber girl sitting alone in the very back row.

The lone girl said nothing. She just shook her head slowly and returned to gazing blankly out of the window. Johanna realised that while everyone else had been talking and introducing themselves, that particular girl hadn't joined in.

Maybe she's shy? Johanna decided that when they switched seats at Grenburg, the next village along, she would sit next to her if nobody else had.

Sure enough, when Johanna climbed into the wagon the next day, there was the mysteriously quiet girl, sitting alone at the back again.

Johanna cleared her throat with a polite cough. "May I sit with you today?" she asked the girl. She met Johanna with striking grey eyes, under a curly tangle of russet brown hair that fell to her shoulders.

"Go ahead," the girl said in a husky, easy tone, shuffling over to make room for Johanna.

Johanna smiled and sat down. She held out her hand, a little stiff and awkward in the confined space of the coach seats, and said, "I'm Johanna."

The girl smiled with bemusement at Johanna's outstretched hand, but didn't leave her hanging for long. "Karly," she said, and they shook. Karly gave such a tight squeeze and held on for longer than seemed necessary, to the point that Johanna had a tiny moment of panic that she wouldn't let go. But of course, she did.

Johanna tried not to show the relief on her face when she got her hand back.

"What you in for?" Karly said, leaning an elbow on the window ledge and nibbling at a fingernail.

Johanna didn't understand the question. "In… what? I'm sorry, what do you—?"

Karly burst out laughing. "Whoosh," she said, sweeping her hand over her head from forehead to the back. "Country bumpkin alert. We got a late one here, I repeat, there's a fish amongst the cows. Haha!"

Johanna stared at her, and realised suddenly why nobody had sat next to her the previous day. The girl wasn't shy, she was *crazy*.

"Sorry, Jo," Karly said, slipping back into that easy, relaxed demeanour as if the previous section of conversation had not occurred. "Didn't mean to rib ya like that. I just assumed since you didn't take the preliminary, you must have been sent as some sort of punishment."

"Oh, really?" Johanna said, glancing nervously ahead to

see if anyone was listening. Now she *really* regretted sitting down here. She thought she'd gotten away with that whole preliminary predicament. "No, uhh, I know Sai Henlowe, the pyromancy tutor." She pointed forwards, in case Karly didn't know who Tabitha was.

"Oh yeah? Special treatment, eh? It's not what you know, but *who* you know, right?"

"Oh no, it's not like that," Johanna said, but even as she said it, she realised that actually yes, it was exactly like that.

Karly knew it as well. "Whatever, I ain't judging." She held up both hands in a gesture of surrender. "I'm only here 'coz my pa was friends with Sai Vanderson, the old pyromancer up at Trinity. I say *was* friends, since they ain't spoken in about ten years, and ever since he and my 'ma found out I was attuned, they've wanted to send me up to learn under Sai Whatshisname, but couldn't bear the thought of me being around that numbnutted fire nincompoop, so now that Vanderson's out of the picture and your buddy Sai Afro is takin' over, pa finally had an excuse to get rid of me. So, ta-da! Here I be."

Johanna blinked. This girl hadn't said a single word all day yesterday, just stared absently out of the window for the entire journey. Now, she was bright-eyed and full of things to say, even if Johanna could barely understand any of it. Karly spoke with a heavy city accent, and used slang phrases that Johanna had never heard before.

In a way, she found it quite endearing, but more than a little exhausting at the same time.

"So, um, what's your attunement specialty?" Johanna asked, wincing in preparation for another bombardment.

"Mind control," Karly said. Then her smile vanished and her eyes widened like a madman, as she leaned forward, pressing her nose so close to Johanna's face that she leaned away in alarm. Karly repeated, in a sinister tone. "*Mind control.*"

They stayed that way for several agonisingly long seconds, then Karly threw her head back and cackled. "Your face! That was bobless. No need to read Jo's mind to tell what she's thinkin', that's the truth." She pronounced truth with an F. *Troof.*

Johanna uttered a nervous laugh, glancing forwards again, hoping for someone to rescue her by joining in the conversation. *Where's Markus when you need him?* She saw him sitting several rows further up, next to Mallory. They were engaged in an animated conversation, which, to her immense surprise, made Johanna feel a sting of jealousy.

Johanna realised she must seem rude, staring up the coach like this, and jerked her attention back to Karly. Karly had her chin resting on the window ledge, staring out at the passing scenery.

"Sorry, I..." Johanna said, unsure where she was going with the apology.

"Huh?" Karly said, jerking her head around.

"Nevermind."

"Sorry, I got distracted by that big nibbet. Did you see it?" Karly asked in wonder.

"No," Johanna said, snorting a laugh.

"It was *huge*," Karly said, turning back to the view.

A quiet settled then, and Johanna found herself with nothing more to say, and no-one to listen even if she had because Karly was staring out the window again, just like she had done the day before. Johanna listened to the conversation happening two rows ahead between Herbert and a lanky boy called Roderick. They seemed to be arguing about who would win in a fight between a werewolf and a minotaur, whatever that was.

Johanna felt a little nudge on her arm, and turned to Karly, who was offering her a small bag. "Wanna hoomie?" Karly said softly.

"A what?" Johanna frowned, peering into the bag. Inside were a bunch of little nobbly brown things that looked like wood chippings.

Karly's eyes did something rather amusing, but also creepy: she bulged them open wide, and let them slowly shrink back to normal. As they shrank, she said, "Troof fruits, Jo."

"Sorry, that doesn't really answer it," Johanna said, frowning and shifting uncomfortably in the bench.

"Shrooms!" Karly hissed, grinning. "Magical shrooms, makes the whole journey more interesting, I can tell ya." She jiggled the bag, and the small mushrooms inside knocked together making a hollow tapping sound.

"Oh, um. No, thank you," Johanna said apologetically. "I'm not really into, you know, that sort of thing."

"No worries," Karly said with a shrug. "More for me." She plucked out a mushroom, popped it into her mouth and began to suck on it.

She's just eating hallucinogenic mushrooms right here on the coach, and apparently thinks that's normal? Johanna was rendered completely speechless. She'd never even tried a puff of Grandpa's pipe back home, nevermind eaten a mind-altering *mushroom* for goodness sake.

Ten minutes later, Karly went completely silent and didn't say another word for the remainder of their ride to Edgehurst. She just stared out of the window, occasionally turning slowly to Johanna with huge, dilated pupils that almost swallowed her grey irises entirely, and smiled at Johanna in a way that made her feel naked again, just like the day before. But this was somehow worse. Whatever Karly was experiencing, it was vastly beyond Johanna's comprehension, and therefore scared the socks off her.

Johanna spent the rest of the journey trying to look anywhere else, but unconsciously kept glancing at the profile of Markus as he talked to Mallory, a million wheels away near the front of the coach.

***

Johanna caught her first sight of the Everdusk Forest at the end of that second day, long after the sun had set. They pulled into Edgehurst village and checked into the inn for their final night on the road. Tabitha suggested that they all go to the roof terrace where there was a viewing platform that looked out north towards the legendary forest.

All of the students piled up the wooden staircase and formed a long line against the railing to have a gander. A wide strip of tall, thick-trunked trees stretched across the horizon, illuminated from within as if by the gentle embers of a bonfire. The foremost trees were dark silhouettes against a twinkling interior, which glowed a very beautiful soft orange, the colour of a pale sunset.

She dreamed of that mesmerising sight, sleeping peacefully for the first time since setting out from Darune without thinking too much of home.

The next morning, they filed back into the coach for the final leg of their expedition through the Everdusk.

The air changed as soon as the coach rolled into the forest. A soft glow engulfed them emanating from a cloud of floating spores that seemed to hang in mid-air. They hovered slowly up and down, oblivious to gravity. There wasn't even a hint of a breeze and the air felt comfortably close, like being indoors with the windows open on a midsummer's day. The air smelled fresh, despite the initial misgivings Johanna had about breathing in the spores. They didn't float into the coach, but rather parted and drifted around it as it passed through.

The road weaved between enormous tree trunks, the biggest Johanna had ever seen. These were the famous superoaks, which grew nowhere else in the province. Most of the trees would have been wide enough to drive through, if one were inclined to bore a tunnel through the bulging trunks. It made the Harbrook woodland seem like a forest of matchsticks.

Johanna was sitting next to Bella this time, a short but comely girl who had the window seat. Bella copied some of the other students and stretched her hand out of the wagon trying to catch one of the glowing spores, but every time she clenched her fist, the spores would drift up and evade her clutching hand. Bella giggled, a sweet melodic sound. "They're so pretty! But feisty. Look, see? Come here!" She giggled again, completely failing to catch any of the glowing sprites.

Johanna's first impression of Bella two days ago had led her to believe she was a bit of a snob, possibly from a rich family, but the ride through the Everdusk changed her mind. It turned out that Bella was just as nervous as Johanna had been, which is why she had been a little overbearing on that first day. And as for being rich, she came from a family that made clocks, and sold them in a store along that bustling road where the McKree's had enjoyed a parting meal at Freddy's. They might *seem* well-off compared to Johanna's family, but life in the city didn't seem worth it when you had to pay so much more just to live. Nobody in Darune grew their own vegetables, for example. They just bought them all from the market. Bella listened intently as Johanna explained how the three farms in Harbrook shared out their food with the rest of the village, in exchange for volunteer helpers throughout the year.

The conversation turned to food.

"You like pentini?" Bella asked with a glint in her eye. "Freddy's recipe is my favourite!"

"We make it at home sometimes," Johanna said. "But I have to admit, it must be nice to have a pub so close to home that serves food as good as that. We don't even have a pub in Harbrook."

"Really?" Bella said, shocked. "So where does your father go in the evenings?"

"What do you mean?" Johanna asked with a hint of amusement. "He comes home of course."

"*Every* night?" Bella gaped.

"Well, most nights. Sometimes he camps out wherever he happens to be hunting. What does your father do?"

"He stays out five times a week with his friends. He has a very strict routine about it. After building or mending clocks in his workshop each afternoon, he puts down his tools as soon as the bell tower strikes four and goes to Freddy's for two pints of ale with *the guys*." She curled two fingers on each hand to symbolise quotation when she said this last part, then continued explaining with bouncy, emphatic hand gestures. "On the weekend he'll have *three* pints and when he comes home his breath stinks which I don't like at all."

Johanna chuckled.

But Bella had a serious expression, her brow crinkled a little, lining her otherwise silky smooth skin. She had a pale complexion and bright blue eyes. Her long blonde hair dangled in a very intricate braided ponytail all the way down to the small of her back.

"I love your hair," Johanna said, abruptly yet somehow naturally changing the subject.

"Oh, you do?" Bella's frown turned upside down and when she smiled a set of gleaming teeth, she went from being just comely to rather gorgeous. "Mallory braided it for me. Want me to ask if she'll do it for you too?"

"Oh," Johanna felt a little rush of excitement, and it would dawn on her later that evening, that this was the moment when she made her first real friend among the students of Trinity Towers. "That would be lovely, thank you."

They beamed at one another.

"Look!" someone cried.

Everyone turned their gaze, following the boy's pointing finger out of the right hand window ahead of them.

Johanna had to lean across Bella to see. What they saw triggered a wave of excited gasps to ripple down the coach.

A tower rose above the treetops in the distance. All they could see was a pointed tip of its conical, tiled roof. It reflected the sun, but dully, suggesting a matte green finish.

"Is that it?" asked Herbert to Sai Henlowe.

"Sure is," Tabitha replied in her exotic drawl. "That's the Sun Tower. The tallest of the three."

"At just over seventy years old, it's also the newest,"

added Sai Clements. "Sai Brockhurst lives in the chamber at the top, but we'll give you the full tour once we arrive. Settle down now, we're almost there."

The road gently curved in the direction of the tower, which went in and out of sight behind the passing trees. The next point of interest was the blockade spread across the road directly ahead. The coach rolled to a stop in front of a densely packed row of thick green plant stalks which sprouted straight out of the ground, rising to at least fifteen feet. The plant wall curved away out of sight in both directions to the left and right of the road. The dirt around their base looked fresh and damp, as if they'd only been planted recently.

"Look at that," Markus said. "The road's completely blocked."

"How will we get through?" said Herbert. "I could cast a fireball at it."

"No," Sai Clements said sternly, turning to give him a warning glare. "It's just our new security perimeter. We need to signal Robert to let us through." She turned to Tabitha and said quietly, "I hope this works. We haven't had time to test their recognition abilities yet." She climbed down from the coach and walked tentatively up to the wall of stalks.

The plants began to *move.*

First one, then the ones next to it, then about four more on either side all bent over towards Sai Clements. It looked as though the plants had sensed her presence and were leaning forwards to look at her with their heads.

Johanna gulped. The plants had *mouths.* And teeth. They were oversized lillysnappers, big enough to swallow a person whole. Each one had a gaping maw at the end of its stalk, and as they lowered into view, the maw opened up, revealing two rows of sharp needles, dozens of them, dripping with a translucent white puss.

"Eeek!" a girl sitting near the front shrieked.

The horses neighed and shied away from the leering plants, taking a step backwards out of fear, jerking the wagon quite violently.

"Whoa, there, easy now," the driver said in an effort to calm his horses. Johanna was reminded of her Grandpa, who spoke to his animals in that same gentle authoritative way.

A low hissing sound began to emanate from the lillysnappers.

"Oh, cripes, fook this!" Sai Clements said, backing away. One lunged for her, snapping its jaws with a sloppy splat.

Some of the students yelped, including Bella.

Sai Clements darted back inside the wagon, cursing and muttering under her breath. "This is all that pesky king's fault, you know. If he hadn't banished us, we wouldn't have needed to grow a wall of titanic fookin' lillysnappers. This is just a pain!"

The boys sniggered at her use of the curse word, but Johanna felt slightly uncomfortable. If the tutor didn't know how to get past the lillysnapper guards, then how were the students supposed to? And since they were clearly meant to stop intruders getting into the grounds, did that mean they would essentially be locked inside too? She remembered Karly's insinuation that Trinity Towers was some kind of prison, and that joke seemed less quirky now, and a lot more troubling.

"Ho! Not that way!" cried a man, dragging everyone's attention to the right hand side of the road. He was spritely, darting across the underbrush and weaving his way between the trees alongside the wall of lillysnappers. As he approached, the plants all leaned towards him in a wave but none of them made any attempt to snap at him. It seemed that they were simply curious.

"Robert?" said Sai Clements. "What are you doing over there?"

He reached the coach and Johanna realised with surprise that he must have been at least sixty years old. He was of average height and build, but carried himself with an extraordinary agility for a man of his age. He spoke with a city accent, like Karly, but softer and a little more refined.

"Sorry Lorraine, we've been having some teething problems with the bloody snappers. These ones at the gate won't let anyone through, not even Wilma! It was her idea to give them an extra potent mix of the Mana compost," he said, shaking his head in agitation. "She said they needed to be bigger and tougher to ward off any government visitors that might come snooping. Look at the buggers!" He waved his arms at the huge plants blocking the road, which, unlike those curious ones around the side, were stretching towards him trying to bite his whole hand off.

"How are we supposed to get in?" Sai Clements said. "I have a coach load of students here!"

"The same way I just got out," he said, cocking a thumb over his shoulder. He turned to the coach now, with a beaming smile. "Welcome, kiddos! I'm Mr Anders. Don't mind the deadly mutant vegetables, grab your bags and follow me. There's a couple of smaller ones round this way which seem more cooperative. Hurry up, everyone's been waiting for you."

The students broke into a murmur of excited chatting, as they gathered their belongings and hauled them one by one out of the coach onto the road. Johanna wasn't the only one with two trunks, and as Mr Anders stood to the side, his eyes gaped wider and wider as each student filed out. "Kella Murphy, you gotta lotta' stuff. Tell ya what, everyone, forget the bags. Leave 'em here and I'll have the boys bring them up to the dorms. There's no way you'll be able to lug them through the forest. Come on, follow me!"

He marched off into the trees, double backing on his own path, following the curve of the lillysnapper wall. "Watch your fingers!" he added in warning.

Herbert led the way, following Mr Anders. Bella, Johanna, Markus and Mallory came next, then the other students, with the weirdo Karly bringing up the rear with Sai Tabitha and Sai Clements.

The lillysnappers didn't know which way to turn, and the

whole wall danced and jostled against each other, shuffling for a good position with which to see the students.

They walked until the coach had disappeared behind the curved wall of mutant plants behind them and then a little bit further than that. The conical tip of the Sun Tower reappeared, poking just above the lillysnappers. Johanna estimated that the base of the tower must be at least two stone's throws away. And judging the curve of the wall, it seemed that they had walked about a quarter of the way around the entire perimeter. *Wow, it really is quite small, then.*

"Here we are," Mr Anders said, stopping next to a batch of noticeably smaller lillysnappers. Smaller, perhaps, but they were still frighteningly large, standing at least ten feet tall. "*Calmus-oprandi,*" Mr Anders said in a firm, commanding voice. As he said it, he waved the palm of his hand back and forth across five of the stalks.

For a moment, the plants went rigid, standing straight upright as if a steel rod had been jammed up through their insides. Then, the five of them slowly bent over backwards, laying their heads gently on the ground, flat against the grass.

"All right, quickly now, head on through." Mr Anders ushered the students on. "Don't worry about stepping on 'em, they're tough as old boots."

Herbert, who went first, leapt over the stalks anyway, and scurried away from the snappers either side of the gap, which were unaffected by Mr Anders strange spell.

Johanna eyed the two snappers either side of the gap, half expecting them to bite her head as she went through, but they only leaned towards her, and she heard a low humming sound coming from deep inside their core.

What weird creatures. They were closer to animals than plants, as far as she could tell. *If I were a thief, I'd certainly think twice about trying to break in here.*

A second wall greeted them on the other side of the lillysnappers, made of great stone bricks. It rose about eight feet high, running in straight lines with intermittent pillars acting as vertices, allowing it to take on an angular curved shape as it enclosed the three towers in its middle. Johanna could see the other two towers now, each about a third the height of the Sun Tower.

They followed the wall around to their left, heading back towards the coach, hidden from view by the monstrous lillysnappers, and soon came to the Trinity Towers main entrance. Huge cast iron gates were swung wide open on great hinges, and as Johanna stepped around the pillar, a burst of colour greeted her eyes.

A cheer went up. There might have been fifty people waiting in the courtyard, and suddenly there were trumpets and a drumbeat, and lots of clapping.

"Welcome to yer new home," Mr Anders announced, winking at Johanna, who happened to glance at him as he said it.

She wore an awestruck smile as she swept her head around, taking in her first real view of Trinity Towers College.

The towers were arranged in an equilateral triangle, with one each to Johanna's left and right, and the taller Sun Tower at the back in the middle. The outer wall encircled them all in a cosy courtyard, decorated with flower beds at the tower bases, and a pebblestone path leading from the gates straight across to the Sun Tower, and branching off to the other two.

She blinked in awe at the sight of it. Standing eight storeys tall, the Sun Tower had a thick round base made of the same chunky bricks that had been used for the outer wall. Climbing out of this rose a straight cylinder of black obsidian brickwork, which had five rows of circular windows staggered up its surface. The upper chamber bulged out wider than the cylindrical body, taking up three of the eight storeys, and had a wide, rectangular window facing forwards onto the courtyard. Johanna imagined the Prime standing up there, overlooking his domain. Right now, nobody could be seen inside the glass, though.

Finally, sitting atop the pinnacle was the tiled cone roof, the one they had glimpsed earlier through the trees as they travelled along the road. The tiles were moss-free, painted a dull grassy green colour, and at the very tip, a little chimney hole jutted out protected by a small rain cap.

The other two towers were each six stories high, but with shallower roof cones that seemed to take off another level when compared to the Sun Tower. They didn't have such large bases, and the main cylinder's that formed their bodies were made of grey, mossy stones. Rather than look dilapidated and unkempt, the moss seemed to be part of the design, giving them a mature, wizened feel, like the wrinkles on Grandpa's forehead.

The welcoming trumpet finished with a crescendo and the clapping petered out. Now, the trumpet let out a long, mournful wail, and each of the staff that lined the pebblestone path turned towards the Sun Tower with their hands clasped behind their backs.

The Sun Tower's front door opened wide and four burly lads with combed back hair and dressed in mourner's black walked out, holding a large stone tablet mounted on a wooden plinth. Johanna could see writing carved into the stone, but had no idea what it said.

The atmosphere had turned from welcoming and celebratory to respectfully quiet.

Mr Anders, who Johanna hadn't even noticed disappearing, walked out of the same door behind the stone tablet. *How did he get there?* Johanna wondered.

The trumpet's mournful tone reached its climax and cut off, triggering a startling silence.

Mr Anders smiled down at the students from the top of the wooden ramp. Johanna could see stone steps underneath the ramp, and wondered why they had covered them like that.

"Welcome one and all, to a new year here at Trinity Towers," Mr Anders said. "Thank you all for your patience, we'll get those pesky snappers in order by tomorrow, or I'll have the whole lot uprooted!"

A small chuckle rippled down the line of staff, but the students were too apprehensive to risk it. Everyone sensed the importance of the ceremony that had just begun.

"It's been a mix of emotions at the college these past few weeks, as we prepared for the start of the new term, we have also faced the unexpected loss of our headmaster. And so today, as we welcome you all to your new home, we bid farewell to our mentor, good friend, and father, Prime Wizard Sai Jason Brockhurst."

As he said this, a smartly dressed lady climbed the ramp and bent to one knee to scratch a mark in the stone. *It's a list of names,* Johanna thought. All of the Prime's that had served the Towers for the last two hundred years were etched onto the tablet.

"And so, taking his rightful place atop the Sun Tower, I want you all to put your hands together for our new Prime, Sai Garrod Brockhurst."

Anders stepped to one side of the door, as everyone started to clap again.

Sai Garrod appeared in the doorway, shorter than Johanna remembered… then she realised that he was sitting in a wheelchair.

A hushed series of gasps went around the students, barely audible over the clapping, but unmistakable.

"Why is he in a wheelchair?" murmured Mallory behind Johanna's left ear.

Bella answered, "I don't know…"

"Shh," Tabitha said gently, pointing forwards and mouthing *listen.*

Garrod came to a stop beside the stone tablet and the clapping ceased. "Greetings, my loyal collective of Sai's, Sir's, Madam's and pupils." He sat perfectly still as he spoke, rigid as a mannequin, not even turning his head. He had one palm face down on the armrest, and the other pointing skyward. It was a very unnatural pose, Johanna thought.

"You will notice I am chair bound. I'll not shimmy

around the fact, I'd rather explain the reason immediately. I am paralysed from the neck down."

Bella gasped the loudest this time, but Johanna must have come a close second.

"I had an unfortunate accident while we were preparing the grounds for your arrival, and fell from the roof. I want to say this here and now, that despite the direness of my injuries, I have absolutely zero intention of letting it stand in my way of tutoring you, the future of attunement in this province."

His speech took on a slightly aggressive tone. "King Victus has declared us scoundrels and fugitives of the law, but we will not back down from our heritage and spit on our ancestors, who have practiced the art for over five centuries. I will not let him get in the way of your knowledge, and I will not let my injuries hinder my ability to teach you."

Anders wheeled Sai Garrod forwards down the ramp now, and onto the pebblestone path, allowing Garrod to roll up close to the students for the final part of his address. "I will do my very best to teach you everything you need to know to become apprentice wizards and mages, and by the time you leave Trinity Towers, people will call you Sai. I'll work hard this year, and I expect you to do the same. Those of us lucky to be attuned, we understand that true power doesn't come from the body, but is summoned from the mind. Even a broken body is capable of greatness, so long as the mind wills it."

A fireball appeared in his upturned palm without warning. Markus and Mallory, who were standing closest to Sai Brockhurst jumped back a little in fright.

Garrod smiled, and his eyes flicked towards the swirling fire in his hand. The fireball changed colours, shifting from deep orange, to a searing blue, then green, purple and red, then it pulsed. The fireball shot up into the air, and everyone craned their necks to follow its trajectory as it flew vertically up and exploded in a dazzling shower of multi-coloured fireflies, twinkling down around the courtyard.

Johanna looked back at Sai Brockhurst, her hazel eyes reflecting the rainbow of colours. Garrod met those eyes and smiled. Johanna started, for she saw colour reflected there also, but it was a tint of yellow. When the fireball had exploded, yellow was not a colour among the rest.

Then the tint was gone, and he regarded her with his natural dark brown irises.

"Welcome to Trinity Towers," he finished.

CHAPTER ELEVEN

Garrod sat alone in his wheelchair at the top of his tower with his eyes closed. A lit candle on his father's desk offered a solitary light in the otherwise dim chamber. A light breeze fluttered the drapes dangling beside the open window. Somewhere above the clouds, a waxing sickle moon looked down nonchalantly at the sleeping forest, but neither did its light make any impression on the moody headmaster's chamber.

He was deep in silent meditation. At least on the outside.

A rap at the door broke Garrod's concentration and he blinked them open, snarling, "Who is it?"

"It's me, Sai," Robert said, his voice muffled through the door. "Come to help you into bed."

"That won't be necessary," Garrod snapped. Then, recalling some manners, "Thank you, Robert. But I wish to be left alone tonight. I can sleep fine in the chair. A benefit of having no feeling in my lower body."

"If you're sure," Robert said tentatively.

"I'm sure. Please go."

"All right. G'night, Sai."

Garrod heard his footsteps clacking down the wooden stair, and waited for them to fade beyond hearing. Then he closed his eyes again and spoke to Corcubus with his thoughts.

Where were we?

Corrrkbusss!

Corcubus screeched and flapped its wings, Garrod could feel them almost as a physical sensation sweeping the underside of his skull. It sickened him.

Yes. Now I remember.

He imagined a whip with three tails, each barbed with razor prongs. He cracked it across Corcubus' back, plucking out feathers and drawing another gash of blood.

COOORRRRKK!

Obey! You will OBEY!

Garrod had meditated for many hours every night since his tumble out the window. He had to understand how the creature was able to survive as nothing but a soul inside his body, and ultimately, find a way to exorcise the parasite altogether. How could he tolerate it after what it had done to him?

Kwi-chak!

The whip snapped again, this time snagging on a wing, ripping out a plume of blood soaked feathers. Corcubus squawked in terror.

Garrod felt no pity. The creature needed to know that it wasn't welcome, and could no longer feed off Garrod's energy supply without severe consequences. He'd had plenty of nights to perfect this ritual and had at least succeeded in locking the creature so far down in his mind that he hadn't lost control of his body to it for four consecutive nights. Tonight was the fifth, and Garrod intended to make it the creature's last.

Tonight, Corcubus would die.

At least he hoped. Garrod may never walk again, but if he could at least regain dominance of his own body, the way it had been before he'd stepped into that forsaken rift, maybe he could learn to adapt to life as a paraplegic.

There was one redeeming factor that had come out of

the fall. Having no physical sensations anywhere in his body, his mind had been able to sharpen to a deadly point, just like a sword on a grindstone. Now, he could do much more than simply sense Corcubus' presence. When he meditated, letting his body relax – but not sleep, no, not until he'd rid himself of Corcubus would he risk *sleep* – Garrod could visit the creature down in the dungeon of his subconscious.

Right now, as his body sat motionless in the wheelchair, candlelit shadows flickering in the crook of his nose and eye sockets, Garrod saw himself standing in the prison cell he had created for Corcubus.

He cracked the whip again.

"*Cooooorkkubuss!*" the vulture screeched, its voice echoing off the dungeon walls.

"Lie down!" Garrod bellowed, whipping it again.

Corcubus cowered in the corner of its cell, head bent low between its legs, wings held aloft in a feeble attempt to shield itself. Blood dripped onto the stone floor from a dozen different gashes, while flaky remnants of the previous night's beating dried on the gate's rusty iron bars.

Garrod walked towards the vulture slowly. It was as big as a cow, with a wingspan that might be over twelve feet wide. It had grown so quickly, probably because of the amount of energy it consumed, energy that it *stole* from Garrod. He clenched the whip in white knuckled fingers, raising it above his head.

This time, you die.

Garrod imagined a short sword, and the whip transformed into it. The tails straightened together and clanged into a sharp metal blade, the leather grip morphing into a simple hilt.

Corcubus lifted its head and looked straight at Garrod with its beady, scared yellow eyes. Garrod glared back with cold determination. He raised the sword, but as Garrod's intention was made clear, Corcubus' will to fight back intensified. It staggered up, talons scratching on the stone floor, and flapped its wings, spraying Garrod with speckles of blood. "*Caaark*!"

Garrod thrust the sword at it. A vicious strike, aimed at Corcubus' breast. The bird writhed and with a heaving flap of its wings, dodged the blow.

"Sit *still*!" Garrod snarled, pivoting after it. He swung the sword in a savage arc, meaning to lop its head off. But again, Corcubus dodged, even managing a petulant snap at Garrod's wrist as it passed its beak.

Every time Garrod's anger flared, Corcubus seemed to invigorate. Garrod jabbed again, trying to plunge the blade into its core, but Corcubus bit Garrod's wrist and the pain was somehow real enough to pull him out of the trance. He caught a snapshot glimpse of the wide rectangular window of his chamber before him, his father's desk lying between him and the view of a sickle moon now shining over the treetops.

Focus!

He slammed his eyes shut again and slipped back into the dungeon. Corcubus had somehow partially healed itself, which seemed impossible, but no less true. The sight of it sent another wave of rage crashing over Garrod, who summoned a fireball without even thinking. He liquefied it, a searing whirlpool of lava swirling in his palm and cast it straight at the hissing condor. Corcubus caught a flaming jet of liquid fire square in the head. It flooded over him, scorching off his feathers, melting his eyeballs and searing his flesh. Garrod sprayed magma from his palm across the prison cell, melting the metal bars in an instant, filling the dungeon with the choking smell of burning flesh and molten iron.

But Corcubus didn't die.

It screeched a deafening cry and lunged *forwards* through the onslaught of lava and flew straight for Garrod with yawning jaws. The beak clamped shut around Garrod's throat. The last thing he saw was the smoking empty eye sockets of Corcubus as it tore Garrod's head clean off his shoulders.

Garrod awoke from his meditation with a violent jerk of his entire body. Even the nerves and muscles that no longer responded to his brain's signals all clenched, including his legs. His feet sprang out in front of him, pushing against the floor and almost tipping the wheelchair over backwards. He teetered on the brink for a moment before tipping forwards again, crashing back down with a thump.

"Fook!" Garrod growled through gritted teeth. *Again!*

He took a few deep breaths, recomposed himself and dived back into the trance to have another go.

But no matter how many times Garrod tried to murder Corcubus, the creature was able to evade his attack. Every time, no matter the method, the creature seemed to feed off his emotion, his desire to kill it, and turn it against him, either by healing itself, or simply summoning enough strength to wriggle out of reach. He tried stabbing it, crushing it, setting fire to it, he even once pictured locking the creature inside a sealed room and flooding it with water in an attempt to drown it. But when the creature went under water, Garrod found he couldn't breathe, and almost passed out before eventually dropping the floor out from under Corcubus and allowing the water to drain away in an instant. Corcubus lay soaking and shivering in his cage as Garrod panted and wheezed in the physical world.

He just couldn't kill the creature.

There had to be another way. He couldn't just let this thing enslave him for the rest of his life. If he couldn't kill it… if he couldn't beat it…

If you can't defeat 'em, join 'em.

The childish catchphrase sprang into his head unwarranted and made him cringe. An absurd notion. He would never *join* with Corcubus. What did that even mean in this context? The fooking condor was already joined with him, constantly struggling for control of his body. A body which was now crippled beyond repair.

Wait.

What if he *could* be repaired?

Corcubus seemed to have the ability to heal itself by using Garrod's energy. What if Garrod could reverse that, and use Corcubus to heal *himself?*

Garrod's eyebrows rose in ponderous excitement. Now *this* was an idea worth pursuing.

He sure couldn't kill Corcubus. But he could at least try absorbing its energy. Maybe even its soul.

He closed his eyes again and concentrated.

This time, he imagined himself standing at a junction in his mind. Two tunnels led off in opposite directions from the junction. Down one dark tunnel was his subconscious. Corcubus' dungeon was in there, down in the depths. A second tunnel led to Garrod's conscious, the active, thinking part of his mind. Light spilled from this tunnel, colourful and vivid. Down there, thoughts manifested themselves from seeds, occasionally sprouting into fully formed ideas or calculations, instructions for body movement, speech and his five senses. That was also where he gathered his energy to use as fuel for his spells. That tunnel was like a pot of gold, constantly drawing Corcubus' eye. He could feel Corcubus striving to get through to that tunnel, yearning to live in the light.

Corcubus appeared now, its head poking out of the darkness of Garrod's subconscious tunnel. Its eyes were back, all of its feathers regrown. It had fully recovered from its onslaught, because of course it had. No matter what horrific injury Garrod inflicted on it, it always reverted to its original state after he left the meditation for longer than a few seconds.

He beckoned it forwards.

That's it. Come out.

Cooorkabuuss?

It sensed a trap, which of course it was. But the bait was too good to ignore. Corcubus cocked its head at the tunnel of light, watching Garrod with one eye and the swirling fireworks of his waking mind with the other.

Crrrk. It made a cooing sound now, not dissimilar to

the purr of a cat. It stepped out of the black. Its talons clacked against the floor. Garrod urged it on, but gently, offering thoughts of comfort. The light inside his tunnel turned an inviting shade of warm orange, like that of the Everdusk. No creature alive could resist such an inviting glow. It was the warmth of a fire on a cold winter's day, a cup of water for a desert pilgrim who has been baking in the sun for days, a mother's embrace for an orphan that has grown up in a cold heartless world, stripped of love and kindness.

Corcubus staggered towards the tunnel with its head bobbing up and down, eager to step into that light and take control of Garrod's body, just as it had done before when it decided to try to fly out the window.

Garrod waited for the moment when he could feel the creature slipping into his neural core. Then he slammed the tunnel closed on its neck.

CORRRRKK!!!

An ear-splitting crack spiked down through Garrod's head, and he felt a bright flash of red and white pain.

He cried out in agony, but no sound came from his voice box and he heard nothing. An ultimate battle for control had begun within his mind. Were Robert still standing on the other side of the door at the top of the Sun Tower, he would have heard Garrod's bones popping and twisting, changing. He writhed in the wheelchair, arms jerking violently this way and that, bending in unnatural ways and his legs darted out straight, tipping the wheelchair completely over and spilling him onto the floor.

His eyes remained tightly shut as his body underwent a grisly transformation.

Across the upper half of his back, behind Garrod's ribcage, something shifted beneath the skin, poking outwards, trying to break through. It looked like a mole probing the surface of the soil, attempting to push its way out, only the soil was Garrod's skin, and the mole was a piece of solid bone. The bone grew out from his spine and split off into two directions, travelling the only way it could go, which was past his shoulder blades and down into his upper arms. When the bones reached the joint of his elbow, they settled into place as if they were meant to be there. Then, that eerie mole-like movement started again, as something else pressed against the soft flappy bit of skin that covered the tips of his elbows. The skin stretched out like a balloon, the shape of something rounded and hard forcing its way out. Something *had* to give…

Plofp!

The skin of both elbows popped against the pressure simultaneously and out flew a pair of gristly poles of bone. They pierced the fabric of his robe and tore it open. The bones protruded out and kept going, extending like gory flagpoles, dripping with blood. A thin membrane spilled down like a curtain as the bones continued to grow, far longer than any human bone, starting out thin but growing thicker as it went. Two knuckled joints appeared, allowing the bones to bend like a finger. The final segment was thickest, a stubby base, closest to the elbow.

At the same time, Garrod's arms opened like a zip, a wound tearing from his elbow up to his shoulder, then ripping down the sides of his chest. The membrane spilled out, creating a triangular web of skin like that between a duck's toes.

The wound didn't bleed. The membrane dripped with goo as the extruding bones ground to a halt. Black feathers unfurled from within the membrane, slimy and oily, creating a curtain that draped downwards.

All of this happened within a few seconds, and when it was over, Garrod had grown a pair of hideous black wings.

He opened his eyes, and instead of dark brown, now his irises were speckled with yellow. He was lying on his side in a foetal position, the two mottled feathery wings spread out behind him on the floor, protruding through the tattered remains of his robe.

Did it work? Did I assimilate it?

He clenched his fists. Realised that he *could* clench his fists.

He pushed himself onto his knees, trembling and giddy, but undeniably strong. *I can feel my hands and legs. I am healed!*

Then his arms snagged, pulling the membrane tight and he found that he couldn't reach very far ahead to pull himself up. He looked back, and saw the wings for the first time. He made a dry choking sound, gaping at the feathery mutations.

"What have you done to me?" he said in a hoarse whisper.

Corcubus didn't reply. What little remained of the animal's soul was now just a few neurons and cells that had merged with Garrod's physical body. Garrod had completely devoured the adolescent condor's spirit and assimilated it into his being. There was *nothing* left of the creature except for those monstrous wings.

No, wait. There was something else.

He wriggled his toes. They felt strange, tough and inflexible. He slumped into a sitting position, and looked down at his sandals. They had been ripped to shreds, protruding out of his trousers were sharp clawed talons instead of feet. He rolled his trouser leg up, to see how far the bird feet went, and saw feather's halfway up his shin. But his knees were human.

Okay… don't panic.

He inhaled three deep breaths to steady his pounding heart. He closed his eyes for a few moments, trying to gather his thoughts.

For the first time since the terrible rift experiment, he found no trace of the alien presence lurking in the back of his mind. His thoughts were his own, and Corcubus really was gone.

His eyes snapped open and he grinned. The moon caught his eye then, peering in through the window. The clouds had drifted away entirely now, leaving an inviting sea of playful stars twinkling across the ocean of sky.

Garrod hauled himself up, rising on wobbly legs and stumbled over to the window for a closer look outside. He had a strong desire to open the window and take a deep gulp of the Everdusk air.

The robe fell about his feet in tatters and as he flung the window open, the cool night air caressed his naked skin. He smiled in bliss, and his wings unconsciously unfurled behind him, filling half the width of the chamber.

Fly.

A simple idea.

Fly home.

Where?

To mother.

My mother's dead.

Home.

My father is there.

Fly!

Before he knew what he was doing, Garrod flung himself from the window. This time he did not hit the ground.

Some newly awoken instinct told him what to do. He fell into a brief nose dive and spread his wings out, filling them with air and levelling out. He soared forwards over the treetops, then lifted his head and aimed for the moon. The wind ruffled his feathers and smothered his naked body in silky kisses.

Garrod banked to the left and glided around until he saw Trinity Towers below and to his left. A few candles lit up several of the tower windows, but he saw no sign of movement.

Garrod took to flying as easily as if he had been born to do it, utterly convinced that he had destroyed all trace of the creature, unable to comprehend that in actuality, Corcubus had merged with him so completely that he no longer could tell where Garrod began and Corcubus ended. They were as one now. Corcubus' instincts had become Garrod's own instincts, and he felt an un-scratchable itch to get back to his home, back to the *other place* where his mother and siblings waited for him.

No, my mother died giving birth to me, an inner voice tried to reason, but Garrod knew that his mother was probably waiting for him in Archdale, in her nest, feeding on the bones of the soldiers that had died trying to steal the egg that he had been born from.

No! We killed the condor! There's nothing for you there.

He shook the nagging voice away and looked around at the sky, which seemed infinitely more important. He was flying. Surely the first human to ever conquer the skies. Even the wizards that had mastered the art of levitation couldn't boast an ability as magnificent as this.

He soared above the trees for an untold number of hours, until the moon had almost sunk beneath the horizon. Then he turned back and headed for his tower. The conical roof leapt up out of the Everdusk like a landing beacon. Garrod swooped onto it and landed hard on his talons, scratching the tiles, and knocking a few off. They tumbled to the ground and smashed upon the pebblestone path.

Garrod cared not. He had an ear to ear grin plastered across his face. Then he cackled. It sounded half laugh, half bird screech.

He scrambled down the roof and swung into the open window. He climbed inside, crashing into the desk.

Robert was standing by the door.

"Sai?" Robert gaped in shock. "What has happened to you?"

"I am healed, Robert." Garrod shot him a mad grin.

CHAPTER TWELVE

Immediately after accidentally killing her father and opening a rift, Ellie managed to drag herself back to the Honeyville bounty office. She gave Huggins a terrible fright, stumbling through his door covered in dirt and blood.

Arrkrussss?

That terrifying voice again. The wolf's voice, snarling inside her head.

Ellie tried to ignore it.

"H-help! M-muh-Mister Hug...my dad! He...He's...!" She fell to her knees, covering her face with bloody hands and burst into wailing tears of anguish.

The burly man came around his desk and hunkered beside her, wrapping a big paw around her back. He managed to get a stunted explanation out of her before embracing Ellie in a bear hug, and carried her down the road to the inn, where her family was staying.

Ellie collapsed into her mother's arms, exhausted and completely spent, partly because of the overwhelming grief of what she had done, but also because the wolf creature that now existed in her mind was siphoning off whatever scraps of energy she had left.

Ellie passed out and fell into a feverish nightmare which

lasted for three days.

While Julia, Grandma and Grandpa waited for Mr Huggins' search party to recover Frank's body, Ellie dreamed of a desolate dead world, populated with blackened, skeletal trees and lifeless grey grass under a greyish-purple sky.

In the dream, she was running, searching desperately for something that she didn't understand. She ran and ran, growing cripplingly anxious, covering wheels of the wasteland, alone and scared and utterly lost.

When she finally awoke, she stared up at a familiar wooden ceiling. She was wrapped in a warm blanket which smelled like home. Because she *was* home. Visions of the desolate land lingered in her mind when she blinked, so she decided to try and keep her eyes open. Ellie tried to sit up, but realised she couldn't. Her arms were bound by hemp rope and she was tied to the bed.

"Eh?" she said, her throat parched and scratchy, triggering a feeble cough.

"Ellie?" Her mother's tired voice sounded close. Ellie rolled her head to the left and saw her mum sitting in a chair. Dark bags hung beneath her eyes, which were blinking away the remnants of sleep, but brightening quickly in relief and love as she leaned forwards and said again, "Ellie! Oh honey, you're finally awake."

"Mum," Ellie said, but her throat was sand.

"Here my girl, you need to drink." Julia offered her a mug of water which she must have prepared in advance as she waited for her daughter to wake up.

Ellie gulped it down, while her mother held it to her lips. When she had finished, she flopped her head back down onto the pillow, looking sideways at Julia. "Mum, what happened?"

"Oh, honey… I don't even know where to start. I've been so worried about you. Here, let me untie those," she said, reaching for the ropes. "Please forgive me, I didn't know what else to do."

As Ellie's hands became free, she sat up, and rubbed her forehead with a sweaty palm. Ellie's stomach gave a long, loud gurgle.

Julia smiled. "That has to be a good sign. You haven't eaten for three days."

"Three?" Ellie said, eyes widening. "I've been asleep for three *days*?"

Aaaaarrkkrussss.

She gulped. *Not again. It's still here!*

"Oh, Ellie, when you came back from the hunt..." Julia's hand went to her mouth, eyes never leaving Ellie's.

"I... Mum, I'm so sorry." Water tried to well in Ellie's tear ducts but they were dry and stung as if a piece of grit had gotten stuck there.

"It's okay, there's nothing for you to be sorry for," Julia said, reaching forwards to embrace Ellie in a tight motherly hug, and they both sobbed, holding each other for a long while.

"Thought I heard voices." Grandpa appeared in the doorway, holding a tray of bread and fruit. "Someone must be hungry by now, eh?" he said. He smiled a warm smile, but couldn't hide the underlying sadness behind his eyes. Grandma followed him in, drifting almost like a ghost.

While Ellie had slept for three days, it looked as though the three of them hadn't caught a wink between them. A lump of guilt formed in her throat.

"I'm so sorry..."

"No," Grandpa said, shaking his head as he placed the tray carefully down on the bedside table. "None of that." He gently caressed her cheek with a leathery thumb. She cocked her head and leaned into it, allowing his comfort to course through her.

"We thought you might never wake up," Grandma said, sitting at the foot of the bed. "I'm glad you did."

"What happened?" Ellie gulped, trying to find the words. "How did, um?"

"Shh," Julia said. "It doesn't matter, honey."

Honey. Ellie felt a cold chill at the word. It summoned up thoughts of the honeyroo she had hunted with her father. The honeyroo that dwelled in the Honeywoods outside Honeyville. The place where she had shot and killed her father. How could she not associate the word with anything other than that devastating accident now?

Aaaaaarkruusss...

A sharp pain stung behind her eyes. She winced, closing them and saw a terrifying image of a black wolf staring at her from an endless abyss. The wolf had four pale eyes, two on each side of its long snout.

She sucked in a gasp of air and reopened her eyes, her heart a pounding drum against her ribs.

"What's happening to me?" she said desperately.

"I don't know," Julia said with such bewilderment in her voice that Ellie found to be even scarier than the wolf. "You are unwell. It's why we had to restrain you."

"Why?" Ellie wheezed. "What did I do?"

"You, well, how do I say it? While you were sleeping, I think you must have been dreaming about something awful. Just awful." Fresh tears were forming in her mother's eyes and Grandpa took over the explanation.

"You thrashed like someone was trying to kill you, Ells," he said, matter of fact. "Your mother had to drive the wagon home, so I could sit in the back and hold you down. We thought you might fall right off the back. Put up a hell'uva fight, lass! You're stronger than you look." He smiled that sad smile again, clearly trying to put her at ease. Despite the troubling nature of his words, that old wise smile did indeed make things seem not quite so bad. That smile said, *I've seen worse. We'll get you through this. Whatever it is.*

A moment of quiet settled over them as Ellie digested this. Finally, she summoned the courage to ask what she needed to know. "What happened to dad?" she said, soft as a mouse.

"He's at peace now, honey," Julia said, wiping her eyes and offering a grief-stricken smile. "We made a pyre in

Honeyville and gathered his ashes. I haven't scattered them yet." Her voice broke, wracked with a sob, but she fought it, determined to say one more thing. "We can scatter them together now. We can say our goodbyes as a family."

Ellie reached out of the bed, pulled her mum close and they cried in each other's arms. Tears flowed now, streaking down Ellie's cheeks in little streams.

***

They scattered Frank McKree's ashes in the woodland behind the cottage. Word of Frank's death spread like wildfire throughout the community, and most of the villagers came to support the family and say their own farewells. A somber atmosphere settled over the village for several days following the funeral.

Ellie retreated to the house afterwards and then sealed herself in her room, entering a deep and all-consuming depression that lasted weeks. She only came out to eat. She regained her strength bit by bit, eating like a horse at every meal. It seemed that no amount of food could satiate her, and the family's stockpiled provisions quickly started to run out. Now that Frank was no longer there to support them with fresh hunts, they would have to find an alternative way to feed themselves.

Julia decided to go to farmer Cribs, Grandpa's old workhand who had taken over the farmstead on the other side of the bridge. She offered what little help she could, mucking out the cow stables mostly, in exchange for some extra meat and eggs. It was mindless physical work, and she found her thoughts always coming back to her poor daughter. She missed her dear husband, and despaired to see Ellie beating herself up over his death. If only there was something she could do to help pull her out of the darkness she seemed to be drowning in.

Julia approached Ellie one morning, as she sat at the kitchen table eating the last of the dried jerky from the deer

Frank had brought home the previous week.

"Ellie, honey, I'm so glad to see you recovering." She touched her daughter's hand across the table, giving it a light squeeze.

"Me too," Ellie said. "I miss him so much, though."

"I know. Me too."

"It's so quiet around here now." Ellie looked around the cosy kitchen, somehow colder than it had ever been before. No Johanna, no Frank. She and her mother were not big enough to fill it.

Ellie pushed her chair back, took her plate to the wash basin and rinsed it. When she was done, she gave her mum a quick, anxious smile and made to return upstairs to her room.

"Ellie, please wait. I need to talk to you."

"O-okay." She hovered by the door.

"He wouldn't want you to be like this," Julia said softly. "You should be out there, under the sky. You *love* the outdoors. When was the last time you practiced your bow?"

Ellie's eyes went wide, and she visibly tensed with fear. "I can't, Mum. I don't think I'll ever go hunting again."

Julia shook her head quickly, "No. It's much too soon for that. I understand. But why don't you just go for a walk? You haven't seen the sun for days. Summer won't last forever, you know."

Ellie hesitated, scratching her elbow. "I… I'm scared."

"What of?" Julia asked gently, her voice full of tenderness.

"I think that if I go out there, I'll run away and never come back."

"Why?" Julia asked, frowning.

Because it's what the wolf wants.

"I don't know," Ellie lied. She couldn't bring herself to tell her mum about the beast that was haunting her. She'd surely think her daughter had lost her mind. And perhaps she'd be right.

The sad irony was that had it been her father asking her

the same question, Ellie would have told him the truth. Frank would have understood, somehow, Ellie knew. He would know what to do about the wolf. Animals were his specialty, just as she'd thought they were hers, too.

But Julia? No. Ellie didn't quite share the same affinity with her mum as she had with her father. They loved each other, of course, but it just wasn't the same.

Ellie turned and took a step towards the stairs.

"Don't push me away, Ellie," her mother said, her voice cracking. "With your sister gone, and now your father… I just couldn't bear to lose you too."

This situation required patience, just like a slow, careful hunt. Ellie came to that realisation suddenly, as if the notion had been pushing against a door which suddenly gave way and burst open.

Ellie went to her mum and wrapped her arms around her waist with her head pressed against her chest. "You won't lose me, Mum. I'm not going anywhere."

Aaaaarkrusss...

Shut up, Ellie hissed in her mind, and the voice quietened. Sometimes it did that. Other times it simply got louder, but this time, mercifully, the wolf obeyed.

"I'll come with you tomorrow," Ellie said. "To the farm. Do you think Farmer Cribs could use an extra hand?"

They pulled apart and Julia smiled at her. "Of course. That would be wonderful." She reached up to Ellie's face and brushed a strand of brunette hair behind an ear, letting her thumb linger on her soft cheek.

Ellie could almost hear her father saying, *that's my girl.*

***

The following day, Ellie worked with her mum on the farm, collecting cowpats from around the paddocks in a chunky wheelbarrow and piling load after load onto the dung heap. Farmer Cribs let the muck rot down over a couple of years and then sold it cheap to anyone that wanted to grow flowers in their gardens.

She worked up a good sweat and at the end of the day her arms ached. A good ache. The wolf didn't bother her all day.

She collapsed in bed that night exhausted and satisfied, feeling better than she had in days.

But that night, the nightmare returned with a vengeance.

She didn't remember it when she woke with a violent jerk, sweating and wheezing for breath in the dark.

Why is it so col-

Her thought broke off because she was outside. Somewhere in the woods.

"No!" she husked, looking around in dismay. It wasn't yet dawn and she was lying in the dirt, shivering and tasting blood. *Did I bite my tongue in my sleep?*

Ellie scrambled to her feet and spun, surveying her location to see if she recognised it. She stepped in something that squelched.

Looking down at her feet triggered a small gasp of horror. Her bare foot was sinking into the open chest of a dead stag. Its intestines were spilled across the ground and something had eaten a good chunk of its flesh.

She licked her lips, and tasted blood.

"Oh no, please no…" It was too dark to see her hands, but they felt sticky, coated in something that smelled like iron.

She had to get home. Wearing nothing but her filthy, mud-encrusted night gown, Ellie picked a direction at random and staggered through the dark woods. The sky began to lighten, enough for her to start to recognise certain trees. She'd played in the woods behind their cottage ever since she was old enough to walk and soon found her bearings and headed for home.

She arrived before the sun had crested the horizon and stumbled in through the front door. She fumbled with the lantern and struck a flint match to ignite it. Under the flickering glow of the lantern she examined her hands and confirmed her fears: they were covered in drying blood.

"Oh no," she said, putting the lantern on the table and looking down at her night gown. Last night when she went to bed, it had been white. Now, it was a mixture of brown and red.

I hunted that stag in my sleep. With what, though, my bare hands? How is that even possible?

"Ellie?" came a croaky voice from the shadowy stairwell door. Her mother stepped into the lantern's light and Ellie saw her eyes widen. She swept into the room full of concern. "What happened to you? Are you *bleeding?*"

"No," Ellie said, holding her hands out in front of her. "I'm okay. Well, not okay, but—"

"You're *covered in blood*!" Julia grabbed Ellie's hands and bent to examine her arms for cuts, then her concerned gaze fell upon Ellie's blood-stained chin. "What have you been *eating?*"

"I think I sleepwalked."

Her mother froze, looking at Ellie as if she had two heads. "Where? Into Joe's abattoir?"

"Ahe," Ellie said, grimacing and stepping backwards away from her mum. "I don't know. I woke up in the woods, though." She hesitated, then added, "Next to a dead stag."

Julia raised a hand to her mouth, clearly at a loss for words. When she did speak, it came out terrifyingly calm. "We should have kept you restrained. You're not well yet."

"I'll be fine, mum," Ellie said with a wavering voice. "I can figure this out." Ellie's intention was purely to take the painful look of worry off her mum's face, but upon hearing the determination in her own voice Ellie realised that she *meant* it. She could beat this, whatever it was. She *had* to.

Aaaaarkruussss!

"*Shut up*!" Ellie screamed, clutching her head in both hands.

Julia looked at her daughter with the anxious expression of one who is seeing her beloved lose her mind. It was an expression built out of sympathy, pity and fear.

Ellie couldn't handle it anymore. She had to get out of there before she slipped back into the festering darkness that had temporarily taken over her life ever since her father's funeral.

Ellie grabbed the lantern, bolted from the cottage and ran into the night.

"Ellie!" Julia cried after her.

But Ellie didn't look back. Her night gown fluttered behind her as she fled into the woods again, retracing her footsteps back to the dead stag. She reached it, panting and wheezing, bent over clutching her knees as she waited for her breath to return.

"All right," she said in as stern a voice as she could muster. "I know you can hear me. I don't know *how* but I can feel you with me." She put the lantern down beside the stag's head and looked down at the carcass. "*You* did this, didn't you?"

Nothing replied. The wolf voice in her mind was silent.

"*Answer me*!"

Rage boiled in her, blocking her ability to sense the existence of the wolf. But she *knew* it was there. She just had to coax it out.

Ellie drew in several deep breaths and slowly counted to five. It calmed her down.

"What are you?" she asked it. This time something stirred under the surface of her thoughts.

Aroo?

It was the unmistakable sound a dog makes when it is scared but curious, and she heard it with her head, not her ears.

"You're a wolf of some kind," Ellie said slowly. Already her heart was trying to accelerate again, she teetered on the brink of fear. But what sort of a huntress could she be if she was scared of a wolf pup? Ellie exhaled another shuddering breath and closed her eyes, blocking out the sight of the dead stag. In her mind's eye, she saw the wolf hiding in the shadows of her subconscious. "I'm sorry if I frightened you," she said aloud. "Please come out."

Absurdly, she now imagined herself standing in a fenced-in yard with an old dilapidated dog kennel sitting in the corner. It was a mental recreation of Farmer Cribs' barnyard, where she'd spent all day yesterday collecting muck.

Ellie saw herself standing in the middle of the yard, looking towards the old dog house, knowing that a scared, lost little wolf pup was hiding in the shadows within.

"Come on out, I won't hurt you," she said, taking a step towards it.

A nose at the end of a long, sleek black snout protruded from the arch of the dog house, followed by four silver eyes, peering out. Yes, *four* eyes, Ellie thought, admiring the way each pair of eyes followed the contours of its snout: the eye behind was larger than the one in front. The young wolf watched Ellie with extreme caution from the safety of the dark kennel.

"Hi," Ellie pushed the word out past the lump lodged in her throat. Even in this strange daydream, she had only a feeble grip on her fear. At any moment, it could engulf her. But her father had taught her that all animals felt fear. And right now, she saw her own fear reflected in the wolf. No matter how scared she might be of it, the wolf was even more scared of her.

That gave her a flicker of courage.

"This is my head, you know that?" she said, trying to sound menacing. "I don't know how it happened, or why, but somehow you've gotten stuck here, haven't you?"

"*Aroo?*" The wolf bent and poked its entire head out of the kennel, its big ears pricked towards her. It cocked its huge head at her, and Ellie was taken aback at how elegant it looked.

"You don't belong here," she said. "Can't you just go away? Please?"

"*Arkroowl,*" the wolf grumbled, and stepped out of the

kennel.

It loped on oversized puppy paws, its thick fur rippled as it caught on the underside of the kennel door. It was impossibly big, far larger than the tiny kennel allowed, but Ellie reassured herself that this was just some daydream, so logic didn't matter here. All that mattered was that they come to some sort of understanding that prevented further horrific sleepwalking incidents like the one that had occurred tonight.

The wolf stood a few feet away from Ellie now, still watching her with its curious, wary eyes.

"Look, Mr Wolf," she said, glancing underneath him to confirm that yes, he was a boy. "I don't want you inside my head anymore. And I know you want to get home to your family, as well. I had to share your terrible nightmares where you were looking for them."

He clearly couldn't understand what she was saying, but the wolf hung his head a fraction, as if maybe sensing the *gist* of what she said, at least.

Ellie's fear was fading. The more she talked, the more empathy she felt towards him. "Who am I kidding? You don't know how this happened any more than me, do you?"

The wolf planted his bum on the ground, and his tail swept around to hug his flank. Wait, *both* tails. There was a smaller tail on top of the main bushy one, mimicking the double set of eyes on its face. Ellie scoffed a bemused laugh.

"You're definitely not from our world." She said it whimsically, accepting it with childlike ease. She sighed. "I guess you can stay here for now, until we figure out how to get you home. You want that, right?"

The wolf made no reply, but he lifted his head, sitting up straight, almost eye-to-eye with Ellie.

"We need to figure this out together. So, no more late night shenanigans! *I'm* supposed to be the huntress. I'm gonna have to get Mum to tie me down to the bed again, until I can trust you."

The wolf cocked his head at her, and looked almost cute.

"Heh. You need a name. I can't just call you Weird Wolf Pup from Horrible Dead Place."

The wolf's tongue lolled out, and growled that now familiar sound: ***aaarkrussss.***

"Arkarus?" Ellie said. "Yeah. Okay. Nice to meet you, Arkarus. I'm Ellie."

"*Ruff!*" he barked. He stood up suddenly and bounded two steps towards her.

She recoiled as a jolt of fear crashed over her. The barnyard disappeared and she was back in the woods, gasping for breath.

Ruff!

Arkarus echoed in her mind. He sounded close enough to touch, but he was locked safely in the imaginary barnyard.

How do I explain any of this to Mum? It's completely insane.

Ellie brushed herself down and went back to the house.

CHAPTER THIRTEEN

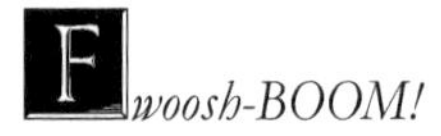

woosh-BOOM!

"Whoa!" cried the class. Then everyone burst into a round of applause.

Sai Tabitha Henlowe spun around to face her students, smiling broadly, and gave a little bow. "There she goes, pupils: a fireball cast without a spellphrase. Your goal for the first term is to master that. But it'll take time, and a lotta' practice. For now, show me what you can do *with* the spellphrases. Who wants to go first?"

Half a dozen hands shot into the air, including Johanna's.

Tabitha pointed to a boy near the front. "Roderick, come now. Stand back, everyone."

The class retreated a few paces against the rear wall of the circular room. They were on the top floor of the Storm Spire, also referred to as the Wizard's Tower, or more crudely the schlong, because the male dorm was situated down on level three. It was one of the two smaller towers that made up the Trinity, and its entire upper half was dedicated to the art of pyromancy.

"*Ignus-spareet!*" commanded Roderick, a lanky boy with spidery arms and mousey coloured hair. A cute little ball of fire shot from his palm and exploded with a soft *puff* on the far wall.

Its scorch mark was swallowed up by the one Sai Henlowe had already created, but she nodded her approval and said, "Well done. Now, pick a fruit and nibble it between rounds. I don't want any attunement jitters in my class."

Tabitha had a table at the back of the spellcasting room dedicated to fruit bowls. Pyromancy lessons were entirely practical, which meant casting a lot of different spells. One could easily use up an entire day's worth of energy in a single hour if you weren't careful. Tabitha had joked that half the college's budget went on purchasing fruit from the farms surrounding Edgehurst. Johanna wondered now whether it really had been a joke, after all.

"Fire is destruction," Tabitha said in a cool, commanding tone, addressing the class. "It is devastation and death. But it is also a healer. Did you know that?"

"How?" Mallory said, frowning. "Fire doesn't heal anything, it just destroys whatever it touches."

"You're right," Sai Henlowe agreed. "But consider a volcanic eruption. What happens after the lava has scorched the ground, and burned every livin' thing in its path?"

Silence lingered.

Johanna hesitated, biting her lip. *New life grows after?* She was too shy to put her hand up, in case she was wrong.

"Anyone?" Tabitha prompted. When nobody spoke up, she answered for them. "The forest regrows, stronger than before. All of the nutrients, the goodness, and the energy that feeds the fire doesn't burn up with it, not entirely. Much of it remains and returns to the earth leaving behind a rich and fertile soil that allows new life to replace the old. Think of fire as one of nature's tools. Like a blacksmith's hammer, or a tailor's sewing needle."

"That's naive," Mallory said. "Fire is dangerous. It shouldn't be idolised."

Most of the class seemed surprised by her nerve to

question the tutor so openly, not least of all Johanna. But Mallory had spoken with confidence and dignity. It was hard not to take her point.

Everyone turned to Sai Henlowe to see how she would react.

She smiled sadly. "What happened? Who did you lose to the flames?"

Mallory turned beetroot red. "Two years ago, my cat was taken… he was burned alive by The Blackfist."

"I remember that scumbag," Tabitha said softly.

"Who was he?" Johanna whispered to Bella.

"An evil pyromancer that liked to murder alley cats." Bella shook her head angrily. "Kella knows why. Eventually he grew bored of cats and they caught him with… nevermind. He's rotting in the city dungeons now."

Johanna was aghast. Darune had serial cat killers? And she wanted to *live* there?

"You show courage to attend my class, Miss Mallory," Tabitha went on. "What level of pyromancy d'ya hope to reach?"

"Honestly, I don't want to harness flames. I have more interest in the power of electro."

"Show us," Tabitha said, extending an arm out towards the firing range.

"Really? But this is a pyromancy class."

"No, it's *my* class. Attunement is about embracing whichever power flows most naturally through a person."

Mallory stepped forwards tentatively and faced the charred wall. She straightened her back, inhaled a breath and spoke clearly, "*Sparkay-illit!*"

A bolt of lightning fizzled from her fingertips and struck the wall. A puff of carbon spat out from the point of impact and drifted to the floor.

"Very good," Sai Henlowe said, leading the applause.

Mallory returned to the group, exchanging a nervous giggle with Bella.

"I wanna see what each of you can do," Tabitha drawled.

"That way, I can personalise my teachings. Every term, I'll take three of you for private tuition. All the other teachers will do the same. We rotate throughout the year until everyone has had close tutoring with every other teacher. It's how we'll get the best outta you, and ourselves."

"You learn from us?" Markus said.

"Of course. Attunement is ever evolving, and you are its future. You'll see things that we miss, and we'll record any discoveries and ideas in the archives so that the next generation can learn from it and continue to develop new techniques. I like to think of the art as undiscovered islands in an ocean. We have charted many so far, but believe there to be many more yet to be located. Help me t'find them, young'uns." She smiled an intoxicating smile. It was easy to like Sai Henlowe, Johanna thought.

After each student had demonstrated their skills against the target wall, Tabitha walked out in front and addressed the class.

"Now, so far we have used our minds to summon the flames," she said. "But there are other, more efficient ways. I wanna introduce you to the art of physical attunement. We will start with a basic example. See this candle."

Tabitha produced a long, narrow candle from the sleeve of her billowing robe, and with a click of her thumb and index finger, she lit it.

"How long will the flame take to burn through the candle? You." She pointed to Johanna.

"Um. An hour, maybe?"

"Yeah, more or less, right class?"

Murmurs of agreement.

"The candle burns slowly, releasing its energy over time. But pyromancers—" She waved her hand across the flame and it jumped into her palm. "—can pull that energy through time and use it immediately." The flame bridged the gap of air between her palm and the candle, burning down through the wick at an incredible rate. Wax dripped onto the ground in a trickle, splattering the floor and creating a little star of gloop.

The candle melted to nothing and the only thing left was a great dancing fireball larger than Sai Henlowe's afro. It was about half the size of the great fireball that Johanna had flung at the wolf to save Ellie.

The whole class gaped in wonder.

"How long can you hold it for, sai?" Bella asked softly, the flame reflecting in her big blue eyes.

"A short while. This energy came from the candle, and requires minimal effort on my part to maintain, but it will burn itself out rather quickly," Tabitha explained. "I don't expect *any* of you to be capable of physical attunement manipulation, but it doesn't hurt to show you what we'll be aiming for during the second term in autumn."

With a flourish, Sai Henlowe rotated one-eighty degrees and sent the fireball down the chamber where it exploded against the wall in a hissing shower of ashes. She turned back to the class to thunderous applause.

"I want to try that!" said Herbert over the din.

The clapping died away and some of the students turned to look at him with doubtful, even derogatory eyes.

"As if *you* could," said the boy standing next to him. It was Ned, the same boy Johanna had seen arguing with Herbert on the coach. They were friends, and never missed an opportunity to jib one another in class.

"I said I want to *try*!" Herbert said indignantly, tipping his glasses up his nose. "Sai Henlowe, you must have some more candles?"

"Perhaps I do," Tabitha said with a wry smile.

"Let him, Sai!" said Karly from the back. She wore a mischievous smirk and her arms were folded as she leaned against the wall. Then under her breath she added, "Could do with a laugh."

Bella and Mallory tutted in disapproval, but it seemed most of the class agreed with Karly, and a commotion ensued as everyone made bets on whether Herbert could do it or not. Ned said he was just going to burn a hole in his trousers.

Tabitha, still smiling, drew another candle from her sleeve and lit it with a snap of her fingers. She held it out to Herbert, pinching the bottom between thumb and forefinger.

Ned gave Herbert a boisterous shove in the back, pushing him out in front of everyone. Herbert straightened his glasses again and cautiously took the candle.

Sai Henlowe stepped aside and a quiet hush settled over the room, all eyes on the freckled kid.

"I read about physical manipulation in a book," he muttered. "I think the spellphrase is…" He waved his hand across the flame, mimicking Tabitha, albeit with less elegance. "*Ignee-tranfee!*"

The tiny flame flared up. It engulfed Herbert's hand for a second, causing him to drop the candle in fright. But even from the ground, the candle was eaten up in a matter of seconds as the fire leapt from the floor into his outstretched palm.

He yelped, and started to spin around, trying to flick the flame away. Everyone screamed and scattered away from him, bumping into each other. The fruit table was toppled over, sending apples and bananas rolling across the floor.

"Wahaiii it's hot!" Herbert screeched, flailing his burning hand around like a madman.

"*Cast it away!*" bellowed Tabitha.

Herbert threw his arm forwards aiming it down the range and cried "*Ignus-projeet!*"

Fwooosh-BOOM!

The fireball exploded, lighting up the room in a flash before fizzling out.

The panic was over.

"Curious. Most curious."

Johanna turned towards the new voice, and gasped when she saw Sai Garrod standing in the open doorway.

"Sai Prime," said Tabitha, stepping towards him as she brushed down her robe. "I didn't expect a visit… *Kella*

Murphy, you're walking!" She gaped at him with a slack jaw.

Her face mirrored that of almost everyone else in the room, including Johanna. *How can he be standing? That's impossible!* She regarded Garrod with deep fascination.

He seemed a little stooped, somehow, and he leaned on a curved wooden cane for balance. He was wearing a freshly stitched hooded robe, thick black fabric draped across his back and hung all the way down to the floor, covering his feet. He stepped into the room, taking small steps like those of an ancient old man, careful and precise, leaning on the cane for support. The tips of some very large leather boots poked out from under his robe as he walked.

"I can see you have your hands full with this rabble," he said in good humour. He stopped in front of Herbert, towering over the boy, who craned his neck to look up. "Tell me your name, little pyromancer."

"It's Herbert, Sai. I mean, Prime Sai. No, Sai Prime!"

Garrod chuckled. "That was rather impressive, what you just did."

He almost killed us all! Johanna met Markus' eyes who gave her a bewildered shrug.

"R-really, Sai? Thank you Sai!" Herbert said, smiling nervously.

"I want you all to take a leaf out of Master Herbert's book," Garrod said, sweeping his gaze around the room. "Out of everyone, he was the only person who had the stones to try. We all have a responsibility to strive for the unknown. It is the very essence of attunement. We have barely begun to scratch the surface of this wondrous gift of ours, and only through daring courage can we learn more. All of us must dive into the unknown, no matter how scary it might be."

He turned back to Herbert, looking down at the blushing boy with those dark, somewhat piercing eyes. Johanna saw the yellowish tint of his iris clearer now. It looked like flecks of dust, not a pleasant golden colour, but a sickly yellow, like that of a withering daffodil's petals.

"I have chosen my first apprentice for the term," Garrod said, smiling. "Herbert, please come to my chamber after class. There will be food prepared for you, so you can replenish your energy. I'm sure you are quite famished after that exuberant demonstration."

Nervous chuckles rippled around the room at that. Herbert gave a sheepish grin, and said "Thank you, Sai."

"Apologies for the interruption, Sai Henlowe," Garrod said, slowly rotating himself around with shuffling, stunted steps. "I will leave you to your teachings now." He shuffled towards the door one careful step at a time.

"Thank you, Sai Brockhurst," Tabitha said as he crossed the room.

"How are you able to walk again, Sai?" Mallory said, voicing the mind of everyone in the room.

He stopped at the door and glanced back over one shoulder. "Let me just say this. In the right body, attunement can be a marvellous healer." With that, he ducked under the door and was gone.

***

After class, the students gathered in the dining hall on the ground floor of the Moon Spire, otherwise known as the Mage Tower. There had to be some slightly old fashioned thinking behind that, Johanna thought abstractly, something that would no doubt put a bug up Ellie's arse were she here to witness it. *Why don't they put the kitchens in the* boys' *tower?* She'd say with an air of indignation. *It's so presumptuous of them to assume that none of the boys would be interested in cooking!*

Johanna smiled to herself as she took a seat with Bella and Mallory next to a window. Together, the three girls gossiped about Herbert and Sai Brockhurst for a while as they ate.

The circular room was split in two by a dividing wall down the centre. What it created were two half-moon shaped rooms: the dining area with a bunch of tables and chairs, and the kitchen in the other half. A rectangular window was carved out of the wall allowing you to watch the cook's working on the other side. At one end of the dining area was a door to the staircase that led up to the girls' dorms. Right now, that door was locked shut. Boys were not allowed in the girls' dorm and vice versa. A rule that had been established many years ago after numerous incidents of tomfoolery among the pupils. Teenagers, whether attuned or not, are wont to engage in experimental behaviour of a more natural kind as soon as the lights went out. At one time or another, it was decided to reduce the number of pupils that lived on the premises to a very select group, to minimise the tension between students. And so they ended up with the current system – a dozen students, six male and six female, each confined to sleep in their respected towers. This year was the exception, with Johanna being the thirteenth.

Johanna found the food to be excellent. She had started with some fruit, a quick way to re-energise after a lesson casting spells, but then the chef brought out a special treat, something he called Everdusk Pentini. It was basically the same as Freddy's pentini, only instead of spices from the south, he had grown a few hot peppers right here in the tower grounds, infused with water from the nearby Mana Spring, which apparently made them especially good for budding wizards and mages.

Johanna zoned out as she ate the pentini, once again being reminded of her family. She missed her sister the most, and wondered how she was progressing with her hunting lessons with Dad.

"Why the frown, grumpy guts?"

Johanna looked up to see Karly standing with Markus. "Oh, nothing. Just tired after that class." It was Karly who had spoken. Were it Markus who had asked, she may have answered with the truth.

"Sai Henlowe sure knows her stuff, eh Jo?" he said. He had *never* called her Jo before. Always Johanna, or occasionally Ellie's name for her, Hanna. She wasn't sure how she felt about that, but decided it wasn't worth making a fuss about. She hadn't seen much of Markus since they had arrived. He'd spent the entire first week ricocheting from one girl to the next, and had apparently saved the weirdo Karly for last. They were both wearing their outdoor jackets.

"You guys going somewhere?" Johanna asked them.

"Yeah, we're gonna check out the Mana Spring," Markus said.

"It's apparently an ancient rockpool in the middle of the forest. Would be soooo good to rip next to," Karly said with a longing in her voice.

"Sai Henlowe said it's not far from here," Markus said. "Wanna come?"

"You're into hoomies now, too?" Johanna asked him, mildly shocked.

"What? Me? No, of course not…" He was reddening. "Well, I'm up for trying things once."

"Hoo, yeah!" Karly said, swaying on her feet. She seemed inebriated already, but then as far as Johanna could tell, that was just her neutral state.

"Look, Jo," Markus said, ignoring Karly. "I just wanna see the spring. It's apparently beautiful. You should come."

"No, I'm okay," Johanna said, turning back to her bowl of food. She *did* want to go, but not with Karly. She imagined them all sitting there on the rocks, Karly convincing Markus to eat a hoomie, then they'd turn on her and peer pressure her into trying one as well, which would just be really awkward. They'd end up getting high and spacing out for hours, leaving her to just sit and watch, alone, and right now, she'd rather just *be* alone. "I'm going to stay here and read a book or something. You guys have fun."

She felt Markus' eyes lingering on her back.

"Come on, hoomie boy," Karly urged. "She doesn't wanna come. I'll get you one day, Jo."

"See ya later then, Hanna," Markus said.

She heard them walking away.

Bella and Mallory turned to her now that Karly had gone. "I really don't know what to make of her," Bella said.

"She's so weird," Mallory agreed. "I can't believe she's attuned."

"I can't believe they allowed her in here," Bella said.

"Me neither," Mallory shook her head.

"Why not?" Johanna asked.

"Because of her father," Mallory said. "Didn't you know?"

"Know what?" Johanna said, feeling lost.

"Her dad's a criminal," Bella said.

"He went to prison," Mallory added.

"Really? What for?"

"Counterfeiting. I heard he robbed a bunch of stores by spending forged coins that he minted himself."

"Wow, that's bad," Johanna said feebly. She glanced towards the main door, regretting not going with Markus and Karly. Markus was her friend, after all. She didn't want him getting hurt, and Karly seemed like trouble.

Or am I just jealous? Ugh, I don't know!

"Excuse me, I'm going to study upstairs."

Bella and Mallory smiled to her as she left them to their gossip. Johanna climbed the spire to the library chamber and buried herself in a book. After a while, she forgot all about Markus and Karly.

CHAPTER FOURTEEN

"Would you consider yourself a well-read student, Herbert?" Garrod asked the boy as he ate his fill of Garrod's personal supply of duskfruit. Garrod leaned back in his father's grand Prime chair, peering at the young student over the steeples of his fingers.

Herbert swallowed a bite and pushed his spectacles onto his nose. Garrod made that the fifth time the boy had done so since he came in the room.

"Yes, Sai, I love to read," Herbert nodded with a beaming smile that made him look about twelve. "I've read all of your father's work! He is an incredible man." His face dropped. "Oh, I meant to say was… I'm sorry, Sai, I meant no offence."

"None taken," Garrod said, dismissing it with a wave. *Father's still alive.* "I'm honoured that you think so highly of my father. Tell me, in your readings, have you ever heard mention of a rift dragon?"

Herbert frowned in thought as he chewed another piece of fruit. He shook his head. "No, Sai." Then his face lit up. "But Sai, I *love* dragons. Me and Ned were just talking about them yesterday. He thinks that a basilisk would be able to kill a dragon, because of its stone gaze, you know? But there's no *way* a fire-breathing dragon would be affected by a stupid basilisk! It'd just burn it to a crisp before it had a chance to stare it down!"

Garrod listened to this with utter bemusement. "What about a dragon that can't breathe fire?"

"What?" Herbert said, scoffing. "All dragons can breathe fire. So the legends say." He gave a wistful sigh. "It's a shame they're not real, eh Sai?"

Garrod smiled at this.

"Sai?"

"My father has seen one. Ever since I was a boy, he told me the story of how Archdale was destroyed by a dragon."

"No way," Herbert said in an awe-struck whisper.

"But it didn't breathe fire. The phrase he used was *pestilence.* The dragon destroyed Archdale with a breath of pestilence." He pulled down the collar of his robe to reveal to Herbert a patch of sore skin which looked a bit like a birth mark on his neck. "This is where the nibbets got me. I have a few more marks like it on my back. I was five years old when we fled from the dragon. I didn't see it myself, but I have vague memories of the nibbets."

"I've never heard about any of this," Herbert said. "The history books say that Archdale was wiped out by a plague, yes. A fell wind blew down from the mountains, raining ash and killed everyone."

"I've read that account as well. The truth is, nobody really knows what happened that day, except the two adult survivors. Robert Anders and my father. And my father believes it was a dragon from another world that came here through a transdimensional rift."

"Why haven't I heard about this from his research?" Herbert said, frowning.

"It was something of a private obsession for my father. He spent the best part of the last thirty years trying to open a rift just to prove its existence. The wizard community is nothing if not pragmatic. Without solid proof, my father was never able to convince anybody that the dragon was real."

"Really?" the boy said, a look of wonder on his face. "So people might have thought him mad? No wonder he didn't record it."

"My father was a proud man. It must have been a great burden to hold onto. A very personal predicament." Garrod recalled the day of the prisoner experiment, and saw a flash of his father's face as he turned and charged away from Garrod to fight the giant weasel monsters. That had been the last time they'd seen each other properly, not counting the glimpse he saw last week through the rift after he fell from the window.

Herbert was looking at him with curiosity now. "Are you okay, Sai?"

"Yes." Garrod leaned forward propping his elbows on the desk. "I'm going to be honest with you, Herbert. I don't know if my father really saw a rift dragon. He witnessed his home being destroyed, and perhaps a dragon was an easy way for his mind to accept what he was seeing. The rift itself however…"

"Have *you* seen a rift, Sai?"

Garrod regarded Herbert, trying to decide whether he had chosen the right pupil for this conversation, and whether the boy would be able to handle what he planned to do with him.

"I've seen two," he said at last.

"What do they look like?" Herbert said. He had stopped eating altogether and leaned towards Garrod with such eagerness to lap up whatever knowledge he could get from one he regarded so highly.

"The rift acts as a gateway to another place, a mirror world, very similar to our own. In fact, I think it *is* our world, but on another plane of time."

"Like a parallel dimension?" Herbert blurted. "Wow!"

"How would you know of such things?" Garrod asked.

"Oh man, it's a key component of the Mystical Collective Battle Cards game that I play. Ned has a set too, we play it every night. The werewolves all come from one dimension, the dragons from another, vampires, elves, orcs, ancient gods and goddesses, there's a dimension for each type! It's awesome!"

"Wait, so you gleaned your knowledge of parallel dimensions from some *game*?" Garrod said.

"Yeah," Herbert replied, cheeks reddening with embarrassment. "But it's not just a *game*." He sounded hurt.

"Who created this game?" Garrod asked.

"His name was Albert Mystwalker. He came up with the concept and created the first set of cards. Back then, there was only the werewolves and the humans, just two dimensions. But over time, the game became so popular because he kept developing the lore and designing expansion cards. I've nearly collected them all!"

"Is he still alive?"

"No," Herbert said with deep sadness. "He died a few years ago. He lost his mind, I think… He was still painting creatures right up until his death, apparently. But his new artwork was scary. Demons and weird abstract creatures that were difficult to relate to. I always preferred the more normal stuff like shapeshifters and hybrid beasts."

Garrod was mildly curious about this fellow, and wondered whether he too had opened a rift. Had he drawn his inspiration from the strange creatures that lived on the other side for the monsters in his game? It seemed a logical assumption. More importantly, it suggested that Garrod was not the first wizard to open a rift by himself. It suggested his father had never needed a hundred prisoners to use as pain vessels. A single mind would suffice.

He recalled his own pain caused by Corcubus as he lay on his back at the foot of the tower. That had been less physical and all emotional. The turmoil of realising he was paralysed had hurt him so deeply that he had opened the rift by himself.

Could he repeat it? Inflicting that pain on himself was out of the question, but perhaps… he looked at Herbert.

"I have my first task for you, apprentice."

Herbert leapt to his feet, adjusted his glasses again. "Yes, Sai, what is it?"

"We're going to conduct a little experiment."

"Wonderful! Where? The schlong?"

Garrod turned his nose up in disgust. "Are you a student of the art or a foolish child?"

Herbert turned beet red. "Apologies, Sai. I'm a student."

"Then act like it and refrain from vulgar obscenities. We will not conduct the experiment in the Storm Spire, we will do it right here in my chamber." *Exactly where I saw father.*

"Oh. Okay then," Herbert said. "What do you need me to do?"

"First, I want to test your mind."

"All right," he said warily.

Garrod reached out to Herbert and immediately sensed the barriers of a wizard with some basic understanding of arcane-self-defence. Where King Victus had an open door to his thoughts, little Herbert here had a quaint little iron gate sealed with a padlock. Garrod could easily smash it down with his superior psychic abilities, but why use force when you already had trust?

"I'll need you to let me in, Herbert," he said.

"Never let another into your mind," Herbert said, parroting the phrase from the Young Wizard and Mages Handbook. He grinned. "You were testing me, right?"

Garrod snorted. "Yes," he lied. "But in order to open the rift, I'll need you to let me in."

"We're going to open a *rift*?" Herbert said, jaw dropping. "How?"

"Like this," said Garrod. As he said it, he tore Herbert's mind gate off its hinges and thrust his conscious inside.

In the physical world, Herbert's body went rigid, as if his muscles had turned to solid ice.

In his conscious, Garrod was spreading like a virus, taking control of the boy's central nervous system and sinking into his brain, searching for his vault of fears.

It seemed that Herbert was afraid of heights, mouldy vegetables and… birds?

Garrod caught glimpses of the boy's childhood, a memory of Herbert hanging from the balcony of the clock tower's viewing platform in Darune City after another kid had bumped into him. Another where he had sneaked into the family pantry and stole a cabbage to eat. It was dark, and he hadn't been wearing his glasses, and as he bit into the rancid cabbage which was writhing with maggots, Garrod could almost *taste* it himself, and hurled the memory away in disgust.

Then he saw the birds. Herbert had been a toddler, perhaps no more than four years old, and he was walking hand-in-hand with a freckled blonde haired man that could only be his father. They were crossing a cornfield, it seemed, walking between the towering stalks. His father bent to speak to Herbert, a smile lighting up his face. "Hey, little man, climb up!" He plucked Herbert up by the armpits and put him onto his shoulders. "Hold on tight, let's scare the birdies!" He ran into the corn and startled a murder of crows that had been pecking at the corn, because suddenly the sky was aflutter with a black writhing mass of feathers. Herbert the toddler screamed, eyes bulging like saucers at the screeching, flapping birds, gripping his father's head like his life depended on it.

Garrod couldn't do much with the vegetable fear, but he could certainly work with the other two.

He retreated out of Herbert's mind, and snapped back to his own body in a flash. Herbert stood opposite his desk, wheezing and panting, clutching his chest. "Sai, that was scary. What was that f—?"

He stopped short, eyes fixed on Garrod, who was shrugging off his robe. He wore breeches and trousers underneath, but both had been ripped to allow room for his recently acquired features. Across his back, the black wings unfurled, stretching to block out the window and the sunlight. He lurched around the desk and staggered towards

Herbert, whose eyes darted between Garrod's hideous wings and his clacking talons.

"Y-y-you're not h-human," Herbert stammered. "You're a shapeshifter?"

"No, dear boy. I'm just me. And I'm no imaginary beast from some *game*." He grabbed Herbert by the shoulders, spun him around and gripped the back of his belt with a talon. At the same time, Garrod flapped his wings and leapt backwards over the desk, dragging Herbert with him. The boy screamed as Garrod took another leap and pulled the boy out of the open window. With three more mighty flaps he cleared the roof, and carried the wailing boy up into the sky.

"No, no, nooo!" he cried in terror.

Garrod flew so high that they could see right to the edges of the Everdusk in all directions, then he dropped into a nosedive, clinging to Herbert's belt with his talons and carrying him back down towards the tower at breakneck speed.

This is rather fun.

He spread his wings wide and gave several mighty flaps to slow their plummet as he soared back to the tower and glided in through the window.

He dropped Herbert on the floor and folded his wings back down the length of his back.

Herbert lay on the ground panting like a dog, his chest hitching in and out so violently that Garrod thought he may have gone too far. His eyes bulged in their sockets, almost rolling like a terrified horse.

He realised then, that Herbert was seeing it. Seeing the rift.

Garrod reached out and laid a hand on Herbert's shoulder.

The chamber pulled back like a stage curtain and transformed into a ruinous version of itself. The air was thick and pungent with a musky scent. The books on the shelves had rotted to piles of dust, but the desk and chair were still present, all chewed up by woodworms and insects.

Standing in the room was Jason Brockhurst. He looked corpse-like, with pale, pock-marked skin and sunken eyes.

He made eye contact with Garrod.

"My son. You found me."

"Father!" Garrod almost lunged for him, but stopped himself. Instead, he reached out offering his father a hand. "Come with me, father. I can bring you back."

Jason shook his head. A flake of skin fell from the tip of his nose and fluttered to the floor. "No, son. I cannot leave yet."

"Why not?" Garrod cried. "This place is wrong! Look at yourself, father."

"No, Garrod," Jason said with a frown. "I am more powerful here than I ever was at home. There's something about this world, my son. I think it may even be the *source* of our power. Look."

Jason extended a palm and ignited an immediate fireball in it, huge and swirling, tinted a sickly purple. "I can't remember the last time I ate, son. I don't need to anymore."

As he spoke, another flake of crusty skin peeled from his cheekbone, revealing the raw flesh beneath. It pained Garrod to see his father in such a horrendous state of health.

Jason flung the fireball away and it shot out of the broken window. It fizzled out on the edge of the husk of trees which should be vibrant and green but here were just lifeless petrified memories.

"It's a lie, father. Whatever you think you're doing here, it's *killing* you."

"I've seen dragons, Garrod. They're *real.* I think one dwells in the forest nearby. I must find it."

"*Why?* Just let it go, and come back home with me!" Garrod felt tears stinging his eyes. It felt like acid.

"I'm sorry, son," Jason said, stepping back. "I thought you would understand. You could stay here with me, and we can uncover the secrets of this place together. I would like that very much." He saw Garrod for the first time, then, really taking in the details of his new body. "You have wings?"

"Yes. A leftover from a creature that lives here. It is nothing but a parasitic slug that tried to feast on me. I destroyed most of it, but it cursed me with these." He unfolded the wings to show them to his father, who gaped at them in awe.

"How did you do it? If I had wings like that, I could fly up to the dragons in the sky and meet with them in the clouds. You must tell me, son!" Jason lunged at Garrod with outstretched arms.

But something faltered. The connection to the rift wavered, and it shrank violently around him, pulling Garrod back through. Jason disappeared as the rift zipped closed.

Garrod was flung backwards and crashed against the bookshelf of his chamber, then dropped to the floor amid a scattering of hardbacks.

Herbert lay motionless on the floor in front of him, a line of drool dripped from the corner of his mouth, and a trickle of blood ran down his cheeks, oozing from his ears.

Herbert's mind had snapped.

"Dammit!" Garrod cursed. He must have been thrown out of the rift when Herbert had lost consciousness.

It worked though. I opened a rift using a single wizard! And a young one at that. Imagine what I could do with a trained apprentice.

He hauled himself to his feet, leaning against the wall for support. Herbert needed to be dealt with, and subtly. There was only one man he could trust to handle such a task.

Garrod hobbled over to the window, and leaned out, waiting for somebody to pass through the courtyard. Two students, a pair of girls came out of the kitchens and were heading for the main gates. He hollered to them and sent them to find Robert Anders.

Robert knocked on the door a few minutes later.

Garrod unlocked it and let him in.

"You all right, Sai?" he asked as he stepped inside. "Is it your legs, again?"

"No, I'm fine. I need you to deal with something." He pointed at the motionless boy lying on the floor.

"Oh dear Kella," Robert said. "Is he dead?"

"Not physically," Garrod said matter-of-factly. "Robert, I saw my father again. He was right here in this *room*."

"Really?" Robert's eyes widened. He looked to the child, then back to Garrod. "You opened another rift?"

"Using the boy as a pain vessel. It worked better than I could have hoped. Although, he couldn't quite handle it, apparently."

Robert was looking at the boy with a hint of unease.

"You disapprove?"

"It's not that, Sai." Robert shook his head slowly in doubt, never taking his eyes off of Herbert. "I'm just not sure if Jason would."

"My father is not of sound mind right now. When I bring him back, he will be grateful."

"Prisoners are one thing, Garrod. But that's just a *kid*."

"The child of a scoundrel. You met his parents, remind me again, who were they?"

"This one," Robert said, crossing his arms as he thought. "He was from Krillbottom. Father operates the town's fishing port, mother runs a small brothel. Though the boy doesn't know about that."

"That's right, the son of a Madame." He nodded to himself. "Our students are the offspring of scoundrels, layabouts and delinquents, Robert."

"Yes, but that doesn't mean their families won't ask questions if they come back as vegetables. We're under enough scrutiny as it is with Victus' new law. Jason would never condone this."

Herbert gave a sudden jerk on the floor. His cheeks turned purple and he started to convulse.

"Oh Kella, he's jittering." Robert hunkered beside the boy and cradled his torso into a safety position. He peered into the boy's mouth. "He's swallowed his tongue." Herbert made a dry clicking noise from the back of his throat and his eyes bulged, turning bloodshot. Robert stuck a finger into his mouth and tried to pry his tongue out, but Herbert's jaw clenched shut around his finger. "Agh!" Robert grimaced in agony and used his other hand to pry the boy's jaw wide enough to release his bloody finger. "He's going to choke!"

Garrod bent down and reached a hand to Herbert's forehead and muttered, "*Calmus-oprandi.*" The calming spell reduced his convulsions to a soft series of shakes, but he still wasn't breathing and his jaw remained tightly clamped.

"Come on, boy!" Robert said in desperation, as he gripped the boy's jaw in an effort to open it.

Herbert's eyes rolled back, and he gave a couple more violent shudders before falling still altogether.

Only then did his jaw slacken.

Too late.

"Oh, Kella, what have you done, Sai?" Robert said, aghast.

Garrod took a few steps backwards and propped himself against the desk for support. He thought about all the people they had sacrificed already to gain access to the rift. Was this child really worth dwelling on?

"I have to save him now. I must bring our Prime back."

"Garrod, you just murdered a child!"

"It was an accident!" Garrod said in disgust. "And besides, would you have me consider his life above that of the Prime?"

Robert opened his mouth to say something, possibly to interject, but he must have seen Garrod's point. "No, Sai. I suppose not."

"This was a mistake, I will admit it," said Garrod, sparing a glance at the dead boy. "My impatience got the better of me. I'm sorry, Robert. We must educate and refine them first. That way, when they open the rift, they stand a higher chance of maintaining it."

"So you mean to try again."

"Of course." Garrod's gaze snapped to Robert, his voice

became a stern whisper. "If necessary, I would sacrifice them all to get back to that place!" He added, almost as an afterthought, "And to save father. Our Prime." He felt Robert scrutinising him from the floor, so he turned away and looked out of the window. "Please dispose of the body. Do it tonight while everyone is asleep. We will inform the other students that Herbert had to return to Krillbottom on emergency family business."

"Is this just about bringing back your father, Garrod?" Robert asked.

"What else would it be?" Garrod said, but even he heard the uncertainty in his tone.

"I saw your father become obsessed with that dragon. He devoted his life to proving its existence. I already see the same glint in your eyes that I saw in his. And I'm not talking about the unsettling yellow specks that you inherited from that creature… I worry about your mental state, Garrod."

Garrod spun to face him. "*Do not patronise me, fool,*" Garrod hissed, his temper flaring without warning.

Robert was taken aback. "All I'm saying, Sai," he said very slowly. "Is that we don't truly know how much of that creature is left inside you. Or what it wants. It makes sense that after assimilating it, some remnant of its will would linger on. You said it yourself, it wanted to get back to where it came from, back to its mother."

My mother! Garrod bit his tongue. *No, my mother died at childbirth. It's Corcubus' mother that resides in that rotten world. Remember!*

"…so if you have any other motive to open that rift, apart from rescuing Jason, you need to tell me," Robert said.

"I don't *need* to do anything," Garrod snarled. Then he closed his eyes, inhaled a breath, and composed himself. "Apologies, Robert. I am just a little on edge after seeing him. I know you only mean to help, and I appreciate the wisdom, but right now, all I need from you is the disposal. There needs to be no trace of his body."

"There won't be," Robert said, letting the subject go for

now. "The snappers don't leave leftovers."

CHAPTER FIFTEEN

"What do you know about wolves, Grandma?"

"Oh, they are wondrous creatures, Ellie. Come, join me in the sitting room. I might have a book to show you."

Great. Books. Ellie had feared this would happen, but with her father gone, she had few others to ask for advice. She'd walked next door to her grandparents' cottage and eaten some lunch. Ellie finished off two servings of her own meal and helped Grandma finish hers too.

Grandpa gave her a quizzical look throughout but said nothing. He was still relieved to see her back to normal after the frightful coma she had fallen into, but even for Ellie's standards, she seemed to be eating like a pregnant sow.

Ellie sat down in Grandpa's cosy armchair beside the bookcase as Grandma settled in the other, so they sat facing each other. She'd seen Johanna sit here with Grandma for hours on end as they discussed whatever book they had been reading, and never imagined a situation where she'd take her sister's place.

And yet.

"Ah, here it is," Grandma said, leaning forwards to pluck a terrifyingly thick tome from the shelf. It looked to have almost a hundred pages. Ellie gulped, forcing a smile.

Grandma held the book out to Ellie. The cover displayed a painted collage of animal heads, all staring out at her from the page. There was a bear, a stag, a honeyroo, a wild pig, a few birds and yes, a wolf.

Arrrrk, growled Arkarus from somewhere deep down. He didn't approve of books either, apparently.

The book's title said "Animal Totems of Darune."

Oh Kella, Ellie thought. *It's some spiritual nonsense. Not even about hunting.*

"I have had this book for over forty years," Grandma said. "There's a section on almost every creature from Nilumb to Krillbottom, all the way up to Archdale and beyond. See what page the wolf is on."

"Okay," Ellie said, biting her lip as she flipped it open to the contents. She thumbed down the gargantuan list, looking for the wolf. Pages 46 – 50, it said.

Four entire pages! Cripes, how much does she expect me to read?

She began flipping through, which made the pages blow a musty smell into her face that made her want to sneeze or gag.

"Okay, I found it," she said, reaching the page titled *Canines.*

Thank Kella, there's pictures!

A black silhouette profile of a wolf filled the top third of the first page, next to a human, to show its size in comparison. The wolf's head came up to the human's waist. Ellie realised then that the one that had almost attacked her in the field was *tiny.* It had been a good forty feet away but she doubted if its head would have been much higher than her knees. Arkarus, meanwhile, *he* was big. When she'd seen him walking towards her from that other place, he'd towered over her. She had been on her hands and knees, of course, but even so, he was bigger than any dog she had seen, closer in size to a bull calf than a wolf pup.

Grandma chuckled. "You look whiter than a bed sheet, Ellie. Books aren't *that* scary, are they?"

"Ahe," she gave an awkward smile. "It's more the

content than the book itself."

"I think you're very brave," Grandma said kindly.

Ellie reddened. "Give me some credit, Grandma. It's only a book."

"No, dear. I mean to confront your fear like this. I know you had a terrible scare that day in the field, and now you're facing that fear by finding out more about it. That's very wise."

Oh, she thinks I'm looking for wolves because of the one that Johanna saved me from.

"What's wise about it?" she asked.

"Well now, don't you know that the biggest cause of fear in the world is not spiders, not sickness, not wolves," she said, smiling knowingly. "Not even death. Those are all simple, tangible things. It's something much more vague than that."

"What is it then?" Ellie said, growing a little anxious about the prospect of learning something she might rather not know.

"It's misunderstanding."

"Huh?"

"Exactly."

"What do you mean? I don't understand."

"And that's why you are scared." Grandma said with a little shrug. "Look at it this way. Why did the wolf attack you?"

"I startled it," Ellie said.

"Yes, probably. What happened next?"

"Um. I fired an arrow at it."

"Good. And it responded, how?"

She remembered its exact thought when it had looked at her: *prey!*

"It wanted to kill me."

Grandma nodded gravely. "It must have been hungry."

Ellie blinked. "Well, not necessarily. Animals don't always attack just because they are hungry. Foxes will tear through an entire pen of chickens just for the fun of it!"

Grandma nodded, smiling. "Yes?"

Ellie realised she wanted her to go on, but didn't know why. "So, the wolf might not have been *hungry*, it just wanted to kill me because… because I had interrupted its nap, or invaded its territory, or maybe it had some pups sleeping in its den or something. Who knows?"

"Who knows?" Grandma agreed.

Ellie stared at her, starting to feel a little annoyed. "Is this how you and Johanna discuss books? By giving each other creepy smiles and talking in riddles? I don't get what you're smiling at, Grandma!"

"But you do, my dear. You *understand* animals. You always have. You haven't even read a word of my book, and you've just explained to me why the wolf attacked you. So, are you still scared?"

"Well, yes! I mean, no, not right now." Ellie frowned. "Grandma, it's not the book that scares me, or even the wolf that attacked me—"

Aaaarkarus!

Ellie tensed up, seeing a flash of Arkarus' face in her vision for a split second. Absurdly, his face had appeared right over her Grandma's, making her look like the sneaky wolf that dressed up as a grandma in that old fairy-tale.

This time she didn't flinch. Arkarus wasn't looking at her the same way that the wolf in the field had looked at her. He was just *there.* She could feel his intentions, sort of, if she concentrated. He wasn't hungry, or startled, or agitated. He was just mildly curious. He seemed to be looking out of Ellie's own eyes at her Grandma sitting in the chair in front of her.

You're part of me now, aren't you? How was that *possible*? It didn't make any sense, and she felt the fear rising in her again, a fear of the unknown. If Arkarus was inside her, how could she ever relax? How could she ever sleep soundly, fearing that he would make her sleepwalk into the forest again to feast? What if he made her attack something that could kill them both, like a bear or a shadowcat?

"Stay calm, Ellie," Grandma said softly. Her smile had finally vanished, replaced with a concerned look of worry. "Take a deep breath. It's okay."

"Grandma, you don't understand… it's inside me." Ellie's breath quickened, she started to gasp, wheezing deep gulps of the musty air. Breathing the smell of the old books. She couldn't stand it. "It's *inside* me!"

She stood up, sending the book toppling to the floor, and fled from the room.

"Ellie!" Grandma cried after her but Ellie just ran.

She bolted to the front door and burst outside into bright sunlight, stepped onto the lawn and inhaled the fresh air in huge gulps. She put her hands on her hips, mind racing with thoughts both her own and canine.

He's inside me. In my mind. Aaaark. Part of me. Merged. Like a twin, an unwanted twin that I can never be separated from.

Arkruusss…

He's an animal. I'm a human. It's not possible!

Arkaaarusss!

"Ellie," Grandma said behind her from the door. She hobbled over to her, placing a gentle arm around Ellie's shoulder. "I didn't mean to upset you. I'm so sorry."

"No, Grandma. It's okay. It's my fault. This is all my own fault."

"No, dear, it's not." Grandma said. "Don't ever think it. Things happen that are out of our control. I know it doesn't help, but there's really no use worrying about those sort of things. All it leads to is anxiety and despair. Come back inside, I'll make some tea. It'll calm your nerves, then we can talk about what you're going to do about this."

Do? What can I do? There's nothing I can do about this!

But something changed then. A deep and powerful emotion that had taken a backseat, re-emerged in that moment, reminding Ellie what she should be doing. All this moping about and worrying, that wasn't her! If she ever faced a problem before, she'd grabbed it by the horns and ridden it with reckless abandon until she figured it out. Even if it meant failing a few times, getting a few scrapes along the way, she always got through it in the end.

This was just like that. A problem that had to be solved. And heck, Arkarus was *just an animal.* Animals were *her thing.* She was a huntress, and if she couldn't figure out how to tame the animal now living inside her, no-one could, and she could just die at the end of trying. But first, she would *try.*

"Thanks, Grandma." She took her Grandma's hand and helped walk her back inside to the kitchen.

The tea was warm, herby and sweet. Just the way Ellie liked it. As she drank, they talked about what Ellie could do to try and get her mind back out of the depression she had sunk into.

"What did you mean earlier?" Grandma said curiously. "You said you felt something inside you?"

"Oh, that." Ellie still didn't like the idea of trying to explain Arkarus to anyone. She didn't even understand him herself. "I don't know how to tell you, Grandma."

"That's okay. I know a way. Come, let's lay some thoughts down, Ellie." Grandma said, patting her wrinkly palms softly on the kitchen tabletop.

Ellie chuckled. "All right."

"Just be honest. Think of three things. The first things that pop into your head."

"Okay," Ellie said, drawing a breath. Three things did come to her mind, and she said them slowly, one by one. "Dad. A forest. Arkarus."

"Okay, good," Grandma said. She frowned. "What's Arkarus?"

"He's a wolf."

"Oh. I see." Grandma nodded, as if that made sense. "Okay, well. Let's start with Frank, shall we?"

Ellie felt tears threatening, but she remembered his last words to her: *Promise me you'll keep trying.* It made her focus.

"I'm really trying," Ellie said. "Trying to not feel guilty."

"That's good," Grandma said gently. "It was an accident.

Your father knew that, as do we all."

"I know, but I still fired the arrow," Ellie said, breathing deep.

"Yes. Because that's what huntresses do."

I'm not a huntress yet. But I will be.

"What about the forest?" Grandma said.

"I don't know," Ellie said, chewing her lip. "I haven't spent enough time there lately. I know I should."

"I'd agree with that. I've never heard of a huntress that spent three quarters of her day in bed."

Ellie blushed. "I know…"

"There's that guilt again. Let it go."

"I know," Ellie said, exhaling sharply.

"Now, this wolf business. Arkarus, you say?"

"He's inside me, Grandma…"

Grandma looked at her then with a troubled expression. "I'm not sure I can say anything to help you with that, Ellie."

You're right, Grandma.

"But there are people out there who might. You just won't find them in Harbrook."

"What are you suggesting?"

Grandma shrugged. "Johanna is attuned. Who's to say you're not, too?"

Ellie blinked. How had she not considered that before?

"Do you want to know what I think you should do?" Grandma said.

"Of course," Ellie said, leaning across the table.

"We still haven't sent a letter to your sister. But she needs to know about your father."

"Yeah…" Ellie said, wiping her cheek.

"Who better to tell her, than you?"

"Me?" Ellie said. But the idea ignited an instant spark in her. *Yes. I should go!*

"A journey would do you the world of good right now, Eleanor. And who knows? Maybe you'll find someone there who knows about this Arkarus."

"I think you're right, Grandma." Ellie felt the sadness

washing away, being replaced by excitement. She couldn't remember the last time she felt such a sense of hope. A journey to visit her sister would be a perfect opportunity to hone her hunting skills, and at the end of it, she could tell her about Dad. She was responsible. "It has to be me," she said softly.

Grandma nodded agreement. "Yes, sweetie."

Ellie went around the table and threw her arms around Grandma's neck. "Thank you. Just, thank you!"

"No need to thank me. I'm yer grandma. Good huntin', Ellie."

***

Mr Huggins looked up from the desk behind a pair of enormous glasses when Ellie walked in through the door of the Honeyville bounty office. "Well, look who it is," he said, putting his quill down and hauling himself out of the chair. He came around the desk to greet her, embracing Ellie in a fierce hug. "I never thought I'd see you again, lil' missy."

Ellie pulsed with warmth. "It's good to see you too, Mr Huggins."

"What can I do you for today?" he said, smiling broadly.

"I want to finish my father's bounty."

His face dropped. "Oh, sweet heavens," he mumbled, reaching for his heart. "That is just the sweetest thing I ever did hear."

"Ahe," she said, scratching her neck awkwardly.

"But I'm afraid the roo bounty was cancelled. Farmer Greenwold changed his mind about the whole thing after what happened to your father. He, well… I'm not sure you need to know the details, my sweet."

Ellie swallowed, half thinking the same thing. But this was a journey of facing her fears, and she'd be damned to stumble at the first hurdle. "Please tell me," she said in a voice more feeble than she would have liked.

"Are you sure? Look, you must know that none of this

is *your* fault, okay?"

"Everyone keeps telling me that," Ellie muttered. "Why was the roo bounty cancelled? Just tell me."

"All right," he said, eyeing her carefully, and removing his glasses. They dangled around his neck on a little string. "After your father died, Farmer Greenwold felt awful. He came in to the office in person, which is a very rare thing, usually he just writes a letter, but in he came standing right where you are now, lil' miss, and he declared all bounty hunters to be forbidden from his land. He didn't want any more…" He hesitated, but went on when he saw Ellie's impatient scowl. "Any more blood on his hands."

"Oh." Ellie considered that. "Well, do you think he'd make an exception if it was me who wanted to complete the hunt?"

"Oh, I don't know," he said. "We'd have to go ask him."

"Where does he live?"

"A few wheels up the road, and down his lane. You're dead set on doing this, aren't you?"

"More than anything."

"Mind if I ask why?"

"I just need to," she said. "I need closure."

He nodded gravely, smiling with empathy. "I thought as much. I understand, I truly do. Come on, I'll walk you to the farmstead."

They made their way to Farmer Greenwold and knocked on his door. He agreed to let Ellie hunt the roo, but made it very clear to Mr Huggins that this was purely out of sympathy for the girl, and under no circumstances would he be putting up another bounty as long as he lived.

"That's fine," said Huggins. "The hunting community will miss your involvement, but I understand."

"Do be careful, miss," Greenwold said to Ellie. "Watch each other's backs. My dog's been barking at night lately. Got a feeling there's a shadowcat out there somewhere. Might've driven all the roos away already."

Aaarkrusss.

Shh, you.

"We'll be careful," Huggins said. "Come along, lil' missy. Let's see if we can't find your roo."

They left and began walking back down the lane towards the woods.

Ellie stopped when they were well out of earshot of Greenwold's house, and said, "Mr Huggins, I want to do this by myself."

He sighed. "I know. I could tell as soon as Greenwold told us to watch our backs. I don't think he'd approve of letting you out there by yourself, and I've a mind to stop you entirely now that I know there could be a bloody *shadowcat* out there. But you're Frank's daughter, and if you're half as reckless as Frank could be, I know you'll just sneak off and go by yourself tonight whether I approve it or not."

Ellie smiled. "My dad? *Reckless*?" The notion seemed absurd, Frank was the epitome of patience and grace.

"Oh you've no idea! He was always going off to collect the biggest bounties all by himself." He added hastily, "This was before he met your mother, of course. And long before you were a twinkle in the stars. But you're his daughter, all right." He put his big paw of a hand on her shoulder, and looked at her dead serious. "You be careful, okay? Don't stay out beyond dusk. Find the roo and come back. If you can't find it today, come back to the inn, stay the night and try again tomorrow. I don't wanna be rummaging through the Honeywoods looking for the pieces of another McKree that the shadowcat didn't fancy. You hear me?"

"Yes, sir," she said. "I'll be careful."

***

Ellie reached the apiaries just before noon. The long clearing looked much the same as it had before, except she could see four or five more damaged hives this time, roofs broken or knocked off completely, lying upside down in the grass.

That familiar sound lingered in the air, the buzz of bees. *Zzzzzzmmmmmmmm.*

She crept along the tree line, retracing her steps with Frank, following the trail of broken hives until she came to a batch that was intact. Five hives nestled together in a little clump, all of their roofs firmly on their tops. If a roo had been systematically working its way through the clearing, then this was the most likely place it would attack next.

Ellie got down on her belly in the grass, with a clear view of the buzzing beehives and waited.

And waited.

And waited…

She sensed Arkarus dozing in the back of her mind. He had been active during the hike, and grown rather apprehensive when they first heard the buzzing of the bees. But since Ellie had decided to lay in the grass, he had apparently felt like taking a nap.

Ellie was glad. If she was to successfully hunt this roo whenever it decided to show its rotten face, she'd appreciate having no distractions.

And Arkarus was nothing if not a pain in the arse. Always growling and barging into her thoughts at the most awkwa—

A rustle. Movement. Ellie spied a set of big flappy ears across the clearing.

Finally!

She tensed up, reaching for her bow in front of her.

Arkarus stirred, making a sleepy yawn that sounded like *rowwll.*

The honeyroo bopped out of the woods away to Ellie's left and sniffed the air with its long, spindly trunk-like nose.

Then in four great bounds, it reached the apiary in front of Ellie.

It *may* have been the same one that she had hunted with her father, but she couldn't really know for sure.

It didn't matter. The bounty had been simple enough:

Kill the roo that's been stealing my honey. Bring back its body for proof, and collect the reward.

The roo picked a hive that was furthest to the left of the bunch. It slid its tail underneath itself, pushing it a little higher off the ground, and flipped off the roof with a dexterous flourish.

He's done that before. He knows exactly what he's doing. It must be the same roo!

Ellie had a perfect shot. She waited for the roo to duck its head into the hive and shimmied onto one knee, moving slowly as she could. Each time the roo brought its head up to swallow, she froze, her leg muscles burning as she incrementally rose into a shooting position.

She nocked an arrow. Took aim. Drew. Inhaled a breath. The roo's head lined up perfectly with the tip of her arrow. Taking distance into account, the arrow should find its way right into the creature's thick neck.

For you, Dad.

Ellie fired.

The roo dropped to the ground like a sack of stones. Its tail thrashed side to side, and it exhaled a horrible, gasping wheeze.

Ellie couldn't bear the thought of it suffering, she cast her bow aside and sprinted out into the clearing, drawing her knife as she went.

She dropped down beside the roo, placing a firm hand against its head and plunged the knife into its throat. "Shhh," she said, soothingly. "It's over now."

The roo gasped once more then its eyes rolled. The tail went still and blood poured from the neck wound. It was dead within seconds.

Ruff! Arkarus woke up, probably at the scent of fresh meat.

"Not now," Ellie muttered, wanting to take a moment to reflect. But between the angry buzzing bees that were now starting to land on her bare skin and the agitated, excited growling and slathering of Arkarus in her mind, she had to cut the moment short.

Grabbing the dead roo by its tail, she dragged it away from the hive, back towards her spot in the tree line.

Meat! Food! She saw Arkarus in her mind's eye, bounding around the barnyard like a playful mongrel seeing snow for the first time. She might have found it endearing, but she *really* wanted to focus on the roo right now, and say a prayer for her father, or something, *anything* so long as she could walk away from this clearing with the roo, knowing that wherever he might be, Frank would be watching this moment with pride.

I got him for you, Dad. And I was so patient! You should've seen it.

Arkarus! Arkrussss! Ruff!

"Oh, be *quiet*, will you?" she said out loud, growing more and more frustrated. She hunkered down and began gutting the roo. No way was she lugging this fat bloater all the way back to town with its belly full.

Ruff! Aarkrursss! RUFF! RUFFF!

He just wouldn't shut up.

"You can't eat it, okay?" Ellie cried, her voice echoing around the clearing. The buzzing bees dimmed momentarily before starting up again. "I need it for the bounty!"

RUFF! RUFF! AAARRRR...

Ellie threw the knife down and grabbed her hair, her head throbbing and pulsing. Arkarus was giving her an enormous headache and if he didn't be quiet she might take the bloody knife and jam it into her temple just to make him stop.

"Be *quiet!*"

Ruff! RROOOWWWWLLL. RUFF RUFF!

The pressure in her mind was unbearable. She thought her skull might explode as she squeezed it desperately between her hands.

"*GET OUT OF MY HEAD!*" Ellie shrieked at the top of her lungs.

The pressure drained in an instant. It felt like a rusty

bathtub of boiling water inside her brain had suddenly collapsed, flooding the water out in a huge torrent. The pressure fell down into her chest, and she had a moment of panic when she thought her lungs were going to burst out of her ribs.

Instead, Arkarus came.

Arkarus, in ethereal form, leapt forwards out of her chest and landed on his paws in the grass beside the dead honeyroo. As he landed, he went from transparent, to translucent, to opaque, his black fur rippling in the wind, his four eyes piercing her as he looked back over his shoulder at Ellie, past Ellie, to something behind her. His ears pinned back against his head, the heckles on his neck rose like electricity and he pounced.

Ellie tried to scream but her throat had gone dry as a desert.

Arkarus leapt *past* her, she felt his thick fur brush against her arms, catching enough of her to spin her around one-eighty.

She caught the glimpse of the shadowcat as it leapt to meet the wolf in mid-air.

Arkarus outweighed the cat by at least double, and the two animals tumbled to the ground in a pile of thrashing paws, claws and fangs.

In three seconds, it was over.

Arkarus sank his teeth into the shadowcat's throat and tore it out in a spray of glistening viscera. The blood sprayed so far that a smattering of red droplets decorated the white wooden beehives twenty feet away.

Ellie felt sick, exhilarated and terrified all at once. How long had the shadowcat been stalking her? She'd had no idea it was even there.

And then there was Arkarus. Here in the physical world.

How is this possible?

Arkarus feasted on the shadowcat, ravenously tearing out chunks of flesh.

Ellie felt like she had stumbled into a waking dream. Not

quite a nightmare. Suddenly, the sight of Arkarus no longer filled her with terror or fear. She *understood.* At least a bit. Maybe her grandma was right, after all?

Arkarus was real. He was a part of her, however unlikely that seemed. But he was also himself, a living entity that she had somehow projected out of herself.

It was almost too much to take in. She wished Johanna were here to see it, this *had* to be attunement, surely? Normal people didn't ingest animals and then project them from their bodies, did they?

So, Ellie really was attuned. Perhaps she'd known it deep down all along, but seeing Arkarus in the flesh, this strange, unnatural creature from some other world, swept away all of her doubts, and she came face to face with that reality for the first time.

Wassat?

She turned to see a squirrel sitting in a tree, staring down at them. She laughed. She actually laughed.

The squirrel bolted, scurrying up the tree as fast as its little legs could go.

"I can hear their thoughts again," she said. With Arkarus no longer taking up all that space in her mind, she found that all those familiar voices returned. She heard the birds in the trees, and sensed a mole scurrying somewhere below her feet. Even the bee's sounded like music in her mind. All singing the same tune, the song of working, collecting nectar and feeding it to their young.

Ellie laughed, a huge weight lifting from her mind. The weight of a monstrous black wolf.

"Ruff!"

She turned to Arkarus who was sitting on his haunches, watching her with his head cocked. Were it not for the blood and bits of meat dangling from his fangs, Ellie might almost have said he looked cute. The four eyes would take a bit of getting used to, and she'd need to figure out how to start training him if she was ever going to bring him home.

She stopped. *What are you thinking? You can't bring him to*

Harbrook! He's a wild animal from another fooking world. Who knows what he'll do! He might eat you any moment!

She looked at him, trying to decide what he was thinking.

Where to? Oh, that's right. She could just hear his thoughts.

He wasn't intending to eat her, at least. He wanted to follow her.

She hunkered over the honeyroo and finished gutting it, pulling out its intestines, stomach, and lungs – collectively known as the offal, her father had taught her – all of which went down Arkarus' gullet. "Ew," she said, glancing at him as he scoffed down the foul-smelling sausage of intestines. He ate ravenously, as if he hadn't eaten in weeks. Then Ellie realised that he probably hadn't! Not real food anyway. When he had been inside her, she felt him feeding on whatever food she ate, and even when he had sleepwalked her into the woods to kill the stag, it had been *her* body that had eaten it, not his.

Another person might feel sick by these musings, but Ellie took it all in her stride as she mulled it over.

And what about before then? She caught a glimpse of his world, and it didn't look very vibrant. His pack had been running through a desolate forest, completely opposite to the lush little Honeywoods. Ellie doubted there was much prey to hunt in there, the whole place seemed barren and inhospitable. Maybe the entire reason he had been drawn to her when that gateway opened was because he could smell the flowers and the greenery (or perhaps Frank's blood, which was even more likely) coming through, like a sweet invitation to his nose.

"You're happier here, aren't you?" she said to him. "I don't think I blame you."

"*Aroowl?*" He cocked his head inquisitively at her.

"Heh," she said. Now he *did* look cute, four eyes and all.

"Come on," she said, hoisting the honeyroo off the ground. She slung it across the back of her shoulders, the weight pushing down like, well, a dead honeyroo. "Let's get this back to town," she wheezed, and set off through the woods.

As she staggered her way through the trees, she listened to the birds tweeting, and their jittery thoughts, as well as those of the field mice, squirrels and grass snakes that mostly went unseen scurrying around her. It was like an orchestra of life, all jumbled together in her mind's ear.

She didn't mind one bit. She had dealt with the noises of the forest ever since she was a child, and could tune in and out of it as she pleased. Right now, after the three weeks of hearing just a single mind, Arkarus, she welcomed the new variety.

Arkarus loped along behind her, sniffing every tree and lapping at little streams as he went. He seemed nervous, apprehensive, and dared not stray too far from his master.

His master? Is that what I am to him? It made sense. She understood that dogs needed an alpha, a leader to look up to. Perhaps that was how Arkarus perceived her. At any rate, he stuck to her heels like a lamb with its mother. Or perhaps just like a dog with its master.

"How am I going to explain where you came from?" Ellie said, as she plonked the roo carcass down on the ground, to take a rest on a fallen tree trunk.

She looked at the wolf, and he looked right back. His front eyes sagged a little, but the larger, rear eyes regarded her with piercing intensity. Without warning, he started to pant as if he'd been running for the last few wheels, and hung his head low.

"What's up with you? Did you eat too much and get a stomach ache? Serves you right, you big porker!"

Arkarus collapsed to the ground on his side and his tongue lolled out in the grass.

"Hey, what's wrong, boy?" she said, now feeling rather alarmed. She slipped off the trunk and knelt beside him.

She went to touch him, and pulled back, a suddenly fearful of some trap. *Don't touch him! He's a wolf! He thinks of you as nothing but prey! Prey!*

She stood up and stepped away from the wheezing wolf, whose chest ballooned in and out so fast, it seemed he might be having a seizure.

He needs my help, she told herself. *I can't be scared of him. I refuse to be scared!*

But her legs were stone. She couldn't bring herself to get any closer to him, fearful that at any moment, he might snap out of this false act of suffering and tear her throat out.

Lying on his side, she could only see the right side of his face, and the two eyes there peered up at her with a desperation that she had never seen on any human before. His breath sounded like a dry choking cough now.

He was dying.

What had caused this sudden affliction, she couldn't even begin to guess, but she couldn't just stand there and watch him suffer. A huntress had a responsibility to never let an animal suffer, no matter the species.

If she had to, she would slit his throat and send him to peace.

Clenching a fist and gritting her teeth, she stepped forward and dropped to one knee next to him. "What's wrong with you, boy?" She reached out a hand and laid it against the top of his head to comfort him.

That touch had a shocking effect. Arkarus stopped panting at once. Ellie felt a rush of energy sweep out of her. The air in her lungs became hot and thick and now *she* was panting, although nowhere near as badly as Arkarus, and she was overwhelmed with an intense nausea.

Arkarus planted his paws in the ground and staggered to his feet.

She let go of his head and her nausea vanished.

Arkarus collapsed again, but this time he lay flat on his belly, as if his head was too heavy to keep aloft.

Ellie's breath returned.

What's happening here? "Did you take some of my energy? You did, didn't you? But how?" She was half mumbling, half squeaking.

Whatever the reason, Ellie knew she had to save him. This lonely, lost creature, the only one of his kind in this world. He was here because of her and she wouldn't let him die.

"Go on," she said, touching his head once more. She lost her breath again, and wheezed, "Take whatever you need."

Arkarus responded with a bark, ignited with Ellie's energy as it siphoned out of her body and into him through the physical touch of their bodies. He sensed her depleting, and grew afraid. Arkarus whined. He shifted beneath her touch, filling with anxiety, knowing that he was hurting his master.

Ellie's head went limp, and she had to plant a hand in the grass to stop from collapsing.

Arkarus whined again, feeling strong, stronger than he should. He was not worthy of this power, this sacrifice.

"*Ruff!*" he barked. "*Ruff! RUFF!*"

He nuzzled against Ellie's chest, holding her up with his hulking head. Then, he pushed harder and something gave way. An invisible barrier seemed to open and Arkarus' head disappeared inside Ellie's chest. His body became ethereal again, transparent and ghostlike. Ellie gasped, feeling a pressure building inside her core.

The voices of the creatures around her shut off like a switch, and she heard Arkarus in her head once again, whining in fear and distress. But she sensed his concern as well. He was trying to help her now, just as she had helped him.

Arkarus crawled inside Ellie like a pea in a pod and his body disappeared entirely.

Ellie's energy returned like a sunburst breaking through the clouds. She stopped trembling, found the strength to stand and blinked away the fogginess. She patted her chest with both hands, feeling for a wound, or for Arkarus. He was gone. She had re-assimilated him and now they were one yet again.

"Kella Murphy," she exhaled an explosive sigh. "That

was intense. Fook."

Arrkrusss! Ruff?

"Yeah, I'm okay," she said, drawing another gulp of air, feeling herself again. In fact, she felt better than herself. When she picked up the roo, she found he weighed less than before, even though nothing about the body had changed. Somehow, with Arkarus inside her, she could draw on his strength and use it for her own. They drew from the same pool of energy now, a bit like the goats and the horses back home that all drank from the same trough.

"We have to share, Arkarus," she said, trundling through the woods. "We can both survive, so long as we share."

Arkarus was quiet now. All she could hear somewhere deep inside was the slow inhale and exhale of his breath. She saw him in her mind's eye, sleeping in his kennel in the barnyard. Resting and contented.

***

A welcoming party awaited her back at the Honeyville bounty office. Mr Huggins had sent word along the road to any hunters that knew Frank McKree, and informed them that his daughter had taken on his final bounty. A half dozen people showed up, some of whom Ellie recognised, but a couple she did not.

They were all men, ranging from muscular to downright monstrous. One guy looked more bear than man, another was missing two of the fingers on his left hand, and another had one eye replaced with a big scar down his face.

"Hello little missy," the bear man said, giving Ellie a respectful nod.

"Heck'uva roo," another said, offering to take the carcass from her. She handed it to him gladly, and he held it up by the back legs so the others could see. This was met by approving nods and a whistle or two.

Huggins stepped forward and removed his hunter's cap, holding it in front of him like a nervous child. "Please share your hunt with us tonight, Eleanor."

"We'd love to give yer pa' a proper send off," said the scarred man. "Everyone here knew Frank, and we never got to say goodbye."

"We're not exactly one for deep and meaningful traditions," said Huggins. "But I just thought at a time like this, it would be good to share the animal that claimed his life."

But it was me who killed him. They knew that, of course, but nobody blamed her for it. If anything, they just wanted to help convince her that what had happened was nothing more than a terrible accident. One that could have happened to any of them. Ellie looked again at the scarred man, and the man with missing fingers, wondering how many of the others had similar scars hidden beneath their clothes. She had that feeling of being a part of something bigger than herself again. Like a family, but somehow different.

Ellie didn't know what to say, she was so touched by their presence. But they were all watching her, hanging on her response. "Of course," she said timidly.

Their faces lit up, and a sense of relief washed over the room.

"Marvellous!" said the man holding up the roo. "Johnny boy, come help me skin this beast. Our little missy here will get the fillet."

And so they feasted. In the centre of the town square was a roasting pit, where they sat around under the fading sky, drinking ale and regaling tales about Frank. Everyone had a story about him, it seemed, and Ellie listened, utterly riveted to snippets of her father's past. She laughed, she cried and she was thankful. It was the perfect way to begin her journey to Johanna. She dreaded how she was going to face her sister and tell her about their father's death, but at least now she had a dozen stories to tell that might somehow soften the news.

At some point during the night, Huggins presented her

with the reward money for the bounty. He said Farmer Greenwold had stopped by in the afternoon with a change of heart. He said that if a little girl like that could face her fear so bravely, then so could he. He'd given Huggins a small sack of bobbins to pass onto Ellie.

Ellie thanked him graciously, and asked if it would be possible to send a portion of the money home to her mother.

"Of course, lil' missy," he said. "I'll send Marvin down to Harbrook first thing in the morning."

Ellie slept soundly at the inn that night. Both she and Arkarus were well-fed, well-rested and feeling a tremendous excitement to hit the road. She left Honeyville behind and set out towards her next stop, the city of Darune.

CHAPTER SIXTEEN

Garrod observed several more classes, and by the end of the week he had made a decision about who his next apprentice pupils would be. The McKree girl turned out to be the most promising pyromancer. Coincidentally, her friend from Harbrook, a boy named Markus showed some natural skill with wind elemental attunement. And although none of the students this year seemed to be gifted with psychic abilities, there was a girl who stood out for her keen interest in the subject, and would therefore be his best chance at producing a telepath. She was the daughter of a fraudulent coin-maker in Darune, and her name was Karly.

He summoned all three to his chamber one afternoon, and they arrived promptly after Sai Henlowe's pyromancy class.

Johanna wore a sky-blue dress and high white socks. Her long brown hair was tied in a neatly braided but practical ponytail, decorated at the tip by a yellow silk bow. Johanna McKree was very pleasing on the eye, for a country bumpkin.

Likewise, Markus apparently knew how to dress, sporting a pair of black trousers and a white summer shirt combo, with his black hair combed back and held in place with a minimal amount of grease.

Standing next to the two Harbrookers, Karly resembled something between a gardener and a homeless drifter one often passed on the road between Darune and Edgehurst. A scruffy, baggy green shirt hung off her chubby arms, sleeves rolled back almost to her elbows, and she wore a pair of brown trousers with numerous pockets sewn down the legs. Her frizzy russet hair stuck up at the back and fell down to her shoulders in knotted curls.

Garrod didn't particularly care how they looked anyway. *It's their minds that I need, not their fashion sense.*

"Thank you for coming so promptly," he greeted them as he sat behind his desk. "Are you hungry?" He gestured to the table of bread, cheese, fruit and cold meats he had prepared for them. Same selection he had offered Herbert, for what ultimately became his last meal. Garrod had no intention to repeat that incident on this occasion. There would be no rift experiments for a while yet. Not until he had a better idea of their limitations.

The students thanked him and each helped themselves to a plate. When they were sitting at the guest table munching away, Garrod explained why they were there.

"As you know, you have been selected to be my new apprentices for this primary term."

Markus raised his hand tentatively. Garrod inclined his head in a gesture of, *yes?*

"Um, if I might ask, Sai. About your previous apprentice..."

Garrod pursed his lips. "What of him?"

Markus hesitated. "Well, what exactly happened to Herbert?"

"Herbert has returned home and will not be coming back," Garrod said matter-of-factly. "You were all informed of this, were you not?"

"We were, Sai," Johanna said, giving Markus a curt glance, as if to shut him up.

Then Karly piped up, speaking through a mouthful of

duskfruit. "Everyone thinks you expelled him, Sai." She swallowed and looked at him with the hint of a smirk. "Should we be worried?"

Johanna and Markus had paused eating and were looking at him too, with almost identical expressions of mild anxiety.

Garrod felt the corner of his eye give an involuntary twitch. Then he broke into a wicked grin. "Only if you underperform. Do you remember what I told you during your welcoming ceremony?"

"You will work hard this year, and you expect us to do the same," Johanna paraphrased.

"Very good," Garrod said. "I cannot ask any more than that. But to put your minds at ease, Herbert performed *above* my expectations, and I was sorry to see him go. But family is family, and when we received news of his mother's illness, I couldn't blame him for wishing to leave. Can you?"

The lie came easy and prompted no further question from the three students.

"That's awful," Johanna said. "I hope she's okay."

"The silver lining is that I now have more time to devote to those who remain," Garrod said amiably. "Now, finish your meals while I give you a brief introduction to what you will be studying under me."

He rose from his chair and sauntered up and down the room behind them. All three stared at him, probably because they hadn't seen him walking without the cane yet. He paced the room, and they listened like enraptured children hearing a bedtime story.

"Telepathy, mind-control, psychokinetic manipulation. These abilities of the mind are all theoretically possible, yet there are very few in the attuned community that can harness them to any meaningful degree. I, however, am one." He chuckled, enjoying the perplexed fascination on their faces. "Relax, I have no intention of reading your minds." Then, after opening the door to each of their heads, he said telepathically, *it's exhausting.*

Johanna gasped and dropped her fork. Markus did a comical big gulp as his eyes bulged, and Karly just broke into a wide, toothy grin.

"When you are done eating, I have a little task I want you all to try." He produced a pack of playing cards from his pocket and started shuffling the deck. He held a fan of cards out to Johanna and said, "Take one, but don't let me see."

She reached out and pinched a card between thumb and forefinger, then leaned back away from him, studying it against her chest. "Okay," she said, pressing it face down.

"Now, think of the card," Garrod said. "Repeat it in your mind."

He leaned his butt against the front of the desk and looked into her apprehensive, hazel doe eyes.

Queen of Rain, Queen of Rain, Queen of Rain…

He heard her mind as easily as if she were speaking aloud.

Garrod smiled. "Too easy. The Queen of Rain."

Johanna's eyes bulged and she turned the card around to show Markus and Karly.

"Ha!" Karly said, slapping her knee. "Brilliant!"

"That's incredible, Sai," Markus said.

Johanna was too stunned to even speak. She dropped the card on their table with a slight tremble in her arm.

"Did I frighten you, Miss McKree?" Garrod said, genuinely concerned. He couldn't afford to let his students fear the arcane until he needed them to. Training their minds was his best chance at reopening the rift, and with so few students to pick from, the last thing he needed was to lose any more.

"A little," Johanna said. "But I'm okay. It's nothing, never mind."

"As your tutor, I do mind," Garrod said, gently enough. "I would hear your concerns, and offer my advice if you desire it."

"Well," Johanna said. "It's just, I didn't know telepathy

was really possible. But my sister, she said she could hear the minds of animals. But we always thought she was just making it up. She's not attuned. Although, now, I think that after all this time, maybe she really is."

Garrod smiled, relieved. "It's common for attunement to manifest in the same family. Your parents, they are not attuned, are they?"

"No. At least, if they are, they hid it well from me. My mother was always suspicious about attunement, and my father is pretty indifferent about the whole thing, although he likes to encourage me. But what you just demonstrated, that was amazing, Sai."

Garrod gave a little bow. "My goal is to teach you to do the same."

"Yes!" Karly punched the air. "Sorry." She absolutely did not look sorry.

Garrod chuckled again. "I'm glad you're so keen. Now, I want you all to practice the card trick. Here." He handed them each a cut of the deck and told them to stand in a triangle around the room. Markus and Karly stood to his right and left and Johanna took a spot directly opposite him. Garrod propped against his desk, leaning on it for support. He winced as he felt his hidden wings pinch against his back. He straightened up and took a small step forwards, freeing the wings within his heavy cloak.

"Are you okay, Sai?" Johanna asked.

"Yes, just a little stiff," he lied, before moving swiftly on. "Markus, let's start with you. Look at the top card and memorise it. You have it? Good, now say it over and over in your head." He turned to Karly. "I want you to pick the card out of Markus' mind. I'm going to help you, by opening the door."

"All right," Karly said, doing a little skip on the spot.

"Stand still," Garrod said.

"Sorry." She stopped. "What do you mean by door, anyway? What door?"

"Perhaps I got a little ahead of myself," Garrod said.

"The first step to reading a person's mind is to rethink your perception of what the mind actually is. Can any of you tell me what the mind is?"

"A door!" Karly blurted.

They ignored her.

"It's consciousness," Markus said.

"Good," said Garrod. "What else?"

"It's our soul," Johanna added.

"Mmm," Garrod made a see-saw gesture with one hand. "What about our thoughts? Where do they come from?"

"The bobbins vault!" Karly cried. Before anyone could even frown, she elaborated like a runaway steam train. "My pa told me that thoughts are the brain's currency, like coins conjured in our head, and the brain is like a bank that has to sort them out. Shiny coins are good ideas, and they go into the world via the mouth, but the dirty, bent or misshapen bobs are the bad ideas, and they get sent to the stomach where you eventually shit them out. I mean poo, sorry Sai. Pa also said that my head bank must be broken coz I'm always spitting out filthy, disgusting coins that no-one would wanna spend. I never really understood what he meant, but I bet you do, don't you Sai?"

A beat passed, where Garrod could only stare in bewilderment. "Possibly," he said at last. "This analogy is quite—"

"So our brains are full of these coin-shaped tubes that sort the ideas and whatnot out," Karly barrelled on. "Then they make a copy of all of them, even the bad bobs, and they all go into the big bobbin vault in the middle of your brain, so deep down that you'd need a trowel to dig them up, and they become memories. Piles and piles of memories, like coins in a sack, just heaped on top of each other. Millions of 'em!"

Finally, she stopped long enough to take a breath and Garrod held a hand up before she could thunder on.

"Well," he said loudly. "Thank you for that unique insight. As a matter of fact, that is remarkably close to how

I was taught to understand how the mind works. Karly's pa must have read one of my father's books, because he also believed that the mind is just like a vault."

The girl beamed with mad delight at this, while Johanna and Markus looked at him as if he'd sprouted wings.

"When I read a mind, I find it helps to picture a door or gateway," he said. "I simply open the door and let myself in. To the unattuned, this is simple, because their minds are like archways, always open and impossible to seal. I'm afraid that's what your minds are like right now. Which is why it was so easy to pick out your card, Johanna."

She blushed and resembled a little girl.

"Don't fret," he assured her. "In time, I will teach you how to secure your minds with a thick door, and lock it shut with iron bolts. We'll turn those open archways into secure vault doors."

Karly cackled gleefully. "I love this shit. Sorry, Sai, I meant poo."

"I'd rather you left all vulgar bodily functions out of my classroom, mm?"

Karly's smile faltered. She opened her mouth to retort but Garrod hastily interrupted, keen to avoid another bombardment of gibberish.

"Now, first things first," he clapped his hands. "The task at hand. Markus, do you remember your card?"

The lad double checked it and then nodded.

"Karly, try to break into his mind."

"How?" she said eagerly.

"Just look into his eyes. Concentrate. And feel for his door. I'm opening it for you now."

Garrod looked into Markus' mind and heard him repeating the name of the card. He picked up the sense of Karly outside the door, looking in. But she hadn't crossed the threshold. There was no way she would be able to hear Markus' thoughts from there.

Karly stared at Markus for about five seconds, then blurted, "Three of Snow."

"Nope," said Markus.

"Four of Snow!"

"Nope."

"Ten of Storms!"

"Uh, nope."

A half hour of increasing frustration began. Taking turns to be the card holder, they rotated partners several times, throwing out wild guesses to varying degrees of failure, all while Garrod continued to hold open the doors to their minds. Despite Karly's enthusiasm, she had absolutely no natural talent at reading minds. Markus and Johanna fared no better. After thirty painful minutes, Garrod switched tactics.

"All right, this is getting us nowhere," he said, slumping back into his chair and biting into a duskfruit to restore some of his wasted energy. Standing on talons, which he had to hide within some heavy, cumbersome new boots, was proving difficult for long periods of time as well. From behind his desk, he told the students to line up on the other side. "I want you all to experience at least some moderate success today. Hand me the deck."

He shuffled all the cards together again, then drew one for himself. It was the Ace of Wind.

Garrod looked at Johanna, standing in the middle. "All right, Miss McKree. I am going to open my door, and let *you* into *my* mind."

She tensed up and a worried frown creased her brow.

"Just relax, and let it happen." Garrod looked into her anxious eyes and reached out to her. He pulled her gently through his mind's door and allowed her to see the recent memory of himself choosing the Ace from the deck just moments ago.

Johanna's eyes widened and her jaw went slack. "I can see it," she mumbled. Then, with more clarity, "I can see the Ace of Wind!"

Garrod smiled. "Very good."

Then something flickered in Garrod's mind that he did

not expect. A lingering dust mote of a memory that should have been destroyed when he assimilated Corcubus crept to the forefront of his consciousness before he had closed Johanna off from it.

Corkabussss...

He shoved Johanna back out and slammed his mind shut. Then he noisily cleared his throat to hide his surprise.

Johanna blinked, her frown returning twofold. "Huh? What was that?" she said, but Garrod spoke over her.

"Yes, very good. The Ace of Wind." He flipped the card around so that Karly and Markus could see it. They both laughed.

"Wow, Jo!" Markus said. "You did it!"

"Who'd have thunk it, a genuine mind-reader!" Karly gushed. "Do me next, Sai, please do me!"

Garrod picked another card and opened the door to Karly. But as he did so, he glanced at Johanna, who was still frowning, no doubt thinking about what she had heard in his mind.

He was extra careful not to let anything like that happen again, and as soon as he had finished his demonstration with the other two students, he brought their private lesson to an end.

"That's all for today. You've each seen a glimpse of the powers of the arcane. Take the cards with you back to your dorm and practice this technique. Try letting each other in, and see if you can pick out cards from each other's memory."

"Isn't it a bit dangerous to let other people go rooting around inside your brain?" Markus asked.

"It could be," Garrod agreed. "But the only way to learn how to keep a fellow wizard or mage *out* of your mind, is to first master the ability of letting others *in*. Remember, a vault is only as secure as its door."

"I geddit," Karly said, nodding with realisation.

"Feel free to show the other students what you have learned today. The more minds you let through your door, the stronger vault you will be able to craft, as you understand different people's methods of opening it."

Garrod figured that the sooner he got them all practicing arcane magic, the sooner he would get a suitable bunch of candidates to open the rift again.

Markus and Johanna left, but Karly stopped at the door, turned around and came back up to his desk. She asked him something that explained a lot about her manic personality. "Sai, do you ever eat hoomies?"

"What? No, of course not," he said.

"But do you think they might help me to widen my mind, and you know, make it easier for others to read it?"

Garrod shook his head bemusedly. "The wider your own mind gets, the *harder* it is for others to read."

"*Ohh*," she said, eyes lighting up. "So you're saying I should eat *more* hoomies, to make my vault extra stro—"

"Mind altering narcotics are not to be trifled with," he advised sternly. "It's true that hoomies can strengthen a person's psychic abilities, but the effect is *temporary,* and wears off quickly. And it can have pretty nasty side effects for those who can't handle them."

He couldn't bring himself to forbid her from taking them. Clearly, she had already built up a tolerance over Kella-knew how many years, and aside from a somewhat frenzied personality disorder, she could probably handle more than most. This made her jump up the ladder of his mental list of potential candidates. Still, he didn't want her to fry her mind before he had a chance to push it to the limit for himself.

He let her go with a bit of a warning. "There are some things the mind is simply not ready to see, and hoomies have a way of bringing such things into focus. Please be careful, okay?"

"Okay, sai," she said, and winked.

"I mean it," he said after her as she sashayed away.

"Will do," she said raising a hand without looking back.

She disappeared out the door and Garrod was left alone

to ponder that memory incident with Johanna. Could a remnant of Corcubus still linger within him, somehow? Or was it just a memory?

He shook off his boots and allowed his talons to stretch out under the desk. The bones clicked satisfactorily as he did so, and the feeling sent a pleasurable tingle all the way up his leg and spine.

I think I'll go for a flight tonight. I'd like to see the stars and the moon reflected on the treetops of the Everdusk.

And while the rest of Trinity Towers slept, that's exactly what he did.

CHAPTER SEVENTEEN

Ellie picked up three more bounties as she made her way along the road to Darune. She did it partly for the reward money, sending the bobbins back to her mum in Harbrook so she wouldn't have to work at Farmer Cribs'. But she mostly just wanted to practice hunting with Arkarus.

In the valleys of Woodhurst, she tracked a bunch of rabbits to their warren on a wide open hilltop. The rabbits bred so quickly that they were invading the local allotments and savaging all the cabbages. Bounty hunters were being offered 2 bob per rabbit carcass they brought back, and could keep the skins for themselves. Chump change, frankly, but Ellie didn't care. Maybe she could stitch herself a new rabbit-skin cloak when this was done.

The Woodhurst bounty officer had been surprised when she said she wanted to take on the rabbit contract. Nobody else had yet, probably because of the low reward money, but that suited Ellie just fine – it meant she would have the area to herself and could practice projecting Arkarus in private so they could try hunting as a team.

"Okay, boy," she said as she climbed a hill with her bow and arrow poised. "You ready to run again?"

Ruff!

In her mind's eye, she saw Arkarus bounce out of his barnyard kennel, his tails wagging furiously, as he tilted his head to the black abyss that was his sky. That blackness lay beyond the wooden picket fence of the yard, forbidden to Arkarus, who had to stay within the boundary. Ellie suspected that when she slept, that blackness changed to something else, something inviting to Arkarus, because she somehow knew that if he crossed the boundary, he would enter the part of her mind that gave him control of her. That's what must have happened when she was lost in the feverish nightmare, and when she had woken up in the middle of the woods after Arkarus hunted the stag.

Since then, he had always stayed within the yard. But for how long? If someone tried to lock her in an enclosure, Ellie knew she'd get pissed off too and try to wander out at the first opportunity. An animal was just the same. Therefore, as long as Arkarus remained spiritually tied to her, she had to figure out a routine that allowed him regular access to her world outside. That way, he should be content to stay in the yard when she was sleeping.

It all boiled down to trust. If she could trust him to stay out of her conscious mind, then she could get used to this crazy arrangement. But in order for her to trust him, first she had to earn *his* trust. They *had* to become friends. There was no other choice.

And what better way to befriend someone than go hunting together? He was a wolf, after all. This should be right up his creek.

She stopped just before the crest of the hill. "Here we are," she said quietly. She turned to her right and pointed ahead, gesturing to the gentle slope. "Head around that way, then go up and over the top. I'll be waiting."

Ruff!

Did he actually understand? Who could tell? Ellie just pointed her chest in the direction she wanted him to go and hoped for the best. She closed her eyes and spread her arms.

Go!

Arkarus projected out of her chest, paws and head first, and landed on the ground running. She exhaled a gasp, feeling the pressure leave her and watched his ethereal form become menacingly solid within two bounds as he moved away from her. He skirted the hill just as she had hoped, but turned left much sooner than she had intended and scrambled in mad excitement to the top of the hill. On the summit, he threw back his head and howled.

"*Arooooooo!*" The cry echoed off the surrounding hills and filled the air with its canine music. He looked monstrous and elegant silhouetted against the moody sky.

A cacophony of anxious little voices flooded in to fill the vacuum in Ellie's mind left by Arkarus, and they all said the same startled word:

WASSAT?

She scampered up the hill and when she reached the top, the sprawling hillside opened up around her. She hunkered to one knee and drew her bow.

Four rabbits had popped their heads up nearby, ears raised high to the sky, all peering away from Ellie towards the terrifying howl.

Arkarus charged down into the valley on her right and the rabbits scattered.

She managed to shoot two that bolted conveniently towards her, then picked off a third which bumped into its friend in the confusion, but the fourth jerked away to her left and escaped.

Ellie leapt to her feet, nocked another arrow and scanned the hillside. Arkarus was a black blur darting through the long grass on the hill opposite her. He paused to dig at a rabbit hole for a few seconds before raising his head and ploughing onwards.

Ellie let out a long whistle, calling him back to her. He completely ignored it. "Dammit! Arkarus, get back here!" She took off after him, following his trail of flattened grass.

Now and then, she passed by little bloodstains, and occasionally saw a dismembered rabbit foot or head. "No!"

she cried. "Don't eat them! We can't get paid if you eat them all!"

After a while, he collapsed in the grass, and she found him panting and wheezing, completely out of breath but with a bulging belly.

"You greedy hog!" she scolded him, planting both hands on her hips. "You were supposed to draw them out, not scoff them down your gigantic throat."

She paused, studying him. He was bigger. Much bigger. When did that happen?

"Huh," she said in wonder. Last time she had seen him physically, he stood about three feet off the ground, but now he looked at least four. And the short stub of his second tail had bulked out, now it was about half the size of his busy main tail. *I guess this whole projection thing is good for him. He's growing with all this extra space or something.*

He looked up at her with his tongue lolling out, four bright eyes watching her with a mischievous intelligence. But there was also something sad about that gaze. Was he longing for his home? Whenever she saw him in the physical world, she couldn't help being reminded that he didn't belong there. If anyone were to see him, they'd assume he was some kind of dangerous mutant, and Ellie wouldn't even be able to honestly dispute it. He had come from another world.

But that didn't matter to Ellie. Wherever he was from, he was here now, and he had no-one to watch out for him, except her. She'd feel just terrible if anything happened to him. She had to take care of him until she figured out how to get him home. Although Ellie didn't much like the idea of parting with him, either.

"Oh, what a mess," she said aloud, wishing her father was here to see Arkarus. Her mind often wandered to him since she set out on this journey, and it never failed to make her want to cry. She exhaled a long, juddering breath.

"*Arowl?*" Arkarus whined, cocking his head.

"Come on," she said, patting her chest. "Back inside."

"*Ruff!*" he barked, jumping to his feet and taking a few steps away from her. Clearly reluctant to go back to his yard. Her guess had been wrong. His head was level with her chest, which would make him at least four and a half feet tall! He might have been the biggest wolf in the world, Ellie thought.

"I know, I wish you could stay out here with me too, but if someone sees you, I don't know what'll happen! It's safer this way, for now," she said. "I'll let you out again as soon as we're on the other side of town. I promise."

"*Arooowl*," he whined again, and coughed. He hacked up a piece of grisly bone that must've been caught in his throat. He bent to sniff it, licked his lips and then started chewing on it with wide, chomping jaws.

She watched him with an amused smirk. "Are you done?"

He swallowed the bone and wagged his tails slowly. The excitement had gone from his body language now, leaked out like water from a holey bucket. His head drooped a little, and his ears flopped limp down the side of his head. When his tongue lolled out and he started panting again, Ellie recognised it as the last sign of his ability to stand upright before he would collapse. She had projected Arkarus four or five times and slowly gotten used to these signs. For whatever reason, he couldn't stay projected indefinitely, and she had to draw him back inside herself so that he could rejuvenate.

"Here, Arkarus," she said, kneeling down to make it easier for him. Ellie patted her chest again and closed her eyes. She imagined she was kneeling in Joe's barnyard, with the old kennel propped against the fence in one corner.

Arkarus loped forwards into her. An observer standing beside them might think he was walking past her, and expect to see his head re-emerge behind her back on the other side, but instead, his body simply vanished, like some surreal optical illusion. Ellie thought it must look like a trick performed by a travelling circus, the one where they walked a full grown horse into a skinny wardrobe. Only here the wardrobe was a slender girl and the horse was a gigantic wolf.

As Arkarus' body drew into Ellie's, he became ghostly transparent. He disappeared inside her and emerged out of Ellie's imaginary self in the barnyard, landing on his paws in the gravel just in front of her. In here, his energy returned instantaneously, and she once again felt the mildly uncomfortable pressure of carrying two souls within her mind.

Arkarus stretched his neck and back legs, and gave a long yawn. He loped over to his kennel and Ellie realised he was far too big for it now. It looked like a toy house meant for a puppy.

Lemme see what I can do about that, Ellie thought.

She imagined a brand new dog house for him, one with a pointed red roof and a great big arched door, large enough for a pony. She pointed to the spot next to the existing old kennel and this brand new one popped into existence. Arkarus' ears pricked as he turned to look at it.

Ruff! He barked excitedly.

Wait, she said, smiling to herself. *I'm not finished yet.*

She imagined a fine leather stag's hide and wrapped it around a bundle of soft feathers, to make a giant pillow bed. This floated past Arkarus and squeezed itself through the door and flopped onto the ground within. Then she turned her attention to the yard itself, which was weedy and layered with old gravel, just like the real thing back at Farmer Cribs'. With the stroke of a hand, she brushed all the gravel into oblivion and replaced it with a carpet of soft green grass, trimmed like her Grandpa's lawn, and decorated the fence line with rows of her mum's flowers, as if they'd been picked straight out of her garden and replanted here.

At one end of the fence was a gate that led to the great old wooden barn, a three-storey behemoth which dominated the view. Ellie liked the barn, because it was made of great cedar logs and built to last, but it deserved a better backdrop, she decided. Here in her mind, the barnyard seemed to exist within an infinite black sea. There was no sky, no horizon, just a slightly daunting amount of nothing.

I know what that needs…

Ellie remembered the night she and Johanna sat upon the roof of their cottage in Harbrook, especially the way the sky had looked. It had been a beautiful sky, streaked with a band of twinkling stars, too many to even count. And just like that, the black abyss that surrounded Arkarus' yard transformed into a cosmos of magnificent beauty. It looked even more radiant than she remembered, with tenfold more stars, a billion twinkling orbs shining down, illuminating the emptiness, filling it with gentle light.

Ellie walked over to the fence and leaned on it with her forearms, gazing into the galaxy she had just created. The stars even went beneath the yard, making it seem as if they were floating on a tiny island through space. Ellie let out a breathless laugh, impressed with her own imagination.

Arkarus sat on his haunches and tilted his neck to gaze up at the new sky. The stars reflected in his four wide eyes like rockpools filled with drifting sea fireflies. The stars were turning slowly, or perhaps their island was. The sensation might have made her feel seasick, but Ellie and Arkarus found it intensely soothing. Ellie thought she could stay here forever with Arkarus, gazing up at that mesmerising sky. But she wasn't really here, was she? This was just a place for Arkarus to live until she figured out what to do with him.

Maybe Johanna will know? Who knows what kind of awesome magic stuff she's learned by now.

The thought of her sister reminded Ellie of her task, and she left Arkarus like that, looking up at the stars and reopened her real eyes.

The rolling rabbit hills reappeared before her, under a tedious grey cloudy sky that seemed completely dull and lifeless. But deep within her soul, Arkarus howled. Not a mournful, sad howl this time. For the first time, that howl sounded content. He howled for the pleasure of it. To Ellie's ears, it sounded like he was saying *thank you.*

She smiled, collected her three rabbits and went back to town to collect the bounty. *Six more bobs for Mum.*

***

Two days later, she arrived at the city gates of Darune City. She passed under the grand stone archway that guarded the south western road and made her way along the cobbled streets heading for the only place she knew: Freddy's.

Arkarus was fidgety and excited in his yard, she sensed him sniffing the air, sharing her senses and listening to the hustle and bustle of many people coming and going, wagons rolling along the bumpy streets, kids chasing each other through grimy gutters, shopkeepers bellowing out of their doors, beckoning people to browse their wares. Ellie passed by a few stores; a man carving the legs of some wicker chairs, another flogging cart wheels. A pair of waifish identical twins with long ghostly white hair, and dressed in flowing robes beckoned her inside to have her fortune read.

"No, thanks," she said shrilly, taking a wide berth around them. She felt their eyes watching her back as she scurried down the street.

She paused for a moment outside a hunter's store. The pungent smell of freshly waxed leather wafted out, and there were various items of clothing hanging on rails; light summer fleeces, jerkins, and trousers. Some of them had little string price tags attached, and Ellie gawped at the gargantuan figures. She'd have to kill more than a hundred rabbits to afford even the cheapest jacket from this store.

How can they justify charging so much for something I could make in a weekend?

The store's owner came out then, noticing her hesitant interest and greeted her with a warm smile. "Hello there, young lady. You look like you know your way around the wilds," he said, looking her up and down. "I love your cloak, is that rabbit skin?"

"Yes," Ellie said, turning to allow him a better look.

"Wow," he said. "May I?" he asked, reaching out a bony, tentative hand. He didn't strike Ellie as a hunter type. Compared to the likes of Mr Huggins and her father's burly friends, this guy resembled a matchstick.

"Sure," she said, unable to hide a smirk.

He thumbed the cloak's hem, admiring her stitch work. "This is splendid handiwork. You're not from the city, are you? I'd recognise any of my peers' work. Where did you buy this?"

"I made it myself," Ellie said in a bemused tone. Why would she *buy* a cloak? There was no sense of achievement in that. *Hunt what you need, and use what you hunt,* her father used to say. The idea of buying any of the gear she saw in this man's store was almost as alien to Ellie as Arkarus was to her world.

The man recoiled slightly, looking at her doubtfully. "You don't say?" he asked. But then he decided she was telling the truth, and put one hand on his hip in a pose that reminded him of her mother, for some reason. It endeared him to her. "You have a talent, my lady. Why, have you ever thought about selling these in the city? You could make a fortune. I'd hire you in a heartbeat!"

"Oh. Um. Not really, no," she said, a little taken aback.

"And this bow, did you make this too?" he said, stepping around her to look at the well-worn ash slung around her shoulder.

"Yeah," she said. "We make everything ourselves down in Harbrook. It's just how we do things."

"Ooh I thought I heard a western accent. I've an ear for things like that," the man said, stroking his little chin.

A stray one-eyed dog approached and sniffed Ellie's butt. She jumped a little and stepped forwards.

"Shoo, you mangy mutt!" the man said, shooing it away with a stick he had propped against the doorframe. He acted and spoke in a way that confirmed Ellie's suspicions that he was not accustomed to dealing with animals. And just like that, the endearment vanished. Why was a man like that working in a hunter's store?

"It's okay," she said, turning towards the dog, but it was scurrying away to the other side of the street with its tail between its legs.

Aroowl? Arkarus whined in his yard.

"The city's overrun with them these days," the man said, shaking his head disgustedly at the stray dog. He turned back to Ellie, forcing a somewhat uncomfortable smile. "Do you take commissions?"

"Erm, what do you mean?"

"For your work. I'd love to know your prices. I reckon I could sell a dozen of these cloaks. How much would you charge?"

"Oh. I dunno. I'm only passing through, on my way to visit my sis—"

"Come now. How about eighty-five, no, make it a clean hundred."

Ellie stared blankly for a moment. "What?"

"A hundred bobbins. For a cloak just like yours."

Ellie's eyes lit up. "You'd pay me a hundred bobbins to make a cloak for you?"

"Well, not just one, my dear," he said, laughing. "I only work in minimum orders of a dozen. How quickly do you think you could make twelve? That's twelve hundred bobbins to take back to Harbrook." He bounced his eyebrows up and down.

Twelve hundred bobs? Ellie was rendered completely speechless. She'd never even heard of so much money in her life, never mind been offered it with such carefree ease.

Another stray mutt wandered over and sniffed Ellie's butt. Absently, she reached behind and petted it on the head.

"Go *away*!" the storekeeper said, whacking the poor thing on the nose. The mutt fled.

Ruff! Arkarus barked. Ellie thought he might be upset

about the man's aggressive behaviour, but she felt the sudden urge to turn and chase after the stray. It took her a moment to realise that thought had come from Arkarus, not her.

"Wait," she said, trying to make sense of the situation. *Arkarus, shh a moment.* "You're saying you'll pay me to make you a bunch of rabbit skin cloaks, to sell at your store?"

"Uh huh," he said, bouncing his eyebrows again. "What do you say?"

"Well, I don't really have the time at the moment."

"How long do you need?"

"Oh. Um. Perhaps a year?"

"*A year?*" he said, aghast.

"Well, yeah." She had slowly crafted her own cloak over a period of several weeks, and even then had needed her father's help to gather most of the skins. He didn't take on rabbit bounties very often, but had made an exception for her once he found out what she was making. Ellie figured if this guy was serious, she could go back to Woodhurst after she'd visited Johanna, camp out with Arkarus for a week or two, assuming he was still with her by then (which a surprisingly large part of her was quietly hopeful about), and gather as many rabbit skins as she could. That might give her enough to make three or four cloaks. After that, she'd figure out where to find more rabbits.

But the storekeeper was looking at her with his arms crossed and bewilderingly shaking his head. "That won't do," he said. "Rabbit is in *this* season, but next year it might be something else entirely. Couldn't you at least make me half a dozen in time for Summer Harvest? That gives you a month."

What planet was this guy from? Did he think rabbits just fell out of the sky whenever it rained? She opened her mouth to say as much, when-

Ruff!

Arkarus barked again, sensing another stray dog. It was a scruffy, matted collie and it waltzed right up behind Ellie and crammed its nose deep into her arsecrack.

She gave a startled yelp and hopped forwards, almost bumping into the storekeeper, who was already reaching to swing his stick again.

But Arkarus was faster.

It all happened in an instant, and Ellie had no time to do anything about it.

She spun around to face the mongrel, possessed by the will of Arkarus, who had escaped his boundary fence while she was distracted counting bobbins.

Arkarus leapt from Ellie's chest in what felt like slow motion. She had time to take in many details before the panic took over.

Several passers-by stopped in their tracks, all staring at the grubby girl in the leather huntress clothes as an enormous, four-eyed ghost monster projected out of her chest.

Others merely froze in their tracks and gaped. One woman dropped her sandwich she had been carrying, and a nearby man fell over backwards in his terror to leap away from the hungry looking wolf.

Arkarus landed on the cobblestones next to the stray dog, which resembled a puppy in comparison, and when the collie fled across the street, Arkarus bolted after it.

"Wait, are you a *mage*?" the storekeeper said in an awestruck voice. He wasn't scared, just completely amazed. Ellie didn't have time to explain.

Someone shouted, "Mage! It's a mage!" and turned to flee, triggering others to do the same.

"Arkarus!" Ellie cried, and ran after the wolf.

She sprinted across the street, following in the wake of Arkarus who had created a convenient gap in the various pedestrians that had scattered out of the way, or been knocked over by his coming. Arkarus bounded into an alleyway between two stores and Ellie chased after him, about ten paces behind, but the gap was growing rapidly.

They emerged on another street at the end of the alley,

this one less busy but still dotted with peasants and beggars, Arkarus caught the collie in the middle of the street, and Ellie reached them as the smaller dog rolled onto its back in submission. The stray looked up at Arkarus as he loomed over her, with wide, desperate, pleading eyes. Arkarus sniffed the dog's butt and wagged his tails. The collie scrambled to her feet and returned the butt-sniffing greeting to Arkarus. She had to really stretch her neck just to reach, because Arkarus was so huge.

"What is it?" someone said in a tone of extreme alarm.

"It's huge!"

"It looks like a *wolf*."

"Why does it have four eyes?"

"And two tails!"

"Sorcery!"

"It's magic!"

"There must be a wizard nearby!"

"Someone, get the guards!"

Ellie noticed people backing away, watching her with wary, scared faces and others pointed at her, talking to one another and looking around, searching for a guard to report her to, while others simply fled.

"Arkarus!" she said, grabbing him by the scruff of his considerable neck. "You have to get back inside me, *now!* You're getting us into a lot of trouble here."

"*Aroowl?*" he cocked his head at her.

"Hurry!" she said, hugging him closer to her.

But he didn't obey. He turned back to the collie, who stared up at Arkarus with her tongue lolling out, panting. No longer scared, the two had already exchanged pleasantries and were now buddies, apparently. Quick to flee, quick to befriend, typical canine behaviour, Ellie mused. But then she heard footsteps approaching and turned to see three armed soldiers marching towards her with spears in their hands.

"Hold it right there, mage!" one bellowed, but their pace faltered when Arkarus turned his attention to them. His ears were pricked in curiosity, not aggression, but that didn't seem to matter to the guards.

"What the fook is that?"

"M-monster!"

"Weapons ready, men!"

The guards squeezed together in formation and lowered their spears, aiming the barbed tips at Arkarus as they approached. Two more guards were approaching up the road from the other side, and Ellie suspected that more would be coming.

She had to get out of there. She would never reach Johanna if she got arrested here and had to spend the rest of summer in a dungeon.

"Come on!" she barked, slapping Arkarus on the head and ran across the road, ducking into another alley on the opposite side.

Arkarus took a final glance at the guards, then bolted after her.

"Hold it!" a guard bellowed.

"Seize her!"

"After them, men!"

And a chase ensued.

Ellie fled down the alleyway which zigzagged between buildings, winding into a darkened maze of the city that smelled like shit and rotten vegetables. Her feet squished in the muck but she kept going, running with Arkarus right behind her, feeling his breath on the back of her knees.

She skidded to a halt in the alley when it seemed that nobody could see them. She figured she had about five seconds before the guards came around the corner and saw her.

"Quick! Get inside me right *now*." She patted her chest and opened her arms. But Arkarus was too excited. He seemed to think this whole thing was a game. And a very fun game at that.

The stray collie came bounding past, sprinting between Arkarus' legs and running on further into the twisting maze of alleyways.

Arkarus slipped past her and gave chase.

"Oh no!" Ellie groaned, and took off after them both.

The collie gave a sudden turn to the right and ran up a sloping wooden board that had been nailed into place by whoever owned the building. It allowed access to a flat ledge that ran along the outside of the first storey of the building.

Ellie followed the dog and the wolf as they bounded up it without hesitation. The plank was connected to several more, which created a narrow gangway connecting this building to the one beside it, which had a flat roof. Looking ahead, it seemed that there was a whole row of flat roofed buildings that went along this street, and all of them had ramshackle shelters built on them.

People live up here? She leapt across the gap from one building to the next and ran on.

A very scruffy, bearded man glanced up as she sped past. He had been snoozing judging by the dazed look in his eyes, then Ellie was gone, jumping over another gap and onto the next roof.

Arkarus and the collie were pulling away from her now, she heard other strays yipping and yapping, leaping out of the shelters to join the game.

By the time they reached the last row of squatter shacks, the pack of dogs had grown to six, all of them dwarfed by the gargantuan Arkarus, whose tongue lolled out, flapping wildly across the side of his face in pure glee.

Ellie's heart hammered in her chest, she was running out of steam and couldn't keep up for much longer, hoping they would finally stop somewhere soon.

But of course they didn't.

The flat roofs came to an abrupt end and the dogs disappeared over the edge of the farthest building. Ellie arrived at the same spot a few seconds later and realised there was an exit ramp leading down into another street, this one wide and spread open across a huge area.

Oh Kella, the city square.

Ellie legged it down the ramp and bounded into the square, which was full of people.

Screams rose up, and a wave of pedestrians scattered. Ellie ran after the dogs, again helped by the fact they were creating a channel through the crowds. She ran past people lying on their backs, presumably knocked over by the pack.

"Sorry!" she cried, feeling more than a little guilty.

By this point, the pack was a dozen strong, as more strays were drawn to the yipping and barking, deciding to join in.

"*HOLD IT RIGHT THERE!*" bellowed the leader of a group of guards somewhere ahead. Ellie saw five of them standing at the northern gate entrance to the square, and they all lowered their spears, aiming them straight at the approaching dogs.

The pack turned left.

"After them, men!" The five guards took off in pursuit, now blocking Ellie's path between her and the pack.

She caught up to the rear guard easily. She may have been running out of breath, but she was wearing light leather and they were clad in heavy mail and couldn't move nearly as fast.

"Move!" she said, bumping the slowest guard aside and pushing her way through.

"Hold it!" he barked, and grabbed her cloak. Ellie felt a moment of panic, sure that she had been caught, but instinct took over and she reached up to unfasten the brooch around her neck, shrugging out of the cloak and jerking away from him.

"Wait!" he ordered. "Come back here!"

Then he fell behind and Ellie was running again. The pack bounded out through the western gate and into a familiar street. She ran past Freddy's, feeling a twinge of regret that she couldn't stop to have another portion of his excellent pentini.

A sudden gasp escaped her lips. Her throat tightened, and she found it difficult to breathe. *Oh no! What's happening?*

She was approaching exhaustion now, but this felt like something else. Her energy had taken a sudden dive, as if the last ten minutes of breathless sprinting had suddenly caught up with her.

Ahead, Arkarus had slowed too.

The other four guards were catching up to him.

Fearing what they would do if they caught him, Ellie fought the urge to stop by grinding her teeth, pumping her arms and legs as fast as they could go, desperate to reach him before the guards did.

The road curved downhill to the right, and she thought she could cut the corner by slipping between two buildings. She plunged into a dim alley off the main street and found a clear path all the way through to the other side. She emerged at the other end of the curve, just as the pack ran past, but in front of the guards.

"Arkarus!" she cried, finally catching up to him. He was panting so heavily, mirroring her own feeling of exhaustion. *He's gonna pass out again, just like before!* "Stop, boy!" she said in a breathless wheeze. "You have to… come back… to me!"

Arkarus glanced back over his shoulder, and gave her a withering look. Then, abruptly, he stumbled, tripped and crashed to the cobblestones, skidding on his side to a halt.

Ellie almost tripped over him, and lost her footing herself. She put out a hand to stop from hitting her head, and landed with a bump on the hard ground next to Arkarus.

"Ouch," she winced, scrabbling on her hands and knees to see if Arkarus was okay. "Come on, boy," she said, kneeling up straight and pushing out her chest towards him. "Get back inside, please! Hurry!"

The guards were only a dozen paces away. They'd be upon them in a matter of seconds.

Ellie reached forwards, plunging her hands into the deep scruff of his neck, and pulled his head towards her belly, trying to force him through her skin.

A burst of energy swept through her, and Arkarus must have felt it too.

Electricity seemed to tingle between her fingers in his thick fur, and suddenly she found she could breathe again.

In a quick jerk of movement, Arkarus shoved his head between her legs, and lurched to his feet.

"Aiie!" she shrieked, falling forwards onto his haunches, as he stood up and took off in a frantic bound down the road, carrying her on top of his back.

Ellie saw the startled and angry look on the guards' faces as they realised their quarry was getting away from them again, and after four or five more desperate steps, they all stopped, bending over to clutch their knees, dropping their spears to the ground in defeat.

Ellie grinned and snorted a laugh of relief. Then Arkarus turned sharply to the right and she almost tumbled off the side of him. Grabbing the tufts of his fur and digging her feet around his thick neck, she clung on desperately as he bolted down another street, overtaking the stray dogs, which all bounded on, tongues lolling and glancing nonchalantly at Ellie as she rode backwards on top of their alpha, lowering their heads to sprint faster, desperately trying to keep up.

Arkarus flew out of the northern gate to shouts of "Halt!" and "Mage!" and "For the king!" as more guards tried futilely to stop the pack of dogs, some tripping over the mongrels as they ran into their legs and onlookers just turned to watch the mad spectacle.

Arkarus ran and ran, fuelled by whatever energy was being shared by Ellie and himself, feeding off the physical connection between them.

Ellie realised then that so long as she was touching him, he could go on for much longer as a projection than if he was by himself.

Arkarus ran and ran, overcome with freedom of his new world, frothing at the mouth with happiness and excitement.

"Arrooooo!" Ellie howled, as she clung to his haunches. *This is insane, and brilliant and wonderful.* She'd lost her rabbit skin cloak, but it was a tiny speck of trouble in the joy of the moment. "*Arroooooo!*"

Arkarus barked back, again and again.

"*Arroooooooo!*" Ellie howled at the sky, watching the city shrink behind them.

CHAPTER EIGHTEEN

Garrod woke up one morning sweating after a dream that he couldn't remember. It left him with the strong desire to go for a morning flight.

This was not unusual anymore. More and more frequently, last thing at night, and first thing in the morning, Garrod took to the skies to stretch his wings. Up there, among the clouds, he could clear his mind and focus on his meditation. He'd almost reached the point where he could meditate mid-flight, as if while flying, some other part of him could take control of his wings and see him safely through the sky. It was almost as if Corcubus –

Nonsense! I devoured that creature. There is nothing left of it.

Garrod went flying because he *wanted* to. That was all there was to it. Any other person would do the same, given his powers.

On that particular morning, Garrod found himself soaring north over the Everdusk as it glowed a deeper shade of orange than the dawn sky to his right. He felt a warm southerly wind pushing him from behind and allowed his body to go with it, flapping his wings only when he felt himself slowly losing altitude.

He soared for half an hour in a daze before realising he

could see the edge of the forest ahead of him.

Archdale. I want to see my old home.

He tucked his neck in and pounded his wings, surging forwards with a hint of urgency. Why did he suddenly have an urge to visit Archdale now, on this morning?

It was that dream. He still couldn't remember it, but something stirred at the cusp of his memory, some lingering thought of the sky. *Yes, I was flying in the dream. That's why I awoke with such a stronger craving than usual.*

The sun rose and illuminated the Northern Province Road, as it wound through the plains beyond the Everdusk, all the way to Archdale City. Garrod followed the road, soaring a thousand feet above it, surely higher than any human had ever been. He flew on through the morning and eventually caught the first glimpse of the city on the horizon. The sun glinted off a window many wheels away. Garrod flew directly at it, and came to Archdale well before noon.

It briefly occurred to him that he hadn't left a message with Robert, but the old servant would probably figure out that he had decided to take the day off. It just so happened to be Sunday, and Garrod had no private tutoring to attend to that day. A fortunate coincidence, which he wouldn't waste any more time dwelling on now that he was several hundred wheels away from Trinity Towers.

Seeing Archdale from above had reminded him of his dream: in it, he was a dragon. Not just any dragon, but the one that destroyed this city almost thirty years ago.

He snorted a bitter laugh, and tucked into a gentle dive, descending to a hundred feet above the city to get a closer look. Garrod soared over the decrepit, abandoned southern gate and followed what was once the main high street. Weeds had overgrown the road, pushing out the cobblestones and scattering them across the path. Likewise, the buildings had green shoots growing out of the windows, strangling vines crept up the walls, and the scent of vegetation rose from the city that had once been home to over ten thousand people, the vast majority of whom had been attuned.

Garrod banked right and flew across to his old home. His parents' home, really. Garrod's memory of the place wasn't foggy, but near non-existent. He had only been five years old when they had fled the dragon. His mother had died giving birth to him down in that house: a large, two storey stone building with a pointed roof and a wizard's turret rising out of the rear section. Garrod circled it a few times, contemplating going inside, but the more he circled, the less inclined he felt to do so.

There was nothing for him down there.

A dragon belonged in the sky, after all.

Garrod turned away from his family home and flew across the town to the old clock tower. He swooped directly for it and landed gracefully on its spire, grabbing the wind vane for balance. It snapped in his grip, brittle as a dried up twig, and he dropped it. He had to give a quick flap of his wings just to stay upright.

He regained his balance and perched upon the slanting clock tower roof. His father had said that the dragon first appeared in the sky somewhere above the tower. He craned his neck to see, but saw only fluffy white clouds far above, floating across the pale morning sky.

As he lowered his head, his gaze passed across the town square and he lost his breath in a gasp.

The circle of rotten corpses lay festering in a circle, exactly where he and Robert had left them after the dreadful prisoner rift experiment.

Mother!

The thought came without warning and Garrod was overcome with a desperation that made no sense yet still filled him with terrible grief. He had to go down there.

He unfurled his wings and glided down to the square, landing in a run on the cobblestones right inside the circle of dead prisoners, and stopped in front of the crumbling well.

Mother?

The nest had been here, on this exact spot in the decayed mirror world. This was where he had been born.

No. Wait. He wasn't born in a nest, he was born in the house on the other side of the city.

That *beast* was born here. Corcubus!

Cooorcubus!

I assimilated it. It's dead.

Crrrk.

No. It lingers within me. It's full of grief. Overwhelming grief.

Tears were streaking down his face, but he was not aware of it until he reached up to cover his mouth with a shaky hand.

What is this torment? Why did I come here? The pain is unbearable!

The world shimmered and swam. The well before him danced as if its stone bricks had turned to marrow.

A rift. A rift is opening!

The darkness swallowed him. Garrod saw the black dome expand around him, filling with purple sickly light. The abandoned buildings around him turned into actual ruins now, decayed brick and mortar, crumbling walls and rotting stone.

Garrod felt wave after wave of suffering crash over him, half aware that it was Corcubus' desire to be here, driven by a desperate need to see its mother again. And so, if only to put a final end to its mewling, he let it have its way.

The rift portal evaporated, but this time he was left on the other side.

Garrod spun around in time to see the last hazy shimmer of his world disappear. He was trapped on this side now.

A brief wave of panic flowed through him, but it lasted only a second before he regained his composure.

It's fine. I got myself here. I can get myself back.

Garrod stood in the desolation of Archdale's twin, a vastly more decrepit version of the abandoned city. A bruise coloured sky loomed down at him, brooding and repulsive to look at, and a thin curtain of dust hovered in the air. There were bones scattered around the square, and to Garrod's horror, he realised that many of them were human. He counted more than a dozen skulls before he forced himself to stop, wondering what good it would do.

It's the soldiers. The ones that came through to protect my father and Prince Leo.

The bird's nest was still there, and the empty, split open eggshells still rested in their place. He even saw the very egg that Corcubus had been born out of.

And then his eye caught on the corpse of its mother.

Little more than a feathery skeleton, with some rotting morsels of meat still clinging to her bones, Corcubus' mother lay on the ground surrounded by several more human skeletons that had been stripped of their skin and flesh by whatever scavengers dwelled in this place.

Garrod felt something die inside him. It was Corcubus' hope.

"You see?" he said aloud. "There's nothing for you here anymore."

But there is for me…

A shadow swept across the square, very fast, and huge. He tilted his head and gazed up at that sickly sky, expecting to see a dragon flying overhead.

Nothing there.

Garrod felt exposed and vulnerable, suddenly paranoid about being observed by unseen eyes. Perhaps more of those weasel creatures were prowling somewhere nearby, or perhaps something worse.

Enough was enough. He flapped his wings and took off, climbing high over the crumbling city, scanning the horizon in every direction. Way to the south he could see the Everdusk, or at least this world's version of it.

That's where his father was. He had to find him.

Garrod flew all the way there, retracing his flight to Archdale, soaring over dead, barren plains. A wasteland of desolation spread out before him, utterly lifeless.

Except it wasn't all dead. Now and then, he'd spy a scabby creature scurrying through the scrubs, unrecognisable from anything he'd seen before. He saw a snarling weasel creature chasing a deformed-looking oversized hare. He even caught sight of another great condor, far away to his right, skirting the edges of the Luna Mountains, which seemed shrivelled and bony. *Whatever doom befell this world, it had the power even to suck the majesty out of mountains*, Garrod thought.

And yet as he flew, he became aware of a strange energy coursing through him. He was flying much faster than he had on his journey up here, even without the aid of a rear wind to propel him. Despite the general repulsion he felt for the air in this world, he recognised a curious power invigorating him.

Garrod reached the Everdusk and shortly after that, he arrived at the other Trinity Towers.

First, the obvious differences: it was no longer a trinity. Only the Sun Tower remained intact. The Moon Spire's pinnacle had collapsed, its pointed roof completely caved in, now a pile of rubble in the tower's centre. And the Storm Spire was nothing but a broken foundation. Ninety percent of the tower had seemingly disintegrated to dust and was gone, only the solid stone base remained, jutting out of the ground like an old petrified tree stump.

Candlelight flickered in the upper chamber of the Sun Tower. The glass in the window was gone, but Garrod could see right in through the frame, and the man sitting at the desk within. Garrod made a wide pass, lining himself up to fly in through the window.

As he did, the man looked up and stared right at Garrod, then he came rushing to the window, leaning out to get a look at his visitor.

"Father!" he cried, finishing his bank and coming in for a direct landing. "Move aside!"

Jason Brockhurst stood his ground for a while longer, his mouth drooping low. He shimmied out of the way at the last moment as Garrod came swooping in to land on his talons. He'd had plenty of days to practice this landing, and despite the window frame in this world being crooked and bent, he managed rather comfortably.

"Garrod? Is it really you?" Jason said, stepping towards his son with a gape of bewilderment on his abysmal face.

"Yes, father," Garrod said, folding his wings away. "My goodness, what has happened to you?"

"I was going to ask you the same thing!" Jason said, stepping closer and opening his arms to hug Garrod.

Garrod recoiled away in disgust. Whatever ailment his father had, he did not want to catch it. He looked like a leper. The skin was peeling away from his face in ragged slices, dry and flaky pieces fell to the floor whenever he moved.

"Wait, father," he said, holding out a hand. "You have some kind of sickness."

"What?" Jason stopped, stared for a moment and then wheezed out a laugh.

Garrod frowned, lost for words.

"Me? *Sick?*" Jason said, and laughed again. "Garrod, my dear boy, I have never felt *better*. Can you not feel it, Garrod? Come son, even the air here is attuned. I haven't eaten in days, because I don't need to!"

"What madness has taken you?" Garrod said, but even as he spoke, he began to understand what he had felt as he flew down here. Usually, after a flight like that, he would need to rest a while, eat some food to regain his strength. But standing there now after making the return flight in half the time, he would expect to need to eat an entire fruit bowl just to stand upright, and yet…

His wings didn't ache. His talons felt strong. He was standing up straight, didn't even feel a need to lean on a cane. And his body felt lighter, somehow, as if his muscles had grown stronger, able to support the weight of his wings with less effort.

Despite the obvious symptoms of some horrendous

disease plaguing his father, he wasn't deluded about this place being attuned. It clearly was. Somehow, it was saturated with the arcane, Garrod could sense it in the air the same way one could smell bread baking in a kitchen. Only this was far less pleasant. It was overwhelming.

His father looked as though he might keel over and turn to dust with the next gust of wind.

"Father, there is something very wrong with this place."

"I found it, son," Jason whispered, ignoring Garrod.

He knew at once what *it* Jason was referring to.

"When?" Garrod whispered back.

"Yesterday. By the spring. It's the same dragon."

"How do you know?"

"I would recognise it anywhere," Jason said, smiling a grim smile. "I've seen others, too. They fly overhead, way up there," he pointed out of the window, aiming his bony finger straight up. "They are magnificent Garrod. Truly, a wonder of this realm."

"You sound like you admire them."

"Of course."

"After what it did to our home, shouldn't you *despise* them?"

Jason didn't seem to hear that. He turned to Garrod with hungry eyes trained on his wings. "You could fly up to meet them. I must know, *how* did you get those?"

Garrod inhaled a breath. "That is a tale for another time, in another place. Perhaps at home." Now he did hold his hand out to Jason, despite his reservations. "Come back with me, Father."

"Why?" Jason said, dismissing the hand completely.

"Because this place is *killing* you!"

"What are you talking about, son? I have never felt more alive! Could a dying man do this?" And he summoned a great sparking rainbow of energy out of thin air. The spell was pure light, a dazzling display of electricity illuminating the ruinous walls in a brilliant glow of multi-colours. For a moment, cast in that fantastic glow, the chamber almost resembled its true form, or at least the version of it that Garrod was familiar with. The walls came alive, shadows retreated to the corners and the room filled with comforting warmth, the cosiness of a home.

Then Jason squeezed his palms together and extinguished the light.

The room blinked back to its cold, grey, dust-ridden self.

"I am stronger here than I have ever been," Jason said, inclining his chin with pride. A chunk of flesh and hair fell away from his forehead, exposing the red raw meat beneath. "Tell me son, what is your ultimate desire? And what are you prepared to sacrifice to get what you want?"

Garrod couldn't remember the last time his father had asked him such a thing. It seemed an important question. What did Garrod want? What was worth lingering in a dying world for?

Garrod had to resist looking away in absolute horror. "You are completely delusional," Garrod said. "Whatever you think you feel, it is the complete opposite! Don't misunderstand me, Father, I feel it too, the allure of being here. It fills me with a sense of power that I fear could take a hold if I let it, but I *can't.* I will not. It is a trick of this place, some foul corruption designed to feed off of us. Were you in my position right now, I know you would advise such counsel, and I beg of you now Father, if my opinion ever mattered, you must listen and come with me. We must get you home. Before…" He gulped, struggling with the words. "Before this place claims you forever."

Jason laughed again. It sent a flare of frustrated rage through Garrod.

"Stop laughing you *fool!*" he roared.

"I cannot help it, son!" Jason said, and Garrod saw with a shock that there was fear hidden behind that laugh. Jason's expression contorted into a grimace, but another bout of maniacal laughter came choking out. "I… can't… help…*myself.*"

"What is this madness?" Garrod said, stepping back.

Perhaps Jason *knew,* or at least a part of him could sense that something dark and backwards had taken hold of him. He was fighting with some unseen force, perhaps similar to the way Garrod had to fight Corcubus for control of his mind. He had won that fight, and now he wondered whether that had been a test for him to overcome in order for him to help save his father now.

Jason had no beast living within his mind, he had simply spent too long in the mirror world, and it was eating his soul like a cancerous growth. He could no longer tell the difference between pain and joy. The two were switched in the dark reflection.

That had to be why Garrod felt so strong here. The air was foul, rancid, and yet his body hungered for more of it. It didn't make sense, but it was still the truth. He remembered what his father had said about the dragon that destroyed Archdale, and how it had a swarm of nibbets living within its stomach. Such a creature could only live in a world as backward as this. Everything he knew about the natural law was flipped here, or at least bent askew.

So, if *pain* opened a rift from his side, how would he open one in the mirror world, in order to get back home? What was the opposite of pain?

Joy. I must create joy.

Garrod scoffed a bitter laugh. How the fook was he going to conjure up enough joy to open a rift in such a depressing place?

He wracked his mind, trying to think. *A memory. I need a memory.*

He had taught Johanna the trick of using memories for attunement energy, but it had been some time since he'd needed to use the technique himself. He had a small bank of go-to memories for this, past events that evoked a strong emotional reaction were the most effective. The caveat here was that he needed to conjure a strong, *positive* emotion. Easier said than done when you'd lived your entire life in the shadow of your father.

Garrod had so few happy memories that finding his happiest came effortlessly. Her face materialised in his mind's eye, a memory of teenage love.

Nia.

Nia was the most beautiful girl he had ever known, and she loved him. They only spent a season together, when he had been sent to Darune City to stay with Robert Anders' family during a blistering summer. He pictured her face – blue eyes, flowing blonde hair that fell about her shoulders, thick-rimmed glasses that accentuated her gorgeous eyes that bored deep into him whenever they talked. They made love in her bed one day when everyone else was out watching a street show. That was his first time. She had claimed to be a virgin herself, and Garrod knew no better at the time. Later, he learned the truth. But for a while, there was blissful ignorance. She had been his, only his, and his heart swelled to the size of the moon. Every day he wondered how life could feel so good, and every day he grew a little happier.

The air around the chamber began to shimmer as Garrod recalled these wonderful memories. His eyes were tightly closed, but he could sense the rift trying to open, felt the electricity of two dimensions pulling apart from one another, the gateway between worlds on the brink of cracking.

But Nia had betrayed him. She said that she loved him, but she also loved others. Garrod could not understand that. It took so much energy for him to love her, he couldn't even comprehend the notion of having feelings for anyone else simultaneously.

He remembered the day he came to her after buying a bronze necklace from a store in the city. He had spent the last of his father's allowance on it, knowing that it would look simply beautiful around her lovely neck.

But when he arrived at her house, he found her with some boy. In the bed. Together. Naked. The same way she made love to him, her on top, him on his back, holding her slender waist. Seeing her with another like that didn't break his heart so much as petrify it to stone.

The rift dissolved before it had even finished materialising.

"Dammit!" Garrod gasped, opening his eyes and seeing Jason's rotting face again.

"What were you doing, son?" he asked in a hushed whisper.

"Be quiet," he said. "I'm getting us out of here."

"But I—"

Garrod tuned him out. He gritted his teeth and remembered that first night again. The first time he made love to Nia. His naivety, his innocence: that was what made the feeling so monumentally happy. The betrayal came later. She was false, but back then he had no idea. He needed that happiness now. If he couldn't remember it, then he would be stuck here with his father, forever, until he too began to rot, his skin would peel off, his eyes would dry up, his skin would crack and flake and he'd slowly fade to nothing.

Concentrate!

Garrod inhaled a humungous breath of the foul, acrid, powerful air, and felt his lungs fill with attuned energy. It felt incredible and terrifying. He channelled that energy into his memories, pouring them into the one specific part of his mind which he thought he had buried long ago.

He saw Nia's face again, looming over him in her bed. He was on his back, she was crawling onto him. She leaned down to kiss him, and then sat up on top of him, brushing away her long blonde hair so that she could see his face. She gyrated her hips against him, smiling a cheeky, intoxicating smile, her glasses sitting askew across her nose, enlarging her eyes to almost comic proportions. She leaned forwards, planting both hands upon his chest and thrust down so hard that Garrod exploded.

The pleasure raced outward from his pelvis and flooded through his torso, down his arms, all the way to his fingertips, then it came again. Wave after wave of intense pleasure cascaded across his nervous system as he stared up at the most beautiful girl in the world, content that if he died right then and there, it would be the best way to go.

Garrod felt the rift sizzling at his senses again. It was trying to open, but that memory hadn't been enough.

Resisting the urge to scream in frustration, he did the only thing he could think of.

He thought back to when he first met her.

The dinner party at Robert Anders place, Nia was the daughter of some old acquaintance of the Anders, and as the adults talked of tedious matters, Nia kept casting glances at Garrod across the table. She had a mischievous smirk that begged him to follow her as she snuck away from the dinner. She kissed him in the gardens beneath a bright half-moon that night, his first kiss. Such happy innocence.

The rift sizzled again, but still it didn't open.

Garrod ground his teeth, forcing himself to replay other memories of Nia.

He saw them lying on their backs in the city park, watching clouds drift by and talking about home. He recalled the day they climbed the clock tower together. Midnight kisses in her bedroom. Walking hand-in-hand through the market square, Nia admiring the bronze bracelet he would eventually buy for her.

Then that first night in her bedroom. Always, it came back to that night.

Garrod replayed the memories again and again.

Unconsciously, he started to multiply their speed. Using the method of meditation he had perfected with Corcubus living in his mind, he recalled these memories as quickly as he could, jumping from one to the next, but always finishing with the first time he made love to her. He remembered barging into the house together, kissing as they clambered up the staircase and burst into her room, she threw her arms around his neck, and before long they were undressing each other in a frenzy. It had been slow and clumsy but by playing the memory faster it became rushed and desperate.

Garrod fed the happy memories into his mind again and again, growing more and more aware of the rift opening around him.

He and Nia finished together, and he started all over again. This time he played the memory even faster, and the whole thing was over in a matter of seconds, but *still* the rift didn't open, but he felt it sizzling around him. He was close.

Garrod repeated the psychological torture again, filling up with pleasurable agony. As soon as the rift opened, he intended to grab his father and drag him back to their world where they both belonged.

He remembered Nia screaming in pleasure as he made love to her again, again, again, again, again ag—

Crrrack!

He sensed the rift open around him.

Panting and with a thin sheen of sweat on his brow, Garrod opened his eyes.

A *dragon* was peering in through the broken window frame.

Its big black eye filled Garrod's vision. The dragon's head was too big to fit inside the window, but he could just about see the line of its mouth, upturned in an animalistic grin.

The rift filled the chamber almost perfectly, a black hazy dome sprinkled with inviting orange fire. The dragon was peering in just at the edge. He tore his eyes away from the dragon, and searched for his father.

But Jason was gone. Garrod was alone in the Sun Tower chamber, alone with the dragon.

"Aaaargh!" he cried in a mix of frustration and torment. He spun around, and saw the candlelit glow of his real chamber beckoning him through, back to his own world, back to sanity.

He turned back to the dragon's eye and a question formed in his mind, but he didn't have time to say it. The question was, *what did you do to my father?*

The dragon answered, speaking in his mind like thunder.

HE YEARNS FOR KNOWLEDGE AND TRUTH. JUST LIKE YOU.

Garrod had time to think, *what?*

HE SEEKS THAT WHICH MORTALS CAN NEVER UNDERSTAND.

"What?" Garrod cried.

IMMORTALITY. OUR GIFT. OUR CURSE.

All the colour drained from Garrod's cheeks, and he swayed on his feet.

In a sudden rush, he knew the answer to his father's question.

"Eternal life," Garrod muttered. His jaw went slack, the single thought of living forever having scorched a brand on his mind. *Eternal life. To live forever, is to gain all knowledge. What a glorious notion…*

He stretched out a lazy hand to the eye, meaning for the dragon to take him. The dragon grinned at him.

But the rift embraced him instead, and yanked Garrod through.

He was spat back out and toppled over backwards, landing on the wooden floorboards of his familiar chamber. He inhaled a gasp of fresh, natural air.

Robert was in the room, and he spun around to face Garrod, with a look of terrible shock.

"Garrod? How did you—?"

"Raggon!" Garrod slurred, gasping and wheezing. "The drag—*dragon!*"

The dragon's voice echoed in his mind like a thunderclap.

IMMORTALITY. OUR GIFT. OUR CURSE.

"E-eternal!" Garrod sputtered.

Garrod saw Robert leaning over him, his mouth frantically working but silent. Garrod couldn't hear him over the dragon's echoing words.

His vision swam. And he passed out.

CHAPTER NINETEEN

The frog was stuck in mid-air and it was the most terrifying thing she'd ever seen.

Johanna tried to scream but had no control of her mouth.

She had no control of anything at all, actually, not even her own breathing. She was trapped in a time loop, that's the only way she could think to describe it. The frog, which had been jumping off a lily pad into the water was frozen before her face, hovering in mid-leap, seeming to defy the very laws of gravity and nature.

Take me back!

She tried desperately to scream again it but simply couldn't. Her mind was a fog of terrified, panicky thoughts, a whirlwind of chaos that she couldn't escape from.

How had she ended up here? She tried to remember, and fragments of it came back to her.

She had gone with Markus and Karly to the Mana Spring pool. Yes, that's where she was right now. Only a half hour stroll from the safety of Trinity Towers, through the superoaks of the Everdusk.

"You're going to love it!" Karly had said while they were hiking through the trees, giving her a huge smile that had been full of optimistic positivity.

Markus, who had allowed himself to be taken completely under the delinquent's spell, mimicked her enthusiasm. "Yeah seriously, Jo, this spring is as ancient as the forest itself. I think it even feeds into the same river that flows down through Harbrook."

"It's the *Mana* Spring," Johanna said. "Didn't you make the connection just from the name?"

"Mana Spring, Mana River… oh yeah!" He shot her a jubilant grin.

That was how they had convinced her to come in the first place. The idea of seeing the source of the river that fed Harbrook its fish and fresh water supply thousands of wheels to the south really appealed to Johanna. That, and she decided a little socialising was better than spending another study session alone.

The spring more than lived up to her expectations when she arrived. It looked manmade, but was apparently an entirely natural formation of rocks that jutted out of the ground. The boulders seemed to have been piled on top of each other by an old giant sculptor.

A jagged cone of rocks pointed at the sky, some fifteen feet above the ground, and out of the top bubbled crisp, clear water. The water trickled down the surface of the rocks and gathered at the bottom in a wide rockpool. This flat, mirror-like pool of water was dotted with flowering lily pads, and an army of frogs had apparently made their home there.

Johanna, Markus and Karly had each found a comfortable rock to sit on, where they could listen to the soothing trickle of water from the spring and watch the frolicking frogs. At the far end of the pool, the water leaked out, forming the stream that snaked away into the trees, heading south, where it would eventually become the Mana River. By the time the water flowed through Harbrook it was a twenty-foot wide torrent which, in the springtime, became rapid and dangerous.

Johanna took off her shoes and socks, and let her feet dangle over the edge, bathing her toes in the cool water.

She sighed. "This is lovely. Thanks for inviting me, guys."

"No problem," Karly said with a dismissive wave. "I just can't believe those other nincompoops don't wanna see this."

She was referring to the rest of their peers, but Johanna suspected she mostly meant Bella and Mallory, who had turned their noses up at Karly's invitation on account of her probably only wanting to come here to "cook their minds."

It was Markus who had eventually convinced Johanna to come, promising that they wouldn't eat any hoomies while she was there. Unless of course, she wanted to…

"Um, no thanks," Johanna had said timidly.

"You sure?" he said. "I've had some pretty amazing experiences. I sorta wish you could see some of the things I've seen this past week."

"Seeing things? You mean, like a trip?" Johanna had a vague idea of what effect hoomies had on a person's mind. Her teacher at Harbrook School had once told them about some of the wild mushrooms that grew in the woods, and which ones were edible and which were absolutely not. She'd described a 'trip' as some vivid hallucination which multiplied whatever dominating feeling the person was currently having, to the point of you losing your ability to speak, stand up straight, or sometimes even move. That sounded absolutely terrifying to Johanna, and she'd never so much as felt any desire to smoke, eat or ingest hoomies in any form.

But something about Markus' new care-free attitude, and his demeanour in general intrigued her. He had changed since leaving Harbrook. He'd nursed a crush on Johanna ever since they were old enough to play together in the lane, but she had never returned the sentiment. She just didn't see him in that way. But after they had come to Trinity Towers, she realised, with some considerable amount of regret, that she missed his attention.

And the hardest part about it was he didn't seem to realise how much it was affecting her. She wasn't jealous of Karly, though. It was simply a case of self-pity, which she recognised as the petty emotion that it was, and felt determined to deal with it.

Markus and Karly were always so *happy.* And now they were offering to share some of that happiness with her, how could she justifiably refuse?

And so, she had gone with them, leaving Bella and Mallory back at the Towers.

At first, it had been utterly worth it. The rock pool was so picturesque, she felt like she'd stepped into a painting. All around, the duskspores hovered, illuminating the forest in their gentle glow, but here at the pool the air was clear. Johanna could look straight up and see fluffy clouds billowing in a bright blue sky. And the constant tipple of water created an atmosphere of tranquil peace.

"Try this."

She looked around at Markus, offering her something in his fingertips.

"It's just a small piece," he said reassuringly.

"What is it?" she asked, when she should have said *No, thank you.*

"A hoomie," he said, and bit his lower lip. "But it's a mild one. I made sure."

Since when were you *an expert on hoomies?* That's what she should have asked. But he was smiling now. He'd never looked more handsome. And Karly was also smiling behind him, watching her from the corner of her eye, probably to see if she would take it or not. And instead of refusing again, Johanna said, "Not alone."

"No, of course not," Markus said, sounding offended. "Me and Karly will be right here with you. It's much better with company. We will enjoy it more if you join us, too." That smile again.

Johanna studied the tiny piece of mushroom in his

fingers. It was about the size of her thumb nail.

It's so small. Surely something so small couldn't affect me too badly.

Her lack of refusal hadn't gone unnoticed by Markus, who took it as an invitation to push her a little more.

"You want to, don't you?" he said, shuffling closer. He sat on the rock next to Johanna and held the hoomie in his palm, lifting it up to her nose so she could get a good look. "Inside this tiny little nugget is another world."

"Really?" she said, skeptical.

"It's true. And there's something about this place, the spring, I mean. It's coursing with attuned energy. I've seen it."

"How?" she said. Both of their voices were slowly lowering. "You can't *see* attunement."

He was on the cusp of whispering. "You can with this." He lifted it an inch higher.

She was staring down at it, regarding the little nobbly ridges. It was brown, speckled with black spots. A simple morsel.

"What will I see?" she whispered.

"Who knows?" he whispered back. "But I guarantee it'll be worth seeing. Join me, Johanna." He squeezed the hoomie chunk with his free hand and it broke into two even smaller pieces. He picked one half up and held it to his lips, waiting for her answer. Perhaps that was what tipped her over the edge. If he was going to eat the same piece as her, then perhaps they could have some sort of shared experience?

She realised with some surprise that she wanted to find out.

Moving quickly, afraid of changing her mind again, she took the piece left in his palm and popped it into her mouth. Markus grinned, tilted his head back and dropped his piece straight down his gullet, not even bothering to chew. "Just swallow it," he said. "They taste nasty."

She had already bitten into hers, and yes, it was foul. Her face screwed up in disgust, and she turned away from him, intending to spit it back out.

"Don't waste it!" he cried, placing a hand on her shoulder and gently, but urgently, turning her back around. "Wash it down with some water."

He scooped water in his palm and offered it to her.

It was such an intimate gesture, she felt her cheeks reddening instantly. She pursed her lips against the edge of his hand and he tipped it upward gently allowing her to take a gulp. She knocked the hoomie to the back of her throat with her tongue and swallowed it.

Johanna's heart thudded in her chest. She had never felt so nervous, so excited, so apprehensive, so… so… *naughty.*

She giggled.

"Wowzer!" Markus recoiled, turning to Karly. "It's working already! You ever seen it take so fast?" He laughed, and scurried across the rocks back to Karly.

"Yep, she's a goner!" Karly howled. "Better send word to the turnip farmers, tell them there's a muncher on the way!"

They both laughed, and Johanna became infected by it, giggling uncontrollably. "Stop it!" she said, blushing. "I can't believe I just ate that. How long does it take to start working?"

"Just relax," Karly said, letting her arms drift out as if floating on the surface of water. "And laugh if you need to. It's all good. Get comfortable, find something beautiful to look at, and get ready to ride the waves."

Johanna wriggled her butt, settling into the groove of the rock she was sitting on, straightened her back and folded her hands together in her lap.

"You call that *relaxing?*" Karly said, bursting into laughter again.

"It's my meditative pose," Johanna said. "This is very comfortable." She saw Markus offer Karly a hoomie now, and Karly winked at him, popped it into her mouth, then helped herself to two more from her little paper bag. Johanna gulped, wondering how much time it had taken for

Karly to build up a tolerance to these things, if she felt a need to take *three* full size ones at a time. She couldn't imagine ever taking more than one herself.

Then Markus took another one!

She felt mildly betrayed. Less than a season ago, Markus had been an awkward neighbour who could barely look Johanna in the eye when he talked to her. Now, he'd transformed into a carefree, happy-go-lucky hoomie-eater. Johanna wanted to be ashamed for him, but found herself feeling a touch of envy instead.

Stop it, she scolded herself. *Where did that giggle go? When this hoomie takes a hold of me, I want to be thinking of something happy, or funny, something that will give me a good experience, if I have one at all. The last thing I need is to have a bad trip on my first try…*

"Lookit!" Karly said, pointing towards the centre of the pool. Johanna followed her arm and saw the frog sitting on a lily pad.

Karly giggled, and said "Ribbit, *ribbit,*" imitating a frog, but it sounded exactly like a human badly imitating a frog.

Markus laughed and said, "That's terrible. Lemme show you." He cleared his throat and burped.

Johanna chuckled.

Karly cracked up. "And that's better is it?" she cried, slapping him playfully on the arm.

"It's better than yours!" he said defensively.

"You're both terrible," Johanna said. Her head was swimming lightly. She wondered if the hoomie was starting to affect her, and felt an urge to demonstrate her frog impersonation before it carried her away. She lifted a finger in the air, looking at them both with a sheepish grin on her face. "*Ree-bit. Reeee-bit.*" She croaked like a frog so well that the frog on the lily pad turned its whole body and looked at her.

Karly and Markus stared for a beat of stunned silence and then burst out laughing. They fell over on their backs, clutching their sides in hysterics.

Johanna laughed too, splashing her feet in the water and kicking up droplets. The world seemed to be slowing down. The splashing water floated up in slow motion and rained down in a thousand tinkling droplets, sending gentle ring waves out from their points of impact, overlapping with each other.

Johanna was mesmerised by the sight. She stopped kicking and sunk deeper into the rock, which felt like a feather cushion under her butt. She stared at the frog, which stared right back, and it made her want to laugh. Her laughter came about ten seconds after she had thought to do it, which made her laugh even harder, but that laugh was delayed by at least twenty seconds.

"Hey guys," she said dreamily, hearing her own voice from far away, as if speaking through a fog. "Heyyy, guys," she said again, waiting for her brain to catch up with itself. She giggled again.

Markus and Karly were sitting upright now, looking across at her, both smiling and pointing. They looked so happy, so relaxed, their limbs had gone soft and droopy, and Johanna felt their floppiness mirrored on herself, as if her bones had turned to jelly.

"What is it, Jo?" Markus said. His voice sounded very normal. Far more normal than Johanna would have expected. It was as if he hadn't turned to jelly, after all, but was somehow still sober, totally himself.

"I think," Johanna started to say, but Karly spoke over her.

"You okay, Jo?" Then she laughed.

"Are you," Johanna started, but Markus interrupted her.

"I think she's—" And then he laughed.

"What's funny?" Johanna said.

"Stop talking over me, Jo!" Markus laughed again.

"I'm not, am I?"

"She's going in!" Karly said, whooping.

"Yes, you are! See, you did it again!" Markus said.

"I don't…" Johanna blinked. Her world turned black for

an unfathomably long time. "I don't feel so…"

She saw the frog again. It jumped off the lily pad and landed in the water with a splash. Except… no, it *didn't* reach the water. It had stopped in mid-air.

That doesn't seem right, Johanna thought to herself, almost seeing the funny side of a frog that could defy the laws of gravity.

Then the frog *rewound.* It arced backwards, landing back on the lily pad. Then it sprang forwards into the air again and froze.

Huh?

She watched the frog with intense curiosity. How was it doing that?

The frog's front feet almost reached the water, but then time seemed to move backwards and it returned to the lily pad.

"Why don't you jump in?" she asked the frog.

It tried again, but just as the tip of its front legs were about to plunge into the water, the frog zapped back again, returning to the lily pad.

Johanna shook her head. It sent an avalanche of rocks tumbling through her skull, making her monumentally dizzy.

"You are!" Karly said shrilly, still cracking up.

Johanna tried to turn towards her to ask what she was talking about, but found herself transfixed on the frog, unable to look away.

Time had become warped. Thoughts began to pile up in her mind, unable to make their way to their destination. She wanted to ask Karly and Markus if they could see the frog, and she also wanted to ask what Karly meant when she said "you are!", and she also wanted to tell them that she was fairly sure the hoomie had started to take effect, and she also wanted to ask Markus if he had lied about the hoomie being *just a mild* one because she really did feel weird right now, and more than anything else, what seemed the most important thing to Johanna right there and then was seeing that frog jump into the water, because it *clearly* wanted to jump into the water but no matter how many times it tried, time kept pulling it back onto the lily pad.

The frog tried again and wound up back on the lily pad.

The frog jumped again and ended up back on the lily pad.

It jumped again, and ended up on the lily pad again.

Just jump in! She sounded a little panicky, but after a while she realised that she hadn't actually said anything at all. The frog tried again, and failed again.

Johanna became more and more frustrated, but then something else was creeping in to override the frustration. A more troubling thought: *what if the frog* couldn't *jump in? What if time had actually become stuck?*

Yes. That's what must have happened. Time had ceased to progress. The frog could jump as many times as it liked, but it would *never* reach the water now, because time had stopped.

And Johanna was stuck here with it.

Oh Kella. I'm trapped.

"You are!" Karly cried.

The fear took her then.

She must have watched that frog attempt to jump into the water a hundred, no, a *thousand* times. Too many to count. She became vaguely aware of the rock pool around her and Karly and Markus's voices, nearby but a thousand wheels away at the same time.

"It's all right, Johanna," Markus said, reassuringly. "I won't let anything happen to you."

What could happen to me? Why would he say that? We were just sitting by the rock pool. Unless…

"You *are!*" Karly said again.

I'm trapped. And they know! They know because they are trapped here too. We're all trapped in time. Oh Kella, how did this happen? How can I get out?

"Markus!" she cried suddenly, and this time she heard it with intense clarity. For a brief moment, the frog disappeared from the lily pad. Not even a ripple on the water's surface marked its entry point. It was just *gone.*

But then something else took its place. Johanna saw clouds, and trees, but they were spinning. The trees and the clouds spun together, forming a colourful whirlpool that enveloped her vision, sucking her into it. And then she realised, with another snap of terrible clarity that she was probably dying. Maybe she had already died.

Yes. I'm dead! That was the only way to explain it. She must have had some terrible allergic reaction to… what was it again?

"It's all right, Johanna, we're here with you."

Markus! We're dead! We're both dead. How can you say it's all right? Why are you so comfortable about being dead?

"It's all right," he said again, reassuringly. He sounded so relaxed, so content with the situation. Johanna couldn't understand why, which sent her into an even deeper state of panic.

It's not all right! It's not, it's not, I'm dead, I'm dead, how can this have happened, oh Kella oh Kella…

The maelstrom took her.

Johanna floated into a whirlpool of colours as she felt herself spinning through time and space. Her brain felt like it would explode from the realisation that was hitting her: she was dead, so was everybody else, and yet, she had to live through it forever. Time no longer existed.

Slowly, acceptance came. Johanna accepted the fact that she was dead, and it made her want to cry forever, but what good was that? She had died, and so had everything else in the universe and there was nothing to do but ride out the intense loneliness and isolation with everyone else *because she is everyone else.*

She snapped.

The fear vanished, or reached such a concentrated pinprick of focus that it no longer mattered, she couldn't tell the difference between terror and ecstasy. Because if she really was dead, and that everything else was with her, waiting to be reborn, then surely she would eventually come back around and become happy again?

Infinity.

That was the word for it. *Infinity.*

YES, said a voice like thunder.

"Who's that?" she said, and heard her say it aloud.

ONE WHO KNOWS ETERNITY.

It was a deep, booming male voice, certainly not Markus, she had a vague idea that it must be Kella, but she somehow knew it couldn't be Kella, because if infinity truly was real, there could be no god like Kella, because in an infinite universe, there was no room for Kella and yet Kella was everything, that was the very definition of god, wasn't it? *Eternity. Infinity.*

I'M NOT A GOD, BUT I APPRECIATE THE COMPLIMENT.

"Where are you?" she said.

The maelstrom morphed into the Mana Spring.

Johanna was still sitting in the same place she had been before, but now her dangling feet were dry. She swivelled her heavy head around, feeling as though her neck had turned to solid stone, and her skull weighed as much as a house.

The actual spring was gone, and yet some shadow of its existence lingered. Where the water pool had been, now a cracked, dried up bed of mud lay.

And a dragon.

The dragon was sitting in the remains of the rock pool, its tail curled around its body, and its head at her eye level, staring right at Johanna.

YOU CAN SEE ME?

It was speaking telepathically in her mind, just as Sai Brockhurst had done when he showed them the card trick.

HOW CURIOUS, it boomed.

It snorted, a puff of black mist wafted out of its nostrils, and then… *scattered.* A high pitched buzzing sound went with it, as the cloud dispersed and Johanna realised, with a considerable amount of disgust, that it had exhaled a plume of nibbets. The flies took off in all directions, several buzzing right past Johanna's ear. She swatted them away with a heavy, rubbery hand, but they were already long gone by the time she lifted her hand to her ear.

IT'S NOT OFTEN I GET TO SPEAK TO A MORTAL, rumbled the dragon. BUT YOU CAN SEE ME, SO WHY NOT?

Two pairs of fangs jutted out of its jaws, and its long snout sloped up to its huge black eyes, which never left Johanna and didn't seem to blink. Its scaly skin was slate grey, shiny in places and translucent in others, she could see dark purple blood vessels beneath its skin. Its underbelly was pale and cream coloured, which streaked down from its neck and folded under its swollen belly. It looked sickly, the aura of the dragon reeked of decay and disease.

WHAT DO YOU EXPECT? The dragon laughed. It sounded like boulders grinding against each other, crumbling under the pressure. I FIND YOUR WORLD DISGUSTING, TOO. BUT THAT'S ONLY NATURAL, RIGHT?

Infinity, Johanna said to herself. *This creature can't exist, and yet it can because in an infinite universe,* everything *is possible.*

HEH, the dragon laughed again. YOU ALMOST HAVE IT, DON'T YOU? I FIND THIS HIGHLY AMUSING. WHY WOULD A MORTAL TRY TO COMPREHEND SOMETHING THAT WOULD LEAD TO ITS DESTRUCTION? BUT THAT IS THE MORTAL WAY, ISN'T IT? OH, HOW I ENVY YOUR KIND.

The dragon snorted again and a much bigger cloud of nibbets escaped, buzzing around its ears, which flapped nonchalantly, before the swarm scattered again, zipping into the air and away.

"I'm dead, aren't I?" Johanna said. She inhaled a long, deep breath of noxious air, not really caring, because she was dead, she could breathe in poison and it wouldn't make a difference, would it?

YOU DON'T LOOK DEAD TO ME, thundered the dragon in her head. Its body remained motionless, apart from the slow expansion and deflation of its bulbous belly, pressing against the cracked mud. Its tail tip gave a gentle wave in the cracked mud.

BUT IF YOU THINK YOU'RE DEAD, the dragon

continued. COULD YOU TELL ME WHAT IT'S LIKE?

Johanna frowned. A flurry of thoughts swept through her head all at once: *It's awful. It's the worst thing that could have happened. I wasn't ready to die, not yet. I'm only seventeen, I'm a virgin! I was attending Mage School, I was supposed to become a pyromancer, I didn't get to see my family again, didn't tell them how much I loved them, my mother, my father, my sister, they won't even know I'm dead until Winter's Feast when I was supposed to come home, but I won't be there. Being dead is the worst possible thing that could have ever happened to me!*

The dragon's head lifted up a fraction, and its eyes finally blinked. IT SOUNDS WONDERFUL TO ME.

"What?" Johanna said. Her voice sounded hoarse and ragged, completely out of breath.

OH, TO FEEL SUCH ANGUISH, SUCH TORMENT. YOU DON'T KNOW HOW TEDIOUS IT IS TO JUST EXIST. I'VE WATCHED YOUR KIND BEFORE, MORTALS SEARCHING FOR WAYS TO EXPAND THEIR LIVES, RECKLESSLY SEEKING THE CURSE OF IMMORTALITY.

"Curse?" Johanna rasped. "How could immortality be a curse? The world is so amazing and yet people die before they've even seen everything it has to offer. That's the saddest thing I could think of."

The dragon responded with another laugh, this one bitter and full of cynicism. It spoke again inside her head. YES! VERY SAD, I'M SURE! AND THEN THEY LEAVE THE WORLD, COMPLETELY FREE AND AT PEACE WHILE WE LINGER ON, FORCED TO WAIT UNTIL YOUR WORLD BECOMES A HUSK, AWAITING OUR CHANCE TO TRANSCEND SO THAT WE MAY DEVOUR WHATEVER'S LEFT AND START THE CYCLE OVER. OBLIVIOUS IGNORANCE: THE MORTAL WAY.

Johanna heard all of this and barely understood it. "So, you're actually immortal? As in, you can never die?"

ETERNITY! AN ETERNAL CYCLE OF PAIN, AN ETERNITY OF PLEASURE, AN ETERNITY OF BOREDOM, AN ETERNITY OF EUPHORIA, THIS IS WHAT IT MEANS TO BE IMMORTAL, AND YOU CANNOT POSSIBLY UNDERSTAND IT.

"No! I don't!"

I KNOW YOU DON'T, BECAUSE I WAS ONCE YOU, JUST AS YOU WERE ONCE ME, AND WILL BE AGAIN. YOU ARE ME, BUT YOU DON'T KNOW IT YET, JUST AS YOU WILL BE YOUR SISTER, AND YOUR FATHER, YOU WILL EXPERIENCE EXISTENCE AS A COMET DRIFTING THROUGH THE COSMOS, AS A BLADE OF GRASS, AS NOTHING AT ALL AND EVERYTHING AT ONCE. THAT IS INFINITY. DO NOT EVEN TRY TO FIGHT IT, BECAUSE IT IS SIMPLY THE TRUTH. ACCEPT IT, EMBRACE IT, OR BE DEVOURED BY IT.

"I… stop…please!"

Johanna's head felt ready to burst. The pressure had risen to boiling point and beyond, she felt like a whistling steam kettle hanging over a fire, that had its lid and spout welded shut, so no matter how hard she puffed, nothing would give until her head simply exploded like a bomb. But it just… wouldn't… give. The pressure mounted, somehow rising and rising, pressing against the inside of her skull with such force, she wondered how she could possibly still be conscious. *Is this hell? Have I already died? I have, haven't I? The dragon said that you feel endless pain, and that's what's happening to me now, I'm stuck here forever oh Kella, this is the end, I'm dead, I'm dead I'm dead I'm dead I'mdeadI'mdeadimdeadimdeadimdeaddeadeadeadededed—*

TYPICALLY DIM-WITTED MORTAL. The dragon sounded bored now.

The pressure didn't burst open her skull as she had feared, but it abruptly vanished. Johanna's fear evaporated with it. Where there was intense anxiety, suddenly there was room for curiosity. She *wished* to understand. What did it mean about *starting the cycle again*?

"What cycle?" she said.

The dragon lowered its head and closed its eyes. It seemed ready to fall asleep. Johanna suspected her arrival here had interrupted its nap.

YOU WOULDN'T UNDERSTAND EVEN IF I TOOK A CENTURY TO EXPLAIN IT.

"I have time," Johanna said with confidence.

The dragon yawned. A cloud of nibbets escaped and flew away.

It continued speaking to her telepathically. JUST CLOSE YOUR EYES AND IMAGINE TWO WORLDS OVERLAPPING ONE ANOTHER. ONE FEEDS THE OTHER. AS ONE WORLD DIES, THE OTHER THRIVES…

Johanna felt a bolt of lightning stab her through the skull. Somehow, she knew the dragon was unlocking her mind, injecting it with a memory from its own vault, and she clutched her head in agony, the pressure returning with tenfold vengeance.

But images appeared, and she saw a vision of overwhelming clarity.

She saw a ball, drifting through the gulf of space, surrounded by stars. At first it was grey and lifeless, but then colour spread across its surface, blue and green. *Oceans and land,* she thought. *The birth of a planet.* She had never seen anything so beautiful in all her life.

Wisps of cloud flew around the planet at lightning speed, materialising out of nothing before wilting away. As she watched, the clouds all evaporated and disappeared, the greenery faded to grey, then black, and the oceans dried up, until the planet looked like the dry, flaky mud that the dragon was sleeping in. An entire world, turned to ashes in the blink of an eye.

Then, just like the frog on the lily pad, the process reversed. She saw the planet rejuvenate, clouds rippled across its surface, and water returned to the oceans, the land erupted in bursts of green, spreading like a flood until the whole planet had returned to its wondrous splendour.

The sequence started over. She gaped in stunned silence, seeing the planet die and be reborn multiple times, until finally, she noticed something else. Whenever the planet became dead and desolate, there was movement. Creatures flying around it in a great flock. *Birds, perhaps? No, they're dragons!*

As the planet reached its apex of desolation, the number

of dragon's also reached its peak. Then, as the planet turned back into its lush, more appealing form, the dragons disappeared, until none were left.

Where do they go when the planet is alive?

She had a vague understanding that the dragon was showing her the planet that she lived on. Her home world. She existed somewhere down there, along with everyone she had ever known, everyone she would ever know, everyone who had ever *EXISTED*.

What a mind boggling realisation.

This was the sort of trip Karly had hoped for, surely.

Because— *oh yeah, that's right… I ate a hoomie, didn't I?*

Johanna laughed. It came out as a croaky cough.

"Jo!"

Johanna's head spun again, but this time it wasn't as terrifyingly nauseating as it had been before. She heard ragged breathing, hitching and gasping in wretched whoops.

Who's that, they sound terrible?

"Johanna! Oh Kella, is she going to be okay? Have you ever seen this before?"

It's Markus, Johanna tried to smile, but heard someone coughing so violently that she frowned instead.

"Yes, puke it up, thank fook," Karly said from far away.

Johanna's vision of the planet had disappeared without her noticing, and suddenly the sky came into focus, somewhere above her. Markus loomed into view, covering up the sky and looking down into her eyes with extreme panic written all over his face. Panic, but also relief.

"Johanna, are you okay? It's all right, you're safe now."

Johanna tasted bile. Her throat felt as if she'd been eating sawdust. She rolled over sideways and coughed, spitting out a phlegmy yellow globule.

"Uggh," she groaned. Her head span like a child's wooden top.

"Kella Murphy, Jo," Karly said. Johanna saw her standing waist deep in the rock pool, arms spread either side of Johanna's legs, which were still dangling in the pool. "I ain't never seen a reaction like that."

Karly looked sober and scared. Johanna felt a pang of guilt wash over her.

That *trip*, if that's indeed what had just occurred to her, was the scariest experience of her life, bar none. But suddenly, seeing Markus and Karly, she came to the startling realisation that they had *watched* her go through it. Whatever fear and pain she had been feeling, they had felt it too.

So we did share the experience after all…

She felt utterly sick, and very ashamed of herself. "I—I'm sorry," she croaked.

"No!" Markus said, shaking his head. "Kella, no, Johanna. *I'm* sorry. I'm *so* sorry. I never should have made you eat that."

Johanna shook her head. "I made the choice. Don't blame yourself."

They all took a moment to catch their collective breath.

After a long while, Karly summoned the courage to ask, "So, Jo… see anything interesting?"

Johanna choked out a laugh. "Yeah. I saw the end of the world." She frowned, remembering a conversation with some huge, immortal creature. "Oh, and I met a dragon."

CHAPTER TWENTY

"You saw a *dragon*?" Garrod leaned forwards across his grand superoaken desk, wondering if he had misheard her.

"Yes, Sai. Yesterday." Johanna bit her lower lip as she stood between the other two pupils.

"Sai Brockhurst, I feel obliged to point out we weren't exactly sober," Markus said.

Garrod, whose mind was still echoing from his own encounter with the dragon, only had ears for Johanna. The taste of immortality lingered. Now he lusted for more. "Where? What did it look like?"

"It was just a hallucination," Karly insisted.

"*Quiet!*" Garrod hissed.

"It felt real enough to me," Johanna said timidly. "We were at the Mana Spring when it happened." She glanced anxiously at the other two before continuing. "It was big. And greyish purple in colour. And it, um… it breathed nibbets."

He searched Johanna's face for any sign of a lie, and saw only nervous honesty.

"It was just a bad hoomie, Jo," Markus said patiently, as if trying to gently pull her out of the delusion.

"So what? You ate it too!" Johanna said. "I know what I

saw."

"Seeing shit is kinda the point," Karly said indignantly. "I saw a five headed flying turtle once, that doesn't mean-"

"Will you *hush*," Garrod interrupted, silencing them. *How is this possible? She opened a rift, this girl that couldn't even pick a card out of a mind a few days ago without my help. And not only that, she actually saw a rift dragon?* Jason had said there was a dragon nesting at the spring. This couldn't be a coincidence. "Please, Miss McKree, start from the beginning. Leave nothing out."

She explained her experience with the dragon as best she could. Garrod listened intently as the others picked at their food. He was hungry for any information that would help him understand the beast.

"Wait," he cut her off when she came to the part where it spoke. "What did it say to you?"

"It didn't speak, exactly," Johanna said, frowning. "I heard it in my head, like when you showed us the card trick."

"Yes, yes," he waved dismissively. "It's telepathic. But what did it say to you?"

"It spoke of two worlds on top of each other…" Johanna frowned, struggling to remember. "It talked in riddles, Sai, I was quite overwhelmed." She shook her head, and gave him a surprised look. "Wait, you believe me, don't you?"

"I do."

"Sai," Markus said, interrupting yet again. "With respect, *we* were there."

"Johanna just ghosted," Karly added.

Garrod glared them both to silence. They both sank back in their seats, looking sheepish and resigned. "Were you scared, Miss McKree?"

Johanna gave a quick, timid nod. "Very."

"Mm-hmm," Garrod said, nodding to himself. "I think you were able to see the dragon while your mind was stretched. And you two, you didn't see it?"

"No, Sai," they both said.

"Even when you touched her?"

They both frowned. Markus said, "What has that got to do with anything?"

Garrod inhaled a breath. "Because in my experience, that's how a rift works. The fact that she was able to open one by herself is what I find most curious."

All three of them spoke at once: "What's a rift?"

He cast his eye over them all, but settled on Johanna. "There is another plane of existence beyond this one, an alternate mirror world."

He let that sink in for a moment. Their stunned silence prompted him to continue.

"It's possible to go there via a gateway of sorts that only certain people have the power to open. My father coined these gateways *rifts*."

Johanna gasped. "And you think I somehow opened one? How do you know that?"

"Because of the dragon. Dragons and other beasts dwell on the other side."

"That's *awesome*," Karly said in a whisper.

"Hush your ignorant mouth," Garrod snapped, wiping Karly's grin off her face. "These are not the fanciful monsters of your childhood fairy tales. They are harbingers of destruction. A dragon came to Archdale when I was a child."

"That's incredible, Sai," Markus said, awed.

"I had no idea," Johanna added. Realisation dawned on her face. "The Archdale Calamity! It wasn't a plague, was it, Sai?"

"No, your history books are inaccurate. A dragon came, and it unleashed devastation that cost the lives of everyone in the city. My father, Mr Anders and I are the sole survivors of the calamity."

Karly raked both hands through her hair, mercifully at a loss for words.

Garrod leaned back in his chair, his mind racing with thoughts of meeting the dragon again. *Eternal life.* With endless time, he would understand everything. He *had* to go back. This thought mingled with his desire to rescue his father and the lust for justice for his home, a drought in his mind that he thirsted desperately to quench.

Garrod licked his lips.

For most of Garrod's life, Jason had worked to prove the existence of dragons, and earned nothing but scorn and ridicule from the higher attuned community because he could never prove it. But now Garrod had the proof he needed at his fingertips. And he didn't need a plethora of prisoners to access the rift anymore. He had three young, attuned minds right there at his disposal.

Jason had been a proud teacher who cherished his pupils. Garrod had the luxury of seeing the bigger picture, and found it easy to see these budding students as tools.

If only my father only had the wit to see their potential, he might have gained access to the rift years ago.

A plan formulated in his mind.

"We are going to open the rift again," he said at last. "And you're going to help me, my talented prodigies." His words referred to three of them, but his gaze lingered on Johanna alone.

"Why?" she said, the fear plain on her pretty face. She had a vulnerable, lost quality that Garrod found queerly pleasing to look at.

"To rescue my father. He is trapped there."

All three of them gasped.

"So he's not dead?" Johanna said, astonished.

"Does anyone else know?" Markus asked.

"A select few," Garrod said. "Now I feel is the time you should know, too. I need your help."

"He's trapped in that horrible place…" Johanna said in a tone of sheer horror.

"Don't be afraid," Garrod said calmly. "As I said to you before, we are only at the beginning of our journey as attuned beings." He tore his eyes away from Johanna and passed his gaze across the other two. "There are so many things we have yet to learn about the ways of attunement, and it will be many years yet until we fully understand all of its intricacies. My father would insist that we do this. He chose to stay there, in the hope of learning what he can about the dragons. We owe it to him, and to ourselves to follow his footsteps. Do you not agree?"

Markus and Karly nodded after a small hesitation. Johanna looked at the floor.

Garrod continued, "Dragons can open rifts by themselves, according to my father. This suggests that they are attuned in some way. They may be the most powerful wizards in existence."

"And we're going to meet them!" Karly gushed. She turned to Johanna rather sheepishly. "Sorry I doubted ya, Jo."

"Yeah," Markus added, scratching the back of his neck. "Sorry, Hanna."

"So then, we have the perfect practical lesson today," Garrod said. "You will help me open a rift, so that I can bring back the Prime. Nobody else can know about this yet, so we will conduct the ritual at the spring."

"The Mana Spring does possess some strong attunement properties, doesn't it?" Markus said.

"The dragon is there," Johanna said softly.

"Yeah, if I were a super advanced attuned being, I guess I would wanna sleep somewhere that could gimme a buzz," Karly said with a dreamy smirk.

"It's settled, then," Garrod said, rising to his feet with a satisfied smile. He gestured towards the door. "We shall go to the spring. Come."

"Sai, might I be excused?" Johanna said. "I don't think I'm up to it."

Karly and Markus stopped halfway to the door and looked back at their friend.

"You okay, Johanna?" Markus said.

"You two, wait for me downstairs," Garrod said.

"Okay," Markus said, offering Johanna a somewhat

nervous look.

Karly followed him out, and they shut the door.

Garrod waited until their footsteps had receded down the tower. Then he propped himself against his desk in front of Johanna.

"I'm sorry, Sai," Johanna murmured. Then, in a stronger voice, "I'm so sorry. I just can't go through that again. And if I may offer some advice, I don't think you should, either. Not at the spring."

"Why not?" His face was stone. "I do not fear the dragon. It is a marvel, something we can learn from. As one of my pupils, I expect you to thrive on the pursuit of knowledge."

Johanna frowned, and looked down at her hands. She muttered to herself, "*As one thrives, the other dies…*"

"What did you say?" Garrod said.

"The dragon talked about two worlds. It implied they were connected somehow."

"Yes," Garrod agreed. "I'm inclined to believe the other side is our own world, but from another time," he explained, remembering the mirrored version of Archdale, as if it had rested there for hundreds, perhaps even a thousand years, slowly crumbling.

"Really?" Johanna said, biting her lower lip. "That makes sense." She clenched one hand into a fist, and slowly encased her other hand around it so she was holding it. "The dragon said that I should imagine both worlds directly on top of each other. The dragon was sleeping in the Mana Spring. Only it was dried up, and some of the rocks had disintegrated away. But it was *definitely* still the spring. So it really could be our world, from another time, like you say. But… *as one thrives, the other dies.* Does one world feed off the other? That's horrible."

"It makes perfect sense," Garrod mused, speaking into his steepled fingers. "Our world is living. The other is dying. At least, that's the way we perceive it."

"Yeah," Johanna agreed, nodding. "It felt terrible there.

It looked dead, the trees were black and had no leaves. It felt like it hadn't rained for years."

"And yet, there is life," Garrod said. "The dragons dwell there. Among other creatures."

"That dragon reeked of death," Johanna said. "What creature can live with *nibbets* crawling around inside it? They *feed* on blood. That dragon was alive, and yet seemed like it could also be dead." She looked on the cusp of understanding something incomprehensible, the verge of madness. "I don't like thinking about this! I'm sorry about your father!" She stood abruptly, turning her back on Garrod and walking towards the door.

"Wait," Garrod ordered. "You are not dismissed."

She stopped, turning slowly back to look at him with that vulnerable, puppy-dog stare again.

"Please, Sai. I can't get this lingering darkness out of my head. I can still sense it if I try, but I don't want to. That dragon, it's not natural, not to us. I fear that it could have, well, *kill* is not a strong enough word. I think it could have *destroyed* me if it wanted to. It was toying with me, it even said I amused it, just by talking to it. But then it grew bored, Sai. That was the most terrible part. It grew *bored*, and showed me a vision, oh Sai, I don't think I will ever be able to get that awful vision of a dying world out of my head for the rest of my life. It will haunt my nightmares."

"So you now have a terrible memory to use," he said, remembering the day he first met her and told her about utilising memories as fuel for her spells.

She scoffed a short, uncomfortable laugh. "Yes, I certainly do."

Garrod nodded again slowly, pondering his options. He could open the rift with the other two students, he was quite sure. But like Herbert, they would probably break before long. With a third, and especially one as attuned as Johanna, he would have more success. "Is there no way I can convince you to come with us?" he said at last.

She hesitated. "I want to, Sai. But I need time, I think.

Just a day or two's rest. Could you give me that?"

"My father may not have that long." He gritted his teeth. She was not going to go willingly.

What are you prepared to sacrifice to get what you want?

His father's voice echoed in his mind and Garrod knew the answer.

He looked around the chamber, and his eyes fell upon the door that led to his bedroom. Nobody would dare enter it without his permission. It would serve. "Johanna," he said, looking her in the eye again. "How is your mind's vault coming along?"

"It's um… a work in progress," she smiled shyly.

"May I see it?"

She hesitated, then nodded once.

He mentally reached out and walked into her mind in a single step.

You forgot what I taught you, didn't you? He spoke in her mind with a calm disappointment.

In the physical world, Johanna's eyes bulged as she sensed his intent before he even had a chance to express it in words.

Relax. It won't hurt. But I will grant your rest, as requested. Walk.

He pointed towards his chamber door, and Johanna turned like a puppet on a string. She staggered over to the door and went inside. He followed her, picking up a duskfruit from Johanna's plate as he passed.

I told you not to let anybody into your mind. Look what can happen when you do. He bit into the juicy fruit.

He made her stop at the foot of the bed. She stared it, each breath hitching her chest with tense jerks.

You need to learn how to defend yourself against external attacks. Can you imagine *what a wizard of a less savoury nature than myself could do to a pretty young girl like you in this position? It is unthinkable.*

He made her turn around and face the wardrobe. A huge, double-doored oaken box almost as high as the ceiling. It would be a dark but spacious cage for her until he returned. If Karly and Markus let him down, he would be able to try again with Johanna. If he succeeded, and truly ended up without a use for her… well, he could cross that bridge later. Either way, Johanna McKree had seen her last sunrise.

She turned the knob on the grand door and swung it open. She stepped inside, and squeezed in between his robes.

Sleep!

She collapsed. As she did, Garrod shut the door, to stop her from spilling out. He turned the key to lock it shut and put it in his bedside drawer.

He calmly finished his duskfruit, eating around the hard stone. As he chewed, he mulled over his long robes and thick boots. *Why should I hide myself anymore?* This was his body now. It seemed absurd to have to hide himself from his own students. He was the Prime, after all. His body was a testament to the powers of attunement, a marvel to behold, and one that the students might be inspired by. He considered walking outside bare-chested, allowing every student to see his glorious wings. It would feel great to be free.

Not yet. Perhaps after.

Markus and Karly were waiting in the courtyard. Several students milled around, pretending not to watch.

Garrod joined his two pupils and gave a short bow. "Thank you for waiting."

Markus gave an apprehensive nod. He asked, "Um, Sai, where did Johanna go?"

"She needed to be alone. I allowed her to remain in my chamber to read my father's research. I hope she can find his notes on the dragon useful."

"Oh," Markus said, relief washing over his face. "That sounds like a good idea. She'll feel better with a book for company, that's for sure."

"Indeed," said Garrod. "Now, let's get to the spring,

shall we?"

***

In truth, Garrod had several reasons to open a rift at the spring. The first was simply because that was where Johanna had seen the dragon, and he lusted to see it again. The other reasons were more practical: firstly, he knew the spring's attunement properties might aid in healing his father when he brought him back through the gateway. He intended to bathe his father's rotting body in the pool the moment he had him safely through. The final justification was to save the embarrassment of asking Robert to dispose of two more cadavers. Perhaps Markus and Karly would survive, but if they didn't, at least they would be far enough away from the Towers to pose no immediate threat of being discovered.

They arrived at the bubbling spring, which was cool and shaded from the afternoon sun. Garrod surveyed the clearing, which was surrounded by thick superoaks in every direction. Secluded, private, perfect. He clenched his teeth, glancing at the rockpool, imagining the dragon sleeping in it on the other side.

"Stand there, and there," he ordered, desperate to get on with it.

They formed a triangle around the spring's pool, Markus and Karly standing at equal distance away from Garrod, who took up a position near the outlet that spilled away into the forest.

"So, how do we open a rift, Sai?" Karly asked eagerly.

Garrod inhaled a deep breath. "With pain."

He attacked their minds simultaneously. Markus put up no resistance. Karly, who had apparently taken his homework task more seriously than the others, surprised him with a brief moment of resistance that felt like pushing through a sturdy wooden door. With a trivial push of force, he barged his way in, shattering the door to splinters and took control of her mind. He dug out a nasty memory of

Karly's mother being raped by a drunken guard. She had been dancing at a seedy establishment in the city, and was taking a shortcut through an alley when the guard cornered her. Forcing the memory to play in Karly's conscious on repeat sent the kid into a frothing fit on the ground, her eyes bulging up at the sky.

He found no such memory in Markus's brain, so simply shoved the same one from Karly across to him, switching her mother for his own. The shock of witnessing his dear mother as a stage girl as well as being brutally forced upon snapped his pathetic mind like a twig. He cried out in anguish, falling to his knees and clutching his head in both hands as he tried to pull his own hair out.

The rift opened on cue.

Garrod sensed it before he could physically see it, and when Karly and Markus both stared ahead, gazing into the centre of the pool, he knew it was opening for them both.

He strolled around the rockpool and laid a hand on Karly's shoulder. Just like that, he saw the rift himself.

A shimmering black dome floated over the water.

Garrod shrugged out of his robe and stretched his wings. He took flight and soared into the gateway.

He emerged in the decayed ruin of the Mana Spring inside a sorry version of the magnificent Everdusk, inhaling a cloud of the dry, dusty air. There was no sign of the dragon, but Garrod could see a bulbous indentation in the mud where it must have been laying.

Nevermind. Go now before the rift closes.

He set off south, soaring low just above the tree husks until he came to the Towers. He flew right into the open window of the Sun Tower, and lying curled up on the floor was a bony, frail figure.

"Father!" Garrod cried, falling to his knees beside him.

Jason Brockhurst croaked a feeble cough and tilted his head to look at his son. "Garrod…"

"Don't speak, conserve your energy. I'm here to save you."

"Why?" he croaked, even managing to imply that he didn't need saving.

Garrod shook his head dejectedly. A quote came to him in a rush, taken directly from one of his father's own research journals. "Even in the face of dire tragedy, one must strive to follow their dreams."

Jason's eyes widened a little at this.

"You wrote that, father," Garrod said. "The day after I was born. After you lost mother."

"I did," he said, nodding almost imperceptibly.

"Even when you had lost the woman you loved, you never abandoned your dream of becoming the wisest wizard in the province. When I read that, I understood so much about my own childhood. Why you weren't always there for me. Why I spent so many days in the care of others. I hated you for it, for the longest time. But not anymore. I understand now, Father."

Jason reached a shrivelled, skeletal hand towards Garrod's face and caressed his cheek. "My son…" He coughed.

"Come with me, Father. I am getting you out of this wretched place."

He scooped his father up in his arms and carried him to the window.

As they both gazed out, a winged creature flew right past.

A dragon.

"Ack!" Jason sputters, his weak grip suddenly jerking to iron around Garrod's neck, as he points with the other hand out towards the flying monster.

Garrod understands something else in that moment. The power radiating from the dragon is almost overwhelming. It feels like its very essence is *made* of attunement itself. He feels its pull, and is drawn to it like a nibbet to a naked flame. He almost drops his father, thinking about stepping out of the window to chase after it, when his father's croaky voice pulls him back to the moment.

"Go to it!" Jason croaks, still pointing at it. "*Take me to it!*"

Garrod adjusts his grip on his father's frail, stinking body and tears his eyes away from the dragon. "Yes, Father. Hold on."

He steps out, cradling Jason in his arms and flaps his wings, beating them hard and fast, pulling them into the sky. Jason wails in mad desperation as they follow in the dragon's wake, heading for the Mana Spring. Garrod sees the rift, a shimmering black haze in the middle of the circle of brittle boulders.

The dragon banks to the right above the spring, and spins around to face them.

YOU AGAIN?

The dragon's voice is like thunder in his mind, all-encompassing, world-breaking in its baritone.

Garrod cuts a sharp turn to avoid colliding with the dragon.

Jason reaches out to grab the beast, and Garrod fumbles his grip, dropping him. He miraculously manages to grab his father by the shoulder with a talon, and Jason dangles there over the rift, as Garrod and the dragon begin to circle it above the trees. Jason continues to reach for the dragon with outstretched arms, like a baby stretching for a bottle.

The dragon is bulbous and monstrous, yet flies with the grace of a bird. It looks wrong, Garrod feels queer looking at it across the space between them.

A FLYING HUMAN. THAT IS SOMETHING.

Garrod utters a hysterical laugh.

KEHKEHKEHKEH.

Is it laughing, too?

YOU'RE THE SECOND MORTALS I HAVE SEEN HERE IN AS MANY SUNRISES.

A vivid clarity hits Garrod as he stares at the wondrous creature, hearing its thunderous voice inside his mind is like a deep-tissue massage compared to the screeching, hissing voice of that wretched bird Corcubus. He feels like he could listen to the dragon for the rest of his life.

Forever, Garrod thinks. *For eternity.*

"Immortality, son," Jason wheezes, as if reading his mind. "Wondrous!"

A flash of fear jolts through him. Why would he want that? That wouldn't be good at all. Forever is so final, impossible to take back.

And yet.

He sees Archdale in his mind, ruined and desolate.

"This is the same creature," Garrod says with certainty. He doesn't know how he knows, but this is the same dragon that destroyed their home. He is certain.

"Yes," Jason agrees. "Thirty years, son! I found it!"

Another, even more terrifying thought comes to him, and Garrod is vaguely aware that the thought isn't coming from his own subconscious, but somehow he is pulling notions out of the dragon itself. Or even *more* terrifying, the dragon is *feeding* him notions. Intricately complicated ideas, almost impossible to comprehend, so many of them at once, making him feel dizzy and lost.

The one tangible thought that he manages to pick out of the insane jumble is that this is *not* the same dragon that destroyed Archdale. And yet somehow, it is. Two contradictory ideas, theoretically impossible, and yet undeniably true.

"A hive mind," Jason babbles. "A connected conscious. "Immortal beings that share each other's experiences, their wisdom, their pain, their joy, their memories." He is bawling as he says this. Tears spill from Jason's cheeks and tumble into the rift below. "Here is a single entity, a dragon, ancient beyond the count of years, a creature that perceives its life not in days, months and years, but in *planetary cycles*, each one lasting a *billion* years or more."

KEH.

The knowledge this creature possesses. I must have it.

Garrod telepathically reaches out to the dragon, hoping to catch a glimpse of its thoughts.

And his mind begins to unravel like a spool of yarn.

He will lose himself soon. Perhaps he already has.

He makes a move to fly towards the dragon. A part of him wishes to bring it through the rift with him, in the hope of assimilating it, like he did with Corcubus.

NO, HUMAN.

Garrod goes rigid in mid-air and his flight falters. He drops Jason, then plummets down after him.

"Nooooo!" Jason wails, his arms rigidly stretched out in front of him, as he plunges into the void and disappears. Garrod falls through a moment later.

Splash!

He spluttered and flapped his arms and wings in the cool water, staggering to his feet and gasping a huge intake of fresh Everdusk air.

A cacophony of jumbled, jittering noises ricocheted around in his head, *kehkehkehkeh*. His arms and legs seized, and he became paralysed, stuck standing in the knee-deep pool, watching his father's convulsing body floating face down in the water. Markus and Karly had collapsed on the rocks, blood dripped from their nostrils and ears, eyes rolled back in their heads showing nothing but the whites.

He was frozen rigid while his mind slowly snapped pieces of itself back together.

Eventually, Jason Brockhurst stopped convulsing. He floated in the water just out of reach.

Garrod could do nothing but watch and wait for the paralysis to wear off.

"Are you okay?" a soft voice said from behind.

Garrod tried to answer, tried to turn around, tried to see who was there, but he was powerless to move. With a monumental effort, he managed to twitch one of his wings, but no more.

From the corner of his eye, he spied movement. A trio of dark furry shapes darted between the trees. He had enough of his senses to ponder why a bunch of dogs were running through the Everdusk, but then an echo of the dragon's laughter hammered his mind again and he let out a grim moan.

At last, Garrod was able to reach out and touch his father's leg. He pulled him closer, and turned him around in the water.

Jason's eyes were bulging like hard boiled eggs, his mouth stuck open like a gaping fish, his blackened tongue lolled out, and flakes of skin peeled off his cheeks and floated in the water. He had the rotten look of a man that died weeks ago, yet only a matter of minutes had passed.

Jason Brockhurst, the true Prime, was dead.

Garrod ejected a painful, low pitched scream through gritted teeth, his face contorted in a twisted grimace. The dragon had done this. Whatever spell it had cast on Garrod to paralyse him had cost him his father's life. He had never felt so humiliated, so enraged.

"I will end you for this," he snarled, his voice a savage, hoarse whisper.

He had never been angrier. He willed a rift to open so he could fly up to the beast and drag it into the rift and assimilate and destroy it. He had no greater desire than that now.

But the rift didn't open.

He inhaled ragged, juddering breaths for several moments, shaking his head and squeezing his father's corpse.

"*Open!*" he cried, spittle flying from his lips. *"OPEN!"*

But the rift eluded him.

"*Aaaaaarrgh!*"

As he screamed, he took to the sky, leaving his father behind.

Up he flew. Higher and higher, until he reached the clouds. He pumped his wings harder and harder, screaming all the way. His screams echoed down across the Everdusk, sounding more like a death wail of an injured extinct bird than a man. He sounded like a dying condor.

Garrod reached an altitude where breathing became

difficult. It triggered a dizziness that threatened to knock him out, but with the lack of oxygen came a moment of clarity.

I can still open the rift because I prepared for this. I can use her.

And down he went again.

CHAPTER TWENTY-ONE

Ellie and her pack of strays spent three days and nights terrorising the road from Darune to Edgehurst. Riding bareback on top of Arkarus, she was able to cover great distances much faster than on foot, and together they hunted a deer for the pack to eat. She spit-roasted chunks of venison over a campfire while the dogs encircled the carcass and stripped it down to the bones. Nothing was wasted. She cleaned the deerskin and sold it to a tanner in the nearest hamlet, who gratefully wished her fortune on the road to the Everdusk.

Whenever Arkarus was being projected in the physical world, Ellie found her mind invaded by many cheerful, scrappy voices – those of the strays she had unwittingly rescued from the city streets. She became adept at distinguishing them from one another, and even gave them all names.

First there was Whisper, the quiet collie with matted brown fur, who never barked, but had incredible eyesight and a sense of smell that outmatched any of the others, second only to Arkarus.

There was Nipper, a Jack-Russell terrier that seemed to think he was as large and tough as Arkarus, despite sounding like an angry chipmunk whenever he barked.

Lappy only had one eye, and liked to rest with her head in Ellie's lap. She was utterly useless at hunting, but adorable when it came to napping.

The biggest stray in the pack was a lean and muscled brown furred ridgeback. He had deep, wise eyes and his bark sounded like a giant pounding a drum. He had taken on the role of being Arkarus' second-in-command, and Ellie was very fond of him, so she called him Frank.

Rounding out the pack were a scattering of flea-bitten lovable mutts she called Moppet, Gunther, Cliff, Lola, Wilson, Mo, Fuzzy, Derek, Toma, Spot, the twins Fang and Bang, Vee, Jay, Kay, and Dug.

When they all howled together, every living creature within a two mile radius either pricked its ears to listen or ran away. The cacophony was music to Ellie's ears. She howled with them, nowhere near as loud as Arkarus or Frank, but coming in around sixth or seventh, somewhere between Toma and Derek. Whisper always lifted her muzzle to the sky during this nightly song, but no sound ever came out.

"You lost little souls," Ellie said one evening, as she lay on her side among them, a fire gently crackling, illuminating her suntanned skin and reflecting in her bright blue eyes. "Good thing we came along when we did, eh?" She scratched Lappy's head, and she opened her eye and wagged her tail.

Ellie had picked out fragments of their individual stories bit by bit, using her telepathy whenever Arkarus was being projected. She had seen how Lappy lost her eye, and nothing had made Ellie feel so revolted in her life. She intended to go back to the city and find the guard that had thought it appropriate to swing a spear at a dog who was only looking for scraps of food under the tables outside a tavern.

Similarly, Fuzzy had suffered a terrible burn when a thoughtless washerwoman had tossed her basin of scalding water from a second storey window into the alleyway without first checking to see if anybody was down there. Poor Fuzzy had been taking a nap and the bulk of the water had landed right on top of him. He lost a lot of his fur, but the parts that had grown back were ragged, clumpy, and well, fuzzy.

Every dog had a similar story nestled in its mind, and Ellie pulled them out one by one, seeing them in her mind's eye as if they were her own memories.

"Some people are arses," Ellie said quietly, rolling onto her back to look up at the stars. Lappy adjusted herself so that her chin found its way into the nook of Ellie's pelvis, a comfortable position for both of them.

They were camped in an empty field a short walk from the road. Arkarus was sprawled out behind Ellie's head, doubling up as a soft pillow and night watchman. As long as her head was touching him, he could stay projected indefinitely.

"G'night guys," Ellie said, and closed her eyes.

***

She reached the Everdusk on a dim, grey, overcast day. The pack entered the woods via the road and followed it as far as they could. Ellie anticipated nightfall to force them to stop and find shelter eventually.

But nightfall didn't penetrate the trees.

"I guess this is why they call it the Everdusk!" Ellie said brightly, admiring the floating little glowing firebug things that seemed to be absolutely everywhere. "The whole place is infested," she said with a grin, enjoying her opportunity to use a detestable word for something that was actually rather beautiful. She liked to do things like that, especially within earshot of her sister, who took words so seriously.

The pack made it deep into the forest without meeting any other travellers along the road.

"I guess they weren't lying about my sister's college being hidden," Ellie mused out loud. Fang and Bang gave her a nonchalant glance from her right as she rode atop Arkarus, the rest of the pack spread out in a jumbled scatter on either side. "You smell any wizards yet?"

All of the dogs were loping along at an easy pace, relaxed and at ease. So it was quite a surprise to Ellie when all of a sudden, she heard twenty voices all suddenly say,

WASSAT?

Every dog, and Arkarus, halted dead and turned their heads to the right. Ellie nearly toppled off him, but clung on to the scruff of his neck.

"What is it?" she whispered, following their gaze, squinting through the luminescent haze.

She could see nothing of note. Just trees. Big ones, all of the trees here were giants, but she saw no movement other than the little fireflies.

"Let me see," she said to Arkarus, dismounting and sliding along his body to his muzzle. He gave a little whine. "Come on, I'll let you back out as soon as I know what it is."

His four eyes lingered for a moment in the direction of whatever had spooked them all, but then he dropped his head and loped into Ellie's chest. He was so big now that he had to hunch in order to fit, like a tall person ducking under a door.

As soon as Arkarus was inside his barnyard, the voices of the other dogs receded and Ellie's sense of smell was invaded by a multitude of scents. She could smell faint traces of a squirrel that had passed by, the musk of bird droppings hidden in the grass, pollen from the various flowers that grew between the superoaks, the ripe odour of twenty stray dogs and of course her own sweat, which always seemed so overpowering compared to when she only had her own nose to rely on.

And then came the sounds. Every rustle of every branch became sharper and defined, she could even hear the direction of the wind before the gust reached her, something she could never do with her human ears.

And there, in the direction the whole pack was looking, she heard footsteps.

Rst…rustle…rst…rustle…

Four legs. Quite heavy. Perhaps a stag. Or something bigger.

Lappy whined. She clearly heard the sound, and was anxiously peering around, as if searching for a place to hide. She crept silently up to Ellie's leg and pressed her neck against it, her ears pricked forwards towards the sound of the footsteps.

Ellie estimated the unseen creature to be about sixty feet away. They should see it any second… now.

Between a pair of gargantuan tree trunks, a lumbering animal's head appeared. It had a big black nose, a clump of stiff whiskers, and a stubby snout. Its midsection was huge, rotund, covered in a coarse bristle of fur, folded over a bulbous body. Its legs were short and muscular, reminiscent of the wide tree trunks that populated this forest. As the head and body disappeared behind the next trunk, Ellie expected to see its tail would also be short and plump, but it seemed to go on forever, dragging behind it like a huge, furry carpet. It was pointed at the end.

She had no idea what sort of animal it was. Never in her dreams had she seen such a beast. Its closest resemblance was to that of a bear, but it was much longer, and had too short a legs. And that tail would look right on some breed of lizard, if it was scaly instead of covered in fur.

So, it's some kind of bear-gator?

That'll do.

She gulped. Bears weren't exactly friendly, and gators were even less so. Ellie decided that they had better leave it alone, but the pack apparently decided otherwise.

"Ruff!" barked five of them at once, followed immediately by most of the others. Fang and Bang led the charge, followed straight away by Frank and Whisper, then every other mutt was bounding into the forest after them.

"No!" cried Ellie. "Leave it alone!"

She gave chase. Arkarus yipped and barked in her mind, so she opened her arms and projected him out. He landed in front of her, and Ellie vaulted up onto his rear to mount him like a horse, and the pair charged into the forest towards where the bear-gator had been.

Ellie and Arkarus chased after the pack, listening to their yips and excited barks for what felt like a few dozen wheels, which wasn't easy now that they had left the beaten track. Arkarus weaved between great trunks and had to leap fallen logs and scrubby bushes. She didn't even see so much as a glimpse of the bear-gator, and soon lost sight of most of the pack as well. Lappy and Nipper stayed close to Arkarus at least, but the others had scattered into the woods in a blind frenzy. Ellie feared she might lose them in the forest, and a sudden panic came to her at the thought of the bear-gator eating any of her new canine companions.

"*Frank!*" she called, her voice quickly swallowed up by the thickness of the forest.

A long howl came back, somewhere ahead.

They hurried on, passing between the trees and came to a slow moving stream that cut a path into the mossy ground. It flowed a meandering route and led away back towards the road, after coming from somewhere deeper in the woods.

After following it upstream for a short while, she found Toma, Wilson and Lola lying on their sides breathing raggedly. "Kella Murphy," she cursed. "You silly things, running off like that." She dismounted from Arkarus and bent to examine them. No injuries, thank Kella. Just worn out. "Where're the others?" She looked around, but saw no sign of them. Arkarus loped out of sight into the trees, sniffing the air. "Bring them back, boy," she called after him.

She glanced around, and decided this quiet clearing was as good a place as any to take a rest. The stream cut a clear segment of trees in either direction, making her voice carry far into the woods. She gave a loud whistle, calling to her pack, and repeated this every few minutes. One by one, some of them returned, but she was still missing over half by the time Arkarus staggered back, panting heavily and dragging his paws.

"Here, boy," she said, laying a hand on his head. The effect was instant, and he perked up, but she could tell he needed more sustenance. "Get inside for a while," Ellie said. He obeyed, lifting his head and pressing it into her core. He faded away and seemed to be pulled into her without needing to move his legs. Ellie wondered briefly at that, shaking her head in bewilderment at these strange, unexpected powers that she had acquired, accepting them the way a young mind can, but still having no real understanding of it.

Lappy went to the stream and bent her head to have a drink.

"Good idea," Ellie said and kneeled down to have some herself.

Lappy snorted violently and shook her head.

Ellie had a palmful of water halfway to her mouth, but stopped to see what the matter was. "What is it, girl? Bad water?"

Lappy's tongue hung out and flapped against the side of her face as she shook her head once more, trying to rid herself of whatever she had tasted.

Ellie gave the water in her palm a sniff, and with Arkarus' extra strong nose to help her, sensed something foul. She dropped the water and shook her hand dry, then stood back up. Lappy looked up at her with what could only be described as grumpy irritation on her face, her one eye almost scowling just like a human. Ellie snorted a laugh and said, "Let's follow it upstream and see what's wrong. Probably just a dead rabbit or something."

Keeping a watchful eye out for the bear-gator, and her unruly pack of hounds, Ellie followed the stream deeper and deeper into the woods. Occasionally, another dog returned. Dug scurried up, drooling and slathering, licked her hand and then bounded away again out of sight. Toma appeared from *behind* Ellie and gave her and Lappy a fright, before loping on ahead with her nose sniffing the ground, following the stream for a while before turning off right. She caught a glimpse of Fang and Bang chasing a squirrel, and Derek chasing the twins.

"Well, they're all still nearby, even if I can't see them all," Ellie supposed. She continued upstream until she spied the source of the river ahead. There was a rock pool with a spring jutting out of it.

And… there was a man standing in the water.

"Hey look, someone—" She trailed off, as she noticed something very, very wrong about him. He was stood rigid in the centre of the pool. At first she thought he had been attacked by a huge bird, but then it became apparent that the wings were sticking out of his own back.

What is that?

Two figures lay slumped over on the rocks. Ellie gasped at the sight of blood trickling down their faces. They could have been sleeping, but Ellie, who had seen her father die in front of her, knew better.

Whatever strange ritual was going on there, she didn't want to get involved. There were stories about the Everdusk which even Ellie had heard about. The place was ancient and mystical, no wonder the wizards had built their college here. Watching that strange, winged man standing in the pool, she had no doubt that he was a wizard, and the two—wait, *three* bodies, she saw another lying face down in the water – suggested that he was a dangerous wizard. Better to avoid being seen if she could.

She veered off to her left, meaning to pass by the spring altogether, when Arkarus caught a scent of something. Sharing her mind, he was able to pick out fragments of her memories, which included the scent of her sister Johanna.

"She was here, wasn't she?" Ellie whispered, eyes widening.

She looked back towards the rock pool, approaching from behind and to the strange winged man's left, out of his eyesight. He was still as a statue, rigid as stone. It frightened

Ellie.

Then she recognised him. Even from behind and without his dark wizard robe, she remembered the wizard that had visited Harbrook to see Tabitha Henlowe and recruited Johanna into the college. What was his name again?

She could see the bodies better now. The two on the rocks didn't look much older than her. The one in the water might have been an older man. Hard to be sure, though.

Wait… one of the bodies. Ellie took a second glance at the boy on the right, lying on his back, dead eyes staring blankly up at the sky.

"Markus!" she wheezed a startled breath. She rushed to him and knelt on the rock to get a closer look. She began to reach for his face, with the intention of checking his breathing, but the sight of his pale, lifeless skin and dried blood oozing down his cheeks from each ear confirmed her fears. Dead.

She lifted both hands to her mouth to halt a shuddering sob from escaping. She looked again to the paralysed wizard in the pool, standing with his back to her, those disturbing black wings protruding from his spine, and shuddered again.

Maddeningly, the empathetic part of her that had manifested as a direct result of being raised in Harbrook, where people looked out for one another, bubbled to the surface as she looked at him. Despite her plan to flee without being noticed, she heard herself say in a soft but concerned voice, "Are you okay?"

The wizard made no reply, and the only sign of movement was a twitch of one wing, barely perceptible.

A dog barked in the distance.

Fool! He's probably the one who killed Markus! Get out of there!

Ellie scrambled to her feet and fled into the woods, following Johanna's scent away from the spring. Her rag-tag pack of mutts followed in a scattered frenzy.

A thousand thoughts reeled through her mind. What was that man up to in the pool? Why was he paralysed like that? Had he really killed Markus and those other two people? If so, why? And what of Johanna? Could Johanna…

These troubled musings vanished when she spied a conical rooftop rising up among the treetops. *That must be one of the towers!* A shiver of excitement rippled through her. She had made it! Harbrook to Trinity Towers, all in under a fortnight. Johanna was somewhere inside the grounds. She had to be.

Ellie faltered when she came to the Towers' boundary. A green wall loomed up before her, but it was *moving*. Half swaying, half jostling, it appeared to be made up of many individual vertical pieces. As she approached she squinted, trying to figure out what it was made of, slowly realising with a considerable level of horror.

Gigantic plants. Plants that had teeth.

The entire wall was a thick growth of giant lillysnappers blocking her way, and Johanna's scent ploughed straight on towards it.

Ellie stopped some distance from the wall, eyeing it warily. As she took tentative steps closer, she saw the plants' behaviour shift, and the ones closest started to *lean* towards her. Their leafy heads didn't have any visible eyes, but she had the disquieting feeling that they could still see her, or perhaps sense her presence. Three of the monstrous things lunged at her, opening their salivary maw of needles and snapping with vicious intent.

The dogs yipped and barked at the plants, clearly agitated. The plants reacted in kind. They started spitting a thick, acidic gloop which singed the grass when it struck. A globule landed on Dug's back, who yelped in fright and bolted into the woods.

"Stop!" Ellie cried, realising the danger her pack were in. "Stay back! Lappy, no!"

But everything was happening too fast for Ellie to control.

Lappy, in her frenzy to defend Ellie from the attacking plants, braved forward barking as loudly as her little jaw allowed. One of the hulking plants bent forwards, opened its drooling maw and snapped closed around the small dog.

"*Lappy!*" Ellie cried.

The lillysnapper raised its head, violently chomping twice, creating a sickening sound of crunching bones. Then it settled back in its spot in the wall as if nothing had happened.

A flash of terrible anger crashed over Ellie, and she unleashed a flurry of arrows at the snapper's neck, firing shot after shot into its stem, but the lillysnapper barely reacted. If it felt the arrows at all, it made no sign. The other snappers continued to rain burning spit at Ellie and her pack, and when Toma yelped in agony, scurrying away with a tendril of smoke rising from the smoking patch of fur on her back, Ellie's blind rage switched to fear for her pack.

Fall back before you lose everyone!

"To me!" she called and retreated into the tree line, out of range of the monstrous plants.

"Cripes," Ellie said, hunkering to inspect Toma's scorched back. The mutt whined and craned her head back in an effort to lick her wound but she couldn't reach. Ellie tipped some of her waterskin over it, and used dry leaves to rub the burning gloop off as best she could. It was a slapdash, desperate fix, but Toma calmed a little after that. Then she found Dug and repeated the process. The two injured dogs lay in the dirt next to each other, licking each other's wounds. Frank, who had been missing, returned from the woods and laid down beside them, panting. Fang and Bang showed up a few moments later. Several of the other dogs milled about, all on their guard, watching the woods and sniffing the air.

Ellie stood and counted eight of them. Still a bunch missing, but Frank's reappearance assured her that the others must be nearby. She hoped so, anyway. It occurred to her that if any of them strayed near to the lillysnappers they'd also be eaten like poor Lappy.

Arkrusssss.

Ellie closed her eyes and peered into Arkarus' barnyard. He was agitated, loping to and fro in front of his kennel, barking at the stars. When he sensed Ellie's presence, he stopped and looked straight at her mind's eye.

"I need your help," she said, knowing he wouldn't understand the words, but hoping he would understand her intention. "We have to re-gather the pack. Can you find them?"

Arkarus cocked his head quizzically, then stepped towards her.

"Come."

Ellie opened her arms and invited Arkarus to project. The wolf obeyed, and bounded towards her mind's eye. As Ellie stood in the Everdusk, Arkarus sprang from her chest and materialised before her, like he had done so many times before. Ellie never failed to find him majestic. He prowled around the clearing, as the pack came up to him in a frenzy, wagging their tails and yipping happily at their alpha. They would follow him into a fire if he commanded it, Ellie realised. Even Frank, Arkarus' second in command, seemed to light up at the sight of him.

"Find them, boy," Ellie commanded.

Arkarus turned to look at her, his four eyes shining with intelligence and understanding. Then he bounded away into the woods. The pack followed.

Ellie turned back to the lillysnapper wall. The tall stone tower loomed behind the plants, and Ellie was damned if she wasn't going to get to it after travelling across the entire province.

She set off walking around the barrier, hoping to find a gap that she could sneak through.

Ten minutes later, she found herself back at the same spot, having walked a full circle. There was no gap. No way through at all.

Alright, then. I'll just have to make my own entrance.

All she had to do was figure out a way past the plant monsters, but that couldn't be that difficult. They weren't fireproof.

She gathered some twine and wrapped a bunch of dry leaves to the end of a sturdy stick to create a torch. Then using her flint and steel, Ellie sparked a flame, lit her torch and hefted it above her head, grinning.

Arkarus howled in the distance as she approached the plant wall. Ellie picked out her target, the lillysnapper that had eaten Lappy, and stalked towards it. She intended to burn that Kella-forsaken monster to ashes. She heard the faint sound of barking in the distance again, but then she heard something that chilled the blood in her veins.

Krrssssssk, skkrreeeeeeessss.

Ellie froze about twenty feet from the lillysnappers.

The noise came not from her ears, but her mind. A strange hissing, scratching sound, like the whispers of ghosts.

Kreessssssssk, skrsssh, skreeshhkk.

She shivered. It was not a pleasant sound at all.

What is that?

She inhaled a deep breath to steady her nerves. The lillysnappers swayed to and fro, not in unison, but still in hypnotic rhythm.

It's their voices…

It made sense. With Arkarus being projected, Ellie's telepathic abilities had returned. She'd never heard the voices of anything other than animals, though. Certainly not *plants.* These creatures must be something in between, she figured.

The hissing sound turned into a raspy rattle, like sand shaken inside a can, then returned to the ghostly whispers. Ellie closed her eyes and concentrated. She focused on the whispering, willing her brain to make sense of it.

In her mind's eye, she saw a row of lillysnappers, rising out of pots in a glass house. A fat woman was tending to them, walking down the line pouring some kind of bluish liquid over the base of the stems. A man was there too, grey hair, a grizzled look to him, watching her as he followed behind.

It's a memory!

Unaware of how she was doing it, Ellie saw the memory of this peculiar, semi-sentient plant as it was just a sapling. The man and the woman were talking to each other now, stopped in front of the one whose eyes she was somehow seeing through (*so they* do *have eyes!*), and through the hazy, muffled sound of its alien sensory system, she picked out their conversation.

"And it'll make them grow three times faster?" the man asked.

"More like ten times. And it increases their intelligence, too. They'll even be able to distinguish between Towers staff and any strangers that might come snooping."

"Marvellous," the old man grinned. He turned towards Ellie now, and she almost jumped back when he reached out a finger towards her. The image of him jerked forwards, growing larger very suddenly, and the man's expression changed to wide-eyed surprise as he jumped back away from the lunging lillysnapper.

"Vicious little buggers, ain't they?" He pointed a finger at himself, jabbing it against his chest. "I'm Mr Anders. You hear me? *Mister Anders.* You better get used to me, because I don't wanna lose a finger each time I walk in and out of the front gate."

The woman chuckled. "They'll know you soon enough. Give it a few more days and they'll have enough neurological brainpower to store basic memories. They'll be the smartest plants in the world, you'll see!"

Think you're a few steps behind, lady, Ellie thought. This plant at least was clearly already capable of building memories, but Ellie suspected that the woman wasn't as smart as she thought she was.

Still, whatever the case, Ellie thought she had a way of getting past the perimeter without being eaten now.

She opened her eyes. The plant wall loomed before her, several of the lillysnappers leaned forwards in wary curiosity. Ellie heard that strange hissing again, the alien sound that represented their thoughts. Unlike the animals that she normally heard, her brain was unable to translate the lillysnappers into anything resembling language. But she sensed their awareness, and realised they were very alert.

The torch. They're afraid of it.

Ellie waved it slowly, and sure enough, the leaning plants leaned to follow it, their maws poised and ready to spit it out if she came any closer. She wouldn't be able to burn them, she realised, not without some level of bitter disappointment.

But now, she had a better idea.

Ellie stubbed the torch into the dirt and stamped it out.

When the fire was out, the lillysnappers leaned back into their positions, still alert and watching Ellie, but far less wary now that the flame was gone.

She looked at the nearest plant and concentrated on it, reaching out with her mind to isolate it. The hissing grew sharper, and flickered with a jolt of electric.

Krrsssseeck, skroooorsk, skkreeeee.

"Shh," she said to it. "Look, I know Mr Anders. I'm a friend, you see?" She put a mental image of the old geezer she had seen in the memory at the forefront of her mind, and pictured herself standing next to him. It was a completely fabricated scene, of course, but she hoped the plant would be fooled by it.

Incredibly, it seemed to work. The plant gave another hiss, but this one was less aggressive and much more submissive. She felt the plant's guard drop, and then in reality, its head lowered. It bent its stalk forwards, lowering its ugly head towards the grass, creating a thin gap between the two neighbouring plants. Beyond, the tower revealed itself, rising up over a stone wall.

She was giddy with excitement.

But looking warily at the gap, she realised it wasn't going to be a safe crossing. She'd have to squeeze through, which would take time, and while she was crossing the threshold, what would stop the other plants from spitting, or worse still, biting her head off?

She reached out towards the plants on either side of the one she had miraculously subdued, and sent them the same absurd image of her with Mr Anders. The two plants went rigid, rising up straight, before joining the first in the extensive bow, tripling the size of the gap in the process.

That's better.

Ellie took a deep breath and began a cautious approach, ready to bolt at the first sign of aggression from the other lillysnappers.

Several more excited barks echoed through the woods, much closer than before. A ripple of movement carried down the plant wall to her right. Something was drawing their attention.

Ellie took her chance. She sprang forwards and sprinted at the gap in the wall. Her feet stepped lightly over the heads of the bending lillysnappers and she jumped through the gap and found herself in a corridor of grass between the lillysnappers and the perimeter stone wall of Trinity Towers.

She ran straight for that wall, terrified that a lillysnapper would turn around and bite her. When she reached the wall she turned and put her back flat against it. Through the gap in the plants, Arkarus came bounding after her, just as the three bowing lillysnappers shrugged off her spell and lifted their heads. Ellie had time to see Frank and Whisper pull up short on the other side, before they were blocked from sight as the wall closed shut.

The lillysnappers went into a frenzy, she heard them spitting and snapping at her pack on the other side. Excited yips and barks echoed into the sky.

"Oh Kella," Ellie said in despair. "Run away, you silly things!"

From this side of the lillysnappers, Ellie could only imagine the scene happening on the forest side. She pictured her poor dogs getting spat on and eaten by the monster plants. Each time one of the lillysnappers bent forwards she expected to hear the sound of crunching bones. But the barking faded away, and the agitated lillysnappers grew still.

The pack's running away, thank fook.

"*Grrrrrr*," Arkarus growled low and sinister. His heckles were up and he was glaring at the wall of plants, which mercifully had their backs to Ellie and her wolf. A few jostled against each other, seemingly trying to turn around to face them, but their thick stalks didn't allow them to do so. They could only guard this place from outer intruders. Once you were behind them, you were apparently beyond their reach.

Ellie exhaled a long sigh of relief.

"What was that?" a voice said from behind her.

Shit!

Ellie spun and saw a boy above her, leaning out a window of the nearest tower. The window didn't face Ellie directly, otherwise the boy would surely have seen her, but he'd only need to take a glance to his right and she'd be caught.

She took cover by flattening herself against the wall, spreading her arms and fingers, willing herself to be hidden. "Arkarus!" she whispered, patting her chest, signalling him to re-merge with her.

"What is it?" she heard another boy say.

"I thought I heard dogs."

Arkarus turned away from the lillysnappers and cocked his head up towards the tower.

"*Arkarus!*" Ellie whispered again, with aggressive restraint. "Inside, *now!*" She thumped her chest again. Arkarus ignored her, he seemed to be gauging whether the boys were a threat or not.

The second voice laughed. "You're going crazy. There's no dogs in the Everdusk."

"Yeh, well, I still heard what I heard, didn't I?" said the first.

She leaned forwards, grabbed Arkarus by the scruff of the neck and yanked him as hard as she could towards the shelter of the wall. He outweighed Ellie fivefold and came to her begrudgingly. She knelt and pulled him into her chest. After a moment, he was back in her mental barnyard, and she was flat against the wall again.

Ellie's heart hammered, and she silently prayed that the boys hadn't noticed them.

Please, just go back inside.

She waited breathlessly.

A minute passed.

Neither boy spoke.

She cautiously leaned out of cover to look up at the tower. Ellie saw the underside of a boy's hairless chin, his arms crossed at the wrists, two hands drooped lazily over the windowsill as he peered out towards the Everdusk.

She ducked back into cover.

Who knew what the punishment was for trespassing on wizard grounds? They might turn her into a toad or something. They could do that sort of thing, right?

Or maybe they'd burn her at a stake…

No! Johanna is here, she will be able to explain. I just have to find her.

After a tense minute or two, the boy went back inside, but he left the window open.

She had to be quiet now.

She spun and looked up at the wall. It wasn't very tall, but was just big enough for her not to be able to reach, even if she jumped.

Come out, boy.

She summoned Arkarus again. Ellie's stomach gave another loud grumble, and she went light-headed. That was what, three? No, four projections in the last hour. She'd need to find food soon.

"Stay close to the wall," she whispered, blinking away the dizziness. "Stand still."

She climbed onto him, pushed her weight against the stone, and stood up on his back. Grabbing the top of the wall with both hands, she slowly peeked over it.

A grin broke across her face when she saw the rest of the grounds. The three towers formed a neat triangle around a well-tended garden courtyard. Flower beds lined the crisscrossing pebble paths that connected all three spires and the main gate to her left. The tower closest to her and its opposite were smaller than the tall, fancy one at the back of the courtyard, away to Ellie's right.

A young man was walking down a path away from her, and two girls sat reading books on the grass about fifty feet away. Other than that, Ellie saw no other people. There was a secluded shadowy area between the closest tower and the stone wall, which she could use for cover.

She lowered herself to sit on his back, and instructed him to move along a bit, so that he was on the other side of that shadowy area.

"Okay, stop," she said, and prepared herself to jump over the wall.

Arkarus sensed her intent, and before she could stand again, he hunkered his legs and sprang. Ellie clung onto his fur for dear life as Arkarus' paws scrabbled for purchase on the top of the wall. He pushed with his rear legs and cleared it. Ellie toppled forwards and tumbled into the dirt on the other side of the wall. Arkarus landed a beat later, almost trampling her with his paws.

"Cripes, you big lummock!" she hissed, scrambling to her feet. She glanced anxiously up at the open window. "Quickly, get inside again," she whispered to Arkarus.

The wolf shook himself off, before trudging into her chest.

Ellie's light-headedness faded with his presence, and her senses re-sharpened.

She sniffed the air. Johanna's scent was stronger now, but it seemed to be coming from the other towers. The strongest whiff led towards the tall one, so Ellie figured that's where she had to be.

With a quick check to her left, she spied the two girls still sitting on the grass, chatting and gesturing to some book that lay between them.

Johanna must love it here. I bet they're all bookworms like her.

With so few people in sight, Ellie figured it was now or never.

She bolted from the shadows. It took five seconds for her to cross the gap between the short tower to the tall one, and she darted in behind it and squashed herself against its stone base, catching her breath.

She froze and listened, half expecting to hear more voices, or approaching footsteps. But there was nothing. She'd gone undetected.

Ellie looked up at the overhanging chamber high above. A square window was ajar way up there, and she decided that would be a better way in than walking through the front door, where anybody might see her.

A sturdy wooden beam jutted out from the underside of the roof. She took an arrow, tied one end of her hempen rope around it and nocked it in her bow. She drew, aiming at the beam straight up and fired.

The arrow buried itself into the beam nice and snug.

She pulled on the rope, now dangling in front of her nose, to test its strength. It felt solid enough.

Here we go.

She grabbed the rope and started to climb. She shimmied her slender body this way and that, scaling the rope like a monkey. Climbing ropes had a funny way of making her feel satisfied, deep in her core. She grinned the whole way up.

Without even pausing to check anyone was inside the room, Ellie tugged open the window as far as it would go, grabbed hold of the top of the window frame and planted her legs on the sill. She swung inside and landed on her feet.

It took a second or two for her eyes to adjust to the dim room, but she quickly realised it was a bedroom. And Johanna's scent was so strong! Was this where she slept?

No… there was another scent, much stronger. A musky, man-smell.

What was she doing up here with a man?

Ellie's eyes went wide as all manner of filthy images immediately conjured in her head. The thought of her sister with a man was utterly vile. How could she!

Nevermind that now. I just have to find her.

Despite the strong scent, Johanna was nowhere to be seen. Ellie left via the door and found herself in a grandly decorated chamber. A huge desk, bookshelves full of tomes, a high pointed roof complete with a glass skylight window, and a desk lined with bowls of fruit.

Ellie's stomach growled at the sight, so she helped herself to a handful of nuts, bit into an apple, and stuffed two more into her pockets for later.

More scents lingered here, Johanna's as well as at least three others. And that man-smell too. His was definitely the strongest. He obviously spent a lot of time here.

There was something else about his scent that gave Ellie pause for thought. Some animal mixed with it. Not the way her father used to smell of deer blood, or boar poop after he'd been hunting, this was different. It was a birdish smell.

Just then, as if on cue, Ellie heard a high-pitched shriek flood in through the open window. It sent an icy shiver down her spine. A birdlike banshee wail of pain. She imagined a huge eagle that had been set ablaze, that's how terrible that cry sounded.

Then, coming from the bedroom she had entered via, came another noise.

A heavy wooden *thud.*

CHAPTER TWENTY-TWO

Johanna awoke with a start when she heard the awful shriek. As she woke, she bumped her head against the side of the wardrobe.

"Oww," she said, blinking in the darkness.

Suddenly, it all came back to her. Where she was, how she had gotten there, and *who* had put her there.

"No. No! Let me out! Someone, *help me*!"

She banged on the door three times, not surprised to find it solid as a rock, and it didn't open.

What she didn't expect was to hear a voice she hadn't heard in almost three months, speaking to her from the other side of the door.

"Hanna? Is that you?"

For a moment, Johanna thought she must be still unconscious, dreaming. How could her sister *possibly* be here?

"Hanna!" Ellie called. "Where are you?"

"Ellie?" she said quietly.

"Yeah, it's me, sis. Where are you?"

"Ellie!" Johanna felt like crying, she was so overcome with relief. "I'm locked in the wardrobe! In here!"

"What? Who did this to you? Wait there, I'll get you

out."

The wardrobe rocked and tilted forwards as Ellie tugged on the door.

"It's locked! See if you can find the key."

"Sod that," Ellie said. "Come, boy."

Boy? Who is she with?

Johanna heard a *thump* outside the door. Or was it two thumps very close together?

Then there was a weird panting noise, like heavy breathing snorting through the keyhole.

"Who's that?" Johanna asked in mild alarm.

"Oh, you'll see," Ellie said, sounding like she was grinning. "Open it, boy."

"*Arowl?*"

"Kella-murphy, is that a dog?" Johanna said, peeking through the keyhole. The view was black and furry.

The door gave a sudden rattle. Either Ellie, or Ellie's dog was tugging at the doorknob.

"Isn't there a key somewhere?" Johanna asked.

"Probably, but don't worry, this will work!" Ellie said cheerfully.

"You sound awfully confident," Johanna said, bracing herself against the rocking wardrobe.

"*Grrrrr!*" said the keyhole.

"How did you even get here?" Johanna asked.

"I climbed up."

"You *what?*"

The door jerked again, shaking the entire wardrobe.

"After I snuck in over the wall."

"How did you get past the—?"

"And that was after I tricked those big green monsters to let me through," Ellie finished.

The whole wardrobe rocked again. The dog outside sounded very big, judging by the sound of its growl.

The wardrobe rocked again, so much this time that some of Sai Brockhursts clothes fell off the hangar and landed on her. Johanna toppled forwards and crashed against the door.

"Ow. This isn't working, Ellie!"

"Come on Arkarus, put your teeth into it!"

"Just find the key!"

"There is no key! That big bird man probably took it with him. I assume he's the one who locked you in there?"

"Bird man? What are you talking about?" Johanna asked, bewildered.

"He's your headmaster, right? I knew there was some animal inside him, didn't I try telling you before you left? He's got bloody wings now, Hanna!"

Johanna was totally lost. "Are you sure it was Garrod?"

"Yes, the guy who tested you in the clearing, that time. It was definitely him."

"What was he doing?" Johanna said, thinking of Karly and Markus.

"Something weird." Her tone changed, became subdued. "I saw three bodies lying around him, Hanna. One of them… oh, Han." Ellie broke off.

Bodies? Johanna was struck dumb. *Did he kill them?* "Markus…"

"We'll talk about it after we get you out of there, Han."

Johanna was taken aback by her sister's commanding tone. She'd never spoken to her like that before.

The wardrobe gave another violent jerk, and the door made a splintery cracking sound.

"Oh no! The handle fell off!"

"What?" Johanna cried.

"Wait," Ellie said suddenly. "Couldn't you just cast a fireball and blast your way out of there?"

Johanna frowned. "What, and bake myself alive?"

"Hmm. Good point."

"*Grrrrr.*"

"You can drop that now, Arkarus."

Johanna heard a metallic *clang*. She closed her eyes, trying not to see the mental image of Markus and Karly lying dead, but couldn't stop it. She *had* to get out of there. Didn't she hear a birdlike cry shortly before waking up? She'd thought it was a dream, but sounds from reality had a funny habit of finding their way into your dreams. He might return at any moment.

An idea came to her. "Get me a candle!" Johanna blurted.

"What for?"

"Just do it, little sis!"

"All right," Ellie said, and walked away. She came back a moment later. "I have one. What shall I do with it?"

"Is it lit?"

"No, hold on."

There was a few quick *skrt, skrt, skrt* noises as Ellie struck her flint and steel.

"Okay, now what?"

"Hold it close to the keyhole. Let me see the flame." Johanna peered through, and suddenly there was a bright orange light as the fire came into view. "Okay, hold it right there. Don't let go, no matter what happens!"

"Is this some new trick you've learned since you got here?" Ellie asked.

Johanna ignored her. She had to concentrate. Sai Henlowe had taught them how to manipulate fire from a candle, but this would be the first time Johanna had successfully harnessed it.

She pinched her thumb and forefingers close to the keyhole and muttered, "*Ignee-tranfee.*"

The flame sucked itself into the keyhole and made a thin tendril of fire, like a very bright glow worm, connecting her fingers to the candle outside the door.

"Holy crap!" Ellie burst. "That's amazing!"

Johanna thought so too, but had to figure out the next part. She dangled the fiery rope onto the metal bolt, which was holding the door locked. With her mind's eye, she saw the candle disappearing in Ellie's hand as she sucked its energy through the keyhole and drooped it onto the bolt.

A strong irony smell stung her nostrils. The metal was heating up.

"It's working," Johanna said, her voice rising to a high nervous pitch.

A sizzling sound came from the keyhole, as splinters of wood near the bolt began to scorch. After a few more seconds, Johanna felt the resistance of the bolt suddenly give way. She applied pressure to the door and felt it move. "Almost there!" she said, wincing. The bolt glowed white hot, softening under the extreme heat. Just before the candle ran out, Johanna gave the door a shove and it popped open.

She tumbled out and fell into Ellie, who dropped the candle and caught her by one arm. The molten bolt sizzled in the door frame.

Ellie hoisted her upright, grinned into her face and they fell into a tight hug.

"It's so good to see you!" Johanna cried, squeezing Ellie around the neck.

"You too, big sis," Ellie said, releasing a long sigh.

Over Ellie's shoulder, Johanna saw a huge, four-eyed, black wolf sitting on its haunches, tongue lolling out and panting lightly. "Who is this?" she said, startled.

They uncoupled and Ellie introduced her to Arkarus. "He's my travel companion."

"He has four eyes, and is that… two tails!" Johanna was bewildered at the sight of him.

"Yeah, he's unique," Ellie beamed.

Johanna clutched her sister's hands, looking Ellie up and down. She was grubby, as usual, and dressed in her leather jerkin and skirt, cotton undershirt, bow and quiver of arrows. Her hands were calloused and rough, the hands of a real huntress. Johanna laughed. "Your hands feel just like Dad's now!"

Ellie's face dropped. The grin vanished and was replaced by something resembling deep pain.

"What is it?" Johanna said, puzzled.

"I—" Ellie croaked. Her mouth was working but nothing would come out. "The reason, why I came here…"

Johanna felt her arms trembling, and Ellie gulped big, her adam's apple swimming in her throat.

Johanna waited patiently, a knot of anxiety forming in her stomach.

Then came a heavy *whump* from the headmaster's chamber. A series of clacks and scrapes followed. They both turned towards the sound, and Johanna saw black ruffling feathers.

Arkarus barked and went to the door. Then he lowered his head and growled.

"What in Kella's name are you doing in my chamber?" Garrod said. "And how did you get up—" He trailed off.

Ellie made to walk over to the door, Johanna started to say "No, stay here!" But Ellie shrugged out of her grip, strode up behind Arkarus and crossed her arms.

"Who are *you*?" Garrod said.

"My name is Eleanor McKree."

Johanna went and stood beside her sister, and met Garrod's surprised eyes. A pair of black wings protruded from his back. Johanna gaped in horror.

"I see the family resemblance," Garrod said. "You are aware that we do not permit visitors to Trinity Towers. I must have you escorted off the prem—"

"We will *both* escort ourselves out of here. Where we come from, teachers don't lock pupils in *cupboards*. Come on, Hanna." Ellie reached back, took Johanna by the hand. "Go, Arkarus."

The wolf prowled into the chamber, his eyes never leaving Sai Garrod, who remained behind his grand desk, like a safety barrier.

"Before you go," Garrod said, wiping his mouth. "Where did you find that wolf?"

"You wouldn't believe me even if I told you," Ellie said, not pausing.

They were halfway across the chamber when Garrod said, "I think I already know. The same place I acquired these." He stretched his wings a bit.

This made Ellie stop. She turned to Garrod with a suspicious frown.

Johanna blinked and muttered, "What are you talking about? Ellie, have you seen the other world, too?"

Ellie turned sharply to her. "The dead place?"

Johanna put a hand to her mouth. "So you have. When? How?"

Ellie hesitated, clearly reluctant to explain it in front of Garrod.

"You must have suffered some unthinkable pain?" Garrod mused, making it a question. "That's the only way to open the rift."

"Y-yes," Ellie stammered. She was watching him, some dangerous curiosity glinting in her eyes. The knot in Johanna's stomach tightened.

"Were you alone?" Garrod probed.

"N-n-no..."

"What happened?" Johanna asked softly.

Ellie turned to her sister, tears welling in the corners of her eyes. "Dad... he's gone. And it's because of me."

Johanna lost her breath. She felt as though a blacksmith's anvil had been dropped onto her chest.

"That would do it," Garrod said, as if explaining some trivial conundrum.

"How did it happen?" Johanna managed to say.

"It was an accident," Ellie said, almost pleadingly. "Please, sis, I need you to understand. I didn't mean to! We were hunting a honeyroo. For a bounty. He finally let me go with him on a real bounty. The hunt was going so well, I was patient, he even said so. But then the roo appeared, and everything just went wrong. We tried to pincer it," she made a gesture with her hands, making a wide arcing sweep motion like an empty hug. "So I was here, and Dad was there, the roo in the middle. I shot an arrow at it... but I missed." She gulped. "I hit Dad instead."

Johanna digested this, feeling a wave of black emptiness engulf her. *Dad's dead. I'll never see him again.*

"He died in my arms." Ellie covered her face in her hands and burst into tears. "You must hate me," she sobbed miserably.

"No," Johanna said straight away, and realised it was true. The black gulf swept aside, and something warmer filled the void in her heart. "No, Ellie, I could never hate you. It was just an accident. A horrible, horrible accident. Come here." She pulled her sister into a tight embrace, feeling her convulsing body wracking with sobs. Ellie pressed her face into Johanna's neck, and warm tears transferred onto her skin there.

As they stood like that, Johanna became aware of Garrod peering at them intently from across the desk. He had an expectant look on his face, as if he were waiting for something to happen. She frowned at him, and his face changed.

"Dammit," he hissed, clenching a fist on the desk. "It's not opening, is it?"

Johanna saw Garrod for the first time, realising the monster that he was. "You are obsessed, Sai."

"Perhaps you're only useful when you're intoxicated. It seems I thoroughly overestimated your abilities, Miss McKree."

"I just found out my father is dead," she said in a soft, flabbergasted tone.

"So what? I just watched my father die, and you don't see me crying about it. The only question is what can we do about our predicament?"

Johanna shook her head, utterly in shock at the callous, cold way he was speaking to her.

"I know what *I* want," Garrod said in a sinister tone. "I will assimilate that dragon."

"Assimilate?" Johanna said, gently releasing Ellie from her grip. "Is that how you got those wings? By assimilating some poor creature?"

Ellie stirred at this, and turned towards Garrod. "You did what?" she said numbly.

"It was a parasite," Garrod said defensively. "It fed on my soul. It *paralysed* me! How could I allow that?"

"Didn't you make room for it?" Ellie said.

Johanna didn't understand how her sister could know about Garrod's bird creature. Surely, it was only something an attuned could possibly comprehend.

"Yes, I made it a cage," Garrod said. "A dungeon. It needed to know that I was in charge."

Ellie shook her head in disgust.

"You don't approve?" Garrod said. "I need no approval from a Harbrook bumpkin regarding my affairs."

"You have no respect for life," Ellie said.

"What? *Animal* lives? Please," Garrod said derisively. "Humanity is more important than any other creature. We should strive to become as strong as possible. Surely you of all people agree with me. How many creatures have *you* slain, huntress girl?"

"None simply for personal gain," Ellie said, but she sounded doubtful. "I hunt only what is necessary, and strive to waste nothing."

"You enjoy the act of killing. I can see it in your eyes. You *want* to kill that wolf."

"Never!" Ellie cried, her voice shaking. Then, she added in a much more convincing tone, "Not anymore."

Garrod blinked. "You bonded with it," he said in amazement. He shook his head quickly. "I couldn't. Devouring Corcubus was my only solution. I have to deal with these." He ruffled his wings, "But they have some advantages."

"You're a monster!" Ellie cried. "How could you destroy an animal's soul like that? You should have just projected it out if you didn't want it inside your head!"

"Projection?" Garrod frowned. Clearly, the notion had never even occurred to him.

But still, Johanna couldn't believe what her sister was saying. "How do you know about any of this, Ellie?"

"Because I'm attuned now. Look." She opened her arms,

and patted her chest. "Come, Arkarus. Inside."

The wolf finally turned his glare away from Garrod, and cocked his head at Ellie. He was panting now, much more than before, and his head was hanging low, as if fighting some heavy fatigue.

Then he took three steps towards Ellie, and what happened next almost gave Johanna a heart attack. The wolf leapt into the air, right at Ellie. Then it *disappeared.*

Just vanished.

"Wuh!" Johanna gasped, stepping backwards.

Ellie exhaled a long breath and turned to Johanna. She bit her lower lip and gave a little shrug. "Surprised me, too."

"Fascinating," Garrod said, holding his chin and staring. "And this creature, it obeys you?"

"He does now," Ellie explained. "I've had to train him. Something you wouldn't know the first thing about." She folded her arms across her chest.

"You're attuned. I can't believe it," Johanna said, a smile creeping into her face.

"Yeah, I could'a come here, shown you up in front of everyone, eh?"

Johanna chuckled. "Maybe so."

"You are obviously an exquisite mage," Garrod said. A dangerous glint was in his yellow-flecked eyes. "I *need* a rift. You have to help me. Between the three of us, there's enough attunement to hold it open for hours." He frowned intently at Ellie.

Johanna realised too late what he was trying to do.

Ellie gave a sudden frown. "What? Stop that!" she cried, pressing her temples. "Get out of my head!"

"Hold still. Let the pain flow."

"Stop it!" Johanna cried. Using what scrap of energy she had left, she summoned a tiny fireball and prepared herself to launch it at her headmaster. "Leave her alone!"

Garrod grimaced. "I can't get in. That wolf is blocking me." He turned to Johanna now. Johanna's mind burst open against her will, and Garrod walked in. She was utterly powerless to stop him.

No! Get out!

Shut up, he said in her head, his essence taking on the feel of black tendrils worming their way through her cognitive tunnels. Her energy was low, and he sensed it immediately.

Show me the dragon, he said, his voice thundering through her mind.

She felt him burrowing into her memories, somehow targeting the ones that caused her great pain. That area of her mind was remarkably small, Johanna had led a good, satisfying life up until recently, the most vivid painful memory being that of when the dragon had spoken to her as she was tripping out on the hoomie.

No, please!

He ignored her, and dragged the memory into her conscious, forcing her to relive a fraction of the madness that she had almost succumbed to.

This all happened in the blink of an eye, Garrod was a master manipulator and worked his way through her head as if he were born to do such nefarious work.

Johanna was reeling from the experience, the torment the dragon inflicted on her when he tried to show her the true meaning of infinity forced its way into her mind again, creating an overwhelming nausea that she couldn't resist.

The only solace she found was that Garrod, who was so deeply connected to her at this point, was experiencing her pain as well. She could sense him on the periphery of her thoughts, like a spectator unable to look away from a gruesome street brawl.

The energy came then. Using the pain of the memory, Garrod took control of her spellcasting abilities and turned his attention to the fireball that still flickered in her palm.

That flame is pathetic, I know you can do better.

Johanna's palm lifted as if being pulled by an invisible puppet string, raising the tiny fireball with it.

Bigger! Garrod bellowed.

The flame grew, pulsing with energy, casting a flickering

glow around the room. Ellie retreated a step away, warily staring at her sister.

Get away from me! Run, Ellie, RUN!

Johanna wanted to scream, but Garrod was in complete control of her body now, and no sound escaped her lips. Her left hand joined the right, and the fireball expanded between her upstretched arms, as she held it high above her head.

Kill her!

Johanna's eyeballs bulged wide in absolute terror. Ellie's did the same. The sisters gaped at each other for a split second.

Johanna's arms dropped in front of her, and the fireball leapt from her grasp with an audible *fwoosh!*

NOOOO!

An ethereal black blur ejected from Ellie's chest.

Johanna met eyes with the wolf a beat before the fireball engulfed his face.

The fire wrapped around Arkarus' head like a death blanket, and the smell of sizzling, burning fur shot up Johanna's nose. The fire swept down the length of his body as he jumped towards her, burning him down to the skin.

Arkarus' charred body fell to the ground in between the two sisters. It thumped onto the wooden floorboards. Smoke rose from his head, neck and back. He gave a feeble kick with one paw, uttered a low whine, and then fell still.

A deafening silence flooded into Johanna's mind. Garrod's presence was gone. She fell to her knees, dumbstruck and devastated.

Ellie blinked. She also fell to her knees, looking down at the smouldering wolf.

"Ar-Arkarus…"

"I'm sorry," Johanna croaked, her voice barely a whisper. "It wasn't… he *made* me…"

"Why?" Ellie said, reaching forwards and touching the blackened skin, the fur had been burnt away in a long, streaking patch. All four of his eye sockets were empty, charred holes. "*Why?*"

Johanna felt her sister's pain then, like a physical force. It overwhelmed her, a grief so strong that it threatened to send her mad.

Garrod silently came around the desk, and loomed over them.

Johanna saw him through a shimmering haze. The air was dispersing, shifting, changing.

Oh no. It's happening again.

A black shadow fell upon the room. In a flash, it swallowed them all. Johanna was faintly aware of Garrod's touch on her shoulder, and suddenly he was in the void with them.

Their world disappeared behind her, and ahead of her, growing and shooting forwards like some phantom vision was a purplish window, an arch of dim fire, rising up around them and changing the ornately decorated headmaster's chamber into a decrepit, decaying version of itself.

The rift had swallowed them.

"Thank you," Garrod said, his voice thick with cold satisfaction.

Then he was gone. He left Ellie and Johanna lying in an abyss of grief.

"Ellie," Johanna said, speaking through the haze. "Are you okay?"

What a stupid question. Of course she wasn't okay.

But she was troubled by another thought, one that somehow seemed more important even than her sister's wellbeing.

He's going to assimilate a dragon. He wants to become immortal. He can't possibly succeed! But what if he does…?

"We have to stop him, Ellie!"

"I'm going to kill him," Ellie snarled. She lifted her head and Johanna saw a terrible burning rage ignited in her sister's face. "Where did he go?"

They both turned towards the window. Black wings were flapping over the trees, heading into the sky.

CHAPTER TWENTY-THREE

Sai Henlowe's little prodigy had proved a bitter disappointment, after she'd shown so much potential. The young mage from Harbrook, who had the near miraculous fortune of meeting the dragon in the first place, couldn't comprehend its magnificence. Her lack of understanding ultimately caused her to fear the dragon, the same way King Victus feared the attuned community. He'd come to expect such cowardice from the common folk, ignorance breeds fear, after all. But to have such a craven reaction from one of his own pupils was tragic.

Garrod had no fear of the dragons because he had figured out what made them so fascinating.

They were the ultimate attuned beings.

His entire life had been devoted to the study of attunement, so he considered himself qualified to recognise the dragons' position in the attuned world. If they were the ultimate attuned being, then he, by right as the new Prime Wizard of Darune, owed it to himself to try and harness their power.

All his life, Garrod had existed in his father's shadow. He respected Jason, even greatly admired his talents, but where Garrod differed to his father was his determination to find his own way. Jason Brockhurst had never truly specialised, choosing to become a Jack-of-all-trades wizard, honing his skills across a wide range of practices, but never mastering any of them. He had still managed to become the Prime Wizard of the province, but without a specialty, Garrod believed his father hadn't truly deserved such a title. It didn't matter what name they gave you, all that mattered was finding the limits of what you could *do.*

Garrod knew enough pyromancy to rival Sai Henlowe, but his core skill had always been telepathy. He was a psychic. Perhaps the greatest psychic alive. He couldn't imagine anyone even coming close to his level of experience in the field, and he couldn't imagine any other more worthy of his new title.

Who else could slip into the mind of anyone and bend them to his will? Who else had traversed the gulf of dimensions multiple times? Who else had assimilated a creature from the dark reflection and used it to mend and amplify his body?

Who else could *fly*?

No-one. Only him. He was the Prime now, and he'd make that title mean something.

He'd capture a prize worthy of the Prime: an immortal riftwalking dragon.

Riftwalker. Yes, that's what they are. Like me.

He left the ruinous version of Trinity Towers behind, and glided over the blackened superoak husks towards the Mana Spring, the dragon's den. It didn't matter if the dragon wasn't there, he had time on his side and could wait for it.

But as Garrod glided closer, he spied it through the branches. The dragon *was* there.

At the sight of its scaly skin, Garrod experienced a wave of giddy excitement that he hadn't felt in many years. He adjusted his wings and descended, making a beeline for the dozing dragon.

The dragon was curled up in the mud, its huge belly rising and falling with every breath. Its head was tucked up beside its back legs, the tail snaking its way around the edge of the dirty spring.

As Garrod flew towards it, he formed a plan of action. It was sleeping, so he had the element of surprise. He'd simply land on it, dig his talons into the dragon's back to awaken it, then he would enter its mind. He'd force it to fly into the sky and open a rift, ride it through to his world, and then assimilate it in the void just like he had done with Corcubus. He'd emerge on the other side with the power of an *immortal dragon.*

He grinned as he approached, priming his talons in preparation for landing.

You're mine!

The dragon's eye opens.

Garrod stares into infinity.

His mind breaks but he doesn't know it yet.

Garrod hasn't accounted for the dragon's own psychic abilities. As soon as they make eye contact, time freezes. Garrod is suspended in mid-flight and thrust into a telepathic-parley.

GREETINGS, MORTAL, the dragon thunders. YOU JUST CAN'T SEEM TO KEEP AWAY, CAN YOU?

"Do not speak to me, beast," Garrod says.

THIS IS NOT SPEAKING, the dragon replies, amused. DO NOT CONFUSE THE PSYCHOKINETIC TRANSFER OF EXPRESSION FROM ONE CREATURE TO ANOTHER WITH THAT PRIMITIVE METHOD OF COMMUNICATION YOUR KIND HAS BARELY BEGUN TO UTILISE.

"I just," Garrod says dumbly. "I didn't expect an animal to be capable of such intelligence."

YOU THINK I'M AN ANIMAL? The dragon sounds mildly offended.

"A mighty animal," Garrod rectifies quickly. "But an animal, nonetheless."

AND THAT WOULD MAKE YOU, WHAT? A TEMPORARY PARASITE.

"A human."

YES, THAT'S WHAT I SAID.

"Human beings are not parasites."

I CHOOSE A TERM RELATIVE TO YOUR UNDERSTANDING. TO ME, HUMANS ARE SIMPLY A HUBRISTIC SPECIES OF PARASITE THAT MANAGE TO SURVIVE PAST THE EMBRYONIC PHASE. BUT YOU EXPUNGE SO MUCH ENERGY IN SUCH A SHORT SPACE OF TIME, SUCKING EVERY ATOM OF POWER FROM THE WORLD BEFORE DYING OUT, BRINGING AN END TO YOUR SPECIES' INANE COUGH OF EXISTENCE.

"You talk nonsense," Garrod says. "Humans aren't extinct."

WELL, THIS BECAME TEDIOUS MUCH FASTER THAN I HOPED. THE YOUNG GIRL WAS FAR MORE ENTERTAINING. WHY CAN'T I SEE HER AGAIN INSTEAD OF THIS WITLESS IMBECILE?

"Watch your tongue, beast! You know not to whom you speak, for I am Sai Garrod Brockhurst, Prime Wizard of Darune. And I'm here to claim you, in the name of Archdale, the Attuned City that you destroyed."

The dragon's curiosity rouses at this outburst. PERHAPS I WAS WRONG, YOU DO HAVE SOME SPUNK AFTER ALL. SO, YOU ARE SOMEONE OF IMPORT IN YOUR WORLD, IS THAT SO?

"Don't patronise me. You will answer for the death of Sai Jason Brockhurst. You will answer for the destruction of my home, and the murder of ten thousand of my kin."

OH YES, I REMEMBER. SUCH FANCIES ARE FROWNED UPON BY MY KIND. BUT OCCASIONALLY, THE OTHER SIDE HAS TO BE KEPT IN CHECK. THERE WAS A LOT OF DRAINAGE EMANATING FROM THAT PLACE, AND IT WAS GIVING ME A HEADACHE. I HAD TO STOP IT SO THAT I COULD SLEEP.

"What are you talking about? Speak plainly, beast!"

Garrod sees a waterfall of flashing images. They snap into his mind like firecrackers, exploding one after another in an ever increasing onslaught. He vaguely recognises each image as a dragon memory, but can't decipher any of them beyond the occasional glimpse of something tangible – a tree, a mountain, various animals…and then he's looking down at Archdale from the sky. He's seen it like this before, when he flew over it. But this time it's different. Through the filter of the dragon's mind he doesn't see just a scattering of lifeless stone buildings and roads. He sees a pulsing, purple light, coursing around the city, like blood vessels beneath the skin.

The people glow with the same light, a purple core simmering in their hearts. And beneath the city, buried in the earth, a mighty glowing orb of energy rests.

What is that? Garrod thinks.

But as he stares, he understands. Perhaps the dragon is allowing him to see, or perhaps Garrod's last remnants of his sanity is putting the pieces together. The purple light is *attunement* itself. Magic, as the commoners say. The dragons can *see* magic.

Archdale rests on top of a natural well-spring of attunement. The city is rife with it, and the dragons know it.

No wonder the wizards had flourished there. Garrod's father and his ancestors had fed from that spring their entire lives and developed their skills under its influence. An invisible bruise-coloured energy lying right beneath their feet.

That colour. Garrod recognises it from the rift portals. The colour of decay. Attunement is the same colour as the sky in this dying world.

YES, the dragon booms. MY WORLD IS WHERE YOUR POWER COMES FROM. THEY ARE BOTH CONNECTED VIA THE COSMIC PLANE, AND THE ENERGY THAT YOU KNOW AS ATTUNEMENT, FLOWS FROM HERE TO THERE, ACROSS THE GULF. NOW, DO YOU UNDERSTAND WHY YOU ARE A PARASITE? YOUR ENTIRE WORLD IS.

"I never knew," Garrod says, awestruck. He tries to remember why he came here. Before he can process the thought, the dragon booms within his skull.

TEDIUM! THE CLOSEST MY KIND COMES TO EMOTION. I FEEL IT AGAIN NOW, GNAWING AT ME. NO DOUBT TRIGGERED BY THIS MOST POINTLESS OF INTERACTIONS. I HAD SENSED SOMETHING DIFFERENT ABOUT YOU, SOMETHING I THOUGHT MAY ACTUALLY BE INTERESTING. BUT I SEE NOW THAT I WAS WRONG. YOU'RE JUST

ANOTHER CREATURE OF HUBRIS WITH NOTHING OF VALUE TO TEACH THE LIKES OF ME.

The insult triggers an automatic response from Garrod. "I will show you hubris!" he snarls. He came here to strike this creature down with his mind. All he has to do is land on it and take control. Any moment now.

The moment passes.

Garrod is still frozen in mid-air. It occurs to him that time has not progressed since he started parleying with the dragon. He is stuck floating mid-flight, looking down at the snoozing dragon in its den. It isn't moving either, and they are locked in this moment, staring at one another.

SO THAT'S WHAT YOU CAME HERE FOR? The dragon sounds amused again.

Garrod senses the fear nipping at the edges of his conscious. He almost comprehends the mistake he has made, but not quite.

A BIG MISTAKE, the dragon booms in agreement. I WILL NOT GO DOWN AS EASILY AS THE CONDOR. HOW QUAINT, YOU NAMED IT CORCUBUS. BUT NOW THIS IS A CURIOSITY. IN ALL MY TIME, I HAD NEVER KNOWN THE EFFECT THE PASSAGE HAD ON A MORTAL'S SOUL. AND WHEN TWO MORTALS TRAVERSE TOGETHER... YOU BECAME ONE? HOW FASCINATING.

"I defeated Corcubus," Garrod says in a brave attempt at defiance. "I will defeat you t—."

I ADMIRE YOUR TENACITY. THE TRUTH IS, THIS NOTION REMINDS ME OF SOMETHING. SOME MORTAL SENSATION, WHAT IS IT AGAIN? YES! EXCITEMENT, THAT'S IT! YOU COULD NOT EVEN COMPREHEND HOW LONG IT HAS BEEN SINCE I FELT EVEN A GLIMMER OF SUCH A THING. EXCITEMENT! TO ASSIMILATE A MORTAL. PERHAPS THAT IS WHAT I HAVE CRAVED ALL THIS TIME.

"W-what?" Garrod says, as a thimble of panic bites a chunk out of his crumbling mind. With time frozen as it is, that tiny speck of panic is left lingering within him, unable to disperse. It becomes the most frightening thing Garrod has ever felt. When will the fear subside? When will time be allowed to continue?

WHEN I WILL IT. DO YOU KNOW HOW TEDIOUS MERE EXISTENCE IS, MORTAL?

Garrod, unable to shake the panic, is paralysed and barely receives the question.

HERE'S WHAT I'VE DECIDED TO DO, the dragon thunders on. WE WILL CARRY OUT THIS PLAN OF YOURS TOGETHER. I WILL GO WITH YOU THROUGH THE PASSAGE, IF ONLY TO SEE WHAT HAPPENS. I CANNOT RESIST. SO FAR AS I SEE, THE WORST CASE SCENARIO IS WE END UP SHARING A BODY, AND I WILL DEVOUR YOU. AFTER THAT, I MAY CONTINUE TO BE MYSELF, AND WELL, I'VE EXISTED FOR THREE TRILLION MILLENNIA, SO WHAT'S ANOTHER FEW AFTER THAT?

HOWEVER, I SEE THE POTENTIAL FOR A DIFFERENT OUTCOME... WHAT IF YOU SURVIVE? WHAT IF TOGETHER, WE BECOME MORTAL? I MIGHT FINALLY BE ALLOWED TO DIE.

Garrod's thimble becomes a teacup of terror. His blood turns to ice. "You want to die?"

NO, I WANT TO LIVE. BUT I CANNOT DO THAT WHILE I'M IMMORTAL. IMMORTALS DO NOT LIVE, THEY ONLY EXIST. EXISTENCE IS A CURSE. ALL I DESIRE IS TO LIVE AS A MORTAL.

"But then you'll die as one too!"

OF COURSE. DEATH IS THE ONLY CURE FOR EXISTENCE. LOOK.

The cascade of dragon memories bombards Garrod again, and he sees the death of so many stars.

THOSE ARE GALAXIES. The dragon says this word in a flippant, playful tone.

Garrod doesn't know the word. All he sees is the birth, life and death of a trillion planets. All within a nanosecond.

Garrod almost comprehends it, but not quite. His mind is full, like a waterlogged sponge, unable to absorb any more information, yet the dragon keeps firing more and more memories at him, none of which he can decipher, they are the memories of an ancient being, one that has existed through an uncountable number of lifetimes, and yet lingers on and on, unable to die. A slave to its own immortality.

Time spits him out at last.

Garrod is a limp bag of meat in mid-air, his wings turn to jelly and he crashes down into the Mana Spring in a crumpled heap, skidding to a halt under the dragon's nose.

The dragon stands, stretches, yawns and snorts out a plume of nibbets. Some of them go straight to Garrod, drawn to his warm blood.

LEAVE HIM.

The nibbets drop dead. The dragon plucks the paralysed Garrod up, where his wings hang limply between its claws. Beating its wings, the dragon takes flight amid a cloud of dust. It heaves itself up and over the dead treetops. In the sky, the dragon stares ahead.

Concentrating on a patch of air, the dragon tears open the fabric of space and creates a rift to Garrod's world.

HERE I COME, SWEET OBLIVION.

It flies into the black abyss, and triggers the assimilation.

When Garrod assimilated Corcubus, the process had taken approximately five seconds according to Garrod's perception of time. He was the assimilator then, exerting his dominance over the hatchling condor with relative ease to become the primary surviving entity.

This time, however…

When the dragon carries him through the rift, it takes barely a second to emerge on the other side. But that single second is stretched thin.

Within a nanosecond, the assimilation begins to merge their two consciousness's into one. Garrod's broken mind snaps together again with a jolting pinprick of pain in his temple that startles him awake.

He finds himself dangling in the claws of the huge beast as they hover in an endless black abyss. He remembers that he came to assimilate the dragon and become immortal.

He experiences time as the dragon does, that is, incredibly slowly.

"What is your name, beast?" Garrod demands, hoping to exert some authority on the situation.

The dragon takes a moment to digest the question, and when it replies, Garrod hears amusement in its voice.

"NO-ONE HAS EVER ASKED ME THAT BEFORE," it muses, speaking aloud for the first time. Then, telepathically, it utters an incomprehensible noise that scratches across Garrod's thoughts like a rake through broken glass.

KRRRRKKKKKKKSSSSSSSSSSSSSSSSSSSSSSSSSSSSSSSSSSSS.

Another jolt of concentrated pain strikes Garrod, this time in his knee. The pain is intense, but only for a microsecond and then it is gone.

"What sort of name is that, dragon? Speak one that I may pronounce."

The dragon considers this. "IN YOUR TONGUE, THE CLOSEST I CAN IMAGINE IS… KRAXIUS." The dragon is clearly impressed with himself. "OH, THIS IS FASCINATING. YOU MORTALS ARE A WONDER, TO BE SURE. NOW I HAVE A *NAME*."

"Kraxius," Garrod repeats, satisfied. If he can name the beast, he can control it. A minor but significant victory. Another flash of agony interrupts his triumph, this one focused in a tiny part of Garrod's right hand. Again, as quickly as the pain arrives, it is gone a moment later. This continues to occur all across Garrod's body, and he focuses his efforts on keeping the dragon distracted as the assimilation continues.

"Only one of us will survive this, Kraxius."

"NO, ULTIMATELY, *NEITHER* OF US WILL." The dragon grins. "THAT IS THE POINT."

Another zap of excruciating pain.

"This agony," Garrod gasps. "We are merging."

"NO. I AM SIPHONING YOUR MORTALITY, ONE CELL AT A TIME."

A cascade of lightning strikes ripple across Garrod's flesh, and he knows the dragon speaks truly. Specks of his skin are now missing, noticeable pieces of himself have already transferred to the dragon.

In that moment, Garrod realises, not that his chance to become immortal had been lost, but that his chance had never existed to begin with. The dragon would devour him.

His life was over.

"*Why?*" Garrod wails, his voice a tiny squeak between the lightning strikes of his body's destruction. "Why would you sacrifice your immortality? Now you're going to *die*."

"NO," Kraxius replies. "I AM FINALLY GOING TO *LIVE*."

"But you could have lived *forever*!"

"I HAVE NEVER LIVED," Kraxius says. His tone is that of a parent explaining to a toddler that walking in the rain will make them wet. "I HAVE EXISTED UP UNTIL NOW. THAT'S ALL. EXISTING AND LIVING ARE NOT THE SAME. MANY CREATURES EXIST IN THIS UNIVERSE, BUT A RARE FEW HAVE THE LUXURY OF LIVING."

"I don't understand," Garrod wails. A myriad of holes the size of bottle caps are now scattered across his body, missing pieces that have been absorbed by the dragon. Fragments of his mind seep into Kraxius, like sand pouring from one hourglass chamber to the next. Garrod's mind is full of unique things that Kraxius had never experienced before: happiness, excitement, fear, pain, frustration, love, embarrassment, hope…

"*EMOTIONS!*" Kraxius says, delighted. "THESE COMPLICATED PHENOMENA EXPLAIN SO MUCH!"

The dragon is processing all of this information at roughly a hundred times the speed of light, and now that Garrod's mind is partially joined with him, the two begin to share consciousness.

Kraxius had always held a morbid curiosity with the mortals. He never understood why or what attracted his attention to them. Until now.

Envy. Jealousy. Bitter resentment.

These words were all new to him, but the feelings they represented were not. He just hadn't been able to label them until now. He had not been capable of emotion, because an immortal being solved all of its problems by simply waiting for them to disappear. Things like discomfort and agitation, they diluted to nothing if you waited long enough. And an aeon dragon had an abundance of time to wait for such things.

But now, as he became mortal, he came to a powerful realisation. All that waiting around had been a colossal waste of…time. The tedium of it. To be an aeon dragon was to be eternally bored.

Bored to his wits end. And, lurking in the human's mind, was a much more powerful description of his condition: depression. Kraxius had been depressed.

Garrod's body resembled a shredded curtain now, flaps of skin dangled loosely in the dragon's grip. One of his eyes and half of his face had been assimilated, so when Garrod spoke, he looked like a ragged, deformed puppet.

"You are pitiful," Garrod said not unkindly, as his ear was zapped away.

"UNTIL THIS MOMENT, I HAVE NEVER FELT THESE… EMOTIONS," Kraxius muses. "THEY ARE LIKE SUPERNOVAS EXPLODING IN MY MIND, EXHILARATING, OVERWHELMINGLY POWERFUL. I KNEW THAT MORTALS HAD IT GOOD, BUT I DID NOT EVER CONCEIVE THAT IT COULD BE THIS INCREDIBLE."

"I can't begin to comprehend the existence you have led, dragon," Garrod said before his right eye disappeared. He sounded pathetic. Full of regret. Kraxius felt a surge of that envious fire again before realising he had no reason to feel that anymore. He was taking this man's mortality for himself. Soon, he could have his *own* regrets, his own bitter memories. Kraxius felt impatient to start creating new memories with meaning, memories that would exist only within his mind for the next, how long? Ten thousand years? A few million?

A feeling of amusement came as the notion occurred to him that he was already thinking in *years* and not cycles – something he must have subconsciously inherited from the human already. However long until the next Equilibrium. Because when the time came again to crossover, Kraxius would stay. He would linger in the dying world as it slowly began to transform back into its primal ingredients of dust and dirt. His body will weaken, he will *age,* his bones will crumble, his skin will peel. And he would at last give his final breath.

He decided then that he would travel the planet in search of a glorious place to die. Somewhere his skeleton would lie untouched for countless years, waiting to be discovered by some human. He would inspire his own stories, feed the mortals' imaginations. Kraxius would become a *legend.*

He liked that idea very much.

"TELL ME OF ONE OF YOUR LEGENDS, GARROD," he asked the human, as the portal to the Other approached. Beyond, Kraxius saw green trees.

"I was a scholar of attunement," Garrod slurred wearily through the remaining quarter of his mouth. "I don't care for bedtime shtories."

"BUT YOU MUST KNOW SOME. TELL ME."

Garrod found he couldn't refuse. The dragon dug into his mind and pulled out a story as easy as taking a cookie from a jar. And Garrod had to tell it. "My father spoke of a monshtrous flying beasht…"

"THAT SOUNDS JUST LIKE ME! WHAT DID HE DO?"

"He laid waste to a city. Ten thoushand people died in a matter of minutes."

"FASCINATING. AND SUCH DEEDS CREATE LEGENDS IN YOUR WORLD?"

"No. This beast is not written in any hishtory books. Nobody knows it even exishted, except for the two remaining survivors. And shoon there will be only one of those left."

"YOU SPEAK AS IF YOU KNOW THEM FIRST HAND?"

Kraxius was toying with Garrod now. He could read Garrod's mind like an open book. He knew this story was about himself. But Kraxius took pleasure in a new sensation – the human behaviour known as cruelty. It brought him great amusement to see the human suffer. It made him feel powerful.

He lusted for more.

"I THINK I KNOW WHAT MY FIRST MORTAL ACT IS GOING TO BE," he said in a sinister whisper. To Garrod, it sounded like a tidal wave crashing over his skull. What was left of his skull, at any rate. The lightning strikes had reduced Garrod to a few dangling patches of flesh and feathers.

"What?" Garrod wheezed, his voice box barely intact.

"I'M GOING TO FINISH WHAT I STARTED THIRTY YEARS AGO. YOUR MENTOR, ROBERT ANDERS. HE IS DEAR TO YOU."

"No," Garrod croaked again. "You can't. Leave him al—" Garrod was cut off as the last of his head vanished, absorbed by the dragon.

"HEH, I CAN DO WHAT I PLEASE. ISN'T THAT THE MORTAL WAY?" Kraxius continued, staring straight ahead at the approaching Everdusk portal. "DO WHAT YOU CAN, MAKE EVERY MOMENT COUNT, RIGHT? LIVE EACH DAY AS IF IT'S YOUR LAST. I AM GOING TO LIVE HARD AND DIE YOUNG. I THINK IT'S TIME TO GET STARTED."

Kraxius had never before experienced the sensation of hate, because time eroded it to apathy. But as he siphoned off the last of Garrod's humanity, as he replaced his immortal existence, Kraxius realised that he *despised* the mortals.

This rage manifested itself as a burning fire in his chest. Not literal, he wasn't one of those fire-breathing lizards that some of the humans liked to tell stories about. He was an aeon dragon, a Grim Dweller, a RIFTWALKER.

But not anymore.

The final remnants of Garrod's body vanished, and the assimilation was complete.

Garrod sees his world appearing before him as the two beings traverse the rift, and the moment before they emerge on the other side, Garrod has a rush of sensation, as if he is being born again.

He finds a part of the dragon's mind that is empty, devoid of memory or thought, and he pounces into it. A space for himself. A blinding white space, vast and empty, and all his.

This is the dragon's mortal memory being created. There's room for me here!

Just as Garrod had created a dungeon for Corcubus, the dragon had unconsciously created a place for Garrod. The blinding white dulls until it becomes a star, a rising sun over the crest of a grassy field.

Garrod soars over the wide empty plain and knows he is home.

Over the Everdusk, the rift spat out a flying creature.

It looked like a dragon, but it had four wings instead of two.

One pair were the dragon's own scaly wings. The other pair was covered in thick, black feathers.

Garrod and the dragon had assimilated into a single entity welded with raging madness.

Kraxius turned in the direction of three manmade towers a short flight away. There, he would begin forging his legend. A legend of torment, fear, misery, and blood.

CHAPTER TWENTY-FOUR

"I'll *kill him*!"

Ellie's face contorted in twisted rage and she grabbed the decrepit, rotten desk with both hands and toppled it over. Half of it crumbled to dust with a dry crash.

"Take my hand!" Johanna called somewhere behind her. She sounded far away.

Ellie went to the window instead and looked out over the black, dead forest. She stared after Garrod, now a shrinking winged monster flying over the trees.

Ellie leaned on the windowsill, stuck her neck out a far as she could and let forth a bellowing howl.

A flock of mangy sparrow-like birds scattered out of a tree and flew away, terrified by the harrowing imitation of Arkarus and his kind.

Ellie's vocal chords thrummed as the howl went on, finally letting go and returning her fiery gaze to the murderer.

Garrod became a small, flapping speck then suddenly disappeared as he dropped out of sight beneath the trees.

"Ellie!" Johanna cried again, sounding desperate.

Ellie tore her eyes away from the window and saw Johanna at the other end of a black tunnel, reaching forwards with an outstretched arm.

Ellie looked at her hands. She felt strange. Energised, somehow. Was it the rage? The grief? No, she was familiar with grief, and this was much stronger. Some alien energy had found its way into her and she knew that if she went back to her sister, who lingered across the threshold in their world, she knew that power would be lost.

She had to use it while she had it.

"Sorry, sis. Not yet."

The rift closed and Johanna disappeared. Ellie was alone in the dead place. Alone with *him*.

She turned back to the window.

Half a click away, some huge, writhing shape heaved itself out of the forest and into the sky. Ellie felt a significant portion of her anger drain away, replaced by a shard of cold fear, because the thing was a creature straight out of a nightmare.

It was a monstrous flying beast, grey and deathly, with clawed wings twice the size of its bulbous body, with a long neck stretching forwards towards her. Its head must have been the size of a horse, with sword-like fangs, and she saw Garrod dangling in its claws. It hadn't eaten him, it was carrying him.

The dragon flew towards her then something strange happened. The air shimmered, flashed, but it wasn't a bright flash, it was more like the opposite of blinding. A sphere of total blackness seemed to swallow the dragon for a second, then it vanished completely. The dragon had gone, carrying its prize with it.

Ellie had barely time to digest what she had seen when an answering howl echoed out of the woods. A pack of wolves, at least ten, if Ellie's ears weren't mistaken, howled one after the other in rapid succession until all of them were singing into the wind.

A pack. They answered my call!

Ellie leaned out of the window and howled again.

They replied with more howls, sounding closer. "Yes!"

she cried. "Come to me! I know your voices, I know your names!" She frowned, unable to explain this strange feeling of connection to the howls. And how could she possibly know their names? She realised she didn't, but that was the closest way to describe the feeling.

She clambered out of the window, and lowered herself down the outside of the tower, which was leaning slightly away from the forest, making a convenient slope, and the rough, jagged bricks made useful footholds.

She dropped the last ten feet and rolled on the ground. She hopped over the low wall and ran into the forest, howling again and calling to the wolves.

A moment later, a wolf bounded up to her and stopped in its tracks. Ellie skidded to a halt and spread her hands wide in a gesture of wary respect. "Hello," she said softly. "I found you."

The wolf was taller than a horse. It towered over Ellie, with *six* eyes regarding her with cool intrigue. Its ears were pricked forwards, ready to pounce at the first sign of deceit.

Can it be? This thought came from the wolf, Ellie heard it in her mind, the most humanlike voice she had ever deciphered from a wild animal. *My son?*

"No," Ellie said, clamping her lips tight. "Arkarus is gone… but he saved me. He saved my life."

Arkrussssss...

"Yes," Ellie said, tears forming in her eyes. "He was my friend. The best one I ever had." She cautiously offered the wolf a palm, and bowed her head, casting her eye down at the wolf's feet. "I'm so sorry."

The wolf licked her outstretched hand with a hot, wet tongue.

My son. I found you.

Ellie choked out a shuddering sob. "No, you're mistaken. He's dead." She looked up then, and met the wolf mother's tender eyes. They blinked slowly, in a little wave – first the smallest front eyes, then the larger middle eyes, then the biggest eyes blinked last. She licked Ellie's hand again and moved closer, rubbing her head against Ellie's chest, in a gesture that could not be mistaken for anything other than affection. Deep affection for a precious family member that had been lost, but now was found.

Ellie didn't understand it. Perhaps the wolf mother scented Arkarus on her, they had spent so much time together, after all. More than that, they had shared their *minds.* Was it even possible to get closer than that to another living thing? Ellie supposed not.

So, she wrapped a tentative arm around the wolf mother's neck, buried her hand deep into her thick fur and hugged her tightly.

"Okay," she said softly. "It's okay."

More wolves approached slowly, from all directions and soon Ellie found herself in the middle of the pack, all watching her. Some had six eyes and three tails, just like the big mother, others had four and two, like Arkarus. All of them were black, streaked with silver. This was undoubtedly Arkarus' pack.

No, not just his pack. This is his family.

The wolf mother looked down at Ellie and licked the salty tears off her cheek. Ellie let out a sweet giggle which brought her crying to a halt. She counted seven pups, although they were nearly all as big as Arkarus had been. Slowly, the anger returned, like a bonfire's embers refuelled with fresh kindling.

"I must get back." She looked around at the depressing landscape. Everything was in a state of decay, even the sky felt wrong, like it had been infected. Not a single leaf sprouted from any of the trees, there was no grass, only dry stony dirt, and though Ellie had seen a flock of birds earlier, right now there wasn't the slightest sign of life other than the wolves. No other tracks, no droppings, and she suspected that it wouldn't matter if she wandered for wheels and wheels, as this pack surely must have, all the way south to the Honeywoods, the scenery would be the same. This world was dying.

And yet the creatures that were here, while not thriving, they were at least feeding on *something*. Ellie knew that creatures as big as these wolves, and that dragon she had seen earlier, and even perhaps the bear-gator thing she had seen wandering in the Everdusk… creatures just couldn't get that large without a food supply to sustain them. Physics simply didn't allow it.

So what in Kella are they feeding on?

She became aware of that strange energising power again, as if the world itself was answering her question. It made her feel stronger, her mind sharper. She felt a tingling in the tips of her fingers, and when she focused on that, it spread up the length of her arms, past her shoulder and into her neck. From there, the pleasurable sensation poured up into her head and when it hit her brain, an explosion of energy surged down through her core.

Attunement coursed through her, and Ellie absorbed it like a sponge. Nothing had ever made her feel *that* good before.

A rift tore open around her and the wolf mother.

The void enveloped them in a dome of darkness. Ellie recoiled in fright and scrambled away from the wolf, terrified that she would be merged with her just like Arkarus. She took a few manic steps away and out of reach of the gateway, joining the pups outside the rift. But this was an opportunity to return home. Greenery and vibrant trees peeked in from the other side, the dusk spores glowed a cosy orange, inviting her back. She had to take this chance! "Go! Go through!" she ushered the wolf mother onwards, encouraging her to enter the vastly more pleasant Everdusk.

The wolf mother stood before the portal to Ellie's world looking back over its shoulder at her pack. She gave a little bark, which sounded echoey and distant coming out of the rift. The bravest pup leapt across the threshold and joined its mother in the rift, then loped onwards, heading for the light of Ellie's world. A second pup followed a moment later, then a third. One by one, all of the wolf pups walked through the rift, glancing at Ellie as they went, some loping calmly, others skipping with excitement.

Finally, the last one traversed the rift, and Ellie was alone in the skeletal remnants of the forest, staring through an abyssal tunnel, guarded by a huge wolf mother. The wolf turned and looked back at Ellie, as if expecting her to come through. "Go!" Ellie said. "We can't go together or else…" *Or else we'll be merged.* It was too much to explain and the wolf wouldn't understand anyway so she just shouted again, "*Go! Now!* Before it closes!"

But the wolf mother didn't move. She lingered, regarding Ellie the way a mother watches her daughter. She was waiting, like a true alpha, Ellie realised she wouldn't leave any of her pack behind.

The rift shimmered. Its edges wobbled, and Ellie sensed its will to close. If it did, she had no idea whether she would be able to open another one, so she had no choice but to risk a second assimilation and go through.

With a big gulp, Ellie bucked up her courage and walked into the shimmering void. She passed by the wolf mother, which didn't move from her spot, floating there in the black tunnel. She crossed into the Everdusk portal and stepped out into fresh air on the other side.

Ellie inhaled a mighty breath, smelling the overwhelming freshness, the abundance of clean air, full of life.

The wolf mother emerged behind her and then the rift snapped out of existence.

Ellie laughed, a joyous gleeful laugh. She smelled the fresh air and wondered if anything tasted sweeter.

One of the wolf pups coughed. It hacked up a phlegmy vomit of mucous. Then so did another. And another. The wolf mother gave a series of nasty wretches and vomited on the ground as well.

As Ellie's euphoria wore off, she became aware of something lurking within her. It felt like a billion tiny insects crawling through her stomach. She was utterly repulsed, and couldn't shake the horrifying visual of creatures, tiny microscopic ones being born inside her.

She hunched over, falling to one knee and retched. Nothing came out. She retched again, making a terrible, choking sound. On the third try, a thick, viscous substance poured out of her mouth, burning the back of her throat and spilled onto the grass.

She looked at it with horror. The mucous was riddled with insect larvae. Tiny nibbet eggs.

She let out a panicked shriek. That euphoric feeling had almost convinced her that the other world was somehow special. But the air, that musky, dusty air was infected with microscopic insects that could come and go as they pleased, using your respiratory systems as roads in and out of your body.

That was how the creatures lived there without food. The insects lived inside the stomach, feeding their host, and yet slowly killing them at the same time. Somehow, the wolves and the dragon had evolved to live in harmony with these parasites.

But here in her world, they had no place. Ellie and the wolves were rejecting them immediately.

It made absolutely no sense to Ellie, turning everything she knew about nature upside-down. That other world was simply wrong.

Someone screamed in the near distance. All the wolves' heads turned together in the direction of the Towers.

"Johanna!" Ellie cried.

Ellie staggered to her feet and ran, and the pack followed.

CHAPTER TWENTY-FIVE

Johanna tumbled backwards and landed on her butt in Garrod's chamber. She sat there a moment, dazed and shocked, alone at the top of the Sun Tower in the headmaster's chamber.

"No… little sis," she whimpered. *She's gone!*

Before she had time to formulate a coherent reaction to this awful realisation, a huge shape caught her eye out of the window. She had seen the dragon before, and so felt not surprise, but a dreadful embrace of cold panic. *Not again,* she had time to think, recognising the oncoming wave of terror. She staggered to her feet and rushed to the window.

Fwuh-wump, fwuh-wump, fwuh-wump. The dragon soared towards the tower at ferocious speed, each flap of its wings creating a strange echoing whoosh. Johanna couldn't tear her eyes away from the approaching beast and quickly realised the source of the strange sound. Since the last time she'd seen it, the dragon had grown an extra pair of wings. One pair looked anatomically correct, wide curtains of thin leathery skin, stretched taut between bony claws. But underneath those, a second pair of wings flapped, looking as out of place as a third leg on a human. The extra wings were black and feathery, like that of a giant vulture, and they moved a fraction out of sync with the dragon's natural wings.

Those are Garrod's!

Johanna gaped at the flying monstrosity, and it turned to look right at her. In that moment, she heard its voice inside her head. It sounded thunderously bestial, but Garrod's voice lingered deep within.

BEHOLD MY MAGNIFICENCE! KRAXIUS IS MORTAL, AND HE COMES TO DELIVER YOUR DESTRUCTION!

The dragon swooped overhead, pushing a foul gust of air through the window into Johanna's face that snapped her ponytail free of its bow and sent her long hair rippling behind her head. She tasted ancient, dry dust and started coughing.

A scream wailed up from below, young and girlish, terrified.

"Bella!" Johanna gasped, and ran for the stairwell. She leapt down the stairs two at a time, her skirt billowing behind her. More screams and cries sounded through the little round windows as she sped past, winding down and down, all the way to the bottom. She ran across the lobby and burst out of the main doors into the sunlight.

Tabitha Henlowe was standing with Robert Anders in the middle of the courtyard, ushering students and low-staff members towards the main gates. They kept glancing up at the circling dragon, which was writhing and thrashing about in mid-air. It looked as though it were struggling to control itself.

Robert spied Johanna and gestured wildly to her. "Stay there!"

The dragon dropped out of the sky and crash-landed on the path, crushing a groundskeeper too slow to dive out of the way, and spraying pebbles in every direction like deadly hailstones. Its head crashed into the grass, leaving a hollow in the ground, and its tail thrashed, whipping against the walls of the Moon Spire, tearing off a spray of stone chunks.

The dragon scrambled into a standing position in the

centre of the courtyard.

"*SUFFER MY TORMENT!*" it bellowed. With its mighty jaws aimed directly at Tabitha and Robert, it spewed forth a belch of nibbets that engulfed them both and dispersed across the courtyard, blotting out the view of the main gates.

Johanna screamed and took cover in the doorway.

A flame exploded out of the writhing black insectoid cloud. Yellow fire erupted forth and scorched a hole in the plague, incinerating thousands of the vicious insects. Robert and Tabitha emerged as the insects receded. Both were bleeding from numerous bite wounds, but as Johanna watched, the nibbets that had escaped the fireblast were also dying, dropping out of the air and landing on the ground, littering the courtyard with a layer of black dust.

Nibbets can't survive here, Johanna thought. *The Everdusk spores keep them out.*

The dragon turned its head towards the Storm Spire and coughed out another plume. Nibbets engulfed the tower, shattering the windows and pouring inside. Johanna heard screams from within but once again, the flying plague quickly dispersed and dropped dead like a flurry of ashen snowflakes.

"HOW CURIOUS," the dragon bellowed in that eerie Garrod imitation voice. "I SUPPOSE MY BREATH HERE IS INEFFECTIVE." Suddenly, its face contorted in a grimace of discomfort and when it spoke again, its voice sounded *much* more like Garrod. It was still thunderously loud, but far more humanlike. "*Run!*" he roared. "*Get away from here. I cannot stop it!*" His words were choked away by a gargling cough as the dragon regained control, and let forth a third plague, this one the biggest of them all. The sunlight was blotted out by the enormous black plume, casting the tower grounds in darkness for the first time in its entire history. Not even the Everdusk spores could illuminate through that terrible fog.

The nibbets swarmed for a few seconds, beelining for whatever living thing they could find. Many found Johanna standing in the Sun Tower's entrance and landed all over her bare skin.

She shrieked again as nibbets tore tiny chunks out of the flesh on her arms and legs and face. With a twirl of her hands she summoned a batch of tiny fireballs and started tossing them, burning any nibbets that flew too close.

Finally, after a few agonising seconds, they began to die off naturally, the Everdusk's mysterious spores poisoning them in mid-flight and the dusky glow returned to the Towers.

"I SUPPOSE I'LL JUST HAVE TO DESTROY THIS PLACE VIA CLASSICAL MEANS." The dragon tucked both sets of its hideous wings down onto its back, like a duck. The feathered wings didn't fit properly, and protruded out from beneath the others in a clump of knotted feathers. The dragon clawed its way across the courtyard in three strides and mounted the side of the Storm Spire. It dug its talons into the brickwork and wrapped its tail all the way around the base, clambering up the tower like a ludicrously oversized living gargoyle. With one swipe of its upper arms, it tore out a huge chunk of the upper chamber, which crashed to the ground in a bombardment of glass, stone and timber.

Shrieks and cries sounded from within. Johanna caught a glimpse of a red and glistening liquid spill out of the gaping hole where the tower's upper floor had been. It looked like the dragon's claw had punctured a giant waterskin that had been filled with tomato juice. A moment later, the upper torso of one of the boys fell out and landed on the grass with a sickening splat.

Johanna lost all sense of thought and feeling. She slipped momentarily into total shock, frozen in gaping horror at the dreadful spectacle.

A wild chorus of barks snapped her back to reality, although she couldn't work out what was happening until she saw a pack of monstrous wolves come bounding around the side of the Sun Tower, heading straight for the dragon.

Five wolves leapt up sinking their claws into its hide and biting at it with savage hunger.

"Bring it down!" cried a familiar voice. Johanna turned to see her sister come charging past riding atop a wolf as big as a stallion. She had an arrow nocked in her bow and as she sped past, drew and fired it at the dragon's neck. The arrow ricocheted off and bounced harmlessly away.

"AAAAARRRGHH *YES!*" roared the dragon. "SO *THIS* IS WHAT PAIN FEELS LIKE! GIVE IT TO ME, GIVE ME MORE, *YES!*" As it bellowed these absurdities, it thrashed its tail and whipped two of the approaching wolves aside, hurling them across the courtyard in a wail of yelps. The dragon let go of the tower and landed so hard that it shook the ground.

Ellie rode away from the thrashing tail, dodged its sweeping arc and circled the Storm Spire. She reappeared on the far side, fired another arrow that sunk into the dragon's neck. The dragon turned towards her, snapping its jaws, but Ellie's wolf dodged again, expertly ducking beneath the attack and they both rushed away out of reach in the direction of the main gate.

"AN ETERNITY OF TEDIUM, IS THIS WHAT I'VE BEEN MISSING OUT ON?" thundered the dragon, and broke into a deafening cough of laughter. "*KEH KEH KEH KEH!*"

"Miss McKree!" Robert Anders had somehow made it across the courtyard to Johanna, and he stood at the bottom of the steps offering her a hand. His eyes were wide and frantic. "Come on Miss, we have to get you out of here!"

"But my sister!" she pointed towards the wolves.

"What?" Robert's expression turned to bewilderment.

"Ellie!" Johanna cried, but there was so much noise in the grounds now that her voice was drowned out by all the snarling, barking, and boom of stomping dragon's feet.

Ellie and her wolf darted behind the Moon Spire and emerged to the right of the dragon, firing arrows at it. Some arrows pinged off its thick leathery hide, but others jutted out like a tailor's pincushion.

The younger wolves were circling and attacking the

dragon in unison, tearing at the legs, the rump, the flanks, mostly coming away with small tears of dry flesh between their teeth.

"Come *on!*" Robert was clutching her arm now and gave a sharp tug, pulling Johanna down the steps. She stumbled after him, reached the flat ground of the courtyard and tore herself free of his grasp.

"No! I won't leave her!"

"That thing is going to destroy this place!" Robert argued desperately.

"Not if we destroy it first," Johanna retorted.

As if hearing their conversation, and perhaps it did, the dragon wheeled about and faced them.

Garrod's voice came out of its snarling lips. "It's me! Robert, I'm trapped in this beast! I…" Then his words faltered behind a hacking cough as the dragon vomited up a grey mucous which burned the grass where it landed.

Robert stared at the beast, mesmerised. "Garrod?" he said softly. "What have you done this time?"

The dragon answered by raising its gigantic head again and lunged at Robert with gaping jaws.

"Look out!" Johanna cried, and raised her hands. Two searing fireballs leapt from her palms and shot straight down the dragon's gullet. It halted mid-lunge and its eyes bulged. Johanna smelled charred flesh and black smoke wafted from its mouth.

How did I do that? She was exhausted, hadn't eaten in hours, and should never have been able to produce a fireball, let alone *two.*

The dragon began to choke. It hacked up more mucous, this time a dark ashen colour, coughing like thunder.

"It's not fireproof!" Tabitha Henlowe cried somewhere out of sight behind the dragon's bulk. Johanna heard a sizzle and a *whoosh,* then more black smoke rose from the other side of the dragon's body. It turned away from her now, snarling and hissing like a furious snake. At the same time, it unfurled its mighty wings.

It's going to fly away.

"Don't let it take off!" Johanna cried, suddenly sure that if it did, they would have no way to kill it. It could fly all the way to Darune and wreak unimaginable damage. The nibbets wouldn't die as they did here. It could unleash a devastating plague across the entire city and nobody would survive.

If it reached the capital, it would be ten times the Archdale calamity.

What if it didn't stop there? What if it travelled along the road, south west, scouring all of the villages along the way until it reached Harbrook?

"*Don't let it fly*!" she shrieked. Lifting both palms towards the dragon, she summoned more balls of fire and hurled them at the beast. They struck the flanks and ribcage making loud slapping sounds, each one scorching a burn mark into the dragon's flesh.

Its wings flapped a hurricane, picking up a whirlwind of dust and pebbles, bits of glass and debris from the broken tower. Johanna screamed as she summoned more fireballs, aiming them at the wings.

Feathers caught fire and sizzled away to nothing, but the dragon kept on moving, scrambling towards the main gates as it picked up speed.

Johanna and Tabitha chased after it on foot, hurling fire at its fleeing backside, and Ellie galloped through the gates shooting arrows, trying to get in front of it and shoot out an eye.

"YES! YES! YEEESSS!" The dragon half-hissed, half bellowed in some kind of demented combination of anguish and euphoria. "THIS PAIN IS EVERYTHING! *I CRAVE MORE!*"

The last of the feathers burned away as the dragon took flight, screaming in agony. Its claws clipped the snapping heads off of the lillysnappers guarding the gates, and their stalks slumped over backwards, decapitated and lifeless. The dragon beat its way into the air and soared over the canopy out of sight.

Johanna wailed after it, a feeling of hopeless despair washing over her.

She didn't notice Ellie come circling back around until she was almost on top of her. "Hanna!" Ellie cried. She grabbed Johanna by the cuff of her blouse and hauled her onto the wolf's back. "Hold on!"

Johanna swung her leg over and sat behind Ellie as the wolf bounded out of the gates, howling. They leapt through the gap made by the decapitated lillysnappers and raced down the road. Johanna craned her neck back and saw the Towers diminishing, Tabitha and Robert joined by a crowd of terrified students, teachers and gardeners staring after them. They flinched and scattered in all directions as the rest of the wolf pack bounded out, giving chase to their mother.

Soon, they were charging at great speed through the Everdusk, a pack of ten giant black wolves. Faintly, Johanna heard more barks and yips. Dogs appeared out of the trees, coming from every direction to join the chase. She saw a brown sheep dog, and a huge lumbering hound, slathering at the mouth as it ran.

"Frank!" Ellie cried suddenly, sounding jubilant. "Whisper! You wanna help us, that's good. Come on!"

"Who are they?" Johanna asked, her voice cracking with every turbulent bound.

"That's my pack!" Ellie cried in glee. She turned to her left. "Toma! Stay back! This is too dangerous for you! And you, Dug!"

Several of the tiny dogs fell behind very quickly, their little legs pounding the grass at lightning speed, but there was no way they could keep up with the wolves.

Overhead, they caught glimpses of the dragon as it flew away south, heading most likely towards Edgehurst, the closest human settlement of any significance.

"You *bastard!*" Ellie yelled up at it, reaching over a shoulder to pluck another arrow from her quiver. Johanna held her tightly around the waist, squeezing in an effort to stop her sister from falling off.

"You're slipping!" she cried.

"Hold onto me!" Ellie retorted, drawing her bowstring. She timed her shot so that the arrow flew up through another gap in the trees. They had no idea whether it found its mark or not, because the canopy quickly closed in again.

"Dammit!" Ellie grunted, holstering her bow over a shoulder, and nearly hitting Johanna in the face with it. "Sorry. Just hang on, we have to go faster."

"*Faster?*" Johanna said, unable to comprehend how that was even possible. But then the wolf under her seemed to judder, her muscles rippled beneath Johanna's legs, kicking in another gear and somehow accelerating even more.

The younger wolves and the dogs fell away behind, and soon it was just the three of them charging at breakneck speed through the forest.

"*Arroooooooo!*" Ellie howled.

Trees whipped past on either side, as the road wound its way this way and that, curving gently, but each turn pushed Johanna's centre of gravity sideways in a mean attempt to shrug her into the dirt.

There was nothing to do but cling on for dear life.

Eventually, way ahead, a light appeared through a gap in the trees.

"We're almost out!" Ellie cried.

The tunnel of light sped towards them, and they burst into the plains south of the forest. In the distance, Edgehurst village sat just below the horizon. Ellie and Johanna both let out involuntary cries of dismay at what they saw.

The dragon had outrun them. It was flying over the village. As they watched, a plume of blackness shot downwards from the dragon and they knew it was raining hell onto the poor people that lived there. Outside the protection of the Everdusk, those nibbets wouldn't die until they had gorged themselves, mated and laid their spawn in every nook and cranny in the village.

"You *bastard!*" Ellie cried again, leaning forwards and giving the wolf mother a kick in the ribs. "Hi-yah!"

They galloped on, and came to the outskirts of the village a few minutes later. A loud, constant humming noise rose up to greet them as they approached, and the sky jittered and danced with a million flecks of movement.

"Fry them!" Ellie screamed, meaning to plunge right into the village.

"I can't!" Johanna cried, clinging her sister around the belly, and staring over her shoulder in sheer terror at the sight of the village ahead, completely engulfed in a swirling mass of insects. Nibbets swarmed everywhere, clumps of them clinging to the walls of buildings, the roofs, the windows, while a million others plagued the sky. "There's too many!"

"Fook!" Ellie shrieked. A beat passed, then she said, "Okay, we have to thin them out first. *Whoa*," she said to the wolf, and it eased up its relentless sprinting, slowed to a gentle lope, then finally came to a stop.

Johanna's head was spinning. As Ellie dismounted, Johanna slipped over the side and stumbled onto the dirt, nearly tripping, but Ellie caught her and held her up.

The wolf mother whined. She looked anxiously back the way they had come, presumably searching for her pups. Then she bounded away back towards the Everdusk.

The dragon belched again and another plume of nibbets rained onto the village.

Ellie and Johanna stared in horror.

"I need you to burn me," Ellie said.

"What?" Johanna frowned in bewilderment.

"Just do it, okay? Somewhere painful. But not my hands!" Ellie quickly added.

"What on Kella—?"

"Just *do it*!" Ellie said, turning away from Johanna, and looking in the direction of the village. It hummed so loud, despite their distance, a quarter of a click away. Ellie closed her eyes, and let out a soft hum of discomfort. The hum turned into a groan, and she reached up, clutching her head with one hand, then both of them. "I can feel them. Inside my head. Do it, Hanna. Burn me!"

Johanna stared, dumbfounded. She glanced at the storm of nibbets and back at her sister.

"*Burn me!*" Ellie cried.

Johanna clicked her fingers and a candle-like flame protruded from her index finger. She touched it against Ellie's bare forearm, the skin instantly turning red. Ellie cried out in pain, and as she did so, a great wave of movement caught Johanna's eye, over the village. A huge writhing mass of the nibbets had taken to the sky and flown straight up, moving away from the buildings.

The hum of their wings grew to a loud deep drone that vibrated through Johanna bones. *She's telepathically hurting them. Sharing her pain with them. Incredible!*

She glanced back at the flame and Ellie's elbow and withdrew her hand in a sharp gesture. Ellie's skin was blistering, turning a horrid whitish red colour, the flesh completely destroyed in a small patch. "Oh, Ellie! I'm so sorry!"

The nibbets reacted to the sudden lack of fire, but warily. They seemed hesitant to return to the village, instead, opting to float around above the village, encircling it with their dragon master, who had now turned his attention towards the two sisters.

"WHAT DID YOU DO?" the dragon bellowed, its voice clear as day even from so far away. He banked until he was facing their direction and then flew right at them. The swarm followed.

Ellie uttered a cry and stumbled to one knee, her burned arm trembled violently.

"I'm sorry!" Johanna cried again, feeling desperately hopeless.

"Nevermind," Ellie said, gritting her teeth. She pointed a shaky finger at the approaching dragon and its swarm and said, "I have to try him now. Do it again!"

"What? No, Ellie, you can't!"

"*This isn't a debate!*" Ellie commanded. "Just *burn me!*"

Ellie turned towards the dragon, and Johanna had a sudden flashback memory of what it had been like to catch a glimpse of the inside of that creature's mind. The mind of immortality. The eternal mind of an ancient being. One that knows the true meaning of infinity.

It had scared her witless. And the only thing scarier than seeing it for herself was the idea of what might happen to her younger sister if she was exposed to the same thing. Ellie may be attuned, she may even be more naturally attuned than Johanna. But she was her *sister*. And Johanna would rather die than watch her sister go insane as the dragon tore her mind apart.

But there was no time.

The dragon was almost upon them. Johanna lifted both palms, outstretched towards the flying monster. It opened its jaws and Johanna saw right down its black throat. It meant to belch another plague right over them. She and Ellie would be riddled with parasites and devoured in a matter of seconds.

They were about to die. It was as simple as that.

Johanna felt a tingling in her fingertips. It was a familiar feeling. Not long ago, back in Harbrook, a similar situation had occurred, and she had a queasy sense of déjà vu. Ellie, facing off against a wolf, while Johanna stood behind, a strong sense of familial duty flowing through her veins. It was her job to protect her sister when she was in danger, and that feeling manifested itself as a swirling mass of orange and yellow flames, cupped in her palms above her head.

Johanna aimed the massive fireball and launched it straight at the dragon, just as it spewed forth its noxious living breath.

The searing fireball plunged through the black swarm and shot into the dragon's gullet. It choked on it.

Any nibbet not caught in the inferno veered sideways in

both directions, fleeing from the blaze. The dragon skipped a flap of its wings and faltered in the sky. Its eyes bulged, its jaws erupted smoke, as the soft flesh inside its throat burned to a crisp, and it screeched a hacking, choking sound.

It tumbled out of the sky and crashed into the earth in front of the sisters.

Its momentum carried it forwards, and Johanna grabbed her sister and flung them both to the side, narrowly avoiding being crushed by the sliding body of the mighty dragon.

The girls landed in the dirt hard, sprawled in a tangled heap of limbs on top of each other. The dragon's huge left claw came to rest just next to them, and immediately it scratched viciously at the ground as it tried to right itself.

"Watch out!" Johanna cried, pulling Ellie backwards over her chest. Ellie rolled nimbly away, but screamed in pain as her burned arm scraped along the ground. The dragon's claw dug a trench into the ground as it hauled itself into a wobbly standing position on all-fours, vomiting up a thick tarry black gunk, which splattered on the grass, instantly turning it an ashen lifeless grey.

"IT BURNS. IT BURNS!" the dragon bellowed. It spoke in a completely nonsensical mix of gleeful agony. "*YESSSSSSSSSS!*" it roared, the word drawing out into a long hiss. Then Garrod spoke up suddenly, sounding very much in pure pain. "*Whyyyy?*" was all he seemed capable of saying, before letting out an insane, blood-curdling scream.

We're hurting Sai Brockhurst, Johanna thought in dismay. But perhaps he deserved this? He had murdered her friends in pursuit of this madness. He had gone after this dragon, and he had lost. He chose this.

"Cover me!" Ellie suddenly shouted. "I can hear him so clearly."

"What?" Johanna said, who took a few beats to understand what her sister was talking about. It could take a long time for her to get used to the notion that Ellie was attuned. And now, as she watched Ellie close her eyes and press two fingers against her temples, she knew that she really was a powerful mage. She knew because as soon as Ellie did that arcane gesture, the dragon responded.

It turned its head sharply towards them both, but its eyes were transfixed on Ellie. Its yellowish irises shrank back as its black hole pupils dilated until they almost filled its eye sockets. They were the intelligent eyes of a rabid beast. Johanna shivered at the hungry look in those eyes and feared what her sister might be seeing now she had entered the mind of an immortal.

She feared for Ellie's life.

CHAPTER TWENTY-SIX

"WHO ARE THEE?" the dragon inquired from across Arkarus' barnyard.

"I am your end." Ellie had a cutting edge to her voice, partly from the fear but mostly because she was so pissed off. The dragon had the loudest voice of any animal she had ever telepathically heard, and unlike every other animal she had ever connected with, this one had actually come into *her* mind. She found herself standing in the now abandoned barnyard that she had created specifically for Arkarus, and it made her feel violated. The dragon was a trespasser standing on holy ground.

The endless starry sky slowly spun above her head. Arkarus' empty kennel lay to her left. The dragon sat on its haunches in front of the big barn with its head slightly cocked as it regarded her. Its wings were folded away behind it, both sets, even though Johanna had burned away its feathered ones in the physical world, they were still present here in this mental version of itself.

"I know you," said another voice from the dragon. The voice of the horrible man that had murdered Arkarus. "You're the younger sister. The attunement radiating from you is magnificent."

"Shut up," Ellie said. "Don't put me in the same category as you. If being attuned means destroying everything, then I want nothing to do with it."

The dragon threw back its head and belched out a series of throaty coughs that could only be laughter. When the creature spoke again, its voice was that of the dragon, all thunderous bass. "SUCH FEIST! ONLY A MORTAL COULD SPEAK SUCH FIRE AND YET REMAIN SO UTTERLY IGNORANT OF HER POSITION."

"Hey," Ellie frowned, offended. Although she didn't fully understand what the dragon had meant, she recognised the word ignorant, because Johanna called her it frequently. "Don't insult me, especially here. This place isn't for you."

"This is where you kept him, isn't it?" the man, Garrod said in a tone of wonder. "It's beautiful."

Ellie was slightly taken aback by this. "Yeah. And thanks, I guess."

"The stars… I didn't even consider stars."

"It was the only thing I could think of to fill the endless darkness." Ellie shook her head. Why was she talking to this murdering bastard? "You *killed* Arkarus. Now that you're trapped in my head, give me one reason why I shouldn't destroy you?" She didn't know for sure whether she could really do such a thing, but it was time to start showing them who was in charge here.

The dragon belched another laugh. "SO FULL OF SPARK. I HAVE YEARNED FOR A CONVERSATION AS THIS FOR LONGER THAN I CAN REMEMBER. YOU HAVE NO IDEA HOW TEDIOUS IT IS TO EXIST AS LONG AS ME WITH NOBODY TO TALK TO, NOBODY TO ADMIRE, NOBODY TO ARGUE WITH, NOBOD—"

"*Shut up!* Kella Murphy, can you *talk*," Ellie cried. "I don't give a shit about you or your existence or your dragon mumbo jumbo. Stop yammering and die." Ellie, for the first time in her life, actively tried to hurt an animal that she had no intention of eating afterwards. She did it by using the technique she had mastered with Arkarus whenever she wanted to project him from her mind. But instead of the gentle nudge she would use for Arkarus, now she extruded every nanofiber of her brain to shove the dragon into the cosmic abyss beyond the barnyard, which in turn would force it out of her head.

That was her hope, anyway.

Ellie imagined a giant fist and punched the dragon backwards. It crashed straight through the oaken barn, splintering its beams like matchsticks. The barn was obliterated, with chunks of it exploding out into the starry sky, carried away like debris in a hurricane.

The dragon flapped its enormous wings and stopped itself from being swept away, and it hovered there on the brink. Ellie was sure it would be caught and taken, but its strength was immense, far more powerful than Arkarus, and she couldn't evict it from her mind so easily.

"WOW!" it boomed, fighting against some enormous force that was trying to pull it backwards into oblivion. "YOU MIGHT BE THE STRONGEST ATTUNED MORTAL I HAVE EVER SEEN."

"*Get out of my head!*" Ellie screamed, furious by the dragon's persistence. "*GET OUT!*"

A shockwave blasted out from Ellie, which ripped every blade of grass from the ground. The shockwave shot across the desecrated barnyard and tore every flower out of the beds along with every fence post. The blast struck the dragon and shoved it backwards. The gentle rotating sky accelerated into a violent spin, and the stars morphed into a blurry spiral of light.

Ellie could feel her mind slipping. She tried to open her eyes in the real world and snap back to reality but she couldn't seem to tear her mental eyes away from the dragon that was tumbling into the starry vortex.

"WOW! " the dragon roared in triumphant madness, as its body was torn apart by the cosmic hurricane. Its wings ripped out of their shoulder sockets, its arms broke off at the elbow joints, its tail thrashed and tore away in a spray of viscous black blood and finally its head was separated from its long neck, the toothy mouth grinning at Ellie in a crazed predatory smile.

Ellie's eyes slammed open in reality and she gasped a huge breath. The angry buzz of nibbets filled the air and she looked up at a sky riddled with them. She was lying on her back in the dirt. Johanna was by her side, staring ahead. Ellie pushed herself up on one arm. She winced in agony, remembering it was horribly burned.

"Ellie!" Johanna cried, her voice full of relief. "I thought I'd lost you!" Tears spilled from her eyes.

Ellie looked past her at the dragon. It was sprawled out on its back with its legs in the air and its wings splayed out on either side. "Kill it." Her croaky voice was sandpaper. She coughed, spat and said again, with venom. "*Kill it, Hanna*!"

Johanna nodded and stood. She strode towards the dragon with her palms pressed together. Her cheeks bled from nibbet bite wounds, her blue dress was torn and shredded. Her long hair billowed out behind her in the wind. She pulled her palms apart and a bright swirling ball of flame ignited between them. She pulled her hands farther apart and the fireball expanded to fill the space. She hefted the flames above her head, the cloud of nibbets shied away from its searing heat. Johanna started to say something. A long, drawn out hum, which rolled into a long, terrible moan. Her arms were spread out in a great V, and the fireball within was surely the biggest anyone had ever produced.

Finally, Johanna swung her arms forwards and aimed it at the dragon, who thrashed around to face her.

Johanna launched the gigantic fireball. It shot forwards in a shallow arc, unleashing a long sizzling hiss.

"YES! END ME—"

His bellowing voice was a perfect mix of dragon and Garrod, and it cut out when the fireball engulfed it. The flames swept over and incinerated the dragon. A horrible stench of charred flesh stung Johanna's nostrils, and thick black smoke billowed upward from the writhing, thrashing dragon, wreathed in flames.

It roared an incomprehensible wail of agony. The air around it shimmered and waved, like ripples on a lake. A rift tore open around the dragon and exploded outwards in a dark spherical wave. The rift swallowed the sisters and the surrounding area, including the entire village of Edgehurst. They found themselves in a barren plain where everything was either dead or dying and the air tried to choke you with every breath.

And yet, Johanna felt her energy return tenfold. She absorbed power from the ground at her feet, feeling it pulse through her. *Like a tree absorbing water through its roots,* she thought. And suddenly, she realised what the dark reflection truly was. She understood its connection to their world, and why it was so important.

Their worlds co-existed on top of each other, just as the dragon had said. *As one world thrives, the other dies.* Johanna couldn't exist without this place. Its slow demise was crucial to her world's growth. As this world fell further and further into decay, Johanna's world sucked the life out of it, feeding off it.

The two worlds swung back and forth on a see-saw of energy. When one was up, the other was down.

And what would happen when the see-saw reached its apex? Why, it would reverse and tilt back, of course. Their planet's roles would slowly be switched. Over eons, their world would begin to die out as all of the energy was transferred back across the dimensions to feed the other, and the dead world would be reinvigorated.

Johanna's world would become the dying mirror of the vibrant, life-supporting place that she had been lucky enough to be born into. Her interaction with the dragon had allowed her this unique insight. A glimpse of infinity.

She looked at the wheezing, scorched creature before her.

How many cycles had this dragon witnessed? How many

more would there be? This creature was a wonder. Unimaginably old, in other circumstances, Johanna could have learned so much from it.

But looking at the smoking, charred body before her, she knew the truth. This was a pitiful creature now, tarred by a human's greed.

She had to put it out of its misery.

Johanna siphoned energy straight out of the ground until it filled her to the brim, and when she lifted her palms to the grim sky, cradled within was a fireball the size of a house.

CHAPTER TWENTY-SEVEN

Garrod died full of regret and sorrow.

Just as the gargantuan fireball raced towards his face, time slowed down, although in reality he was merely utilising the dragon's remarkable ability to see things as quickly or as slowly as it wanted. Garrod could have spent several lifetimes learning and mastering this skill, had he managed to assimilate the dragon into his being. But instead, he only had this final hour of utter madness and he would die without even touching the surface of this creature's potential.

But he deserved no less, really.

Faces drifted into his thoughts. First was Herbert, the young wizard that he had sacrificed. *The boy had his entire life left to live and I snatched it away.* Then came Markus and Karly, two more victims in his greedy pursuit of power. They had trusted him and he betrayed them. Finally, he saw Jason, materialising out of the shadowy vortex that had become his memory. *I couldn't save you, father.*

Then came a face he didn't recognise at first, and yet when he looked into her eyes, a warm sensation swept over him.

"Mother?" he said, almost choking on the pain.

Her face burned away when Johanna McKree's fireball careened into the dragon's body. Garrod's mother screamed with him, as if she was feeling the same scorching agony rip through her bones.

Garrod and Kraxius thrashed against the ground, as nibbets belched out of their throats and fled into the sky. When the fire burned deep enough into their belly, Garrod felt a terrible flooding feeling in the pit of his stomach. The lifeblood and heart of the dragon's body was literally pouring out through a fissure in the beast's skin. An unholy smell of rotten carrion burst out of the dragon's guts, and a great sloshing brood of nibbet larvae came with it, oozing gelatinous bile and puss that spread across the ground, hissing and steaming around the flames. Then the fires caught hold and boiled the bile into poisonous steam.

"ETERNAL SLUMBER COMES FOR ME NOW!" Kraxius roared its deathcry, drawing it out as a long, ear-splitting screech.

Garrod's mind was torn apart in his final moments as infinity took him. The last thing his conscious comprehended was a swirling vortex of fire and stars, sucking him into oblivion.

And then he was gone forever.

CHAPTER TWENTY-EIGHT

As the dragon burned, it exhaled its final breath. Every nibbet either dropped dead or fled into the sky. They rained down for a few seconds, littering the dirt with tiny insect bodies.

The smouldering dragon twitched a final time and then went still.

Ellie inhaled the fumes of the smoking carcass and decided it was the worst thing she had ever smelled. Barbequed ribs this was not. She cast her eyes across the black-charred skin that ran along its spine to its head. Both eyeballs had vapourised, and its tongue lolled out, also charred and smoking, curling between two black fangs.

"I swear never to piss you off again, Hanna."

Ellie only said it because she was too taken aback by the horror of what she had just seen, that trying to make light of it seemed the only way to possibly deal with it. The last thing she expected was for Johanna to burst out laughing.

Johanna bent over double, gasping her weird little laugh usually reserved for one of Grandpa's jokes. "Don't!" she gasped. "This isn't the time…" And with that, her laughter ceased, and she gazed at her hands with an expression of fearful wonder. "Oh, *Kella*."

"That was crazy," Ellie said. "You gotta be the most powerful wizard in the world."

"Mage," Johanna corrected absentmindedly, still staring at her hands. She flicked her fingers and a tiny jet of flame spat out from every digit. She clenched her fists together, stopping the fire and turned to Ellie. "What about *you*! I've never seen a telepath do what you just did. You… *attacked* it with your mind. You have to show me how to do that."

"I don't know how."

"You must!"

"I'll try to explain to you after we get out of here." Ellie looked around. The dragon's enormous rift lingered even after its death. "*If* we can get out…"

They both looked around searchingly, then turned towards where Edgehurst should have been. In its place was a barren field dotted with leafless, prickly bushes. With nowhere else to go, they headed in that direction. A couple dozen survivors of the nibbet plague were wandering around in a daze, victims of the dragon's attack. Many were crying, clutching the corpses of loved ones.

Ellie wandered through the field as if in a waking nightmare. Bodies littered the ground, lying all over the place, covering an area as large as Harbrook. Edgehurst's population far outweighed her home though, judging by the number of corpses. Ellie had seen death before, of course. But nothing like this.

"Ohh, what is this hellhole?" cried an Edgehurst woman. Like most of the survivors, her skin was scabbed and bloody from dozens of nibbet bites.

"How did we get here?" said a man, eyes darting around.

"My home! It's gone!"

"Help! Someone please help my boy!" wailed a woman, cradling a lifeless child in her arms.

"This is awful," said Ellie to Johanna.

"I know," she replied. "We have to help them."

After gathering up as many people as they could, the sisters set out north, leading the villagers back towards the

Everdusk, or at least this world's depressing version of it.

The rift caused by the dragon was so big, it had apparently swallowed the entire village of Edgehurst, and a huge chunk of the Everdusk. The group reached the rampikes that marked the outer limits of the grand forest and stopped.

Howling echoed from deep within, as well as the yips and barks of several large hounds.

"I hear wolves!" someone cried.

"Me too!" said another. "We must turn back!"

"It's okay," Ellie said, trying to calm them. "They won't hurt us, I'll make sure of it."

"How can you protect us?" said a man with a permanent grimace, thanks to the huge flap of torn skin that had been ripped from his left cheek. "You're just a wee girl."

"She's a telepath," Johanna spoke up, defending her sister. "She already saved you from the dragon. She can protect us from whatever's out there."

Ellie exchanged a not so convincing look with her sister, but she appreciated the vote of confidence.

"We can't be saved," moaned another man with crazy eyes, cradling the unconscious body of a small boy. "We're already dead."

The wolves howled again, seeming much closer than before.

"*Arroooooo!*" Ellie howled back, startling the villagers.

"What are you doing?" someone cried in dismay.

"She's leading them right to us!" bawled another.

Some of the people backed away from the two sisters, panic growing in their eyes.

"I reckon it was *you* who brought the dragon upon us in the first place!" snarled a man with blood streaked across his face like war paint. He lunged at Ellie with violent intent. Johanna instinctively reached out her hand to stop him, jets of fire shooting from her fingertips.

The flames made a wall of fire between Ellie and the man, whose lunge was too far gone to take back, and he tipped forwards into the fire head first.

Johanna panicked and clenched her fists to quell the flames but not before the man had burned half of his face. "I'm sorry!" she blurted in horror. "Oh Kella, I'm so sorry!"

"Aaaaaaaggh!" the man shrieked. He fell to his knees, a trembling hand reaching up to his smoking cheek. Then he just screamed again.

"Please, I didn't mean to—"

"Mage!" the first woman cried, pointing an accusatory finger at Johanna. "They're mages!"

Ellie had never been called a mage before, but she would remember this first occasion for as long as she lived, because it was spat at her with such ferocious venom and fear that she almost wished she had never discovered her attunement in the first place. Nothing but grief had come of it.

A huge creature leapt into the clearing making a loud gurgling roar. It skidded to a startled halt when it spotted the group of people. It had the body of a bear and the tail of an alligator, and Ellie immediately recognised it from the glimpse she had seen back in the Everdusk on the day she arrived at Trinity Towers.

The wolf mother came bounding after it, followed by her pack of pups. Apparently, they had been chasing the bear-gator, and now the villagers were caught in the middle of a ferocious pack-hunt.

The bear-gator gave a high pitched growl and started running again, deciding to take its chances with the villagers as it fled from the wolves.

All hell broke loose.

Panicked villagers scattered in every direction, screaming and running for their lives.

"Wait!" Ellie shouted in vain. "Stay together!" Then someone barged right through her, yelling at the top of his lungs, and she was flung aside. The bear-gator stomped past her in pursuit, its giant paw narrowly missing her head. Ellie instinctively rolled away, and she sprang nimbly back to her feet.

Without breaking stride, the bear-gator chomped a man's torso and flung him out of its way in a shower of blood before charging onwards. Other villagers darted left and right away from the monster as it stampeded through the clearing and out the opposite side it had entered. Three of the wolf pups chased after it, yipping excitedly, but the wolf mother stopped beside Ellie.

"Hello girl," she said, reaching out to let the huge wolf sniff her fingers. Ellie heard the wolf mother inside her mind.

Follow?

"Follow you where, girl?"

Follow. Must go.

"Where to?" she repeated, but instinctively sensed the answer. The wolf mother wanted to lead her to safety. She turned and pointed her nose into the trees, then looked back over her shoulder at Ellie.

"This way!" Ellie called to anyone close enough to hear. "Follow the wolves, they won't hurt us. They can show us the way out!"

The wolf mother bounded away and Ellie, Johanna, and a handful of villagers followed her into the trees, leaving the carnage behind. After a while, the screams faded and they were wandering through the desolate quiet of the skeletal forest. Soon, Ellie sensed a barrier ahead. A shimmering wall of watery air seemed to hang in front of them, stretching all the way from the ground up beyond the treetops. On their side of the barrier, the trees were all dead, but through the haze, they could see greenery and the soft orange glow of the Everdusk.

"What is that?" asked a villager tentatively. "I've never seen anything like it before."

"I think it's our way home," Johanna said.

"How can that be?" the villager asked.

"It's difficult to explain," Ellie said. She exchanged a glance with Johanna. "I'll go first. You all follow after."

Johanna nodded.

The villagers tentatively agreed to this, Ellie's confident tone giving them a reason to hope.

Ellie turned to the boundary and stepped up to it, close enough to feel the pull of her world, drawing her back to where she belonged. But there was something else, an invisible force trying to hold her back in this dead world. What was that?

She didn't want to know.

Ellie stepped across the rift boundary and was sucked through as if a huge muscular hunter was pulling her by the shoulders. There was a flash of stars, and then she fell forwards onto her hands and knees, inhaling a deep gulp of startlingly fresh air and looked up to see a plethora of lush green leaves and thick tree trunks. The Everdusk, the way it was supposed to be.

She turned around, and could see the wobbly visions of Johanna and the villagers still on the other side in the dead place. This rift was beyond her abilities to explain. She could barely comprehend it. When she had first encountered the phenomenon, it was a tiny gateway that swallowed her in the Honeywoods. It was no taller than a cottage door, and seemed to affect only herself. But the dragon had created something vast. Craning her neck upwards, Ellie couldn't even see the top of the rift, but somehow sensed it did indeed have a peak, somewhere far above the trees. And glancing left and right along the visible wall, she could see it curving away from her. So, it had to be a dome shape.

A giant dome of darkness.

She waved, beckoning the others to come through. One by one, they did. Ellie helped pull them to their feet, as they inhaled deep breaths of the air and turned their eyes in wonder at their surroundings. Some thanked her with tears in their eyes, squeezing her tightly. Others simply staggered off to quietly throw up behind a tree.

The last one through was Johanna. They shared a quick hug, Ellie feeling a very strong urge to cry, but managed to hold it in.

When they parted, Johanna's cheeks filled like a balloon and she turned aside to vomit on the grass. Ellie patted her sister on the shoulder, and looked back at the giant rift.

"Is it stuck here forever?" Ellie asked quietly.

"I don't know," Johanna replied.

Movement caught Ellie's eye. She could see the wolf mother and her pack approaching the rift wall from the other side and sitting down on their haunches just in front of the two sisters.

Ellie peered through the haze at the mother.

"Can you hear them?" Johanna whispered.

Ellie wanted to. But she could no longer reach them.

It didn't matter. She knew what they'd be thinking.

We are home.

The wolf mother stood, turned away and led her pups back into the forest.

Ellie did cry a little, then.

EPILOGUE

The dragon's death created a seemingly permanent rift to the mirror world which covered over six hundred square wheels. Edgehurst was engulfed by the rift and subsequently cut off from the world. Its surviving residents were forced to abandon their homes and sought refuge in the numerous villages along the western road.

Johanna and Ellie travelled with a ragtag group of survivors as far as Grenburg, where they met a local doctor that setup a makeshift aid camp to tend the victims of the dragon attack. Johanna received treatment for her nibbet bites, and sat with Ellie as the doctor examined her burnt arm.

"So, what now, sis?" Ellie said with a sheepish grin.

"I don't know," Johanna said with a heavy sigh. "But we'll have plenty of time to decide on the journey home."

Ellie frowned indignantly. "Excuse me?"

"It's a four day journey from here, at least," she glanced at the doctor, as if seeking confirmation.

"You from Harbrook?" the doctor said. "In your conditions, I'd say at least six days. Hold this." She handed Ellie a cloth bandage while she rummaged around in a bag of supplies.

"Right," Johanna said. "Six days is more than enough time to figure out what to do next."

Ellie's jaw flapped wordlessly for a moment. The doctor took the bandage and began to wrap it around the burn, making Ellie wince. "Ow!"

Johanna covered her mouth with one hand, and muttered, "I'm so sorry."

"Don't be!" Ellie scolded. "Look around! None of these people would be alive if it weren't for you!"

At the outburst, several of the Edgehurst villagers glanced towards them. The weary doctor had done a good job patching them up, but many were lucky to still have both eyes. Most had been disfigured from nibbet bites and would be permanently scarred. Still, they *were* alive.

"My sister's a fookin' hero," Ellie said as the doctor finished applying the bandage.

The doctor nodded and stood up, gathering her supply bag. "Try telling them that." She walked away before Ellie could react.

"Ellie," Johanna said softly. "They lost their homes because of attunement. I don't think I want to be praised for my involvement. I honestly want to forget everything and just go home."

"But this has been your dream for years, Hanna!" Ellie said. "You can't leave until you've completed the first year, at least."

"I know, but I really want to see mother." Johanna tried to protest.

"She'd be furious and you know it!" Ellie insisted. "Putting her through the torment of leaving home and then returning *without* the mage qualification. She'd be heartbroken."

Johanna smiled. "You called me a mage."

Ellie gave a long pause. "Did I?" she said, breaking into a grin.

"You're one too now," Johanna pointed out.

"No way. I'm a wizard. It's a much cooler word."

Johanna laughed and looked at the ground.

Ellie added quietly, "Not to mention Markus. He'd want you to become a mage, too."

Johanna nodded without looking up. Her voice cracked a bit. "You're right." Then she was struck by an idea. She looked up with a glint in her eye. "Why don't you come back with me?"

"What?" Ellie said, frowning.

"Come to Trinity Towers! You're attuned, you could teach us how to hear animals!"

Ellie's eyes went wide and she shook her head. "No way. I don't know anything about this stuff, Hanna."

"You do," Johanna insisted. "You may even be more of a natural mage than me."

"Wizard," Ellie corrected, and her cheeky smirk returned. "You really want me to come with you?"

"Really. In fact, I think it would be amazing to spend the rest of the year with my little sister. At the very least, I'll be able to keep an eye on you. Who knows what could happen if you went home without knowing what you were capable of."

"Heh. The cottage might be a crater when you return."

They both laughed.

"I'll go if I can bring some friends." Ellie looked across the street to where her pack of unruly hounds were tied up, eating their fill of meat scraps.

But the matter was settled. Ellie went with Johanna to Trinity Towers.

***

After Garrod's death, the Towers fell into the hands of Robert Anders, who, with the aid of Tabitha Henlowe, continued to operate it under a new set of principles, amended from the ones laid down by five generations of the Brockhurst family. Anders donated all of his salary to the kin of Herbert, Karly, Markus, and the numerous other casualties of the dragon attack. The Brockhurst name died in disgrace.

Four of the surviving students left Trinity Towers the day after the attack and returned home to recover from the trauma. But within a month, new students had been chosen and escorted to the grounds from Darune. This was no doubt thanks to the lifted ban of attunement. King Victus was forced to acknowledge the influx of curious travellers that came from all four corners of the province in hope of seeing the mysterious dragon rift. So, taking advantage of the business prospects, Victus declared magic study legal once again, coined the rift the Dome of Decay and began to offer subsidiaries to any inns that could provide hospitality to the city's new visitors. Johanna thought naming the rift was vulgar and insensitive, considering how many people had died in the incident, but was ultimately pleased to no longer be considered a fugitive.

A new extension of the road was built around the rift, bypassing the dome and taking a wide berth in both directions until it joined up again at a junction within the Everdusk. This led to even more frequent visitors to the Towers.

Anders decided the lillysnapper defense wall was no longer necessary and ordered Tabitha to destroy all of the monstrous plants. Nobody opposed this idea, other than Mrs Kerrick, the Towers botanist, and their creator. Tabitha and a small band of pyromancers burned them all down one afternoon. Ellie's pack of hounds were free to come and go as they pleased without the risk of being eaten, which is probably why she didn't speak up about the notion of destroying sentient plants that had memories. She told Johanna about it, who then informed Mr Anders, who advised them not to think about it too much. Mrs Kerrick quit and left a couple of days later.

An attuned architect and his crew of labourers visited the college and offered their services to rebuild the devastated Storm Tower, boasting to have it done before

Winter's Feast. Anders hired them on the condition they would allow the students to witness the building process, because telekinesis-aided-construction made for a very good practical lesson. The building work went on throughout the year while Ellie and Johanna trained and honed their mage skills.

The remaining summer consisted of theoretical studies at the top of the Moon Tower, which Johanna adored and Ellie despised, and numerous field trips all across the Everdusk, which Johanna tolerated and Ellie revelled in. They occasionally visited the Dome of Decay, studying it from a safe distance and not daring to cross the boundary for fear of being stuck in the dark reflection. During these trips, Ellie always had a subtle desire to go back and find the wolves…

Then one day, six weeks or so after the dragon attack, the rift simply disappeared. It left a gigantic circle of lifeless ground in its wake. Anything that had been caught inside its circle of influence had apparently choked to death. The grass was brown and crusty, any Everdusk superoaks that had been inside it turned ashen grey and all their leaves had fallen off. And when an expedition of wizards ventured inside the circle to study the area, they discovered several human skeletons, presumably victims of Edgehurst, part of the band that Johanna and Ellie had tried to save.

The dragon's carcass laid at the centre of the circle, in the road between the ruins of Edgehurst and the Everdusk forest. A reminder of the link between the two worlds. Attuned visitors continued to flock for wheels across the province to see it, and eventually the body was stripped away, its various parts taken for study.

But the grass never grew back within the circle. Nothing could live there anymore.

***

By the time winter arrived, Ellie had become an apprentice

telepath, capable of picking out simple thoughts and feelings from other people. This creeped her out at first, but as soon as she learned how to filter the thoughts and choose when to listen to them, she began to delightedly tease Johanna with it. The sisters grew closer than they had ever been, sharing in the joys of learning and practicing their abilities in the safety of the Towers.

Before they knew it, the time had come to return home to Harbrook. Trinity Towers closed for the Winter's Feast holiday and the two sisters made the long journey home along the westward road. They stayed for a long weekend in Darune City to enjoy the new Attunement Festival. The whole city was lit up with lanterns and ribbons, celebrating the approach of New Year. Pyromancers set off fireworks and there was much drinking and merriment in the streets.

They journeyed along the east road, passing through Honeyville, where they paid a visit to Mr Huggins and the other hunters that knew their father, before making the final leg back to Harbrook.

Julia McKree burst into joyful tears when they walked in through the front door.

"Oh my goodness, welcome home!" She wrapped her arms around both of their necks and squeezed so hard that they could hardly breathe. But it didn't matter, it just felt so good to be home, and Johanna and Ellie had beaming smiles spread across their faces. Their mother caressed their cheeks in the only way a mother can do, after looking upon her daughters' faces for the first time in several months.

Ellie noticed a glint of sadness in her mother's eyes as she regarded them both, and she couldn't help but gently open her mother's mind to hear what could be troubling her.

She sensed a strong feeling of loss.

"Mother, what happened to Grandma?" she asked very softly.

Julia's mouth squeezed shut and she gave a long blink that nudged a tear down her cheek.

"Oh no," Johanna said, clasping both hands to her mouth.

"She got sick," Julia said, tears welling in her eyes. "It was peaceful though, and quick. We buried her in the garden."

"Why didn't you send a letter?" Johanna asked softly.

"Because we knew you'd be home for the Feast. I didn't want you leaving before you got your certificate." She eyed Johanna expectantly.

Johanna smiled, and took out a roll of parchment from her bag. It was wrapped in a ribbon. "First year apprentice pyromancer."

Julia smiled so proudly it lit her face, and she embraced Johanna in a fierce hug. "I knew you would do it!"

Ellie, standing nearby, said off-handedly, "I'll get mine after next term, they said."

Julia broke away from Johanna and gave Ellie a quizzical look, which made both sisters laugh.

"I'm as surprised as you," Ellie said with a shrug. "Hey, where's Grandpa? He'll love to hear about this."

They went outside to the back garden and found Grandpa McKree dozing in a rocking chair in the afternoon sun. He was snoring, but stirred when the ladies approached. He smiled at them, but it was a subdued, sorrowful one that almost broke Ellie's heart. She didn't need to read his mind to understand that he was feeling some unimaginable sense of loneliness.

"What a pleasant sight to wake up to," he said, pulling himself out of the chair. "A year away from home, and you're more beautiful than ever."

"Grandpa, I missed you so much," Johanna said, hugging him.

Then it was Ellie's turn.

"Look Grandpa, I brought you some friends." Two of Ellie's pack loped along at her side. "This is Whisper and Frank."

Grandpa gave her a knowing smile and hunkered to

receive a few enthusiastic licks. He fell into the grass as more dogs scurried up, and soon the garden was alive with the sound of excited yips from all of Ellie's little pack of strays.

After, the McKree's stood together in the garden as the wind rustled the remaining brown leaves in the trees and the sisters caught up on two seasons worth of Harbrook news, which wasn't much. Then the matter of Ellie's attunement came up, and they explained is as best they could to two unattuned Harbrookers who couldn't possibly understand, but revelled in hearing all about it anyway.

Ellie's stomach grumbled.

Grandpa chuckled. "Sounds like someone's ready for Winter's Feast," he said.

"You both look like you could use a good meal," Julia added. "But that goose isn't going to cook itself."

"Leave it to me," Johanna said. With a wave of her fingers, five flickering flames danced into life.

"Too bad mind powers don't help with peeling carrots," Ellie said.

They were a family again. Broken, but strong in each other's company. And with that, the McKrees went inside and feasted together.

THE END

A NOTE FROM THE AUTHOR

Well, this feels good. Third novel in the bag!

I want to thank you for reading this story, and I hope from the bottom of my heart that you enjoyed it. If you've turned to this page without reading it, I can only assume you are a terrible human who likes spoilers, and we can never be friends.

Only kidding. We probably already are friends and I'm standing nearby as you read this. See how annoyed I look, right now?

I wrote most of this story on a farm near Ottawa, surrounded by the sweetest herd of dairy cows you ever did meet. Thank you so much to Robert and Petra, the kind farmers that put up with me for several months as I bumbled my way through my WWOOFer duties before locking myself in the top floor bedroom to write down the crazy nonsense that fills my head every evening.

I actually planned this one. If it weren't for the marvellous Snowflake Method by Randy Ingermanson, I would never have managed to get it all done in such record time. I had the first draft of this story finished in a little over a month. If you're a budding writer, I can't recommend the Snowflake Method enough.

Thanks to B. Aynsley for my incredible cover image. I mean seriously, just look at that thing!

I need to mention Mum, for once again being the first person to read it all. She hates scary things, and isn't much into wizards or dragons, so it's even more impressive that she made it to the end. Thanks Mum.

So, what now? I set out six years ago to write three novels, and it feels rather surreal to have made it. Also exciting! I think I'll carry on.

Care to join me?

M A Clarke
January 5th, 2020

ABOUT THE AUTHOR

M A Clarke is a 33 year old English bloke who now resides in Canada. He has written three novels, which was always the goal after he quit his full-time career job as a web-designer and animator. He did a spot of travelling for more years than he spent at that job, and regrets none of it because life is short and there is a lot to see and do. He is an avid fan of dogs, mountains, space, time-travel and has to rely on his mother to send him boxes of Wispa chocolate bars because they are not easily available in the Canadian Rocky Mountains.

When he's not writing, he can usually be found eating soup in cafes.

You might like his website: www.mattclarke.co.uk

For more information about other work by M A Clarke please visit:

www.tekamuttmedia.com

Cover art by B. Aynsley

Made in the USA
Columbia, SC
15 January 2020